READERS LOVE
Moonlight Over Mayfair

★ ★ ★ ★ ★
'With a wonderfully
eclectic cast, the story just
reads itself off the page'

★ ★ ★ ★ ★
'I was swept away'

★ ★ ★ ★ ★
'I just loved it . . . A great
book to lose yourself in'

★ ★ ★ ★ ★
'Very evocative of
the era'

★ ★ ★ ★ ★
'Perfect!'

★ ★ ★ ★ ★
'Another fabulous read'

★ ★ ★ ★ ★
'Fantastic'

★ ★ ★ ★ ★
'Beautiful . . .
a perfect read'

★ ★ ★ ★ ★
'Enthralling'

Moonlight Over Mayfair

ANTON DU BEKE, household name and all-round entertainer, brings the charm and style he's famous for to this, his second novel, the follow up to his *Sunday Times* bestseller, *One Enchanted Evening*.

Anton is one of the most instantly recognisable TV personalities today, best known for his role on the BBC's *Strictly Come Dancing*, which he has featured on since its inception in 2004. His debut album reached the Top 20, and his annual sell-out tours have been thrilling dance fans in theatres nationwide for over a decade.

www.antondubeke.tv
 @TheAntonDuBeke
 @Mrantondubeke
 www.facebook.com/antondubeke

Moonlight Over Mayfair

ANTON DU BEKE

Moonlight Over Mayfair

ZAFFRE

First published in Great Britain in 2019
This edition published in 2020 by
ZAFFRE
80–81 Wimpole St, London W1G 9RE

This is a work of fiction. Names, places, events and
incidents are either the products of the author's
imagination or used fictitiously. Any resemblance to
actual persons, living or dead, or actual
events is purely coincidental.

A CIP catalogue record for this book is
available from the British Library.

Paperback ISBN: 978-1-78576-781-4
Hardback ISBN: 978-1-78576-783-8
Trade Paperback ISBN: 978-1-78576-782-1

Also available as an ebook

1 3 5 7 9 10 8 6 4 2

Typeset by IDSUK (Data Connection) Ltd
Printed and bound in Great Britain by Clays Ltd, Elcograf S.p.A.

Zaffre is an imprint of Bonnier Books UK
www.bonnierbooks.co.uk

List of Characters

At the Buckingham:

Raymond de Guise AKA Ray Cohen – lead male demonstration dancer

Nancy Nettleton – a chambermaid

Hélène Marchmont – lead female demonstration dancer

Frank Nettleton – Nancy's brother

Vivienne Edgerton – a permanent guest, Lord Edgerton's stepdaughter

Lord Bartholomew Edgerton – director of the board of the Buckingham, Vivienne's stepfather

Maynard Charles – the hotel director

Billy Brogan – a hotel concierge

Louis Kildare – a saxophone player in the Archie Adams Orchestra

Archie Adams – the leader of the Buckingham's orchestra

Aubrey Higgins – Maynard Charles's partner

Abner Grant – a hotel detective

Emmeline Moffatt – the head of housekeeping

Rosa – a chambermaid

Ruth – a chambermaid

Edie – a chambermaid

Sofía LaPegna – a demonstration dancer
Gene Sheldon – a demonstration dancer
Diego – the head cocktail waiter
Mr Bosanquet – the head concierge

Beyond the Buckingham:

Georges de la Motte – Raymond's former dancing mentor and friend
Arthur 'Artie' Cohen – Raymond's younger brother
Arthur Regan – an Irishman and occasional guest at the Buckingham
John Hastings Junior – an American businessman
Sidney Archer – Hélène's late husband and Sybil's father
Sybil Archer – Sidney and Hélène's daughter
Maurice Archer – Sidney's father
Noelle Archer – Sidney's mother
Mary Burdett – the matron of the Daughters of Salvation

To Hannah, George and Henrietta,
my joy, my world, my inspiration,
the loves of my life

Prologue

8 December, 1937

The Grand Ballroom, the Buckingham Hotel

FIRST THERE COMES THE CONFUSION.

Moments later: the screams.

Welcome to the Grand Ballroom of the Buckingham Hotel, a place of music and magic, of magnificence and splendour. Strung high with decorations for the Christmas festivities, today it is flanked by a dozen miniature Norwegian firs, all of them bedecked in crystals and lights – while, gathered around its chequered dance floor are the great and good of London town.

There is nowhere else, no other dazzling palace or mansion in Mayfair, that the finest members of society would rather be.

But now . . .

The guests cease their toing and froing and turn to the head of the ballroom, where arched doors lead to a place of enchantment beyond. It is from these doors that the proud musicians of the Archie Adams Orchestra make their daily march. It is from these doors that the Buckingham's feted dancers glide and twirl to take up their positions on the hotel's legendary ballroom floor.

And it is from these doors, now, that a chaos of black smoke erupts.

The doors explode outwards, disgorging frightened musicians and dancers. On a tide of roiling black smoke, they come, clinging to each other as they escape the blaze behind. Soon, the guests are flocking to the edges of the room, making for the doors. Sensing danger, they take flight, up and out of the Grand Ballroom itself.

In the middle of the dance floor, one dishevelled figure stops. Doubled over, taking great gulps of air, he gathers his composure and draws himself to his full height. His black hair is unruly, his stature imposing. His sad, dark eyes suggest a certain, tragic kind of beauty.

He looks back.

Through the dressing room doors, beyond the churning smoke, somebody is screaming.

Somebody is screaming his name.

'Raymond!'

Raymond de Guise, lead dancer at the Buckingham, barely misses a beat. His eyes pan around, taking in the guests and hotel staff who are rushing to the ballroom to lend what assistance they can, and pick out one figure among them. Nancy Nettleton tries to push through the crowd to reach Raymond – but Raymond is already resolved, his mind already made up.

He turns to face the doors that just cast him out. The flames are fiercer now, advancing angrily through the smoke.

'Raymond!' the voice calls. '*Raymond!*'

There are moments in life when you act without thinking, when you forget all thoughts of the future and act *now*, because you *must*, before it's too late.

Lives change in moments like these.

For Raymond de Guise, this is one of those moments.

So he plunges into the fire . . .

Eight Months Earlier . . .

April 1937

Chapter One

THE INAUGURAL SPRING BALL AT the Buckingham Hotel was about to begin, and in the Grand Ballroom, strings of yellow lights were arranged in garlands.

The saxophonists, trumpeters and trombonists of the Archie Adams Orchestra had already taken their places on the ballroom stage when the doors opened up and there, framed in their light, stood Archie Adams himself. Distinguished and grey, wearing his trademark black bow tie, with eyes the cobalt of the skies above Berkeley Square, he soaked up the applause of the guests who filled the ballroom. Then, taking up his stool behind the grand piano, he ran his fingers along the ivory keys . . . and the ballroom came alive.

For a moment, Archie seemed imperious, the king of the ballroom: a god with grey hair and a suit of tailored white silk. Under his direction, the old Duke Ellington number, 'In a Sentimental Mood', filled the cavernous interior of the Grand. Excitement stirred around its edges, where lords and ladies – and every debutante recently presented at the royal court – had been holding their breath in anticipation. Conversations were silenced. Heads turned. As one, the hotel's guests watched, rapt, as the Buckingham's dancers flocked out onto the floor.

Hidden among the debutantes stood a tall girl with immaculately sculpted auburn hair and a gown of golden satin, embroidered with rows of pearls along its every seam. Although she looked young enough to be a debutante herself, Vivienne Edgerton could scarcely tolerate the shrieks of delight which filled her ears when, down on the dance floor, the elegant Hélène Marchmont twirled around her partner. Hélène had been a star at the Buckingham ever since the Grand opened its doors, but Vivienne's eyes were fixed, instead, on Hélène's partner – the Buckingham's male principal, with his wild black hair and sad, almond eyes. A girl could get lost in those eyes, thought Vivienne. They invited you to fall in, deep and fast. And those arms . . .

'In A Sentimental Mood' was coming to an end. The orchestra exploded in a rapture of trombone. On the ballroom floor, the hotel dancers fanned apart, reaching out to partner up with the guests waiting on its fringes, while in its heart Hélène and her debonair partner came to the climax of their dance. Arms around each other, they turned and turned again. Vivienne watched the way they gazed at each other, with such exquisite longing. Then, with the final flourish from the orchestra, they came apart to soak up the applause.

In the middle of the ballroom stood Hélène Marchmont . . .

. . . and Gene Sheldon, formerly of the Imperial Hotel, newly made the principal dancer at the Buckingham itself.

Vivienne watched, with something approaching amusement, as Sheldon waltzed away to accept the hand of the first debutante who reached him. He was a serviceable dancer, she supposed. He'd made a name for himself, romancing the guests at the Imperial. But he was no Raymond de Guise.

8

The band was lurching into its next number when Vivienne felt a tap on her arm – and turned to discover Billy Brogan standing at her heel. Brogan was still like a faithful hound, Vivienne decided, even though this new season found him in the smart black uniform of the hotel's concierges, not the forgettable grey that the hotel pages all wore. Sixteen years old, and two years Vivienne's junior, Billy had been a page until his recent promotion. He was not a bad sort, but he had a tendency to hang about like a bad smell.

'What is it, Billy?' Vivienne asked.

'Mr Charles sent me for you. He's asked for an audience.'

Asked for an audience? Vivienne tried to stifle her smile. Ever since Brogan had accepted his appointment as a new concierge, he had been adopting strange airs and graces. *The boy thinks he'll be hotel director one day, if he plays his cards right.* But Vivienne knew that, in an establishment like the Buckingham, social climbing would only take errant Irish lads like Billy Brogan so far.

'Haven't you outgrown being Maynard Charles's errand boy, Billy?'

Billy drew himself to his full height and beamed. 'I'm always eager to be of service, Miss Edgerton.'

Admitting defeat, Vivienne strode up and out of the Grand, while behind her Gene Sheldon glided effortlessly from one side of the ballroom to another, a beautiful debutante in his arms.

The Grand Ballroom may have been launching into its spring spectacular, but that did not mean the machinations of the broader Buckingham Hotel could grind to a halt. As Vivienne crossed the glittering reception hall, a party of guests fresh in from Salzburg were being attended to by one of the day

9

managers, while the doors of the golden lift opened to reveal an elderly dowager, weighed down by a gown of ivory silk.

With the music fading behind her, Vivienne crossed the check-in desks and, following a familiar corridor, came to the office at its end. Many were the times she had attended this office and stood outside its doors as if she were still a despairing schoolgirl awaiting a scolding. But she'd been quiet – quiet and *clean* – for three months now. The staff and the guests at the Buckingham Hotel must have thought she was a ghost, so rarely was she seen among them. It had never been Vivienne's decision to come and live at the Buckingham Hotel. *That* had been the doing of her stepfather, Lord Edgerton himself – who had forced upon her not only his name, but a new residence, a new country, dragging her away from New York and keeping her at arm's length from her own mother. But she had resolved, after last Christmas, that she did not want any more trouble.

So what am I doing here at all?

She knocked and waited for the deep, baritone voice to summon her through. Maynard Charles, the hotel director, was sitting behind his desk – as he did every evening – filling in a variety of ledger books and memos. He bade her to sit. A portly man, nearing sixty, he was wearing his usual pinstriped shirt and braces over his not insignificant belly. A tumbler of brandy was perched on the edge of his desk.

Vivienne waited until he was done, her eyes roaming the shelves. There were row after row of ledger books, chronicling in columns of profit and loss the peculiar history of the Buckingham Hotel. The head of a stag, shot by one of the hotel's first directors, was mounted on mahogany and glared down from above Maynard's desk.

10

'Miss Edgerton,' he said at last, 'I'm sorry to take you from the festivities.'

Maynard Charles had a paternalistic tone, but Vivienne knew it was calculated; he had never become a father, because his life had been devoted to the smooth operation of the Buckingham Hotel. All twelve hundred of its staff were his children, from its elegant dancers to its porters and pages.

'Am I to understand that I've done something wrong?' Vivienne tried not to, but she needled him further. 'Committed another great sin, perhaps?'

Maynard raised an eyebrow, pointedly refusing to be baited. 'I received a telephone call from your father's secretary this afternoon – on a matter grave enough that she had thought to query me before involving your father.'

'My *step*father,' Vivienne interjected, with ice in her voice.

'Forgive me,' said Maynard, standing at last. 'Might I pour you a drink?'

'I don't care for brandy. I was happy with the Moët they're serving up down in the Grand. Mr Charles, if I haven't done anything wrong – and I haven't, I'm quite certain of that – might I be permitted to return? I've kept myself clean since Christmas. I'm trying my best to . . . go unnoticed. But I've been anticipating the Spring Ball and I was looking forward to dancing.'

'This is important. Lord Edgerton's secretary feels she must take it to him, unless I can tell her robustly that nothing is amiss.' He paused, composing himself as if for a grand announcement. 'It hasn't gone unnoticed, in this hotel, that since the debacle at Christmas – when, let's not beat around the bush, Vivienne, you were close to perishing from your *overindulgences* – you have withdrawn from life inside and outside the Buckingham. You haven't been on lavish spending missions into the Regent Street arcades. You haven't frequented the Queen Mary, the Candlelight Club, nor any of our other restaurants and bars. Why, I believe your appearance at tonight's Spring Ball might be the first time you've worn a ball gown all year.'

Vivienne bristled. 'What of it?'

'Miss Edgerton, you haven't drawn on your stepfather's allowance in one hundred and eleven days. The generous stipend he permits you is simply accruing in an account – and his secretary is questioning *why*. Why would Vivienne Edgerton suddenly stop spending? Why is she ordering simple room service meals instead of sitting at the table of honour in the Queen Mary? Why isn't she dragging a hotel concierge out with her into the boutiques of Mayfair?'

Vivienne felt herself growing angry. It was just like her stepfather to have his minions watch her like this. Wasn't it enough that she was banished from his Suffolk estate so that he could have her mother all to himself?

The words were rising up her pale, swan-like throat of their own volition. She blurted them out.

'I'm eighteen years old. Nearly nineteen. I'll not be a kept woman. He's turned my mother into his pet and he tried to do the same to me. Well, I made a resolution, Mr Charles. I'm through with it. All the money in the world doesn't matter to me.'

Maynard Charles remained silent.

'Oh, I know what you think. I'd be thinking it too. Who *is* Vivienne Edgerton without a new outfit every single night? Well, I'll tell you who. I'm *me*. All of that money he throws at me – it isn't for my benefit. It's to keep me quiet and compliant. And all the while it's been ... rotting me. Yes, that's the word. *Rot!*

You spend and it fills a hole inside you. But the next time you spend, the hole's a little deeper, so you need to spend more. Soon enough, you're destroying yourself – just like I did last Christmas. So I don't want his money, Mr Charles!'

'Vivienne,' Maynard began calmly, 'money doesn't have to corrode. Money makes the world go round.'

'I'm a leech, Mr Charles. Oh, he makes sure I pay my way in this hotel, and of course you benefit from it too. A permanent guest in the finest suite! But I do not want to remain a leech any longer. I want to *contribute*. I'm worth more than dresses and pearls, aren't I? I can . . . help.'

'Help?' To Maynard, the idea was patently absurd.

'Not the hotel,' Vivienne went on, 'but there has to be *something* for me. Some way of *mattering*. Not like my stepfather and his parties and his hunts.'

Maynard rounded the desk and perched on its edge, close to where Vivienne sat. She shuffled backwards; it was just like Maynard Charles to come and patronise her. The old man meant well, and she knew he'd covered for her indiscretions on more than one occasion in the past, but how could he ever understand what it felt like to be trapped like this, trapped in her own skin?

'Let me tell you something, Miss Edgerton. Your stepfather and those like him, men of great means – they do contribute. Without men of great wealth, establishments like the Buckingham would evaporate. Thousands of livelihoods would vanish, just like that. Thousands of families would be back on the breadline. And, without the money they earn, thousands more would feel the effect – all the bakeries they go to, all the haberdashers they frequent. Great wealth doesn't sit still. It ripples out, like a stone dropped in a pond. It *provides*. That's why—' He paused. 'That's why what we do here at the Buckingham is so important. That's why it has to survive.'

Was Vivienne mistaken, or was there something faintly anxious in the way Maynard Charles had started to speak? Whatever the case, she had not come here for a lesson in economics. 'My stepfather doesn't care for the people this hotel supports. He cares for the way the manager at Lloyds fawns all over him each time he makes an appearance. No, profit isn't good enough for me, Mr Charles. I want to *help*.'

Nodding, Maynard returned to his desk and picked up his fountain pen once again.

'Find a way to satisfy your needs – but, if you would, do it without provoking the attention of your stepfather. There are choppy waters ahead for the Buckingham Hotel. I would rather navigate them without my eye being drawn to another one of your "problems". Are we agreed?'

Vivienne stood, smarting as she smoothed down her gown. Only when she was back at the door, listening to the sounds of a Viennese waltz drifting up from the ballroom, did she look back.

'Is everything all right at the Buckingham, Mr Charles?'

Maynard barely looked up as he constructed his reply. 'We must achieve some sense of balance, Miss Edgerton. Some new normality. Since King Edward abdicated, we are without our principal benefactor. Reputation matters in an establishment like ours. Hence, efforts like our inaugural Spring Ball. Hence—' He laid down his fountain pen and looked up. 'You must already know, from rumours in this hotel if not from your stepfather himself, that we are seeking new investment. Our eyes have turned to America, Miss Edgerton – because if I am right, and war is to come to the Continent, we will not be able to count on our German dignitaries for very much longer.'

His tone was grave, and now Vivienne understood why. All the time she had once spent dallying in the Candlelight Club and hotel restaurants had to be filled, and for the first time in her life she had lately deigned to look at the broadsheets. She had read all about Mr Hitler. *But all-out war?* She was too young to recall the Great War itself, but surely men could not be so foolish as to risk it again?

'Our Spanish business is already at a standstill. Imagine what happens next. The Buckingham needs more ballast if we're to weather whatever's to come. But there's hope. There is a man called John Hastings – Junior, you understand. Perhaps you're familiar with the type. He's a New Yorker like yourself. He's to come to London this summer, sizing up new investments, and ...' Maynard petered into silence. 'We need the Buckingham strong, when he arrives. We need equilibrium. So the very best way that you might help the good people of this hotel – the good people, Vivienne, who have themselves helped you when you've been at your lowest ebb – is to play your part. Act your role. Am I understood?'

Vivienne would have spoken, then, but a lump had formed in her throat. She remained frozen in the doorway, until finally she uttered the single word, 'Understood,' and slammed the door behind her.

In the reception hall, the check-in desks were clear. Billy Brogan was waiting patiently with the other concierges as one of the night managers arrived for his shift.

Vivienne passed them all by, holding herself rigidly as Maynard's words played over in her mind. *Play your part. Act your role.* Be a good little girl and keep out of the way, would you, Vivienne? The grown-ups are working . . .

The music of the Archie Adams Orchestra was still floating up from the ballroom, but Vivienne stopped before crossing its threshold – then turned away and walked into the golden cage of the guest lift.

Suddenly, she didn't feel like dancing at all.

Chapter Two

THE TRAIN HAD BEEN SITTING on the platform for ten minutes by the time Nancy Nettleton flailed across the concourse at Euston station, late from her morning changing sheets in the Buckingham's uppermost suites. By the time she reached the platform – her bad leg slowing her down, as always it did – the passengers had already disembarked and were tramping their way through Euston Arch, catching omnibuses to take them further afield. Only one person remained on the platform: diminutive and slight, with his haversack on the floor and his cap placed in his lap like some sort of penitent.

'Frank!' Nancy gasped, and – ignoring the complaint of her leg – gambolled over to take him in her arms.

Frank Nettleton had been on the 6 a.m. out of Lancaster, which was itself an hour's ride in the back of a farmer's wagon from the little mining village where Nancy and her brother had grown up. Consequently, he was bleary-eyed as he found himself smothered in his elder sister's arms.

'Gerroff me, would you?' he said, wriggling free.

He stood back. Nancy could see he was trying to stifle a smile, so she took him in her arms again. Then, choking back tears, she whispered into his ear, 'I've missed you, Frankie.'

She took him by the hand and, together, they joined the throng leaving the station.

The London Underground was alien to Frank, and Nancy could tell that he was frightened. She remembered only too well the way his face had screwed up every time a storm shook open the skies above their village when he was small, and he wore the same expression now. Creases appeared around his left eye every time he was trying to be brave, and he played with one of the hazel curls that hung down around his ears, a nervous tic he'd had ever since Nancy used to bathe him in the tin bath by the fire. Those curls, Nancy knew, would have to go. She'd find a barber to take care of it, or else take the kitchen scissors to it herself. If her little brother Frank was going to join the ranks of the Buckingham, he was going to have to look the part.

It had been nine months since Nancy last saw Frank, but it seemed another lifetime ago. Last summer, Nancy herself had stepped off that same train and made this same pilgrimage across London, all to take up her post as a chambermaid under Mrs Emmeline Moffatt at the Buckingham Hotel. And now – thanks to a kind word Billy Brogan had put in with management – Frank was to do the same, enlisting as a hotel page. It was honest work, and it was a way of rescuing Frank from the miners' hostel he'd been living in since their father passed away and Nancy set off for London. The guilt that she'd felt at leaving him behind had always been assuaged by her ambition to bring him to join her – and now here he was, little Frank Nettleton, his school bag carrying all the possessions he had in the world. Somewhere in there, no doubt, would be the teddy bear their mother had made for him before she passed away, when Frank was barely a babe in arms.

'Are you tired, Frankie?'

Frank slumped against her shoulder. It was the most natural thing in the world. He smelled of engine grease and sweat, but Nancy didn't care. 'I didn't sleep last night. The boys in the hostel wanted to give me a send-off, but I knew what that'd mean – they'd 'ave me drinking ale they'd dipped all sorts in – so instead I slept in the hedge back outside Farmer Garrison's. It was him who drove me to the station before dawn. I gave him the last of my wages, so I haven't eaten either.'

'Mrs Gable didn't pack you sandwiches?'

Mrs Gable was the old widow who kept the lodgings that Frank had been calling home.

'She did, but the other lads got to 'em first.'

Nancy pondered it as the train rattled through another station. 'Might be you could catch twenty winks in my quarters, Frankie.' Was Nancy mistaken, or was she sinking back into her Lancashire accent, just because her baby brother was beside her? 'We could probably smuggle you something up out of the kitchens too. Rosa and Ruth – they're the girls I share with – they've got friends in the kitchens. They save us scraps. But, Frank, what's *scraps* to guests at the Buckingham, it's complete *luxury* to us. So we'll see you right.' She hesitated. 'You might have to wait until tonight to have a proper fill. Billy's got to get you sorted with a uniform and he'll be the one showing you the ropes, making some introductions. It's Billy's family you'll be bunking with. They're down in Lambeth. You can walk it from the Buckingham – it's scarcely a couple of miles, nothing to us, is it, Frank? But you'll see – it's a different *world*.'

'You've been on an adventure, haven't you, Nance?'

'What do you mean?'

'Well, you talk like all this is *normal!*'

'You'll get that way too, Frankie.'

'All these men in . . . bowler hats. They're carrying *umbrellas*.'

Nancy couldn't help it; her body shook in a fit of uncontrolled laughter.

'Look at that one,' Frank said, indicating a man sitting further down the carriage. 'He has a *pocket watch*.' He hesitated. 'You haven't really seen the King of Great Britain, have you, Nance?'

'I've seen the King of Norway.' Nancy shrugged, as if it was the most natural thing in the world. 'The thing you've got to learn about the Buckingham, Frankie, is it's all the world, wrapped up in one. There might be kings and queens, but there's chambermaids and hotel pages, just like us, as well. There's ministers for the Crown, but there's folk scratching a living scrubbing stains out of carpets. And in the middle of it all . . .'

'Your friend, Raymond de Guise?'

Nancy stalled. There was only one more station to go. The truth was, she'd been about to talk about Maynard Charles, and how, somehow, he kept the whole of the Buckingham afloat – like the captain of a vast ocean-going liner. But the image of Raymond popped into her mind, and Frank's expectant face beseeched her to say more. She'd written to Frank and told him about Raymond – how they'd first met, how they used to dance together in the little studio behind the Grand Ballroom, how the feeling of love had crept upon her without her truly recognising it for what it was. But putting it down in writing was easier than saying it face to face. For the first time, she flushed red.

'You won't meet Raymond. Not yet. He's been gone from the Buckingham for two months, Frankie. He's . . .' This was the unimaginable part. 'He's in Hollywood, Frankie. Hollywood,

California! His old mentor in the ballrooms, Georges de la Motte, wrote to him with an opportunity. Georges, he's to star in a movie with his new partner . . . and, well, where Georges goes, Raymond follows. Georges wanted to make introductions. He thought that, perhaps—'

'Raymond de Guise – star of the silver screen?'

Nancy shrugged. 'Perhaps.'

She was still uncertain what she thought of the idea. Georges de la Motte, the exiled French baron who had, once upon a time, introduced Raymond to the delights of the ballroom, had found himself a new paramour, Laurana St Clair. The studios believed they might soon be known across the world, more famous than Fred Astaire and Ginger Rogers themselves. Georges had travelled to the Hollywood Hills to take a role in a new film, *A Ballroom on Broadway* – and, as keen as ever to help Raymond in his own path towards stardom, he had invited his old protégé across the Atlantic to effect introductions.

'And maybe even take auditions,' Nancy added. 'Well, as you can imagine, Maynard Charles – that's the Buckingham's director – wasn't easy to convince. Losing your ballroom star for months on end – even for the night of our very first Spring Ball – was difficult to accept. Only then—' She paused. 'You should know, there are wheels within wheels at the Buckingham. Keep your ear to the ground and you'll hear so much. And the hotel board, they're courting a new investor. An American, by the name of John Hastings. It won't mean anything to you, Frank – it doesn't to me – but he's a financier in New York City, and the word is he's looking for an establishment like ours to invest in. Something outside the United States. A place he might bring business associates. Well, that's what financiers do, isn't it?

They think themselves kings and queens of their own moneyed worlds. And when Mr Charles realised that John Hastings was due to make a visit to London to size up potential investments, he realised he had a secret weapon. He could send Raymond to meet him, in New York City. Raymond's the sort of man who can *impress*.'

It was what had swayed Maynard Charles in the end. On his way back from his Californian sojourn, Raymond would visit New York City, and there meet the financier John Hastings. Together, they would get the steamer to Liverpool, where a chauffeur would bring them to the hotel itself. If Maynard's ploy worked, by the time they reached English shores, Hastings would be so enamoured by Raymond de Guise – the debonair dancer, the master of the ballroom, purveyor of charm – that the other hotels he planned to visit on his trip would already be forgotten.

'It's the sort of plan only a mind like Maynard Charles's could dream up. The whole of life is an endless game of chess to a man like that. But Raymond can charm anyone.' Nancy paused, dwelling on the idea for a moment. 'He's extraordinary. If anyone can work his magic and get John Hastings to invest in the Buckingham instead of the Imperial Hotel, it will be Raymond.'

The train rattled onwards.

'I miss him, Frank,' Nancy softly said. 'It's like a *need*. I didn't know it until he was gone.' Her words petered out. Embarrassment caught up with her. Perhaps she'd said too much. Frank was scarcely seventeen; there was still so much he had to learn about love.

'Hey, Frankie.' She grinned. 'You might find love yourself in the Buckingham.'

22

'Nancy!' Frank protested.

'If it can happen to me, it can happen to anyone.' At last, the train pulled into a station. 'Look alive, Frank, this is us!'

Then the doors opened and Nancy hauled her little brother onwards, up and into the sunlit Mayfair spring.

Chapter Three

FRANK'S FIRST IMPRESSION OF THE Buckingham Hotel was of some great fortress, reaching skyward above the green expanse of Mayfair's Berkeley Square. Its gleaming white façade put him in mind of the fairy tales Nancy used to tell him when he was small (the same stories, he was afraid to admit, that he still told himself when he closed his eyes at night), and the colonnade in front, where the taxicabs lined up, made him think of some palace out of Greek myth.

Frank was striding towards the sweeping marble steps that led to the hotel's famous revolving bronze doors, but Nancy caught him by the arm.

'First lesson,' she said. 'We use the tradesman's entrance.' She led him across the green of Berkeley Square, to a narrow mews he hadn't noticed until this very moment. 'I've been stung before, Frank! There's so much you'll have to learn.'

The staff entrance was halfway along Michaelmas Mews, and opened into a small receiving hall where boxes and trunks were piled up. From here, Nancy led Frank into the warren of corridors behind the hotel reception. This was the beating heart of the Buckingham Hotel. Here was the housekeeping lounge, the auditors' office, the concierge station, and the basement stairs.

Nancy pointed out the old laundries beneath the hotel, where the pages often congregated.

They came, at last, to the head concierge's office. Inside, the newly appointed head concierge, Mr Bosanquet – descended, or so he proclaimed, from a line of Flemish lords – was working on the season's rotas. But outside stood the cheery, dimpled face Nancy was longing to see: Billy Brogan himself.

'This him, is it, Nance? You brought me another one for the slaughterhouse?'

Nancy flushed scarlet. 'Billy Brogan, you *promised*!' Stepping aside, she revealed Frank, looking sheepishly at the floor. 'Frank, he's teasing. That's all he does. Taunt and tease.' She paused. 'Billy, this is my brother Frank. Frank, this is Billy Brogan. Until a month ago, he was doing exactly the job you're going to be doing – so trust in what he says, but don't let him think he can boss you about.'

Billy looked Frank up and down. 'You stick with me, Frank, and you'll be all right. I'll see to it. Trust in us Brogans. You got me at the hotel, and my ma to cook and clean for you at home. There, how's that for a new life?'

Billy was grinning inanely – it was just his way – and something in it inspired Frank to reach out his hand. Billy shook it vigorously.

'I'll show him around, shall I, Nance?'

Nancy edged her way between Billy and Frank and smothered her brother in her arms again.

'I'll find you later,' she whispered. 'I made Eccles cakes, especially for your coming.'

It must have touched a nerve deep inside Frank, some memory of childhood, because for a second his eyes shimmered with tears. Then, remembering himself, he nodded and drew away. In a second, Billy's arm was around Frank's shoulders, as if to shepherd him away.

Yet something stopped him.

'Here, Nance, I almost forgot!' he announced – and, reaching into his smart black concierge's jacket, he produced an envelope. 'I nabbed it from the hotel post room. It's from your Ray—'

'Yes,' Nancy interjected, not meaning to sound as prim as she did, 'I know who it's from.'

'He getting on good out there, is he?'

Nancy glared. 'Be off with you, Billy Brogan! And you make sure my brother stays out of mischief. Frank, remember what I told you about this one, you hear?'

Nancy watched as Billy led Frank away. Part of her wanted to follow them, but she reined herself in. She would see Frank again soon. She'd see him every day. He was here now, right where she wanted him to be, and she could get on with the business of being a big sister again. But he had to learn to go his own way too. They weren't in a small town in Lancashire anymore.

She watched as they disappeared from view, and it was only then that she turned to the letter in her hands.

My dearest Nancy,

Since my last note, I've received the most exciting news: I am to audition for the producers of A Ballroom on Broadway. For the past three days I have been working on set, standing in for Georges between takes so that cameras and lighting and various other technical disciplines (of which I am a keen student!) can be concluded. To think that my foxtrot has caught the eye of the upper echelons! This matters, Nancy, for this world in Los Angeles is every bit as dictated by one's station in life as the Buckingham Hotel – and, if you are to climb, you must have the right patrons . . .

Nancy was lost, imagining Raymond's honeyed voice as he told her about his new life under Californian skies – but then she felt a tapping on her shoulder. She turned, expecting to see Mrs Moffatt about to admonish her, or else pass her one of her inexhaustible supply of barley sugars – and there stood Vivienne Edgerton.

She was dressed down this morning – but, then, she always seemed to dress down these days, as if going unnoticed was now as important to her as standing out used to be. She was wearing a simple tan house dress, with scarcely any rouge upon her cheeks or kohl around her eyes. She was beautiful like this, Nancy thought. *If only Vivienne could see it herself. For Vivienne, it's all a kind of punishment: as if she needs to atone for who she used to be.*

'Miss Edgerton, is everything all right?'

Vivienne coughed, nervously. Yes, thought Nancy, that's it – *nerves.* It was an aspect she'd never seen in Miss Edgerton before. She'd seen her high and she'd seen her low, but she'd never seen her nervous.

'Nancy,' Vivienne began, 'I'm in need of some help. And I believe you're the only one in the whole of the Buckingham to whom I might turn.'

27

Chapter Four

MIDNIGHT IN THE BUCKINGHAM HOTEL: somewhere, a clock began to toll out the hour.

One . . .

Behind the reception hall, Maynard Charles made his last tour of the offices, bidding goodnight to the porters and concierges whose duties went on into the small hours. At the reception desk, the night manager took a register and skimmed through it, searching for potential problems he would face during the night.

Two . . .

In the Grand Ballroom, where the last waltz had been danced an hour ago, the waiting staff were still shutting down for the night. In the morning, the sprung ballroom floor would be treated with wax, and before that happened there was much to do: tables and chairs to be packed away, scratches on the floor to be marked out for special treatment.

Three . . .

Outside the revolving bronze doors, the doorman awaited the arrival of his replacement for the night. The Buckingham did not sleep. It was ever-present and ever-watchful, a bastion for the great and the good.

Four . . .

From kitchen to Candlelight Club, from Queen Mary dining room to French brasserie, the hotel was turning towards its slumber. But not everyone slept, not in an enterprise as vast as this. It would not be long before the ranges in the kitchens must be fired up in anticipation of breakfast.

And, on the hotel's seventh storey, a figure flitted, unseen, from corridor to corridor. At each door they passed, they rested a gloved hand upon the handle, as if to test whether it was locked. The first one held fast. So did the second and the third. Onwards they went: past the Atlantic, the Pacific, the Crown Royal suites. When voices could be heard coming from behind, the figure pretended to fumble with keys, and waited as two lovers – an elder statesman and his much younger paramour – passed by. They paid the stranger no mind, so rapt were they in each other. It was just as well – because the door the intruder had reached was unlocked. Its handle clicked and turned under the gentlest pressure – and then the stranger was through, into the chamber's opulent surrounds.

Past the bathroom with its porcelain bath, its taps and pipework plated in gold, through the lounge area, where thick Persian blankets had been thrown upon the chaise longue. There lay the four-poster bed. From the darkness, where the intruder lingered, the sleeping guest could be seen. The intruder remembered the hotel manifest – this was the dowager princess of the former Bohemia. Yes, it was to be a fortunate night. This nocturnal foray would present a great reward.

The intruder stole nearer, close enough to hear the princess's breath. Only once they were certain she would not wake, did they reach out to the armoire at the bedside.

And opened the drawer.

∽

Maynard Charles, his face purple with a rage he could barely conceal, slammed down the telephone receiver in his office and opened his mouth wide, as if he might scream up at the heavens.

He got to his feet, poured himself a glass of brandy, and drank it in one smooth, fiery gulp. There was a time, he thought, when nothing had affected him like this. Running a luxury hotel had more in common with being a general in His Majesty's army than it did anything else, and Maynard had learned to cope with almost any calamity the hotel threw his way. Good God, he'd kept the Buckingham alive through the Great Depression, when all twelve hundred of its staff depended on him! He'd barely broken stride in those devastating years. In fact, he thought now, he'd *relished* the challenge. *Cometh the hour, cometh the man.*

Why, then, did he feel like he was on the verge of breaking down?

It wasn't the second swallow of brandy that settled his nerves. It wasn't even the third. Only when he was feeling the warmth of the fourth did he feel like he'd come back to solid ground.

In the corner of the room, the wireless was buzzing with news from the BBC: the Condor Legion, the Nazi Luftwaffe's elite squadron, were in play over the skies of Spain. He marched over and turned it off. *That* was it. That was why he was so on edge: the creeping sense that another war was coming had been growing in intensity with each passing day. He had gone to bed the previous night and, on closing his eyes, all he could see were the banks of barbed wire that had characterised his own time at war. Twenty years had passed since those hellish days, but it took so little to bring back the sight, the sounds, the *smells*.

The Buckingham Hotel had endured the Great Depression. But if it came to war . . . Maynard shuddered at the idea. Every time he tried to confront it, it was like he was back in Flanders, being dragged down into the thick, suffocating mud. The thought of another generation being devastated was almost too much to bear. And all day, every day, he was plagued by the thought of what would become of the hotel when the first shots were fired. The borders would go up on the Continent. The English Channel, would, once again, become a battle scene, isolating the little island of which Maynard was so proud. Travel would grind to a halt. What that meant for the Buckingham was surely calamitous: empty suites and empty halls; restaurants scarcely half-filled; a ballroom unattended.

Get a hold of yourself, man! It hasn't happened yet. There's still hope. There's a long game to play in this hotel, and you're playing it to win. You've got to keep focus.

He dialled the number again, and this time a voice crackled on the other end of the line.

'Imperial Hotel.'

Maynard floundered. 'I'd like to speak to Mr Abner Grant.'

'Room, please?'

Maynard despaired. 'He isn't a guest. He's one of your members of staff.'

There was the briefest pause. 'May I ask who's calling?'

No, you may not! Maynard wanted to roar.

Despairing again, he put down the phone.

It had started at dawn. No sooner had he been up than Mr Bosanquet, the new head concierge, had appeared with the most frightful news. At some point during the night, a stranger had crept into the King Edward Suite where Beatrice, dowager princess of what had once been Bohemia, was staying, and taken a string of pearls from her bedside dresser. Maynard Charles was a deft hand at controlling occurrences like this. Thefts were simply a cost of business, and had to be dealt with swiftly and sharply.

31

The problem was that it wasn't the first robbery reported this year; it was the fifth. And reputational damage like that was hard to contain.

Making a quick decision, Maynard Charles picked up the telephone and dialled for reception. Moments later, Billy Brogan stepped into the office with an inscrutable look on his face.

'You called for me, Mr Charles?'

By now, Maynard had plucked his fountain pen from the pot on his desk and begun scribbling a note, which he slipped inside an envelope. This he sealed with a drop of wax from a flickering candle, and pressed into Billy's hand.

'It's to go to Mr Abner Grant at the Imperial Hotel. Abner Grant, and no other, do you understand? Deliver it to him forthwith, wait while he reads it, and then ask to take the letter back. Mr Grant may give you something in return; he may not. That's of no consequence – not at this juncture. But it's imperative that you bring this letter back to me, or else destroy it on the way. A gutter would do, Billy, but make sure it's destroyed. Do you understand?'

Billy hesitated. 'I do, sir, but isn't this work better fitted to a page?'

Maynard rolled his eyes. 'I should never have signed off on this little change of career of yours, Master Brogan. You were more use where I had you.' He paused. 'This job, it's of critical importance.'

As Maynard's words petered out, Billy's eyes flashed with a bright new idea.

'There's a new page, sir.'

Maynard remained silent.

'He can be trusted, Mr Charles. I'd vouch for that myself.'

Billy fancied he could see a big blue vein, as fat as a caterpillar, throbbing on Mr Charles's temple. Then, finally, the old man acquiesced.

'It's on your head, Brogan. This letter is to reach Abner Grant and no other. It isn't to be left with a proxy. It isn't to disappear into the Imperial post room. It's to go directly to Grant's hands. Anything less, and you're to answer for it. Do you understand?'

Billy Brogan puffed out his chest and accepted his commission with inordinate pride. Then, leaving a distinctly harassed Maynard Charles behind, he headed out into the hotel.

Frank Nettleton was where Billy had last seen him, in the old hotel laundries – long since decommissioned – that doubled as a pages' lounge. Less than a week into his service, he already looked like a native. He had Billy to thank for that. He was wearing the simple grey uniform that all hotel pages wore, and the heaviness of his eyes was less to do with the intensity of work at the Buckingham than it was the cacophony that Billy's vast brood of brothers and sisters made at night, robbing Frank of any sleep. The Brogans were grateful of the contribution Frank was making to household expenses – and Billy himself didn't mind making a bed for Frank in his own room, since he was so rarely there. Billy had been taking great pride in introducing Frank – just like Nancy had told him – to the secrets and mysteries of London town. Give him another few weeks, and Frank would know all the alleys between Lambeth and Mayfair, have met every hospitable shopkeeper and flower seller, and even know the intimate histories of every last one of the Buckingham's regular clientele. By the end of the summer, he'd be another Billy Brogan in the making – and then, no matter what the future held, the Buckingham wouldn't be able to live without him. He'd be indispensable, his future secured.

Frank looked up wearily when Billy dropped the letter into his hands.

'Wh-what is it?'

'It's an education!' Billy declared.

Frank turned the letter over. The name on the front was written in cursive script, and barely legible to Frank's eyes.

'I don't know, Billy. I'm not g-good with my letters. Didn't Nance say?'

'You don't got to be. That name on the front there is Abner Grant. Now, listen, this is a special directive, courtesy of Mr Maynard Charles himself. He's entrusting it to you – for the future prosperity of the Buckingham Hotel itself!'

Frank blanched. Billy thought he had never seen a boy look so pale and white.

'You're to get up and out, and down to the Imperial – it's not far, and I'll point you the way. It sits up on Lancaster Gate.' He paused. 'Look, come with me, Frank, I'll set you straight.'

Up the stairs, out of the old laundries, and at last Billy and Frank came to the staff entrance. There were wild flowers on the banks of Berkeley Square. Soon, the whole place would be a riot of colour. Berkeley Square in the summertime was – or so Billy insisted – the most beautiful of all London's parks. Hyde Park itself had nothing on Berkeley Square.

'When you get there,' Billy repeated, 'look for Abner. You won't miss him. He's as round as he is tall. A big white beard, and mutton chops to boot. Put him in a sleigh with some reindeer and you'd mistake him for Father Christmas. Only, he isn't nearly as friendly.' He paused. 'Now, you understand what you got to do?'

'The letter to Abner Grant.'

'Indeed. But here's the important bit, Billy. You got to destroy it. Don't let anybody see it. Don't even let Abner Grant keep that piece of paper – on honour of your life! Get it off him after he's read it, and tear it up so that nobody could ever read it again.'

Frank had taken only two steps along Michaelmas Mews before he stopped and looked back. He had the inalienable feeling that, no matter who had commissioned this, he was doing something *wrong*. Frank had always had a strong moral compass – he got that from his sister.

'What's in the letter, Billy?'

Billy gave him a knowing look. 'Page's honour, isn't it, Frank? Don't ask, don't tell.'

Frank nodded. London suddenly seemed so incalculably vast. If he wasn't careful, he'd lose himself among its towers and spires. He had to keep his head screwed on. He had to *think*.

Two steps later, Frank looked back again.

'*Why*, Billy? *Why* would Mr Charles want to write to Mr Grant this way?'

Billy preened. 'I couldn't possibly guess—'

'But who is he, Billy?'

'Well, that's where the mystery thickens, young Master Nettle-ton.' Billy strode up Michaelmas Mews, putting an arm around Frank. 'Mr Abner Grant is the Imperial's detective. They say he's the best in London. That he can catch any crook in a hotel, root out any wrongdoing. But the thing about old Abner is . . . he and Mr Charles, they've hated each other a long, long time. The way I heard it, they fought together in the Great War and, well, there's been bad blood ever since.' He paused. 'So what does Mr Charles want with Mr Grant now, twenty years after the fact? *That*, Frank, I couldn't tell you.' Billy's face opened in the most glorious, preposterous grin. 'But it's going to be fun finding out . . .'

Chapter Five

S OMETIMES, HÉLÈNE MARCHMONT EVEN DREAMED of the ballroom.

Tonight had been one of those nights. Leaving the Grand after Archie Adams and his orchestra came to their final crescendo, she had felt weariness wash over her even before she was out of her ball gown. Sometimes, the dancers and musicians gathered to toast the night's success – but, more and more often, Hélène sloped away gracefully, back to her quarters and the comfort of her four-poster bed. It wasn't just the dancing, she knew. It was the concentration she needed to keep her secret: the secret that whisked her away from the Buckingham, over the river Thames, and into the back streets of Brixton. The secret who cried and squawked and asked for her mama, and went by the name of *Sybil*.

Hélène had retired, wearily content in the knowledge that tomorrow, she would catch the omnibus south and be reunited with her daughter. Even a few snatched hours were worth all the world to her. In vain, she hoped she might even dream of Sybil, but, instead, she found herself back in the ballroom, being swept along in the arms of, first Gene Sheldon, and then Raymond de Guise. She missed Raymond. She'd danced with him for so long that she could anticipate not only his every move, but the very *feelings* that fed into them. Not that she begrudged him his Californian serenade. If what Raymond wanted was the life being promised to him by his old mentor Georges de la Motte – well, that was what he should go after. Life was nothing without dreams.

Hélène felt her heart twinge for Nancy Nettleton, the chambermaid with whom Raymond was in love. Romances were ruined because of ambition. It was such a familiar story.

One moment, Hélène was waltzing through a dream, she and Raymond dancing on air across the floor of the Grand Ballroom, kings and courtesans turning around them. Then she opened her eyes, sat bolt upright in bed.

Somebody was knocking at the door.

By the time she was wrapped in her dressing gown – burgundy flannel, embroidered with the copper crown crest of the hotel – the knocking had grown in urgency. Hélène opened the door – and there stood the Spanish dancer Sofía LaPegna, her eyes red and raw.

'Sofía!' Hélène gasped. 'Sofía, what is it?' She reached out to take Sofía's arm, and it was only then that she noticed how she was dressed: in a plain brown house dress and coat, fastened with a single silver brooch. On the floor at her feet was a leather holdall with a golden clasp. 'Sofía, come in.'

Sofía resisted Hélène's hand. 'I came only to say goodbye,' she said, the Spanish inflection in her words becoming stronger the more emotional she became. 'Oh, Hélène . . .'

Something broke inside Sofía. She drew in deep, ugly breaths, but even that could not control the crying. Hélène stepped into the hall and put her arms around her. Sofía's tears were an unstoppable cascade.

'They destroyed Guernica,' she finally whispered, with what little breath she had left. 'The Condor Legion. The Nazis. It is all over the BBC. They razed Guernica to the ground.'

Every day the wireless trilled with yet more reports from the war in Spain. Ordinarily, Hélène put it out of her mind – but every time she saw Sofía, she remembered, starkly, that on the other end of every news story were real people: people living, people dying.

'My brother was in Guernica only last month. That is where we last had news.'

Hélène took her by the shoulders, shook her fiercely. 'Listen to me. *Listen*. It doesn't mean a thing. He's survived this long, hasn't he? Well, *hasn't* he?'

Sofía stepped back. There was suddenly a new steeliness about her, as she disentangled herself from Hélène's arms.

'No, Miss Marchmont. *No*. I have come to tell you goodbye, and that is what I must do. I'm . . . leaving, Hélène.'

'Leaving?'

'I will cross into France, and then back home – to Spain, or what's left of it. I must know if he lives or dies.' She paused. 'I wanted to thank you. Of everyone at the Buckingham, it has been you – you alone – who I have needed. You have been like a sister to me, and I will always remember.'

'Sofía, please—'

'My mind is made up. Only, I would not let the Buckingham down. It has been a home from home. And there is a gentleman, a guest, who requested my favour tonight. He wanted to dance, and I made a promise. He is a gentleman – a charitable man. Arthur Regan, from County Cavan. I wanted to ask – if you are not promised already, might you take my place tonight?'

38

Hélène was silent.

'Miss Marchmont,' Sofía began. Her eyes were dry now, and she picked up her leather holdall with the air of a businessman about to depart. 'Miss Marchmont, I'll remember you fondly.'

'And I you, Sofía,' Hélène whispered.

And then she was gone.

Later, Hélène would feel the emptiness of knowing that here, right here, she had witnessed the way a faraway war could chip away at the Buckingham itself. But right now, as she trudged back into her quarters, her mind was dominated by only one thought: *I wasn't meant to dance tonight at all. I was meant to be in Brixton – where I belong – with my daughter . . .*

What the Buckingham gives, the Buckingham takes away, she thought, and summoned the new page Frank Nettleton to deliver a message.

Once the afternoon demonstration dances were finished, Hélène returned with Gene Sheldon to the dance studio behind the Grand Ballroom. Standing in for Sofía LaPegna meant more than just turning a few foxtrots with Arthur Regan; when Hélène had an off-night, Sofía danced the evening's opening number, and consequently, there was a routine to rehearse.

Fortunately, Gene was one of the most consummate professionals Hélène had encountered in all her years on the ballroom circuit. Tall and handsome, he was airy and light on his feet, and the way he took guests in hold suggested a man without a doubt in his ability. Light of voice, a man of few words, what he lacked in conversation, he more than made up for in balance and poise.

'It's a simple number, Hélène,' Gene began as they box-stepped around the studio. 'Poor Miss LaPegna has been so distracted, we barely conceived anything at all.'

For a time, they danced – but Hélène's heart was four miles away, over the river and up the long Brixton Road, and no matter how hard Gene tried, the *feeling* was not coming to her this afternoon.

'Are you worried for Sofía, Miss Marchmont?'

Hélène said, 'I'm worried for us all,' for, if war was a reality, and the Buckingham one of its casualties, what did that mean for Sybil? Without the money Hélène sent home, the Archers – Sybil's grandparents, who devoted their lives to her well-being – would be lost. Without the Buckingham, there was every chance Sybil would . . .

Thoughts like these did nothing to lift Hélène's spirits, so she was grateful when the studio door opened and Louis Kildare walked in. Big and broad, with his saxophone in one hand and a fistful of sheet music in the other, Louis stopped when he saw Hélène and Gene turning around each other, and would have left if Hélène hadn't broken out of Gene's hold, whispered, 'Shall we take five minutes?' and hurried after.

'Louis Kildare, I haven't seen you in *days*. Where have you been hiding?'

Louis could not ignore a taunt like that, not from Hélène Marchmont, the Ice Queen of the ballroom herself. When he turned to face her, he was beaming. When he smiled like that, he reminded Hélène of Sybil's father, Sidney. Louis and Sidney came from the same sun-kissed Caribbean isles and their friendship, forged in the clubs and dance halls of Soho and the East End, had been like the relationship between brothers. There was

40

no other in the hotel who missed Sidney like Hélène did – but Louis Kildare came close.

'I'm sorry, Hélène. Archie's delivered us his new compositions. I was going to sneak in an hour rehearsing before tonight … I wouldn't dream of interrupting you and Mr Sheldon though.'

'Oh, we don't need to rehearse. Tonight's hardly going to be a Buckingham classic, I'm afraid.'

Louis's face creased. Then, in a low whisper, he said, 'I thought you were in Brixton today?'

She whispered, 'Plans change.'

Louis opened his fist, letting the sheet music float to the floor, and laid his hand gently on her shoulder. 'I'm sorry, Hélène.' He knew, as few others did, what she was missing out on to be here for the Buckingham's guests.

'I have a taxicab coming, as soon as the final dance is over. I'm going to see her, Louis, no matter what. One hour, two – whatever I can get.'

Louis nodded. 'I'll share that cab with you, if I may. After I'm through here, I've a spot at the Baritone in Knightsbridge.'

Hélène squinted. 'The Baritone?' She knew of it, but only by reputation. 'That's a—'

'Classy affair,' Louis interjected.

'Isn't it—?'

'Too classy for a black man?' Hélène reeled back, but Louis smiled. 'The world's on the change, Hélène. If a black man has talent, he can play in the most garlanded of halls – just like our own Buckingham Hotel. Lord help him if all he can do is rattle some spoons.'

'Are you all right, Louis?' She had detected something in his voice, some timbre she did not recognise. Was she wrong – or

41

was there something *gloomy* hiding behind the eyes of Louis Kildare?

'I been doing myself some moonlighting, Hélène, that's all. The Baritone. The Nest. Anywhere they're in need of a man of my talents.' He lifted his prized saxophone. 'I love the Buckingham. It's only that, sometimes you start . . . hungering, I suppose, is the word. You need something *more*. For you that's Sybil. But for an old dog like me . . .'

Hélène watched as Louis sauntered away, kicking his heels as he went. There was something heartbreaking about seeing Louis Kildare dejected; it was, she decided, like listening to the mewling of an abandoned puppy. A sudden thought occurred to her and she called out.

'It isn't . . . You don't have *romantic* trouble, do you, Louis?'

Louis looked over his shoulder. His dark eyes met Hélène's of glacial blue. 'The lack of romance is the only romantic problem I've had for a lifetime!' He laughed, and walked away with a new spring in his step.

But still, the feeling that nagged at her, the feeling that all was not right in the world of Louis Kildare, would not go away.

Across the Grand Ballroom, the lights went up.

The guests turned, raising their glasses to the rainbow of colour refracting through the ballroom's manifold crystal chandeliers. Among the throng, where Maynard Charles paced, the anticipation reached its peak. Conversations faltered. Eager looks were shared. Then, the stage doors opened – and the Archie Adams Orchestra marched to their seats.

When the first number reached its peak, Louis Kildare taking centre stage with a triumphant saxophone solo, the doors opened again – and, in pairs, the Buckingham dancers waltzed out into the Grand. Last among them came Hélène Marchmont and Gene Sheldon. At the heart of the other dancers, they glided and swooped, describing a grand romance on the ballroom floor. Then, to a stirring round of applause – and rampant trumpets and trombone – Hélène and Gene came apart, each twirling to the edge of the dance floor where their promised guests for the evening were waiting.

Hélène knew who Arthur Regan was only from the description Billy Brogan had delivered before the dances began. A tall, rakish gentleman with red hair, and whiskers to match, he was standing at the edge of the ballroom floor in a crushed velvet dinner jacket, with a champagne flute in one hand. As Hélène approached, his eyes – green, and dazzling in the ballroom light – seemed to widen, as if to take her in. *You're not Sofía LaPegna*, they seemed to be saying.

A nervousness with which she was not familiar settled in the pit of Hélène's stomach. It was unlike her to feel nervous with a guest, and yet something about Arthur Regan prickled, deep inside her.

'Mr Regan,' she began. 'Might we begin?'

Arthur Regan paused, before finally saying, 'Madame, we might,' his Irish lilt so strong – and yet so refined – that it took Hélène quite by surprise.

He was an adept dancer. Hélène had danced with beggars and fools, with princes and kings, and few of them turned a waltz with the same fluidity as Arthur, his beautifully poised body sailing across the floor of the Grand. Hélène was even more impressed when the Archie Adams Orchestra struck up their own version of 'Puttin' on the Ritz' and Arthur transitioned expertly into the shorter, syncopated movements – the lock-steps and hops and skips – of the classic quickstep. What Hélène had expected to be a chore – as it so often was with dancing guests – had, somewhere along the way, turned into a genuine joy.

She did not know she was smiling until Arthur slowed and whispered, 'Am I doing it right, Miss Marchmont?'

'You're doing it splendidly, Mr Regan.' She'd have said it whether he was dancing like a professional or bucking around the ballroom like a runaway horse – but it brought her great joy to actually mean it for once.

They were in the middle of their third dance when suddenly Arthur asked, 'Miss Marchmont, might we take a break?'

Hélène had heard it before. Wealthy men thought they could buy anything they wanted – and, when they found it could not buy them grace on the ballroom floor, they looked to buy certain *favours* away from it. Hélène could hardly remember the number of times she'd been propositioned in the Grand, so she politely demurred.

'A glass of champagne,' Arthur went on. 'That's all. Then we can resume.' He paused. 'I'm old,' he said – though, to Hélène's eyes, he could have been no older than forty. 'My wife, Lord keep her, has been ten years in the ground. Let me delight in your company, Hélène. One drink – and then the ballroom can have you back.'

Hélène knew what Maynard Charles would think. *Mr Regan is a valued guest, Hélène. Were he making an inappropriate suggestion, you can count on the Buckingham to support the dignity of its dancers. But if he is not . . .*

Hélène nodded. 'I'm partial to champagne.' And Arthur's smile, as he led her from the dance floor, was the smile of a true angel.

44

Some time later, a magnum of Moët et Chandon on ice between them, they sat at one of the circular tables on the edge of the Grand. As Archie Adams and his orchestra launched into 'Sweethearts and Rye', one of Archie's own compositions, Arthur coaxed Hélène to tell him a little of her own history. Careful as ever to avoid any mention of Sybil, she regaled him, instead, with the story of how she had once stared out from the covers of both *Harper's Bazaar* and *Esquire* in the very same month. Shallow nonsense, Hélène knew, but it was what men liked to hear.

'And you, Mr Regan? What brings you to our hotel?'

'You mean to ask' – Arthur smiled – 'if I'm to become a regular patron?'

It wasn't what Hélène had meant, but the twinkle in his emerald eyes made her forgive him the assumption.

'Since my Agatha passed on, I have tried to do some good in this world. In her memory, you understand . . .'

Hélène hardly caught the next words, because the idea of Arthur's dead wife ripped her out of the Buckingham and put her back at Sidney's side: what it had been like to have him, to hold him, to stand weeping at his grave.

'I have, you might say, a private income, of sorts. A collection of the estate bequeathed to me when Agatha passed on, and what my own grandfather – a brewer of some renown from where I hail – left behind. Some men might squander it on drink and horses. Some men might fritter it away and end up derelicts. But I saw an opportunity to do something greater. I began to do what I could for the rural poor back home. But then . . . Well, then I came to London.'

The London Irish, Arthur explained, were among the sorriest examples of his countrymen he had encountered. A proud

45

people, come to seek their fortunes in the big city – and yet, in London's streets, his fellow men were spat upon, derided and beaten, simply for being who they were.

'All across London, men little different from me are being treated like animals. I have set myself the not insignificant challenge of improving conditions for all the London Irish – to ensure, in my own lifetime, that what opportunities this city presents to others, might also be presented to my fellow Irishmen . . .'

He paused. Hélène was not surprised when his fingers danced across the table as if to brush against her own – this, after all, was how wealthy men behaved – but what *did* surprise her was that her hand did not automatically retract. It wasn't only the way his eyes were dancing across her. It was what he'd said. She looked back at the ballroom floor and her eyes lit upon Louis Kildare, there upon the stage with his saxophone in hand. It wasn't long ago that men like Louis, and her own Sidney, would not have been able to play in an orchestra as distinguished as this – and all for the crime of being black. *And still, if it were known I'd given birth to a black man's child, what would that mean for me? The Board would think it a disgrace. I'd be besmirching the good name of their ballroom.*

'Mark my words,' Arthur Regan went on, 'one day equality will prevail. That, Miss Marchmont, is the promise I've given the world.'

Hélène was silent; there she sat, in a daze, until finally Arthur stood and took her hand.

'Might we finish our dance?'

This, she decided, was easier than trying to process whatever feelings Arthur had stirred in her. Because it was not just the recollection of Sidney. It was not just the passion he had for righting all of London's social wrongs. It was something else, something she could hardly admit, even to herself: an instant affection. An instant admiration. An instant . . .

Up on her feet, Hélène was able to put the thought out of her mind. You could lose yourself in dancing. That was only one of the many things that she loved about the ballroom floor: a few brief moments, basking in the music, and everything else evaporated away.

So she and Arthur danced, long into the night, until the Archie Adams Orchestra wound down. To Hélène, it seemed the only thing she could possibly do.

That night, when the ballroom finally closed its doors, Hélène and Louis climbed into a cab out on Berkeley Square and sat in companionable silence together as it wound its way, first into Knightsbridge – where Louis, looking back gently at Hélène, climbed out and made haste towards the Baritone – and then further south. When she had finally reached her destination, Hélène climbed out at a row of terraced houses, and rapped gently on the door. Soon, it drew back – and there stood Sidney's parents, Noelle and Maurice Archer. On the ground beneath them, more confident than ever on her feet and wearing the brightest, toothiest smile, was Sybil herself.

'You're up late, little one,' Hélène began, sweeping the child into her arms. 'Are you teething again?'

Then she was through the doors, breathing in the scents of this, her secret second home. It would have been perfect, if only it hadn't been for the feeling nagging away at the back of her mind that all was not right.

It took her an age to understand what that feeling was, and longer still to admit it, even to herself.

It was guilt.

She was feeling guilty.

And it was because of Arthur Regan.

She'd been thinking of him all the way back home.

Chapter Six

NANCY NETTLETON COULD ALREADY HEAR Rosa and Ruth clucking about the kitchenette, getting ready for the evening gathering in the housekeeping lounge downstairs, but the carriage clock on her bedside table told her there were still seven minutes left. Reaching under her pillow, she drew out the latest envelope.

It was approaching dusk over Berkeley Square, and the final hints of sunlight illuminated Raymond's beautiful penmanship. The letter had been waiting for her last night, delivered from the hotel post room by Billy Brogan himself. She had read it twice already, but this evening – after a long day flitting between the hotel's various suites – she needed to savour it again, if only to feel Raymond's words washing over her from so far away.

> Dearest Nancy,
>
> I can hardly describe the beauty of the sun pouring over the Hollywood Hills, so let me instead describe the moonlight . . .
>
> I have spent the last week on the set of A Ballroom on Broadway, dancing with Laurana St Clair's stand-in, Ruby, while lighting rigs are lifted and scaffolds set up. The industry of making movies is as

involved as the industry of running a luxury hotel. Maynard Charles himself might be able to marshal a film set.

I have learned so much. The demands of dancing on screen are quite different to the demands of the ballroom – where, no matter who is watching, one might get lost in a fantasy world of one's own. Here, the fantasy must be shared with cameramen, lighting technicians, directors, producers, and all the many thousands who will one day be watching. Georges de la Motte has taken great pleasure in introducing me not only to his representatives here, but to Mr Havelock Meyer, the head of the studio which will finance A Ballroom on Broadway and, should the tide turn his way, all the future movies in which Georges will be a star.

Yet I am not only learning about making movies. In A Ballroom on Broadway, Georges and Laurana are playing two dancers from the Mid-west, down on their luck and looking to catch a break in the big city. They visit the clubs of Harlem, New York . . . and there they discover a new dance. The jitterbug. By the end of the movie, they are dancing the jitterbug on the stages of Broadway. So, two nights ago, the producers arranged for Georges, Laurana and I to experience it for ourselves at the Lion's Den, a private dance hall high in the Hollywood Hills.

This is no Midnight Rooms or any of the other clubs you and I have danced at together in Soho, Nancy. A mansion, framed by white colonnades, sits looking down on the Californian valley, and here the high and mighty of Hollywood gather to dance under sparkling California stars. I have heard of the jitterbug, but I have never seen it like this: the joy in it, the liveliness, the freedom as heels rock back and forth, as partners turn and kick and swing, their hands held not like graceful figures of state in the ballroom – but like lovers. To see Georges give himself to the lively, pulsating music – this has been one of the most singular joys of my life.

I can hardly wait to teach you the jitterbug, Nancy, when I am back in England.

I am soon to cross America by land. By this time next week, I will be driving back across the orange groves of California and east. Ten days later, I am due in New York to meet Mr John Hastings Junior – or, as Maynard Charles described it, to 'romance and delight' him as I would any other feted guest of our Buckingham Hotel. I admit I will miss these Californian skies. I wish that I could share it with you, other than in these words.

New York is the first port of call on my journey back to you. After that, I will be at sea – and, though my letters must end, I will still speak to you, as if you are there with me. Let us hope I will be bringing back with me the man who will help restore the Buckingham to its former reputation – and be a bulwark for us all in the years to come.

I am longing to see you.

Yours always,

Raymond

There came a knock at the door. Quickly squirrelling the letter away, Nancy got to her feet to find Rosa standing there. Four years Nancy's junior, her golden hair was tied back in a bun and her eyes were dazzling blue.

'You coming, Nance? Mrs Moffatt won't like us being late.'

Once a week, the entire housekeeping staff gathered for dinner in the housekeeping lounge. It was a chance to feel united, said Mrs Moffatt, but the truth was it was a chance for her to spot any rivalries, any problems, anything that might disrupt the department. Yes, Mrs Moffatt was as much an army general as

Maynard Charles – only she did it with a benevolent smile on her face and a pocket full of barley sugars.

'I'm excused tonight, Rosa.'

'Excused?' Rosa asked, in mock horror.

'It's—'

'No, I remember now. It's your *special* duties with Miss Edgerton, isn't it?' Rosa shook her head, as if in sympathy. 'Nance, you never did learn how to keep your head down in a place like this!' Then, as she scurried down the hall after Ruth, Edie, Vera and all of the others, she turned and called back, 'Say, Nance, I been seeing your Frankie around the place. Up and down these halls like he's always belonged here. Got a bit of your pluck and derring-do, has he?'

Nancy was silent. 'Pluck' and 'derring-do' were not words she naturally connected with herself – but to think of anyone describing her Frank like that was absurd.

'You be nice to him, Rosa,' she said.

No matter what front he's putting on, Frank won't feel a part of this yet. It's going to take him a lot longer than me.

Vivienne Edgerton was waiting just outside the storeroom door at the staff entrance. As Nancy approached, she saw Vivienne was dressed in a pair of navy lounge trousers and a simple satin blouse. The short coat in her hand was woollen, with a simple fur trim. Only the pin in her hair, dazzling and bright, gave the impression that Vivienne was a person of any means.

I shouldn't be doing this, thought Nancy. *If Maynard Charles were to find out – Lord help me if he were to tell Lord Edgerton or any of the board – I'd be hauled in front of Mrs Moffatt. Who knows if I'd even be here when Raymond gets back.*

But it was too late anyway. Vivienne's eyes lit up when she saw Nancy approaching.

'I was beginning to think you wouldn't come.'

'I always keep my promises, Miss Edgerton.'

'I'm glad you do.' Vivienne reached out a hand and squeezed Nancy's.

Nancy wasn't sure if she would ever get used to the idea that Vivienne Edgerton was so eager to be her friend. *Six years younger than me, but six social strata higher. The Buckingham never ceases to amaze.*

'Shall we?'

Nancy nodded. Then they were off, through the staff door, up and out of Michaelmas Mews – where the taxicab Billy Brogan had summoned for them was already waiting.

Arlington Road stretched north into the warren of streets that was Camden Town, the rolling dell of Regent's Park on one side and a chaos of tenements and terraces on the other. As Nancy helped Vivienne out, the driver turned and scowled.

'Are you sure this is the place?' he asked with the unmistakable accent of the Dagenham docks where he lived.

'Quite sure,' replied Vivienne. Then, reaching into her purse – black leather with a handle studded in pearls – she passed back a single pristine banknote. 'I'd like it if you remained. We shan't be more than an hour.'

'Just wait here?' the driver scoffed. 'I'm your personal chauffeur, is that it?'

Vivienne arched an eyebrow, witheringly. Nancy was impressed with the way she carried herself; her voice was still strong with the accent of her native New York, but the way she

53

looked at the cab driver was British and imperious in its every expression, surely picked up from her haughty stepfather.

'As I say, we shan't be more than an hour.'

Vivienne took Nancy by the arm and together they strolled further up Arlington Road, Nancy's bad leg aching as they walked. The tenements glowered at them. Figures appeared at windows high up. Laundry was strung in the dirty air. The smells that came off the road were of smoke and petrol and, underpinning it all, something riper – like the hotel's kitchen waste, left to go off in the sun.

After some time, Vivienne consulted a piece of notepaper secreted in her purse. Then she looked up and permitted herself a smile. There had been no real need to take such a fastidious note of their destination. The building above was a veritable fortress of red brick and iron railing, an Industrial Age manor house, almost as vast as the Buckingham Hotel itself.

Nancy stared up at the building's austere façade.

'Are you certain about this, Miss Edgerton?'

Vivienne paused. 'I know what they think of me at the Buckingham. That I'm a spoilt little rich girl whose only real interests are ball gowns and boys, and how loaded I can get. Well, that's about to change. I'm doing this, Nancy. And I need someone at my side. They call it the Rowton House. A hotel for working men. Well, it isn't quite like *our* hotel, is it, Nancy? But . . .' For a moment, her nerves evidently bettered her. 'We're here to meet a Mr Ross, the house's general manager. Nancy, I believe this may be it. My way to pay back, for all the good things I've had.' Defiantly, she went up the steps. 'And if I happen to be doing it with my stepfather's allowance, well, that's simply the icing on the cake. To take from the rich and give to the poor. Who could belittle me for that?'

Through the doors was a receiving hall laid with oak block floor-ing, in which an elderly man sat behind a desk. It was dark within, but light spilled in from a multitude of passageways funnelling deeper into the house. Oak seats ran around the room, and the bare brickwork was glazed the colour of chocolate, rich and glossy. On the walls hung murals of forests and islands, factories and mills.

Nancy was aware of Vivienne whispering beneath her breath, as if to give herself courage. Finally, she approached the desk, introduced herself and asked to be presented to Mr Ross. Obediently, the man shuffled off along one of the pas-sages, returning some moments later with an instruction that Vivienne and Nancy should wait.

'I read about this place in the *Daily Herald*,' said Vivienne. 'They were championing its virtues – a place of dignity for the common man. When Mr Ross discovered who I was, he was very accommodating. This name my stepfather forced on me, it has to be good for something, wouldn't you say?'

Nancy was lost in thought. The Rowton House might have been vaster, but it was not so very different from the place she had left Frank when she first came to London.

'Miss Edgerton, I presume?'

The voice belonged to a man who had materialised from one of the inner passageways. He was in the throes of middle age, with the protruding paunch and thinning hair to prove it. He was dressed like any city banking clerk, thought Nancy, and there was something undeniably kind about his soft, grey eyes.

Vivienne took his hand. 'Mr Ross?'

'The very same. I'm charmed to meet you. It isn't always we have the chance to show off our work here to a potential benefactor. I'm glad you could come down.'

'I've been intrigued, ever since I read the piece in the *Herald*,' Vivienne replied.

Nancy was sure Mr Ross himself wouldn't notice, but there was a tremble to her voice that Nancy had rarely heard before.

It means she thinks she's out of her depth. But Vivienne doesn't know the kind of power she has. With a little more self-confidence, she could be a force to be reckoned with.

'Well,' Mr Ross went on, 'I must send the girls at the *Herald* flowers.' A moment later, Vivienne beamed – an affectation, but an affectation that seemed to put Mr Ross under a spell. 'Shall we begin our little tour? There's much that I can show you' – he stuttered to a halt, before finally he concluded – 'before we come down to business.'

Vivienne nodded – but she had not taken two steps before her face blanched, and Nancy could see the kind of fear she was try-ing to conceal. Perhaps it was only the act of following this man into the darkness that unnerved her, or perhaps it was some-thing deeper: the realisation that she was taking the first step on a journey that might take her away from the life she'd been promised – and in which, until a few scant months ago, she had been happy to indulge.

Fortune favours the bold, Miss Edgerton, Nancy thought – and, stepping forward, took her by the arm.

'It's all right, Miss Edgerton,' she said quietly. 'Isn't this why you brought me along?'

Vivienne hardened, as if ashamed of how much Nancy had seen. 'Nancy, I haven't the faintest idea . . .'

Nancy grinned. 'Stay close to me – I'll remember the way out.'

Something melted inside Vivienne – and, at this, she herself tittered.

'Thank you, Nancy,' she whispered – and, arm in arm, they followed Mr Ross deeper into the maze.

What had appeared as one grand red-brick manor from outside was actually six different constructions, each nestled around the other. Mr Ross showed them a dining hall that put Nancy in mind of the Victorian workhouses she'd read about in the stories of Mr Dickens. He showed them the reading room, where men were slumped around with newspapers in hand. He showed them banks of bedrooms that put Nancy in mind of stables, with hard concrete floors and swing doors opening onto each.

'We can sleep more than five thousand destitutes when we are at capacity,' Mr Ross proudly declared, as he opened the door to one of the bedrooms, where small partitions separated bed from bed, and dozens of men were already reclining. 'Iron bedsteads. Horsehair mattresses. Yes, these men – and women, in a separate block – sleep well here.' He stopped, turning on his heel. 'They may be penniless, but our policy is simple – man needs dignity. When he loses his livelihood, his dignity is the first thing that falters. And we believe that, if you restore a little of his dignity, the rest of life will follow.'

He led them between buildings, past concrete courtyards, and into pavilions where yet more bedrooms were laid out.

'Our costs are low. Seven pence a night for a cubicle in one of our dormitory rooms. Less, if our guests are staying with us longer than a week. If it's a demarcated bedroom you want, well, that's a little dearer. Here men have a chance to reclaim a little of their souls, wouldn't you agree?'

Mr Ross was about to lead them on when Vivienne called out, 'Mr Ross, I've seen quite enough. As I think you know, I didn't come here merely for a tour of your estate. I've a gift I should like to make.'

Mr Ross's lips curled in a smile. *He's been waiting for this*, thought Nancy, *all along. He knows how to play this game.*

'Miss Edgerton, let us make a very welcome retreat.'

In Mr Ross's office, Vivienne reached into her purse and produced a single sheet of paper: a banker's draft, drawn from Lloyd's that very afternoon. As she handed it over, Mr Ross took in the inky signature and figures printed on its front with something approaching delight. His fat black moustache trembled as he nodded his thanks.

Then, as if to speak of money at all was uncouth, he opened a drawer, placed it within, and met her with a smile.

'The good your kindness will do for the destitute of London is unparalleled. Might I ask,' he ventured, 'if we might see you again?'

'You may, Mr Ross. I have to admit, I have become enamoured of your work here.'

Mr Ross folded his hands. 'The Lord moves in us all,' he said. 'He is moving here tonight.'

By the time Mr Ross showed Nancy and Vivienne back through the doors, night had hardened across Camden Town. The smell in the air – the smoke, the petrol, the faint tang of sewage – was given new, crystalline clarity by the cold air. *April*, thought Nancy, *and by night it still has the whisper of winter.*

The taxicab was still waiting, further down the road. After bidding farewell to Mr Ross, Nancy and Vivienne were about to head in its direction when, from the darkness on the other side of the street, two figures appeared. They lurched across the road, one propped up against another, until they were almost at the steps of the Rowton House.

'I must beg your pardon, ladies,' said Mr Ross, with a stiff formality.

Without waiting a second longer, he descended the steps and met the two strangers where they were staggering onto the kerb. By now, bathed in the orange lamplight, Nancy could see their faces starkly. Both appeared hungry and gaunt, but that wasn't what drew her attention. Nor was it the ripe smell that, even from a distance, she could detect coming off them.

No, thought Nancy. *It's their eyes.*

Their eyes, rimmed in red and yet wide and glassy, did not seem to see Mr Ross as he approached. They seemed to be looking straight through him, as if they were in some other world entirely. These men looked hungry in body, but they looked hungrier in their souls.

She thought of her father, how he'd been in the weeks before he passed away, his body given entirely to the laudanum keeping his pain at bay.

She thought of Vivienne Edgerton at Christmas last year, the special powders the last head concierge used to source for her from that crooked little den in Soho . . .

'I'm sorry, boys,' Mr Ross intoned. His voice was bigger and heavier than Nancy remembered. He had opened his arms wide, as if to sweep the two strangers on their way. 'I'll have to ask you to move on. It would be a crying shame if I was to have to call the constabulary.'

One of the strangers tried to lurch past Mr Ross's open arm, as if to make for the Rowton House door.

'*No!*' Mr Ross declared.

His voice must have acted as a summons because, a moment later, three of the hostel's residents were running down the steps to help usher the men on their way.

After it was done, the men retreating into the outer darkness of Camden Town, Mr Ross rejoined Nancy and Vivienne on the hostel steps.

'Those men,' Nancy ventured. 'Why did you turn them away? There are still beds, aren't there?'

'I'm sorry you had to witness so unseemly a spectacle, especially after your kind donation. Yes, we have room at the inn this evening – but our house is for the destitute of London, those who have fallen prey to the scourge of our time – poverty, and its manifold traps. Yet some men have fallen prey to different scourges. I'm sure two delicate things like yourselves have little experience of such, but . . . drink, and worse, drags men down. These are vices which a man of character can fight himself. We must not let it pollute the good work we do at the Rowton Houses.'

Nancy caught Vivienne's eye.

'You would turn them away?' Vivienne asked. 'People in need? But isn't that—'

'Some people are beyond help. We must not squander what little we have in the pursuit of lost causes.' Mr Ross paused. 'Let me escort you to your taxicab, ladies.'

The taxicab driver was snoozing, his face pressed against the window, when Nancy and Vivienne climbed into the back seat. Suddenly stirred, he fired up the engine – and soon they were cutting their way back south, over Euston Road and into more familiar terrain.

As the houses grew more noble around them, as Fitzrovia turned into Mayfair and the gleaming town houses gazed benevolently down, Nancy turned to Vivienne.

'It's a good thing you did tonight, Miss Edgerton. Not a soul can deny it. And yet—'

Vivienne stopped her. 'I saw them too, Nancy.'

'To turn men away, when they're in need . . .'

Vivienne's head snapped up, her eyes open in a fiery glare. 'I said I saw them too!'

Momentarily taken aback, Nancy struggled to gather her composure. 'Miss Edgerton,' she began, more sheepish now, 'I overstepped my mark. Forgive me. I forgot myself.'

For a time, Vivienne was silent. Only slowly did her anger begin to subside.

'No,' she finally whispered, 'forgive *me*, Nancy. It's only that . . .' Her voice turned cold again, as cold and flinty as it was before – only, now, it was not directed at her. 'He seemed an upstanding sort when he took my stepfather's money, didn't he? He seemed as if he *cared*, when he was showing us around. And yet, the way he looked at those men, that's the way people looked at me. Oh, the setting might have been different. It might have been in the Grand or the Candlelight Club, or the dances at the stately homes in Suffolk my stepfather would condescend to take me to – but the looks, they're all the same. It's hatred, isn't it, Nancy? Hatred for those you think are *weaker* than you, less *pure*. Less than . . . *human*. Because *those* people don't need a helping hand, do they, Nancy? Those people – they can just be left to rot.' She hesitated. The taxicab had turned a corner, and the greenery of Berkeley Square drew them on. 'Like *I* was left to rot,' she finally uttered.

61

The taxicab pulled up in front of the miniature colonnade, and the Buckingham doorman – on seeing Vivienne Edgerton behind the window glass – made as if to come down and open the door.

But Vivienne wasn't finished yet. She took hold of Nancy's arm, and her fingers were vice-like in their grip.

'I won't rot again. You're the one who helped me last time, Nancy. You picked me up and set me straight, where every other soul would have left me. Well, it's time I was the one picking people up. Mr Charles said something to me, earlier this month. He said – there has to be balance. There has to be equilibrium. Well, I'm going to find *my* equilibrium, Nancy. I'm going to find a way of balancing my own scales. And if it isn't the Rowton House, well, I'm going to go out there and find it somewhere else.'

May 1937

Chapter Seven

Maynard Charles was standing by the window, a glass of brandy in hand – it wasn't yet lunchtime and it was already his second – when there came a knock at the door.

'Come in,' he announced – and, on turning, he saw one of the hotel footmen presenting Mr Abner Grant.

He was not the kind of man who changed with the passing of the years. Neither Maynard nor Abner had been young men when they found themselves running the supply lines in Flanders, but in the twenty years since, Maynard had aged considerably. Abner, meanwhile, had looked as beastly back then as he did now. He had always put Maynard in mind of a slug given human form, with thick white whiskers borrowed from some West Country farmer, and eyes permanently circled in red. His natural expression was a scowl but, as he stomped into the office, Maynard thought he caught a glimpse of a smile.

Well, Maynard thought, *there's a first time for everything*, and took a second glass from a shelf to pour Abner a drink.

'How long has it been, Maynard?' Abner Grant drawled. He still had the bass Scots rumble of his youth. In France, the rumour had been that he was descended from dethroned Celtic royalty – though how far back the descent, Abner had always refused to say.

Just another person with a past to hide, Maynard had always thought. *But then, haven't we all?*

'Ten years, Abner, if it's a day. Would you take a seat?'

Abner Grant descended into the chair in front of Maynard's desk with the air of a bear settling down to hibernate for the winter. In one second, the brandy Maynard had poured him was gone. In another, he was reaching for the decanter to pour himself another. Ordinarily, insolence like that would not have gone unpunished – but Maynard Charles had need of Abner Grant.

'Your boy brought me your letter, Maynard. I must say, I was surprised to hear from you. I wasn't going to respond. I told that boy of yours – what's his name, Nettleton? – to sling his hook. He's as easily frightened as a little mouse, that one. But then I thought – if Maynard Charles wants to see me, it has to be something serious. Something *interesting*.' He paused, rocking back in his chair. 'Well, what is it?'

Words, Maynard decided, would not do this moment any justice. Instead, he searched for one of his notepads, wrote a sequence of digits across it, and revolved it so that Abner could see.

It was with some satisfaction that Maynard saw Abner's eyes open wide. He had, he decided, played his gambit well.

'To poach me from the Imperial?'

'Why not? You've been poached before. The Savoy thought you were theirs until the Imperial dangled their coin in front of you. Or have your loyalties deepened since then?'

'I have grandchildren, Maynard. Not something somebody like *you* would ever know about. My loyalties are to them, and their inheritance. But what need have you for somebody like me? I thought it was a matter of pride that the Buckingham never had the need of a hotel detective.'

'Times change. A good hotel director responds to the things happening in his hotel, not the things he *wants* to happen. We have experienced five robberies in the months after the New Year's Ball. I have dealt with each as I must, making recompense to guests inconvenienced and allowing the Buckingham to bear the burden of revenues lost. But I can do it no longer. A man of your talents is more cost-effective for the Buckingham Hotel – not, perhaps, in terms of pounds paid, but in terms of *reputation*. Scandal is the one thing I cannot afford.'

It was what Maynard Charles did not say that mattered most: *there can be no scandal here, not when Raymond de Guise brings John Hastings Junior back to these shores. The Imperial Hotel is also vying for Hastings's investment, and if its great detective just happens to leave it exposed to scandal and insinuation of its own – well, so much the better.*

All of business is a game, thought Maynard Charles, *and I intend to win.*

He had been silent too long. Abner Grant's red-rimmed eyes seemed to demand further explanation.

'In ten days' time, Abner, a new king is being crowned. Just as I'm certain the Imperial has its suites filled for the occasion, so does the Buckingham. King Haakon of Norway is return-ing, alongside the Crown Princess. The Count and Countess of Flanders. Prince Kyril of Bulgaria. You, of all people, understand what that means. The Buckingham has built its reputation on serving the greatest among us. If scandal were to break when they were in attendance . . .'

Abner grunted. 'You were always given to grand soliloquies, Maynard. I understood you from the start.'

'Do we have an agreement?'

Abner reached out for a fountain pen, wrote another sequence of digits upon Maynard's paper, and returned it to the fuming hotel director.

Maynard loosened his collar, flushing crimson.

'An inconvenience payment,' said Abner. 'One-off, to go alongside my new salary.'

Maynard opened his mouth but was unable to utter a single word. All he could do was nod.

'I'll need to complete a survey of the hotel. I'll need to know its every nook and cranny. The rooms you shut up, so that nobody sees. Well, every hotel has them. Old laundries, or derelict offices. The corners where chambermaids sneak off with whichever porter they think they're in love with. Every hotel has them – those in-between places, places nobody ever really goes. If you have a thief here, he'll be using them, you can bet your final farthing on it. Oh, and I'll need the guest books as well. There are patterns in guest books. You can see traitors as they come and go . . .'

By now, Maynard had composed himself. 'You'll have every-thing you need, Abner.'

'Send me a boy as well. I'll need to settle my affairs at the Imperial, to bring my things over. I'll need an office.'

Maynard bristled. 'I'll find you one. Just end this, Abner, once and for all.' Maynard sank back into his chair and, lifting the tele-phone receiver, dialled for reception. 'Have Frank Nettleton sent to reception. Mr Grant will be with you shortly,' he uttered, before hanging up. 'Consider him your personal page. What errands you need running, send Frank. He's docile and obedient – but treat him properly, Abner.'

Abner Grant levered himself out of his chair. Only when he had reached the office door and was closing a meaty hand over its handle did he say, 'Your staff here. The night managers. The heads of department. They'll need to know who I am, of course. But if you tell a soul about Flanders, if you tell a soul about what I did out there – well, I'll spill your little wartime secret as well. Do you hear me, Maynard?'

Maynard drew himself upright. 'I hear you loud and clear, Abner. This is a business association. We weren't friends then, we haven't been since – and, with my own heart as my witness, we're not friends now.'

Abner nodded once. 'Then it's settled. I'll stop the rot here, Maynard. Leave it to your old *friend* Abner.'

Chapter Eight

THE EARLY SUMMER SUNSHINE BROKE through the clouds, illuminating the towers and spires of London. In Berkeley Square, the crocuses in the flower banks turned slowly to drink in the light. In the underground stations, ticket sellers scurried to their stalls, ready for the morning rush. From opulent mansion flats to boarding houses, from the palaces of Westminster to the vagrant camps beneath Battersea Bridge, the city was stirring to greet another day.

And in a tiny cemetery south of Streatham Hill, Hélène stepped out of a black taxicab with Sybil in her arms and, steeling herself, set out between the graves.

Two days was as much as Hélène ordinarily got with Sybil and her grandparents, Maurice and Noelle Archer. Two days: the compromise Hélène had had to make, when Sybil's father passed away. Ordinarily she would have relished this, the third morning she had awoken to hear Sybil babbling in her crib. But this morning was different. This morning she stepped between the gravestones, the bouquets of flowers left to wither on every grey slab, until she stood in front of a stone that chilled her, even in spite of the early summer warmth. On the stone were the words:

SIDNEY ARCHER

BELOVED BROTHER, HUSBAND AND SON

1908–1935

Hélène looked over her shoulder. Maurice and Noelle were making their way slowly through the graves, but they stopped some distance away, as if to give her privacy. Hélène felt a rush of love towards the elderly couple. It hadn't been easy for them. At sixty years of age, they had every right to expect their child-rearing days were long behind them. And yet . . .

'We couldn't have done it without them,' she whispered into Sybil's ear. 'A white dancer and a black musician, and a child conceived out of wedlock. Maynard Charles would have skinned me alive. He pays me for decorum and elegance, not to bring the Buckingham into disrepute.'

Hélène had often said that, one day, she would find a way to repay them. But Noelle and Maurice were adamant: they needed no repayment. The love of this new family they were helping to build was everything they could ever need.

Hélène knelt at Sidney's grave, gently guiding Sybil down onto the grass. She had brought with her two golden daffodils, and she handed one to Sybil. They had been Sidney's favourites.

'Your father came so very far, little one,' Hélène said, and showed Sybil how to lay the flower on the grave. 'Halfway across the world, of course, but so much further. From immigrant boy, and all the way to the Buckingham Hotel. From playing for paupers to playing for princes . . .'

All those signs he must have seen, thought Hélène, *as he first looked for places that might let him try out his talent with the trumpet. NO DOGS. NO BLACKS. NO IRISH. Turned away from clubs and halls, and all because of the colour of his skin.*

The thought brought back memories of Arthur Regan and everything he had said. *One day equality will prevail.*

Well, thought Hélène, *it prevails here*. She took in the sights, the sounds, the smells of the cemetery. *We all end up in the ground, no matter the colour of our skin, no matter the place we were born.*

Sybil was threatening to toddle off between the graves, so Hélène put an arm around her and brought her to her breast. She had made a promise, on the day that Sidney perished: their child would hear about her father so vividly that it would almost be like she could remember him herself. So she began to whisper into Sybil's ear:

'It was your father's birthday today. He would have been twenty-eight years old. I remember his last birthday. We took a train out to Southend. Oh, Sybil, we felt *alive*. So far away from the Buckingham, with the smell of the sea air and the sun on the sand. Oh, we got some looks. A white woman in the company of a black man always will. But we didn't care, not for any of it.'

She paused, and when next she spoke, she was directing her attention to the grave.

'We'd have moved away, wouldn't we, Sid? Somewhere you could play your trumpet and I could look after our children, hang up my dancing shoes.' She reached out and traced his name in the stone. 'You're still missed at the Buckingham, Sid. Archie Adams never did find a trumpet player to replace you. And . . . I'm still dancing. Six afternoons a week. Five evenings. All the balls. I'm still sending everything I can back to your parents. But I'm saving too – a little every week. And one day I really will give up the Grand and be the mother I've been dreaming of. And, Sid, Sybil and me, we're never going to forget.'

Sybil let out a sudden squawk and, turning to follow her gaze, Hélène saw that another figure had joined Maurice and Noelle Archer on the trail between the graves.

Louis Kildare was dressed in a suit of charcoal grey, with a starched white collar and a simple homburg hat, his saxophone case in the grass at his feet. As Hélène watched, he stooped down to lift the saxophone from it and clasped Sidney's father's hand in his own.

Hélène met him halfway to the grave. 'Louis, I didn't know you were coming.'

'I have been before. I play a little something for Sidney. I just like him to know the music he would have been playing.'

Louis's voice trembled as the sentence petered away, but Hélène lifted a hand and let it dance on his shoulder. Something in the touch seemed to embolden him. He lifted a finger to tickle Sybil's chin and she beamed in reply.

'She's looking more and more like him,' he said. 'Hélène, do you mind?'

'Be my guest, Louis,' she breathed – and, retreating from the grave, left the two old friends to parley together.

Standing with Sidney's parents, Hélène listened to the first notes from Louis's saxophone. She closed her eyes and, for a moment, she was not in the South London cemetery at all, but back in the practice room behind the Grand, three or four years ago, watching while Louis, Sidney and a ragtag of other musicians from the Archie Adams Orchestra practised their new standards, joking and improvising as they went. Those had been *perfect* days. The feeling of *knowing* somebody as intimately, in

73

body, mind and soul, as she had known Sidney. The feeling of *knowing* where life was heading.

And now . . .

She opened her eyes to find herself back in the cemetery, as Louis Kildare's mournful lament rose up over Sidney's grave. From a nearby willow, a succession of starlings was frightened into flight. They sailed over the cemetery, propelled by the music, and then they were gone.

Afterwards, Louis accompanied Hélène back to the Buckingham while Maurice, Noelle and Sybil stayed behind to clip the grass around Sidney's grave. *One more year without him*, thought Hélène. She was going to tell herself that it didn't get any easier – but the terrible truth was that it did. She still thought about him every day, but a life full of demonstration dances, of evenings in the Grand, of working diligently to keep her secret – and all with the fear that, if she was ever exposed, she would have no way of supporting Sybil – all worked to crowd out the memories she cherished.

Today had been the first time since Christmas that she'd visited Sidney's grave, and the realisation that so many months had passed was like a thorn in her side.

Sidney wouldn't want you to live a life of regret, she told herself, as the cab drew into Berkeley Square. She turned to Louis, who had been lost in the same kind of reverie.

'You'd better go in before me,' she whispered, squeezing his hand. 'It's expected of you, but people might ask questions, if they knew I'd been at Sidney's grave. It's better we're not seen together.'

Hélène might have been mistaken, but for a fleeting moment it seemed that Louis was crestfallen. Then, with a few simple words – 'Sybil couldn't have a better mother, Hélène' – he made for the staff entrance on Michaelmas Mews.

Hélène climbed the marble steps and stepped through the revolving bronze doors. Inside, the scents of the Buckingham crashed over her. She glanced through the ornate archway that led down into the Grand, but no amount of elegance could make up for what she'd left behind, south of the river.

The demonstration dances would begin in an hour. Hélène was hurrying for the lift when a little voice – meek as a mouse – called out her name, and she turned to see one of the hotel pages appearing from behind the reception desk.

'Miss Marchmont?'

Hélène recognised Frank Nettleton only very vaguely. Tall as he was, there was something timid about him. He certainly did not have the courage of his sister. His hair, which had been cropped short, was turning back to curls around his ears, and the nervousness in his eyes was only too apparent.

If Nancy Nettleton hadn't asked for a favour, this boy would never have found a place at the Buckingham, thought Hélène. *He isn't nearly bold enough to impress Maynard Charles.*

Frank handed her a slip of notepaper. When Hélène opened it, the words 'SIMPSON'S IN THE STRAND, Wednesday 7 p.m., in return for the dance of a lifetime' were written in an elegant hand – and, beneath it, the signature, ARTHUR REGAN.

'The gentleman asked for you by name, Miss Marchmont. When you weren't here, I promised I'd pass on a message.'

Hélène was momentarily shocked. She'd danced well enough for Arthur, but it certainly demanded no reward. Only then did the full flush of embarrassment come.

'Thank you, Frank.'

75

Thanks were all he needed. His face transformed, full of pleasure at a job well done, and in seconds he had darted away.

In a fever, Hélène folded the invitation and made haste for the service lift. Only when she was rattling upwards, bound for her quarters, did she dare unfold the invitation again. *Wednesday 7 p.m.* That was still two days away. She could only look at it for a moment before she needed, once again, to secrete it away.

That night, the Grand was a kaleidoscope of lights. Hélène had been promised to one of the lesser Flemish dukes, a man who had come to London in anticipation of King George's coronation. With Hélène in his arms, he waltzed elegantly across the ballroom floor.

But the music was not with Hélène tonight. She dared not admit it, not on this day of all days, but every time she closed her eyes, the memory of dancing to these same songs with Arthur Regan came, unbidden, into her head. More than once, she tried to shake it away. More than once, the memory came back with renewed vigour. Perhaps it was only the invitation Frank had delivered. Perhaps it had put him back into her head.

Three years ago tonight, she had finished the dancing for the evening and met Sidney out on Berkeley Square. They had walked until dawn. She had told him she loved him, that – no matter what it cost her reputation – she would spend the rest of her days with him, dancing to the music he created. She would be the belle of the ballroom; one day, Sidney would lead his own band. Their stories would be entwined forever.

She closed her eyes again, allowed the Flemish duke to lead her on. Hélène did not need to see the ballroom tonight; it was her feet doing the dancing, not her heart. It was just as well – for, when Hélène next opened her eyes, she found them filled with tears. The ballroom was distorted, and whether she was crying for the man she had lost, or for the way Arthur kept intruding on her thoughts, she dared not say.

Chapter Nine

'THERE YOU ARE, FRANK. GET stuck into that. The way they got you running around, you'll soon be wasting away!'

It wasn't often that Frank spent the night in Nancy's quarters. Ordinarily he traipsed home at the end of each day to the Brogans' terraced house on the other side of Lambeth Bridge. But on occasion, when the guests or concierges were running him hard, he crawled upstairs and curled up on some blankets beside Nancy's bed. When she could convince him, she'd give up the bed itself – just like she used to when they were small, and he'd creep into her bedroom at night, scared of the old hawthorn tree clawing at the windows. Last night had been one of those nights – and now, with dawn rapidly approaching, Nancy fussed around him in the kitchenette, laying out tea and a hot cross bun slathered with fresh butter and jam.

As Frank was filling his belly, the other chambermaids began to appear. It was Rosa, her golden hair tied back in a band, who spotted him first. She tousled his hair, as if she herself was his big sister, and sunk into the big duck-down sofa beside him.

'You still with us, Frank?'

'J-just about,' said Frank, through mouthfuls of hot cross bun. He was trying hard not to blush, but Rosa was just about the prettiest girl he'd ever seen and she wielded some sort of magic over him. It made him feel about eight years old.

'I'll nab you some room service leftovers if I can. You can take them back to the Brogan house. They'll treat you like a king.'

As the other girls fluttered about, Nancy sat down beside Frank.

'Look here,' she said, and brandished Raymond's most recent letter. 'He's reached New York.'

Although Frank took the letter, his face had blanched. Quietly, so that the others might not hear, he whispered, 'You know I'm not good with my reading, Nance.'

'It took him ten days to cross America. The Buckingham paid for a driver, of course, but can you imagine a country being that vast? Here we are, Frank, thinking Lancashire's the other side of the world. And Raymond's out there . . .'

'What's he been up to, Nance?'

Nancy opened the letter and read a snippet, careful to omit all the professions of love with which Raymond liked to fill his letters.

New York, Nancy, is like no place I've been on Earth. All the towers in London are nothing compared to Manhattan. Even the skyline is a thing of beauty: the Empire State Building, barely five or six years old, will one day be counted among the true wonders of the world. New York feels like the future. And all of the world is here, Nancy! There are corners for the Italians, corners for the Irish, corners for the Jewish and the African Americans and, yes, even for we Englanders! Once upon a time, I thought London was the City of the World. I was wrong. All roads lead to New York . . .

Nancy stopped. 'I think he's excited,' she said.

Frank nodded, polishing off the final scraps of hot cross bun.

At the Cotton Club last night, Cab Calloway was playing with his band. And, oh, Nancy, how the room came alive! The jitterbug is a dance that . . . how can I describe this? I can say nothing else but that it speaks to the soul. Oh, the dances of old, they speak to tradition and grace and elegance. But the jitterbug speaks to joy, and there is surely not enough joy in this world. If Maynard Charles is to be believed, joy will soon be in very short supply in Europe, so I am doing everything I can to embrace it now. If you were here, we would jive our nights in New York away, and I would count myself the luckiest man in Manhattan.

Nancy realised she was going too far – *Frank doesn't want to hear about what Raymond and I might do!* – and folded the letter back in its envelope.

'I can't wait for you to meet him, Frank. I've told him so much about you.'

Frank himself wasn't sure what to say. Raymond de Guise was a famous dancer. Frank was hardly succeeding as a hotel page. Not for the first time, he wondered if *everybody* found London quite as daunting and exhausting as him. Sometimes he still hungered for the rolling green hills and vast open skies of home.

'Frank,' chirped Rosa, who was about to dart back through the kitchen door, 'why don't you just curl up here, for a bit? I bet they wouldn't notice if you were a little late.'

Frank's cheeks had turned scarlet again.

'I . . . c-can't,' Frank stammered – and, at once, he was on his feet. 'I promised Billy. He's g-got a special job for me. I don't want to let him down.'

Nancy looked at her little brother, her heart brimming with sisterly love. Poor Frank – his stammer always came back when he was nervous, and, of all things in the Buckingham, Rosa seemed to make Frank most nervous of all. She stepped forward, straightened Frank's shirt – 'If you're going to stay again, you really ought to bring some pyjamas' – and brushed the crumbs away from the corner of his lip.

'Stay sharp, little brother. That Billy Brogan will run rings around you if you're not careful.'

'He already is, Nance. But it's how he started, isn't it? And he says that, one day, he'll be a night manager – and, who knows, even a hotel director himself. So I've got to work hard, haven't I? And maybe I could be the same.'

Nancy furrowed her brow, holding back her disbelief. She'd have to have a word with Billy, tell him not to fill her brother's head with all his nonsense.

But, 'On your way,' she said, and planted a sisterly kiss on Frank's cheek. 'Be good today, Frankie.'

'I will, Nance. I promise.'

The fact was, Frank didn't have a clue how to be anything other than good. He'd tried, he really had – the lads in the boarding house back home were all miners, and enjoyed playing practical jokes, some of them pretty grisly, against each other – but it had never suited him. So, when he reached the ground floor of the Buckingham, he sought out Billy straight away. Whatever his task was, he was adamant he was going to do a good job.

Billy was waiting at the reception desk, and quickly spirited Frank around the corner.

'Look, Frank,' he began. 'I got an important job for you. It comes courtesy of Maynard Charles himself, so hopefully that gives you a measure of how important it is. Reckon you're up to it?'

Frank was about to stutter, 'I don't know, Billy,' but Billy had already heard his own answer.

'Now, you know what's happening in two days, don't you?'

Frank did. There was gossip about it all over the hotel. In two days' time, on 12th May, a new king would be crowned in Westminster Abbey. Some of the kitchen porters said they were going to go out and watch the procession – that is, if they could force their way down the Horse Guards Parade. Maynard Charles had declared the demonstration dances cancelled for the afternoon, and the Grand Ballroom was going to be flowing with champagne for the hotel guests, the BBC radio broadcasting the coronation for all to hear. And Rosa had said that Edie had overheard Mrs Moffatt telling one of the other housekeeping mistresses that Maynard was having a *television* installed in the director's office, specifically for the occasion.

'A coronation like this, it brings all sorts to town. The Crown Prince and Princess of Norway, they arrived only last night. Michael I – he's the heir apparent, virtually the *king*, of Romania – he's booked into the Pacific Suite this evening. Hélène Marchmont's to dance with him in the Grand tonight – and that, Frank, will be an evening neither one of them's going to forget!'

Frank had never thought much about kings and queens, not outside of fairy tales. Oh, he knew they existed. He knew they made the world turn round – and Nancy, she'd written to him often enough about the lords and ladies she'd seen when she first came to the Buckingham – but, to Frank, it was all so far away and unreal. Nancy used to say that Frank could never really look further ahead than the end of his nose.

'There's somebody else coming to dinner tonight. You'll have heard of Mr Baldwin, of course?'

'Mr . . . Baldwin?'

'The prime minister, Frank! Well, word is he won't be Prime Minister for long. He's already declared it, hasn't he? That he's going to step aside once the new King's on the throne. We'll have a new prime minister then – Mr Chamberlain, I shouldn't wonder. And, yes, he's made use of our hotel as well. Well . . .' Billy paused. The inscrutable look on Frank's face gave him the impression that the boy was following scarcely half of what he was saying. 'There's a dinner in the Queen Mary tonight. Mr Baldwin and his ministers. And Conte Grandi.'

Billy announced it as if Frank ought to have known to whom he was referring, but Frank's silence begged further explanation.

'Conte Dino Grandi. The Italian ambassador. He's to represent the King of Italy at the coronation – and he's here tonight. Well, these ambassadors, they like to put on a show, Frank, and there's no better show in London than right here at the Buckingham. After dinner, no doubt they'll be drinking and dancing in the Grand Ballroom. And that's why I need you.'

'Me?' Frank asked, incredulous.

'Listen here, Frank. When I was a hotel page, I used to run various little errands on behalf of Maynard Charles. A page can get in places others can't. Nobody ever notices a page. And when an important man – a man of European extraction, you understand – was to come in, it would be my job to listen to what he had to say. And then to tell it, each and every last bit of it, to Mr Charles.'

83

'But . . . why?' wondered Frank.

'That's for Mr Charles to know. That isn't for the likes of us. All we have to do is get close and make careful notes. Mr Charles, he can do the rest. Think you're good for it, do you, Frank?'

Frank just stood there, stunned. He remembered Nancy's edict: that Billy Brogan was a good sort, that Frank should listen to everything Billy said and made sure he did his absolute best. But surely she did not mean *this*?

'I don't know, B-Billy. It doesn't s-sound honourable.'

Billy stood back, appraising Frank with a wry eye. 'Listen, it's for Maynard Charles. You do good deeds for Mr Charles and he'll do 'em back for you. How do you think I'm turned into a social climber? It's on account of my good deeds. So . . .' He stopped, because Frank's eyes had dropped; he was fixated on a spot on the ground, directly in front of his feet. 'Come on, Frankie. It's for the good of the hotel, isn't it? You want to get on in life, don't you?'

Frank had spent the day up and down the Buckingham halls, but in every idle moment Billy's words shuddered through him. It wasn't that he didn't want to help. Billy had been kind to him in the last few weeks – and his family, well, they'd been kinder still. Frank had never known what it was like to have a mother – Nancy had been the closest he'd ever got – and there was something so magical about watching Mrs Brogan, feeding and watering and just *loving* that gaggle of children that she called her own. It sang out to parts of him he hadn't known existed.

What if I don't do what Billy asks? What if he tells his family? What if they think I'm ungrateful, or lazy, or what if they think I'm not good enough for them?

It was thoughts like this that drove him to the doors of the Grand Ballroom, just as the early summer darkness was settling over Berkeley Square.

The Archie Adams Orchestra was already swinging their way through Tommy Dorsey's 'The Morning After'. Tonight there was no guest vocalist, just the soaring saxophone of Louis Kildare. The guests were still drifting down from the Queen Mary and the Buckingham's other lavish restaurants, and the ballroom's outer doors were open to the balmy summer scents floating in from Berkeley Square.

Frank had never seen a place as exquisite as this. Nancy had tried to describe it in her letters, but how could she ever have captured the sights, the sound, the *atmosphere*? The chandeliers glittered overhead like a constellation of stars. Waiters waltzed from table to bar, bedecked in suits of brilliant white. There was Hélène Marchmont, in the arms of Prince Michael of Romania. There was Gene Sheldon, clasping the Crown Princess of Norway in a classical ballroom hold. And there, his big hands clasped around the balustrade as if he was the captain of a ship, was Maynard Charles himself.

The old man always made him anxious. Frank had known plenty of old men in the mine, but here was an altogether different class of man. He held himself imperiously – as if he was himself one of the dignitaries who thronged the Grand Ballroom tonight – but there was something reserved about him too.

What am I doing? thought Frank. *Why me? Billy said that Maynard Charles could never do this kind of work himself, on account of he's always* noticed. *Whereas I can slip in and out. Kings don't look at beggars – that's what Billy says. And yet . . .*

Frank took a deep breath. That's what old Mrs Gable always used to tell him: 'When things are getting on top of you, Frank, just take a step back, take three deep breaths, and listen to your heart.'

Well, now his heart was hammering. It was hammering in time to the strident music. The Archie Adams Orchestra had burst into a new song now: 'The Camberwell Waltz'. Frank felt it carrying him onwards, between the legs of passing royals. Suddenly, he felt three feet tall.

But I want to do this, he thought. *If it's for the good of the Buckingham – if it's a way I can repay the Brogans for everything they're doing for me – it has to be the right thing. Well, doesn't it?*

He searched the room for signs of Conte Grandi. Billy had taken Frank into the corner of the Queen Mary during the dinner-time service and pointed out the hawkish Italian ambassador, with his black hair swept back and that dark beard erupting from his chin. 'One of those whose looks could kill.' That was how Billy had described him, and Frank had concurred. His eyes seemed all-knowing as they had taken in his dinner companions, Mr Baldwin on his left, Mr Chamberlain to his right. *The great and the good*: that was what people had said – but to Frank there wasn't much about Conte Dino Grandi that seemed good.

'The Camberwell Waltz' came to its uproarious end and, down on the dance floor, Prince Michael I stepped out of Hélène's arms. With the slightest incline of his head, he retreated from the floor. It was then that Frank saw Conte Grandi. He had been lurking at the edge of the ballroom, but as soon as Prince Michael ascended the steps and crossed to the polished walnut balustrade, Conte Grandi approached him.

This was it, thought Frank. This was what Billy had sent him in here for. *No time to feel afraid now, Frank. You've got a job, haven't you? Well, do it!*

He took off into the throng, weaving unnoticed between two couples consorting on the edge of the dance floor, until he was almost at Conte Grandi's side. Prince Michael of Romania was tall and lithe, but it wasn't until Frank got close that he realised quite how young the heir apparent was. He seemed no older than Frank himself – and very possibly even younger. His eyes were a beatific blue, and there was so little stubble darkening his chin that Frank counted him sixteen or seventeen years old, if he was a day.

What's the difference between him and me? thought Frank. *Only nobility. Prince Michael's not just a prince at all – he's a king in waiting. No wonder he can dance with someone as beautiful as Hélène Marchmont and not bat an eyelid. Me, I could hardly look her in the eye . . .*

'Of course,' Conte Grandi was saying, his voice half-obscured by the orchestra, 'the Italians and the Romanians have such long ancestry between them. We fought the Ottomans, did we not, bravely and side by side? And in troubled times like these, we should not forget the flames of that friendship.'

'My people have always been grateful for the solidarity of yours during the Great War,' Prince Michael began. 'I was not yet born, and yet I am indebted as well. But—'

Conte Grandi raised a hand. 'You're right. We must speak of the bonds of the future, not the bonds of the past.'

Bonds of the future, thought Frank. *How am I ever going to remember all of . . . ?*

'Of course, what the future holds – well, that is very much a question in search of an answer. The future, Your Highness, is in flux. Will it go one way, or will it go another?' Conte Grandi raised his round shoulders in an exaggerated shrug. 'Spain is already in flames. So might the rest of Europe be, if the balance tips the wrong way.'

'What the British position is – that, dear Prince, is the burning conundrum. The old King Edward had the right of it – he knew what was his kingdom and what was not. He knew that Great Britain was at her best keeping her nose out of other nations' business. Yes, King Edward was always very *sympathetic* to the European cause. You should know, he is due to visit his old confidants in the Third Reich just as soon as his marriage to Mrs Wilson is official.' Conte Grandi paused. 'Now, of course, there are voices in the British government who will be seeking to bend the new King George to their will. They will try and make him believe that Europe is Great Britain's preserve, that Britain has the right to direct what is happening in our own countries, that Britain should . . . overstep her boundaries again. But this is morally improper, and we in the Italian court will not stand for it.'

Frank watched Prince Michael stepping backwards, as if to extricate himself from the conversation – but Conte Grandi moved in rhythm with him, as consummate as any of the dancers on the ballroom floor.

'Of course, we still hope that wiser heads will prevail and that Great Britain will step back from the brink. That is why we wait for Mr Chamberlain to succeed Mr Baldwin as the King's first minister. Mr Chamberlain knows that Great Britain is an island nation, and that its interest in Continental affairs should be but fleeting. If he gets his way, as he must, Britain will soon retreat from its constant meddling in Continental affairs of state. We will tend to Europe while the British are left to tend to their Empire. Europe will become the preserve of my own Mr Mussolini, and of course Mr Hitler will look to the German peoples across the Continent. As for the rest of the European states . . .' Conte Grandi pitched even closer to Prince Michael, and Frank Nettleton had to strain to hear. His heart was beating, panicked as a baby bird's, but somehow he found the resolve to creep closer. 'That is why I ask – no, I *implore* – you to think carefully about Romania's next step. Mr Mussolini has already made a formal invitation that you should visit him in Rome. It is an invitation your regents should make haste to accept, Prince Michael. Make friendships that *matter*. Make them soon. Because the map of Europe is yet to be written in stone, and – mark my words – we will soon be writing it ourselves. Italy would welcome the renewed friendship of Romania in the east. And, if war is to come once more, Romania could find no better ally than in my own strong nation.'

The tango came to its triumphant conclusion. Across the Grand Ballroom, conversations were stilled by sudden flurries of spontaneous applause.

Conte Grandi's eye must have momentarily wandered – because, the next moment, Prince Michael had retreated into the wider throng. Frank watched as Conte Grandi's face darkened; then, lest he himself be spotted, he scurried back to the edges of the room.

What did it all mean? Frank thought as the band struck up a new number. The Italian ambassador, putting pressure on a prince of Romania to . . . what? Make an *alliance*? Was that the word? An alliance in anticipation of war in Europe? And all that talk of Mr Chamberlain, destined for the premiership as soon as Mr Baldwin stepped aside – what did *that* mean?

Up on the stage, the orchestra turned from Viennesse waltz to Argentine tango to cantering foxtrot and back again; elegant ladies in flowing chiffon and silk swept past, their necks encrusted with diamonds; all around him was beauty and refinement, elegance and grace – but, not for the first time, Frank Nettleton wondered if life would have been more simple if he'd just stayed up north, back where he belonged.

Later, when the night was coming to its end, Frank watched Conte Grandi disappear through the ballroom doors, out into the balmy Mayfair night. Then, remembering Billy's edict, he ran to the reception desk and began to commit to paper everything he had heard.

I should know my letters better than this, he thought, as he scrubbed out each second word, certain he had made mistakes. But it was no good. He'd just have to find Nancy. She'd be able to help. *Maybe she can even do the writing for me.*

Then a thought struck him.

Eavesdropping. Spying. Telling tales. What Billy Brogan had asked him to do was hardly the work of a respectable gentleman. It was hardly the kind of thing that would make Nancy proud. She'd been so careful to instruct him in his morals. She'd made sure he grew up good and right, even without a mother to call their own.

The kernel of guilt that had been sitting in Frank's stomach all day was suddenly sprouting. No, he could never tell Nancy. He'd have to find another way.

Frank was about to take flight when a hand clapped on his shoulder. He spun round to see Billy Brogan himself.

'Frank Nettleton, there you are!' Billy beamed. 'I was beginning to think you'd done a runner.' Seeing the ghostly white of

Frank's face, Billy stilled. 'What is it, Frank? What's happened?' He paused again, as realisation dawned. 'You've heard something, haven't you, Frank? Something disreputable? There was *conspiring* going on in the Grand tonight, wasn't there? Well, come with me' – he wrapped an arm around Frank's shoulders, as if to shepherd him somewhere more private – 'and you can tell us it all. Maynard Charles is going to be very pleased with you, Frank. Very pleased indeed . . .'

Chapter Ten

Emmeline Moffatt, the head of housekeeping, had called the Buckingham home for longer than most of the chambermaids had been alive – but not once had she presided over a breakfast in the housekeeping lounge quite like this. As the long oak table filled up, the excitement on the faces of her chambermaids was unparalleled. Not even on Christmas mornings – when the under-kitchens and housekeeping lounge would open up for the festivities, while the *corps d'élite* danced on above – were they gripped with anticipation like this. She had to try three times before the girls were quiet enough that her own voice could be heard.

At the countertop, Nancy and Ruth were hurrying to fill their bowls with porridge – while, at the end of the table (and to general consternation), Edie spilled a jug of fresh cream and upended the sugar pot in her fever to clean it up.

'Girls, really!' called Mrs Moffatt. 'The King doesn't leave Buckingham Palace until almost eleven. That leaves you five hours of strong, solid work to accomplish before there's a hope of getting out there. And remember Mr Charles's edict – there are no excuses for beds unmade, for floors unpolished, for guests unsatisfied. The world might have stopped what it's doing, girls, but the Buckingham hasn't.'

Nancy and Ruth found their places at the table. At the front of the room, Mrs Moffatt was still speaking – but, no matter how strict her words, Nancy could tell that she, too, was dazzled by what the dawn was about to bring. It was there in the way a smile played on her lips, even as she cajoled Rosa – one of the only chambermaids lucky enough to be off shift this morning – to take her seat.

It was 12th May, 1937 – and, in only a few short hours, a new king would be crowned.

The Buckingham Hotel had been anticipating this moment for months. Out there in London town, streets were closed and cordoned off. By the time the sun broke in full over the slums and mansion houses, the procession would begin: up the Mall, through Admiralty Arch, down the long, wide barrel of Whitehall and into Westminster Abbey itself. The gossip from the porters and pages was that London had ground to a standstill several days before. Daily the trains disgorged well-wishers from further afield; by night, the streets surrounding the planned procession were thronged with spectators staking out the best possible vantage points from which they might catch a glimpse of the new King, gliding by in his golden carriage of state. They said that more than ten thousand would throng the city streets as royalty from Europe's manifold palaces, the princes of India, the premiers of all Britain's Dominions, moved in convoy to the abbey.

But Maynard Charles would see none of it. The Buckingham Hotel was his domain, and there he would stay.

The procession through London was being managed by a team of close to one hundred from the Palace and the Metropolitan Police, but the Buckingham Hotel had only Maynard Charles. He would be ensuring the Grand Ballroom opened its doors, just as the procession embarked from Buckingham Palace, overseeing the celebrations in the Queen Mary, the Candlelight Club, the French brasserie – everywhere that the guests might congregate, to listen to the coronation being broadcast. *By God*, thought Maynard – and resisted the urge to reach for his decanter – *I ought to dance the foxtrot myself! I'm doing everything else . . .*

The clock in his office struck six. Berkeley Square was already buzzing with the taxicabs the hotel had ordered, ready to take its prized guests to the abbey. Everything was in order. Maynard felt certain of that.

Why, then, was that nugget of fear still hard in his gut?

At least there hasn't been another robbery. All thanks to that blackguard, Abner Grant, no doubt. Sometimes just having a hotel detective is deterrent enough. Get through the coronation, he told himself, *and see what happens next.*

What would happen next was written in ink in front of him. The latest missive had arrived from New York only yesterday. Raymond de Guise had reached the East Coast of America, and had ensconced himself in the life of John Hastings Junior, just as Maynard had instructed. Soon, they would be boarding the steamer to Liverpool. Once John Hastings was in the United Kingdom, staying at the Buckingham itself, Maynard could influence things. But right now, the sensation of being powerless was impossible to ignore.

It was that same sense of powerlessness that drove Maynard up, out of his office, and into the hotel. All around him, the

94

Buckingham was waking up. A page darted past, head ducked down. In the reception hall, the night cleaners had just finished polishing the black and white chequered floor. He fancied he could hear the pipes groaning as a hundred different baths were filled.

The rhythms of the Buckingham Hotel, so wonderful, so familiar. It has to survive.

As he passed the housekeeping lounge, two dozen chambermaids erupted out. The sight cheered him. *This*, he decided, was the life's blood of the Buckingham: the people who flowed through its veins. Not one of them understood the import of John Hastings's arrival, but that was as it should be. He, Maynard Charles, was the bridge between them and the board, the bulwark between them and disaster. The unadulterated joy on their faces set his own heart to wonder. Even Maynard Charles had been young once. There had been an age when the coronation of a new king would have been enough to fill him with pride and amazement, just as it was doing these girls.

As the chambermaids fanned out, he heard Mrs Moffatt's voice chasing after them. Soon, she joined Maynard in the hallway.

'We're all set, Mr Charles. The girls have just got to contain themselves for another few hours. I've laid down the law – those on split shifts are not to leave the hotel premises, though the wireless will be blaring in the housekeeping lounge for the service itself, and they're more than welcome to crowd around and listen. As for the girls working the morning only, or with the day off – well, I shouldn't think we'll see them until the morrow, but they've each had their lecture. If they're not fit and rested enough for their next shifts, well, there'll be explaining to do.'

'Thank you, Emmeline,' said Maynard.

He was about to drift on when Mrs Moffatt called back, 'Is everything all right, Maynard?'

She was the only person on the whole of the Buckingham's roster who dared to call him by his Christian name. He stopped, turned back to face her.

'The whole of life is a balancing act, Emmeline, but this year more so than any. Let us survive the day. Then, perhaps, we can focus on surviving another.'

'You're allowed to enjoy the day, Maynard. You're allowed *one* day where you aren't a master tactician, always thinking six steps ahead.'

Maynard folded his hand across hers. 'I should like it very much if you were to watch the coronation with us, Emmeline.'

Mrs Moffatt gave him a benevolent wink. 'There's no place else I'd rather be. As soon as my girls are finished, I'll see you in the Park Suite.'

Vivienne Edgerton had been among the first to leave the hotel on this, the morning of King George's coronation. It wasn't that she had any particular interest in royalty – in fact, as a born-and-bred New Yorker, she considered herself ancestrally bound to denounce the King of Great Britain entirely – but to explain such a thing to her stepfather and mother (who was rapidly losing her American accent and replacing it with an abominable approximation of the English) would have invited the kind of anger she was studiously trying to avoid. It was better, she had decided, not to give her stepfather any more cause for complaint; some day soon, he was going to find out that she had used her allowance to support the Rowton House on Arlington Road, and the result was going to be incandescence.

Her father's driver had been waiting out on Berkeley Square. The gleaming black Bentley had delivered her to a restaurant on the Strand where the family was taking breakfast. Though it had been some weeks since Vivienne last saw her mother, there was no fond reunion. Her mother had primly asked how she was – 'and let's not have a scene today, shall we, Vivienne?' – and turned, without waiting for reply, to the menu. Lord Edgerton had brought along William, his errant son – who had spent much of the year on his tour of Europe, returning home only because he believed his father would gain admittance to Westminster Abbey itself – and with William had come a French lady, Arielle, some ten years William's senior. Vivienne soon came to understand that they had grown fond of each other on the Côte d'Azur, and that they had even spoken of marriage. Nobody seemed to be taking it very seriously; William, Vivienne was given to understand, became engaged to a new friend at least once every year.

'She'll be investigated, like all of the rest,' was all Vivienne's mother would say on the matter. 'We can't have the family fortune in danger.'

Soon, the Edgerton family were joined by others: a succession of hawkish men, each dressed in their finest morning suits. Some of these faces Vivienne recognised as members of the board of the Buckingham Hotel; others she had seen at the Edgertons' country residence in Suffolk, on the rare occasions when she had been invited to join her family for one of their soirées. Yet more were strangers – business associates, she decided, of her stepfather.

Not one of them spoke to her.

Lord Edgerton himself was holding court. He had trimmed back his silver whiskers since Vivienne last met with him, and his small dark eyes were pronounced by new spectacles, but, despite his patrician air, there was something . . . aggressive – yes, that was the word – about the man. Vivienne got the impression that, even when he was in the throes of cordial conversation, he might reach out at any moment and slap the man he was speaking to sharply about the face.

'For myself,' a warthog of a man, with teeth like tusks, began, 'I believe Mr Charles is putting altogether too much stock in this Hastings character. I've said it from the beginning – new investors mean diluting our own interests. And why would we do that? Mr Charles's fantasy of war in Europe may be just that – *fantasy*. Now we have Mr Chamberlain moving into Downing Street, who's to say there won't be a guaranteed peace before the summer's end? Europe's doors would remain open. The Buckingham would thrive. We have German dignitaries lining up to stay in our suites. All we'd be doing is inviting Hastings aboard for nothing. And then—'

Lord Edgerton lifted a hand. 'We all want peace, Uriah. What we want more, however, is profit.'

'Can these things wait for another day?' Vivienne's mother interjected. 'We're gathered to celebrate the crowning of a king.'

Vivienne watched as the menfolk turned their scathing eyes on her mother. For herself, she wasn't certain which she loathed more: the way that her mother, after such a short time in Britain, had become enslaved to the royal family – or the poor impersonation of the King's English that she was trying to adopt.

I wish I'd ordered pancakes for breakfast. Big, thick, fluffy pancakes, drizzled in syrup, just like they used to serve up in New York. Why, I bet Raymond de Guise is having his fill of New York pancakes, right now.

Lord Edgerton was purpling. He might even have formally admonished his wife, if, at that moment, his driver had not entered the restaurant and whispered in his ear, 'The procession moves through, my lord. We should, perhaps, make ready.'

'As you would, Alfred. We'll be with you shortly.'

The cars were waiting outside: five open-topped Rolls-Royces to lead them along the Strand, through the crowd amassed in Trafalgar Square, and along Whitehall. Vivienne sat beside her mother in the back of the first car, trying to summon up a modicum of enthusiasm for what was about to follow – but, somehow, the thought of a day spent among her stepfather's associates, all slowly getting *sozzled* on a Whitehall roof terrace and growing in bitterness that they were not attendees at the abbey itself, held little appeal.

The crowds were already heaving in Trafalgar Square. The Metropolitan Police were out in force, lining the banks of the road as the Rolls-Royces moved through. A great Union Jack rippled from the peak of Nelson's Column and, in the sea of people around it, a hundred more were proudly being held aloft.

They were turning onto Horse Guards Parade, when Vivienne noticed that two Metropolitan Police had retreated into an alleyway along the side of a public house. What Vivienne saw was only fleeting, but it burned into the backs of her eyes. There was a man lying there, in the gutter, with the same faraway look in his eyes as the men she and Nancy had encountered outside the Rowton House. But the Metropolitans were seizing him by the arms. He was begging them to leave him where he lay, but instead they were hauling him aloft, their truncheons at their sides, and forcing him deeper into the alley – deeper, where he would not be seen.

Vivienne looked around. By the scalding look on her face, she could tell that her mother had seen it too. She rolled her eyes.

'Those fine policemen have spent days scouring these streets clean of ne'er-do-wells, but there's always one to spoil the occasion. Well, good riddance to bad rubbish, that's all I can say!'

The fraudulent accent became more imperious – and more obviously *fake* – with every word, but it wasn't this that made Vivienne burn so fiercely. Now that she thought about it, every street she'd passed through this morning was curiously *clean*, curiously *polished*. There wasn't a beggar anywhere.

It's like my mother said, she thought. *These streets have been scoured clean. But where have they all gone? Not to be looked after. Not to be cared for or sorted out. Just shovelled along, like the human detritus they are . . .*

The man she'd seen in the alley, that look in his eyes – if Vivienne had any insight at all, she knew it was more than just the demon drink. There would be no Rowton House for him. He was enslaved to darker gods. And, because of the coronation, there wasn't even the comfort of his familiar place in the gutter. He would just be moved and moved again, an unsightly blemish not to be seen in the company of princes and kings.

Lost, dispossessed people like him did not, it seemed, belong anywhere in London.

She would have to tell Nancy about this.

Maynard Charles stood in the silver archway that opened out into the Candlelight Club, the Buckingham's premier cocktail lounge, peering into the darkness beyond. Yes, he was satisfied. The Grand Ballroom was in full swing, the Archie Adams Orchestra playing a roster of slow, respectful waltzes while Hélène Marchmont, Gene Sheldon and the rest put on an understated show. Many of the guests – those who had not gone out to catch a glimpse of the procession – were content to celebrate the coronation there, with the BBC broadcasting the service itself while the orchestra took a break; but those who wanted something a little more sublime reclined here, while Diego, the Argentine cocktail waiter, marshalled his troops to keep the cocktails flowing.

All of this, thought Maynard, *and it's not even high noon.*

He had drained his glass and was gesturing for Diego to bring him another, when he noticed a figure on the terrace. The lounge's doors opened onto a broad patio of exotic ferns and shrubs from all of Britain's many great dominions. And there, on the terrace, corpulent and altogether out of place in such beautiful surroundings, was Abner Grant.

It was too late. Abner had seen him. He tramped back into the lounge and joined Maynard by the door.

'It's quite a show you're putting on in this hotel, Maynard, my old friend. They've got decorum up here, but down in the Grand Ballroom, they're making merry hell. Of course, that makes it the perfect time for a thief. All those rooms and suites left unattended.'

Maynard stilled. 'What have you found, Abner?'

Abner lifted his enormous shoulders in a pronounced shrug. 'I've been doing my reviews, Maynard. It takes time to get to know a place. I dare say I walk a marathon every day through these halls, just getting the *feel* of the place. At the Imperial, I could have walked from under-kitchen to bridal suite with my eyes closed. I can feel the changing textures of the carpet.'

Maynard remembered: he was like this in Flanders too. He always thought he knew best. And then came that fateful night when everything went awry . . .

'And you've found nothing?'

'A spate of burglaries is almost always a member of staff, Maynard. You know that.'

Maynard was growing restless. 'That's what you're here for, Abner.'

'If he's here, I'll find him.' He stopped. 'Or *her*. Chambermaids are just as greedy as concierges. *And* they've got access to all the rooms. On which note, Maynard, you must have *plans* – drawings of the hotel?'

The architect's drawings were still in Maynard's office; brittle and yellow with age, they reminded him of a time when the hotel was bright and optimistic, when life was not about survival, pure and simple.

'I'll have them for you presently,' Maynard began, but Abner still lingered.

'You'll have beaten the Imperial hands down, today.' Abner grinned. 'Yes, the Imperial likes to put on a show, but nobody puts on a show like Maynard Charles. Well, the whole of your *life* has been a show of sorts, hasn't it?'

Abner Grant was whistling a discordant tune as he left – and, not for the first time, Maynard Charles wondered what had possessed him to invite that odious man into his hotel.

The clock on the wall was approaching midday. Maynard slipped silently out of the Candlelight Club, rode the empty guest lift up to the Buckingham's highest storey, strolled nonchalantly past the Atlantic, the Pacific, the Crown suites – and, turning a corner, arrived at a plain, unmarked door.

There were but two keys to this door. No caretaker's skeleton key, nor housekeeping master key, fitted this lock. Emmeline Moffatt was in possession of one – and the gleaming silver key in Maynard's pocket was the other.

He slipped it into the lock, and vanished beyond.

Inside, the windows were open to the summery scents of Berkeley Square. Once upon a time, they had called this the Park Suite – but it had been an aeon since a guest was last here. Instead, as Maynard rounded the corner, he saw Mrs Moffatt fussing around a man in a velveteen armchair, an oxygen tank at his side, a breathing mask over his face. With every step Maynard took, another ounce of his worries sloughed away. It was like shedding a skin.

When he reached the old man's side, he bowed down and planted a loving kiss upon his brow.

'Maynard, my dear,' began Aubrey, lifting the mask momentarily from his face. 'I was beginning to fear you wouldn't make it.'

'I wouldn't miss it,' Maynard said softly. 'The hotel can cope without me, for a few hours at least.'

Mrs Moffatt, who was fixing lunch on the silver room service tray, reeled back in mock astonishment.

'It truly must be a day of celebration!'

Maynard drew a chair up alongside Aubrey and turned to face the crackling box in the corner. On the screen embedded in its walnut surround, black-and-white images were strobing, like the lights in a theatre.

How the world changes . . .

It had been a challenge to have the television set installed, but Maynard had spent many long years practising the arts of secrecy. He'd simply let it be known that a BBC engineer was visiting the hotel to install one of the new 'television' sets in the hotel director's office – and, using this to explain the presence of the man and his equipment, neglected to tell anybody that he also had a second, secret set to install while here.

He'd wanted to do it – not for himself, but for Aubrey. Maynard glanced down at the oxygen tank by Aubrey's side. His eyes followed its tubes up to his oldest friend – the only man he'd ever been able to love in the way his heart told him he must – and fought hard not to picture the day when he would not be here.

You survived this long, Aubrey. But what happened in Flanders, it's still with you. Our war isn't over, not after what the mustard gas did to your lungs.

'I have something to tell you,' Maynard began, taking Aubrey's hand. 'I've been meaning to tell you for weeks already. Abner Grant is here, in the hotel.'

Fleetingly, Aubrey drew back his hand. Then he threaded his fingers back through Maynard's own.

'I thought it was best,' said Maynard, 'that he might put an end to the robberies, and any brewing scandal, before Jack Hastings comes. And, well, leaving the Imperial exposed without their hotel detective, that was in my thinking too. I *need* Jack Hastings to choose us. Not just for me. For—'

'Maynard,' Aubrey said gently, 'you mustn't worry. The chances are, Abner Grant thinks I'm dead – if he remembers me at all.'

'Oh, he *remembers*. He didn't say as much, but it's all over his face. But he'll keep our secret, if I keep his. Besides, he doesn't know you're here. How could he? The only people who do are right here, in this room, right now.'

Mrs Moffatt was serving up smoked salmon and rare beef. For a time, they sat in silence, Maynard cutting Aubrey's food into tiny pieces and holding him steadily as he poked scraps between his lips, letting them melt on his tongue.

Then, as if from nowhere, there came a rousing cheer. Maynard fancied he could hear it coming through the open windows, the joyfulness rippling in waves across London; perhaps he could, but the real cheering was coming from the flickering screen.

Such a magical contraption: a window into the world out there. It's going to change Aubrey's life – what's left of it, at least.

On the screen, the image showed the crowded Mall, where a carriage was moving through the heaving throng.

'Look,' said Aubrey – and Maynard had rarely seen such simple delight on his face. 'Maynard, my love – it's beginning.'

'Quiet, girls!' exclaimed Ruth. 'I can't tell what's happening!'

The housekeeping lounge might not have been blessed with a television set, but the wireless was all the girls needed. Nancy angled her ear so that she might hear more clearly. The procession had been making its way to the abbey since breakfast, but now the King himself had embarked from Buckingham Palace in his golden carriage – and, with his wife Elizabeth at his side, he was being drawn slowly to his coronation.

'They're onto the Mall,' Nancy called out. 'You'd better keep that champagne cold for a little while yet.'

None of the girls had been expecting it. A gift of this magnitude from Maynard Charles and the board of the Buckingham was unheard of. And yet this was a day like no other – and the housekeeping lounge had been given two bottles of Maison Veuve Clicquot for the celebration. Ruth said that old Mr Charles must have gone mad – he'd been so dour of late, tramping around trying to hide his hangdog expression – and, finally, he must have snapped.

Not that any of the housekeeping staff minded.

Nancy was concentrating on the wireless so hard that she did not notice, at first, when Billy strolled in with his arm around Frank's shoulder. It was only as Billy shepherded Frank through the girls that she saw her brother standing there.

'Frankie!'

'We thought we'd share these festivities of yours,' Billy cut in. 'The pages have all fled off into town. Mr Charles is going to have a fit if he finds out – but it ain't as if there are many guests asking for errands. They're all getting on with these celebrations themselves.'

'You all right, Frankie?'

Frank was silent, but that was often his way. The truth was, he'd been feeling anxious for days now. Ever since Billy had cajoled him into eavesdropping in the Grand Ballroom, he'd been beset by this terrible feeling that he was about to be *found out*. Directly afterwards, Billy had dragged him into Maynard Charles's office – Maynard Charles, the hotel director *himself*! – and asked him to spill everything he'd heard. In the end, he'd been stammering so much that Mr Charles had asked him to write it all down – and this only disturbed him more. He'd sworn to himself, there and then, that he'd never do anything as hasty again – but Mr Charles seemed so pleased that he'd given him a whole pound note.

'Frank said he'd rather come down here with *me* than sneak out with the other pages,' said Billy. 'My folks are down there somewhere. Got all the Brogan brood on the Embankment. They've been champing at the bit for days, haven't they, Frank?'

The children had been so excited, it had been a task of Herculean proportions to get them settled in bed the night before. Frank was exhausted.

'Frankie, you should be out there!' Nancy exclaimed.

Frank kneaded his eyes. Truth was, London still frightened him – and the thought of London, already so crowded, crowded further still by the untold thousands, was roiling his tummy.

'Can't you come, Nance?'

'No such luck,' Nancy answered. 'Mrs Moffatt was very clear. But *you*. If the other pages have gone, you should ...' She stopped. 'Rosa's out there somewhere, with some of the other girls who were off shift. You can't get lost, Frankie. Imagine – if you're swift, you might catch a glimpse of the procession coming back.'

Frank was silent. It wasn't the idea of kings and queens that was tempting him. It was Rosa. Rosa, with the golden braids. Rosa, who tousled his hair and made him feel ... *runny* inside, in a way he hadn't known before. It was simultaneously frightening and exciting, and that unholy cocktail was making him nauseous.

'Right,' said Billy, 'that's it. I'm turning this into an order. I'm going to stay here with my girls, and you're going to get on out there and live a little!' Then he bent down and whispered in Frank's ear, 'Get on with you. Rosa and those girls, they'll be on the Embankment. You got to be bold, Frank. It's your new life! It's London!'

What if what I want is my old life? gulped Frank. *And my bed in the lodging house. And gin rummy with the lads at the end of the day?*

But then there was Rosa.

So he took off, as fast as his legs could carry him, before common sense prevailed.

By the time he'd fought his way to the Embankment, midday had come and gone, and that meant that the royal procession would soon be wending its way back to Buckingham Palace. The Embankment Gardens, where the pink blossoms of early summer were just beginning to show, were so crowded that Frank could hardly pick a route between the people who had gathered here.

It's no use, he thought. *How am I supposed to find one person in all of this?*

Some time later, Frank was fighting his way through the crowds – but the closer he got to the river, the more packed the people became. Buffeted from both sides, he began to feel as if he was back down the mine, the walls closing in on each side.

Remember what Mrs Gable taught you, he thought. *Get your head out of the mine, even if that's where your body has to stay. Breathe, Frank. Just breathe . . .*

In the end, it was breathing that undid him. He was holding himself rigidly, trying to control his panic, when the crowd shifted too suddenly around him. Somebody wheeled into his shoulder. Somebody else's legs entangled with his.

Frank felt himself falling. For a second, he stayed upright, held in place by the press of bodies on either side.

Then, the crowd parted just enough for him to plunge down to the cold, hard ground.

Lights exploded in front of Frank's eyes.

He felt a boot in the small of his back.

He tried to pick himself up. Now the roar of the crowd was a distant thing, as if he had plunged his head into cold, roiling water. He lifted himself again, only to discover that the crowd was moving unthinkingly around him. Not a soul among them seemed to know that he'd tripped.

So this is London, he thought. *Nancy, I want to go home . . .*

Then he heard his name being called through the chaos.

'Frank? Frankie? *Frank?*'

Frank dared to open his eyes. He looked up. At first, all he saw was a hand – dainty and pink, with beautiful, shining nails – reaching out. Then he saw Rosa's face, banked in golden curls, the sun shining behind her like a halo itself.

In an instant, he came back to his senses. He took her hand, felt himself being lofted back to his feet. The roar of the crowds had suddenly returned in full force.

'Frank, what on earth were you doing down there?'

'I t-tripped,' he stammered. 'I f-fell. And then—'

'Then, nothing, Frank Nettleton!' Rosa put an arm around him and turned him bodily around. 'You almost missed it, you fool! Look, they're coming!'

And coming they were. He could tell it in the way the cheering changed. It moved along the Embankment like a joyful wave, and in its wake came a carriage cast out of pure gold, drawn by eight elegant grey horses.

'I came to find you,' gasped Frank. 'And here you are . . .'

But Rosa could hardly hear. She was hauling him to meet the other chambermaids who'd managed to get out of the Buckingham for the day – but they were too far away, and eventually she relented.

'I guess it's just you and me,' she said, with a grin.

It seemed, to Frank, that there was more joy in that little path of the Embankment than he had ever seen in his life. Something in it melted the panic he'd been feeling. He raised himself on his tiptoes to see the carriage gliding into view. It was adorned with rich gilded sculptures of cherubs and Greek tritons carrying swords and crowns and sceptres. Those Greek gods cast in gold seemed to be drawing the carriage onwards, trumpet-like shells put to their lips to herald the coming of the new king.

And there he was! Frank saw him now, sitting in the window of the carriage, his queen beside him, waving to the passing crowd.

He looks nervous, thought Frank. *Nervous like me. Can it be that kings get nervous too?*

'Oh, Frank!' Rosa exclaimed. He was staggered to find that she had thrown her arms around him, that her lips had been planted on his in a perfect kiss. 'He waved right at me! He looked me in the eye. The new king, Frank, and there he goes!'

The carriage had passed them only fleetingly. Now it was being drawn further down the Embankment and up towards Trafalgar Square, where the revelries continued. Rosa meant to go after it, but the crowd was thick and it held them fast in its grip.

Frank didn't mind at all. Moments ago, he had been lying on the cold stone ground, resigned to being trampled. Now, he was holding Rosa's hand, her lips had been for a moment on his – and, most miraculous of all, he didn't feel anxious at all.

London, he thought. *Perhaps London might work out for me after all.*

Chapter Eleven

I REALLY SHOULDN'T BE HERE, thought Hélène as she stepped out of the taxicab and breathed in the heady scents of the twilit Strand. It was the night of King George's coronation and London was slowly beginning to empty. Rags of revellers still moved up and down the wide avenue, but the coaches and trains were gradually drawing the crowds away from London.

I should be being drawn away as well. I convinced Maynard Charles that I could be excused coronation night in the Grand – told him all manner of lies – so that I could sneak back into Brixton, spend one more night with Sybil. And yet . . . here I am.

She was standing outside the window at Simpson's, the hastily written invitation from Arthur Regan in her hand.

Inside, the restaurant was heaving. Hélène followed a waiter dressed entirely in white as he weaved between the tables. There were gentlemen dining with their paramours, and landed families who had come in from the country for the coronation. Some diners had tumbled in from the Savoy next door, preferring Simpson's whole and hearty fare to the Savoy's own restaurants.

I suppose I should feel like a traitor being here at all, thought Hélène. *A traitor to the Buckingham Hotel.*

But that, she decided, would only be to ignore the true guilt that she felt.

She and Sidney had never dined in places like this. Theirs had been a private romance, picnics in the summer grasses on Parliament Hill, or meetings in the public house on Brixton Hill where Sidney's family knew everyone. Compared to all that, Simpson's was the very definition of luxury. Its diners sat on plush red leather, and the tables were of gleaming mahogany. The smells that billowed out of the kitchens reminded Hélène of her own childhood, back on her father's estate. She had not seen her own family for three years and more, but the smells of Simpson's made her feel six years old again, lingering outside the kitchen door while the cook busied herself basting the beef.

The waiter led her to a corner table, stepped aside with a minor bow – and there sat Arthur Regan. He looked good in his charcoal suit, his flaming hair trimmed back, and his whiskers tamed. His eyes, alive with admiration, lit up as they took her in.

'Miss Marchmont,' he said, standing, 'I'm delighted you could come.'

Hélène descended into her seat.

'I almost didn't,' she confessed. 'I had plans, Mr Regan.'

'Please, call me Arthur.'

'And, I have to admit, I wondered why you might want to have dinner with me at all.'

Arthur Regan had already ordered champagne. A 1922 vintage sat in ice on the table and he motioned for a waiter, who sashayed over and poured her a glass.

'You fascinated me when we danced, Miss Marchmont. Or . . . Hélène – might I call you Hélène?'

Hélène nodded, and together they raised their glasses.

'I enjoyed dancing with you too, Arthur. You aren't the first guest to invite me to a supper. And yet I wanted to come. I'm glad you asked.'

'I don't have much company when I'm in London. There are my business associates, of course. And those at the various charities in which I invest. But with these, I am always "at work". I have to put on my official Arthur Regan face. Sometimes I should rather relax and be *me*, in the company of someone I don't have to pretend to admire.'

'I know how that feels,' said Hélène, thinking of all those nights in the Grand Ballroom when she did exactly the same.

The whole of my life is putting on the 'Hélène Marchmont' show. All except those precious few moments when I'm in Brixton with Sybil.

Where I should be tonight.

If only to stop that thought, she said, 'What is it you *do*, Arthur?'

'That's a long old tale.' He winked. 'Let's order, shall we?'

Over oysters and clams, monkfish and mullet, Arthur tried to explain the long trajectory of his life.

'I'm sure you can't imagine what it was like when I was a bairn. Slumming it on the estate with the local boys in County Cavan. My history was written – I'd inherit the brewery my grandfather founded, look after the lads there and retire content, if I didn't drink myself to death first, o' course.' Here he smiled playfully. 'But that all changed when Agatha came into my life. We met when I was hardly nineteen – oh, a quarter of a century ago now. Agatha was everything I was not. She was refined. Lord knows what she saw in me, but we were married within a year. It was Agatha who first brought me to London. She opened my eyes to the fate of the London Irish. To lads like me, come to seek their glory – and spat on by any who'd look. You mightn't have seen it, not in a rarefied place like the Buckingham, but London is a den of inequality. We Irish are no better than dogs to most men here. But I couldn't do a thing about it.'

Hélène dared not ask more. Arthur was in full flow now – and, between mouthfuls, he told her the rest. How Agatha had fallen ill, here in London on one of their visits. How English doctors had treated her but found no cause for her fainting fits. How Arthur himself had barely got her home to Ireland when the last fit took her away from him forever.

'I might have lost myself in the drink. I had every intention to. But, you see, she'd written a will. Her father made her do it. I hadn't a clue. She left me everything she had, everything bequeathed to her by her great-aunt. And I knew what she wanted – for me to be a good man.' He paused. 'So here I am. I have a little foundation. We scour London's streets for organisations of interest. Those promoting the Irish cause, first and foremost. Helping the London Irish stand on their own two feet. Helping them find work, helping them organise – helping them butt back against the yoke of British oppression.'

He saw the look of incredulity on Hélène's face, and began to laugh. She remembered what he'd said, back in the ballroom: one day, equality will prevail.

If equality had prevailed already, I would never have had to keep my love for Sidney a secret. I wouldn't have to hide my daughter in shame. I . . . would never have met Arthur Regan.

She scarcely dared voice it, even to herself.

'But that's enough about me!' Arthur declared, with a flourish. 'I want to know about you. Oh, you've already spun me the legend, of course. Hélène Marchmont, who graced the cover of *Harper's Bazaar* and *Esquire*, and every fashionable women's weekly from London to New York. And yet, that can't be *everything*, can it? Take any person in this room, for instance. Take *me*. There's a story behind the story, isn't there? The real, authentic *you*. That's the person I want to hear about.'

Hélène breathed deeply.

The real, authentic me? The me who fell in love with a black musician and gave him a child? The me who kept it a secret, even after that careering bus ended his life? The me whose life would come crashing down if, for a second, I thought about telling the truth?

The me who shouldn't be here at all – because, damn it, I'm still in love with Sidney. Aren't I?

Well, aren't I?

This was going to take some telling, but it was not as if Hélène was not practised at lies.

'My story isn't really as exciting as you may think, Arthur. But I'll tell it, if that's what you want. You see, I was only a little girl when I first attended a dance . . .'

Later, after Hélène had spun Arthur a story about the first tea dances she'd gone to and how they'd drawn her into a world she had no desire to leave – even for the stardom of the silver screen – they stepped outside. On the Strand, Arthur hailed a cab and, opening the door, took her hand. Though he meant only to help her inside, some deeper instinct drove Hélène to draw back.

She had acted too soon. A look creased Arthur's face – as if he was wounded – and another dagger of guilt pierced her side.

'Arthur,' she said, gathering herself, 'I had a marvellous evening. Thank you for dinner.'

Arthur nodded, and she was surprised at how happy she felt when the smile returned to his face.

'I hope you shall do me the honour again, Hélène. My work brings me often to London. At least I know which hotel I shall now be frequenting.'

He planted a single kiss on the back of her hand, and stood back as the taxicab drove away, taking Hélène with it. Inside, she fought the urge to look back through the window. She could still feel the impression of his lips on the back of her hand, the touch of his whiskers on her skin.

At the Buckingham, the Grand Ballroom was finally closing. Maynard Charles stood sentry as the guests filed back out into the night, or into the guest lift and the Buckingham's uppermost floors.

Hélène kept her head down as she sashayed through the doors, losing herself among the departing guests as she made for the dressing rooms at the back of the Grand. She could not go to bed yet. Not with the recollection of Arthur Regan's lips still playing so fiercely on her mind.

It was only dinner, Hélène. It doesn't mean the world.

She had been hoping to find Gene Sheldon and the rest of the hotel dancers celebrating backstage, but the exertions of the day must have exhausted all and sundry, because only a few members of the orchestra still lingered here. Perhaps it was for the best. Hélène did not trust her own tongue tonight. And yet . . .

'Hélène!'

It was Louis Kildare. He'd been crouched by Archie's practice baby grand, laying his saxophone back in its velveteen bed, but now he stood up.

'Louis, you frightened the life out of me.' Then a thought occurred to her. 'I need to talk.'

Taking him by the hand, she led him into one of the dressing rooms' many alcoves and made him sit down.

'I thought you were with Sybil tonight, Hélène. Something hasn't *happened*, has it?'

She saw the consternation on his face and something melted inside her. Louis cared for Sybil as much as any of the Archers themselves. Not for the first time, she remembered how close – not to mention how alike – he and Sidney had once been.

'No,' she said, clasping his hand to reassure him, 'nothing of the sort. Louis, I've been ... frightful. I've been the worst mother.' She took a deep breath to embolden herself. 'I went out for dinner tonight, with Arthur Regan. I danced with him here, weeks ago, and he wrote to me, asking for my company. I ...'

Something broke inside her and the sob she'd been trying to control forced its way up through her throat. She buried her head in her hands.

'Louis,' she said. 'Louis, I'm sorry.'

Louis grasped her hand tightly, forced her to look up.

'I don't ever want to hear you call yourself a bad mother, Hélène. Your life, it's built around that girl. And I don't ever want to see you like this. You're allowed a life. You're allowed to be ... you. Sidney would never have wanted you wasting your years, thinking of him. He was in love with you for your light. Don't—' And here it seemed that Louis might let out a sob as well. 'Don't give in to the darkness.'

Those words cut through all the pain she'd been feeling. Such a little thing, but what a difference they made.

'Thank you,' she whispered. 'I've always been able to count on you, haven't I? Somehow, you always have the right words.' Standing, she straightened her gown. 'Louis, my friend—'

'Did you enjoy his company, Hélène?'

It took all Hélène's strength to speak a few simple words. 'I'm afraid that I did.'

Then, unable to dwell on the thought any longer, she turned and was gone.

After the dressing room doors closed, Louis stood there for a long time. Perhaps emotion was infectious, because the agony that had been on Hélène's face had, somehow, wormed its way into Louis himself. He breathed until the agony was numbed, but even then the image of Hélène sitting across a restaurant table with somebody who wasn't Sidney Archer kept coursing through him. Hélène with Sidney he could understand. Sidney had been his best friend; they'd practically been brothers. But Hélène with Arthur Regan? Hélène with almost anybody else? Why did such a thing pierce him so?

Louis was the last out of the dressing rooms behind the Grand Ballroom that night. Alone he tramped out onto Berkeley Square. Alone he wandered through the moonlight streets of Mayfair. And when, finally, he arrived at the Camden Town house where he boarded and threw himself back to his bed, he realised that he could still smell the perfumed scent of Hélène Marchmont. It was all over his hands.

June 1937

Chapter Twelve

ON THE FIRST DAY OF June, Frank awoke from a dream of the rolling hills of his Lancashire home.

Frank was always comfortable in dreams. When he was a small boy, almost everything in the waking world had had the capacity to frighten him – but, whenever he slept, his head was filled with the warmest images: Nancy taking him out on a stroll; playing conkers with his father in the back yard; his mama, the mama he had never known, taking him foraging for brambles so that she might make him a pie.

The younger Brogans were already bustling around the breakfast table by the time Frank picked himself out of bed. Mr Brogan, who worked at the fish market in Billingsgate, was long gone – but Mrs Brogan was dishing out porridge oats from the big pan on the range. It was Frank's job to sprinkle brown sugar over each bowl as the younger children lined up.

One day, he thought, *I'll be a father myself. I'll do for my own bairns what Mrs Brogan does for hers, and what Nancy did for me.*

'A big day for you up at the Buckingham, isn't it?' asked Mrs Brogan.

'Every day's a big day,' said Frank. 'That's h-how Billy tells me to think of it.'

Today was big because Mr Chamberlain, newly made the prime minister, was in attendance. Only last night, Mr Brogan had rhapsodised about what a grand man Mr Chamberlain was, and how much the country needed a man of his mettle.

'You see, young Nettleton, Mr Chamberlain knows *people*. He knows what they want and he knows how to get it. And, by God, what they want is *peace*. You mark my words, with Mr Chamberlain in charge, all this bluster and talk about war is going to ebb away. Leave Europe to fend for itself. That's how it has to be.'

Frank didn't like to say anything, because he knew that Mr Brogan had been in France for the Great War. He'd come back unscathed – but the thought of another war to come, one that might sweep all the many Brogan children into danger, was too terrible to imagine. Yet, as Mr Brogan spoke, all that Frank could think of was what he'd heard Conte Grandi saying in the Grand Ballroom that night.

If only I was cleverer, thought Frank, *I'd understand what it all means. And maybe I'd know why Mr Charles needs to know as well. All these things Nancy didn't tell me about working at the Buckingham! Worlds within worlds. Secrets within secrets. It was easier up north.*

'No,' Mr Brogan had concluded before he tottered off to bed, 'Mr Chamberlain's the man. He has his head screwed on, you mark my words. Not like that Mr Churchill.' Mr Brogan had rolled the name around his mouth as if it was some sort of a curse. 'Calling for catastrophe, that's all he's doing. Agitating and exacerbating. A man like Mr Churchill, he almost *wants* a war.

But a man like Mr Chamberlain? Well, let's simply say, I'm glad Mr Chamberlain has the ear of our new king.'

Around the breakfast table, the Brogan children were finishing their porridge oats and – ignoring the protests of their mother – were busy lapping their plates clean with long, lolling tongues. Frank had one more task to do before hurrying off – so he helped Mrs Brogan line the children up, organised each of them into their day clothes, and made sure each had an apple in the bag they'd be taking to school. Under Billy's direction, Frank had brought back a basketful last night; the apples were perfectly edible, but marked by unseemly bumps or bruises, so that they'd been rejected from the kitchens at the Buckingham Hotel.

By the time the children were all ready, Frank was enormously proud.

I could be a schoolteacher, he thought, *if only I had the brains. I'd like that. A class of my own, and a family to come back to. All I really need is a girl, somebody nice to be my wife. I don't think I'd worry for anything in the world if I had someone to look after and someone to look after me.*

The image of Rosa popped back into his head: her hair the colour of the wheat in the fields back home, the touch of her fingers as she tousled his hair. Her arms around him as they watched the new king sailing by.

Don't even start dreaming of it, Frank! Surely you've no chance with a girl like that. She thinks of you as a baby brother, pure and simple.

But . . . she stepped out with you, didn't she? And wasn't she as happy as it's possible to be, just standing there with you, waiting for the new king to ride on by? She put her arms around you! She kissed you. Just think about that!

The last lunch bag was for Frank himself. Mrs Brogan had made sandwiches with the nice crusty end of the loaf. She knew that Frank could easily graze on the finer fare they threw away in the Buckingham kitchens, but somehow she knew, without having to ask, that Frank preferred the simple stuff. It reminded him of home.

By the time he arrived at the Buckingham, the sun was already spilling over the rooftops of Mayfair – and Frank's first assignment for the day was impatiently waiting.

Abner Grant was lurking in the reception hall, looking through the notes left by the departing night manager. Frank was given to understand that Mr Charles had promised him to Abner Grant as a personal servant. Frank was hurrying by when Abner grunted his name in the gruff Scottish drawl that always made his skin crawl, and when Frank turned around a single meaty finger summoned him near.

'I'll be in the office, Nettleton,' Abner grunted. 'Make it my usual.'

The usual was smoked salmon and cream cheese, freshly pressed tomato juice and a pot of tea brewed so dark and meaty it was practically undrinkable. Frank nodded glumly and made haste for the under-kitchen beneath the Queen Mary, where the morning prep chef was, at least, an amiable sort.

Some time later, Frank made his way, with the tray in his hands, to the office Maynard Charles had unearthed for the hotel detective, one of the old audit rooms that was scarcely used except for meetings of the board. Here, Abner had made his den. Every time Frank set foot in here, it seemed that old Abner had imported some other trinket. On the wall hung the head of an elk that Abner claimed to have killed on a hunting expedition in his youth. A King James Bible, bound in calfskin, took pride of place upon a shelf. The desk was home to a portable Underwood typewriter – because Abner Grant insisted on typing up his own reports.

'Ah, Nettleton!' Abner exclaimed as Frank teetered to the table, carrying the tray. 'All present and correct, I see.'

Frank nodded nervously. 'Chef sends his regards.'

'I'll wager he doesn't,' said Abner, and proceeded to devour the smoked salmon. 'You can pour the tea, son.'

Frank hated this part. He trembled as he poured the tea – he always did – but, this time, he managed not to spill it all across the table. *That* had been a disaster, the first time he did it.

With the tea successfully poured, he scurried to the door, as if to slope away and get on with the other errands of the day.

'Frank?'

'Wh-what is it, sir?'

'Humour me, Nettleton. You're one of the only ones I can talk to.' Abner paused, registering the look of horror on Frank's face. 'Oh, it isn't because I *respect* you, boy. Heaven forfend! No, I can talk to you about these matters because ... well, you weren't here when these robberies happened. So you're above suspicion. And, besides' – here Abner beamed, as if conjuring up the most delectable joke – 'you haven't got enough brain cells to under-stand. Come here, boy. Let me show you.'

Frank's insides were squirming as he moved closer. Stretched out on the table in front of Abner, pinned down by coffee cups in every corner, was an architect's drawing of the hotel, with every one of its rooms and suites marked out in Abner's own spidery hand. On top of that was a brochure from the Buckingham's opening year: 1889. Frank concentrated hard to read the words:

WELCOME TO THE BUCKINGHAM

ROYAL BY ASSOCIATION

220 ROOMS, 26 LUXURY SUITES

'Well?' grunted Abner.

Frank had no idea what Abner Grant expected him to say.

I'm only a page, he thought. *Just do as you're told, that's what Nancy said. And now . . . spying for Billy Brogan, and 'personal servant' for Abner Grant.* Where did it all end? Only the thought of letting Nancy down stopped him catching the next train back to Lancashire. That, and the wild idea that he might one day get to spend some time with Rosa again. *Fat chance*, he thought, *but it's nice to have a dream.*

'You don't know what you're looking at, boy, but it's not your fault. Now, you see this number?'

Abner's fat finger landed on the '26 Luxury Suites' on the front of the brochure. Then he proceeded to count each suite down on the architect's drawing.

'Twenty-six, you see. *Twenty-six.*'

'Yes, sir.'

'Well, now look here . . .' Abner reached under the table and, from a box, pulled up one of the old hotel ledgers. 'I've been through these books for the last five years. You never know what you might find. You got to cross-reference – you won't know what it means, but don't kill yourself on account of it. You got to check who's where and when. You can see patterns – guests coming, guests going, staff being hired, staff being fired. I've caught

126

plenty a conman just riffling through a hotel's ledgers. Well, here in the Buckingham, I didn't find a pattern, Frank. But do you know what I did find?'

Frank murmured, 'N-no, sir.'

'Well, it's the damnedest thing. But for years and years, there's only been *twenty-five* suites being taken at the Buckingham Hotel. The Atlantic, the Pacific, the Crown – all of these suites, occupied by dukes and duchesses, foreign dignitaries, Royalty from near and far. But only ever *twenty-five* suites.'

Frank stammered, 'But the brochure says that there's t-twenty-six.'

Abner Grant flurried up. 'So!' he declared, tapping the side of Frank's head. 'There is an intellect in there!'

'Yes, sir.'

'Secret places are aplenty in hotels like this – but a good hotel detective, he needs to know about them all. Where secrets lie, so does criminality. Maybe it isn't these robberies, but it's *something*, and I'm appointed to sniff those *somethings* out. So I've been prowling. I've been marking the suites off, one by one. I know which the missing suite is. And, Frank, that's why I need you.'

Inwardly, Frank cringed. *Nothing good could come of this*, he thought. *Not a single thing.*

'Me, sir?'

'You, boy. You've got the ear of the pages. You get into all the nooks and crannies. There must be gossip. There must be rumours. And what I want to know is . . . why, in the past five years – perhaps even more – has the Buckingham Hotel never welcomed a guest to the Park Suite?'

Chapter Thirteen

THE LETTER WAS WHERE NANCY had left it, hidden under her pillow. It was right that she should savour it. The girls didn't stop asking when they knew she had a letter. As if the idea of her, country mouse Nancy Nettleton, having won the heart of the dashing Raymond de Guise wasn't bizarre enough, the idea that she was receiving missives from *Hollywood* was simply too exciting to ignore. But there was nothing sweeter, to Nancy, than being alone with Raymond's letters, imagining the words spoken in his dark, dulcet tones. It sent a shiver through her every time.

My darling Nancy,

This is the last chance I shall get to write to you before I see your face again. I am sorry it has been so long, but I have every hope that this will only make our reunion sweeter still. By the time you receive this letter, I shall already be on the steamer bound for Liverpool — and back to you . . .

New York grows warmer by the day. Even its nights are balmy now and, so I am told, soon its days will become swelteringly hot. Quite unlike old grey London, where the rain is our constant companion! Over the last days, I have wined and dined with John Hastings and his family. John is a young man, not yet thirty years of age, and yet he has wealth beyond the likes of us. I believe he has grown to like me, though he is guarded — as many great men are. I have accompanied him to dinners and soirées, but this evening, I feel certain, I had a breakthrough of sorts. His wife Sarah has fallen quite in love with my stories of the Grand Ballroom, and of all the courts and palaces in Europe where Georges and I used to dance. Sarah has been busying herself raising their two small boys for so long that my stories inspired something in her, and — knowing that I have also been frequenting the Cotton Club — she laid down a gauntlet: would I, she asked, take her and her husband out . . . dancing?

As you can imagine, John Hastings himself was reluctant — men of money are sometimes so guarded that they cannot possibly comprehend of giving themselves over to music and dance — but, for his wife's sake, he agreed to join us on an expedition. And tonight we have been at a dance hall on Clinton Street, on New York's Lower East Side. From the outside, you would not think the Sunset Lounge much to write home about. It is a narrow cocktail bar, with scarcely enough room for a dozen revellers to stand. And yet, open the doors at the back of the bar, and a whole new world is revealed. And it was here that John Hastings, Sarah and I have whiled the night away.

The music, Nancy! If only I could do justice to such music in words! How carefree it is, how loose, how the dancers get lost in the emotion and let themselves take flight. I am in love with the jive. I am in love with the jitterbugging. And I am resolved to spend the next few months living it myself, throwing myself into the music just like these New Yorkers do. For what looks uncontrolled at first is actually an instinctive exuberance. It is the very heart and soul of dance itself: the embodiment of joy! Nancy, when I am back, I will take you to *the studio behind the Grand and teach you what I have learned. You must feel this, Nancy. The jitterbug is truly a dance of the heart.*

One day, perhaps I will jitterbug in the Grand Ballroom – and what would kings and lords and crown princesses make of that?

Enough! I must sleep, for soon the dawn will come, and I must make preparations for our departure. The last time John Hastings made the Atlantic crossing he did so on the Hindenburg line: by Zeppelin straight into Europe's heart. But only last month one of Germany's proud Zeppelins combusted right here, outside New York City, and Mr Hastings, I have learned, is a superstitious man. He would not tempt fate, and so I am to take, once again, to the oceans. And though I will not be able to post my letters to you, not a day will pass when I will not put pen to paper. Nancy, I . . .

Before she could read any further, a knock came at her door and, springing to her feet, she found Rosa looking sheepish in the hallway.

'You have a guest,' Rosa whispered.

It was not like Rosa to be so simpering. Rosa was usually one of the most outspoken chambermaids in their quarters – she'd been reprimanded by Mrs Moffatt on no less than three occasions for gossiping too loudly in the corridors, where the guests might hear.

Could it be he's back, already? Raymond's . . . here?

Rosa, having done her piece, scurried back into the kitchenette – and Nancy saw, lurking a little further down the hallway, the imperious figure of Miss Vivienne Edgerton.

'Nancy,' Vivienne began, 'might I have a word?'

Nancy, who was still trying to conflate the image of Vivienne with her surroundings – really, it was like seeing a swallow in

130

winter! – had no time to reply. Already Vivienne was sweeping into her tiny chamber. Nancy felt a sudden burst of shame, and immediately scolded herself. Her room might have been nothing compared to Vivienne's majestic suite – but everything Nancy had, she'd had to *work* to pay for.

As Nancy closed the door, she could hear the girls tittering in the kitchenette.

'Nancy, I'll come straight to the point,' Vivienne said. Then she hesitated, her eyes taking in the diminutive room and opening in surprise, as if to register the fact that Nancy had so little. Nancy thought she sensed some sort of *shame* ghosting across Vivienne's face too. 'The Rowton House, up on Arlington Road. I've been sending my allowance there for weeks now, but . . . it isn't right. It isn't enough. That is, the amount I am sending them is everything I have – but the work it's being put to, giving beds to those in need, helping the down-and-out back into society – well, it's good work but it isn't . . . *enough*. Not for me.'

'Miss Edgerton, I'm not sure what you're saying. Am I to—'

'On the day of the coronation, my stepfather was hauling us through Whitehall when I saw two Metropolitans setting upon a beggar man. They'd cleared them all out, you see. Purified Westminster, so that the King's splendid day wasn't ruined. They just shovelled them up and shovelled them on, like so much horse shit. And the look in the man's eye . . . It was like those men outside the Rowton House, you see. He was addled, Nancy. So far gone that it wasn't just Metropolitans who didn't care to help him. It was the very charities themselves. Oh, Mr Ross put on a good show, didn't he? He led us round like two dainty little things with more money than sense, said all the right things. But when it comes down to helping people,

131

helping people who *really* need it – people, Nancy, who need helping even in spite of themselves. People like . . .' She paused, as if it was going to take great courage to say what she had to say next. '. . . *me*. Well, nobody's interested in helping *them*, are they? All the do-gooders in London, what they're really interested in is just *looking good*. Nobody's interested in getting their hands dirty. Nobody except . . . Well, *you*, Nancy.'

Nancy had listened to Vivienne's words coming at her with the force of a gale. Now, as the storm subsided, she began to wonder what it was all for.

'Come,' Vivienne interjected, 'I have a taxicab waiting out on Berkeley Square.'

'Miss Edgerton?'

'Simple charity isn't enough, not for me. I should have known it from the second we left the Rowton House – and perhaps, in my heart, I did. But, these past weeks, it's been preying on my mind. I've been thinking that there ought to be somebody to help *those* people, people who don't have anybody else. And I've been thinking . . .' For the very first time, Nancy thought that Vivienne's eyes were sparkling with a real zest for life. 'I've been thinking it ought to be . . . us.'

'*Us?*' ventured Nancy.

'Of course, us!' Vivienne paused. 'Well, I'm not doing this alone, am I, Nancy?'

Chapter Fourteen

I T WAS ALMOST AN HOUR later, weaving through East End traffic, that the taxicab pulled up at its destination, and Nancy helped Vivienne up and out into the Whitechapel night.

East London after dark was not like Mayfair. In Berkeley Square, silver light cascaded over the perfectly manicured flower beds, and miniature rainbows formed in the fountain. Here off Whitechapel Road, the intermittent street lamps made halos of light in the inky blackness, and the air of menace was palpable. Somewhere in the distance, a horse and trap rattled by. A chorus of drunk voices were caterwauling a shanty.

The taxicab had deposited them in an alley off Whitechapel Road, at the foot of a set of red-brick steps. Nancy's eyes panned upwards, taking in the face of a squat brick chapel, reminiscent of the factories and mills she'd known back home. The door to the building stood ajar, spilling lamplight out into the night. Beyond it, she could see figures milling – but this was no chapel in the middle of a service. The sounds that came from within were stern conversation, the occasional muted howl.

Vivienne turned back to the taxicab, its engine still rumbling.

'Stay here, won't you?' she said. 'You may leave your meter running, no matter how long we are.'

'I haven't eaten all night, miss. I'll need to find myself some grub.'

Vivienne rolled her eyes. 'Then be back sharply,' she instructed. 'And your meter isn't to run while you're hunting down your sausages.'

As the taxicab left, Nancy felt suddenly a long way from home. She was surprised – and not a little comforted – when Miss Edgerton reached out and touched her hand.

'They call themselves the Daughters of Salvation,' Vivienne began, looking up at the red-brick chapel. A wicked wind whipped up through the street, and on it came the pungent smell of stale beer. 'Only a penny a bed, *if* you can afford it, and . . . there's no questions asked. It doesn't matter whether you're drunk or addled or, I dare say, on the run from the police themselves. Mary Burdett – that's the lady who oversees everything here – has never turned a soul away.'

Nancy caught herself thinking how strange it was that London, giddy London, could be the home of both the Buckingham Hotel and this place, with its crumbling mortar, the boards up in its windows, the stains on the step where some poor vagrant must have hawked up his guts.

'I found it in this,' Vivienne said, and produced a scrap of newspaper, *Socialist Commentary,* printed in bold black type at its top. 'I had Billy Brogan searching for me. He and your brother brought me back all manner of pamphlets, but this one pleased me most. Why, imagine my stepfather – staunch capitalist Lord Edgerton! – discovering his stepdaughter reading the social-ist papers?' Vivienne beamed at the idea. 'It had a list of all the charitable endeavours in which people of little means engage. People who have nothing, giving what little they can to those even less fortunate. Now, *that's* the sort of folk I want to help, Nancy. Those who'll help people at their very lowest ebb.' She paused. 'Well, shall we?'

It doesn't look like much, thought Nancy. *Just four walls and . . . scarcely even a roof. But who's to say what goes on inside? And there's only one way to find out.*

So they stepped inside.

If this had once been a practising chapel, it had long since fallen into a state of disrepair. All of its pews had been torn up. Those few that remained were used as benches around the periphery of the room, and across its floor were laid rows of beds, little more than mattresses on the stone. In them lay various men, either snoring deeply or staring, glassy-eyed, into the airy vaults above. In another corner, a group of men were crowded around an electric bell heater – and, from somewhere beyond that, came the rattle and roar of a petrol generator. In another corner, a brass brazier held glowing coals and a big, fat log in its cauldron. On top, a kettle of water was being boiled.

The lady tending it was big and meaty, with untamed white hair and features that seemed altogether too large for her face. She was so busy making what appeared to be half a dozen pots of tea that, for some time, she did not notice the interlopers to the chapel. It was only when one of the vagrants shuffled over and began to play waiter to the men lounging around the hall that she walked over to them.

'Miss Edgerton, I presume?'

Nancy noticed how Vivienne had to take two deep breaths before she spoke, and it took all her self-control not to jump in and speak for her. Vivienne needed to do this herself.

It might be the first time in her life she's felt in control of any-thing. All of her life, being told what to do and where to go . . .

'Mrs Burdett,' Vivienne began.

'*Miss* Burdett, actually,' the white-haired lady began. 'Well, I never did meet the right fellow. None of them ever quite took my fancy.'

'I can quite understand *that*,' said Vivienne.

Mary Burdett's face opened in a smile. 'I can see I have a kin-dred spirit in you, Miss Edgerton. Come on, let me show you around. I was pleased to get your message. It isn't often that people take any interest at all in what we're doing here.'

After Vivienne had introduced Nancy as her friend and com-panion, they walked the edges of the room. In truth there was so little to see that they could have taken in every last corner from where they had been standing. The delinquents who came to the Daughters ranged from an elderly vagabond – 'sixteen years on the streets, and now he wants to get help' – to a pair of much younger men that Mary explained had fallen prey to the scourge of opiates when they worked on the East India Quay.

'I can't offer much, but I offer what I can. Three years ago, this chapel was an abandoned corner of London. The vagrants broke in sometimes and called it their home. Well, back then, I was employed by the diocese to clean the place. Nobody used it, but they still wanted it clean. The problem was, that was a losing battle. And eventually I said to them – why don't we put it to good use? If vagrants want to sleep here, well, why not *let* them? And why not help them while we're at it? That's when I christened it the *Daugh-ters of Salvation*. And for three years, I've been here day and night, doing what little I can, with what little I have. Who needs a hus-band when you have life's work as fulfilling and enriching as *this*?'

'And the men here, they're—'

'Good men,' Mary intoned, as if Vivienne had been about to come out with some insult.

'Yes, but, even so . . . troubled men. Men with vices.'

'We don't need to pretend here, miss. Before they were lounging here, these men were lounging in dens of depravity somewhere else. There, they were being fed the very things that destroy them. But here, well, it's tea and toast and what soup I can provide. Lord knows, it isn't much. But if I can keep their bodies intact while their minds battle those demons, if I can provide sustenance for the spirit while they wage their private wars . . .'

Nancy saw Miss Edgerton stiffen.

'I mean to help you,' Vivienne announced.

Mary Burdett was not like Mr Ross from the Rowton House. She seemed genuinely surprised.

'That is to say, to donate what I can. And perhaps to . . . volunteer my time.'

'Miss Edgerton,' Mary began, cautiously, 'you do understand what I do here? It isn't pretty. It isn't—'

'I know it isn't pretty. I was down there with them, once. It is only the good nature of my friend' – here Nancy blushed – 'that set me back on my feet. They say you should repay debts, do they not? Well, short of indulging her with money – which is not what she wants – I have no way of repaying my friend. So instead I intend to repay the world.' Her voice cracked. 'I want to help these men, Miss Burdett. I want to learn how, and to be here doing it with them. But until I learn, perhaps my money will suffice.'

Reaching into her coat, she pulled out an envelope, in which was stuffed a full three weeks of her stepfather's allowance.

Mary Burdett accepted the package with what seemed to be apprehension. When she looked inside, her face – already white and pallid with age – blanched.

'Miss Edgerton, I couldn't possibly—'

'Why, don't you need all the help you can get?'

Mary stammered, 'But the donations we receive are mere pennies, not whole pounds!'

Vivienne dared to touch the back of Mary's hand.

'There shall be more where that comes from,' she began. 'I ask only one thing. I want to come. I want to do the good work.' Vivienne paused, for there was something on Mary's face that made her doubt herself. 'You would be pleased for a little assistance, would you not? Mightn't you be able to help more people, with a servant – for want of a better word – at your side?'

Mary's face crinkled, her aged lines deepening with confusion. 'A servant who pays for the privilege?'

Vivienne trembled. 'That's exactly what I mean.'

For a moment, Mary was silent, as she dwelt on what Vivienne had said. Then, her eyes opened fractionally and her face brightened.

'I think the least I can do for you fine ladies' – she nodded – 'is to provide a hot cocoa on a cold East End night. Come on, I keep sugar cubes too. Sometimes our visitors can't take anything down, but hot cocoa and sugar never fails to bring some cheer.'

Later, as they made their goodbyes and stepped back through the doors, Nancy took Vivienne by the arm.

'Miss Edgerton,' she whispered, 'you mean to help them *yourself*? Not just to donate your allowance but to become like Mary Burdett?'

Vivienne stopped, rooted to the spot. 'You sound as if you don't think I have such a thing in me.'

I've hurt her, Nancy realised. *I didn't mean to, but . . .*

'I meant no such thing!' she gasped, though inwardly she wondered if she'd meant exactly that. 'Miss Edgerton, I'm quite certain you can do almost anything you want. It's only that we're so far from the Buckingham. This world, it's so very different . . .'

Outside, the night had grown colder. The skies over Whitechapel were wide and open and marked with stars, and a frigid moon hung beached over the endless terraces. Nancy and Vivienne pulled their shawls around them as they came to the bottom of the steps.

'It's everything the Rowton House wasn't. The Rowton House was already provisioned. It didn't need me at all. But here? Here they need every penny, every ounce of help they can get. And, Nancy, they're doing the *important* work. They're doing for these people what you once did for me – finding them at the bottom of the pit and helping them climb back up.'

Nancy had been so caught up in Vivienne's words that only now did she realise that the taxicab was nowhere to be found.

'Maybe he's down there,' Nancy ventured. 'Miss Edgerton, we should . . .'

Vivienne nodded, and threaded her arm through Nancy's own. 'And let's be swift about it.'

Arm in arm, they came to the end of the alley and onto the wide open thoroughfare of Whitechapel Road. Nancy looked one way, then the other – but still there was no sign of their taxi-cab, nor any other.

'How long can finding some "grub" take?' Vivienne muttered. 'We should wait, shouldn't we?'

Nancy nodded. This far from the familiar contours of Berkeley Square, there didn't seem any other choice.

The darkness along Whitechapel Road was made up of a thousand different textures. There was the darkness around the halos of the street lamps; the darkness where the thoroughfare opened up onto the countless lanes and alleys that twisted away from it; the darkness under the shop awnings, where Nancy could discern the outlines of vagrants, curled up in their makeshift tents. Then there was the darkness that hardened at the end of the road: the wild, impenetrable darkness at the edges of her vision.

Suddenly, Vivienne shrieked. Nancy clung to her tight, wheeled around – and saw a fat, black rat that had emerged from the alley behind them.

'Let's walk,' Vivienne began. 'He must be here somewhere. Which way is home?'

Nancy was uncertain. 'It's a long way, Miss Edgerton. It would take all night.'

'We'll find another taxicab soon enough.' Vivienne shuddered. 'But, Nancy, we can't stay here.'

We could go back to the Daughters of Salvation, thought Nancy, *spend the night there if we needed to. Only, I'm on shift in the morning, and if Mrs Moffatt were to find me missing . . .*

Together they took off up Whitechapel Road. Past one alley they came, past a second and a third – and yet the endless road still plunged into the further blackness ahead. From the shelter of a shop awning, somebody cried out, propelling Vivienne and Nancy on their way. Somewhere above them, a window opened and, from within, came the thunderous roar of a husband braying at his wife.

Nancy felt Vivienne's arm tighten on hers.

'A penny!' somebody crowed. 'A penny, madam, and I can be on my . . .'

Nancy felt the hand on her arm before she saw the figure. The fingers had grasped her tightly, wheeling her around – and she, in turn, wheeled Vivienne around with her.

The figure, hidden by fronds of entangled beard, had risen out of the refuse bins at the side of the road, and now he held her fast. In the inky dark, Nancy could see so little – only the way his eyes rolled madly in their orbits – but she could smell and feel more. His hand was a vice. He brought the other up, as if to tug at Vivienne's shawl.

Nancy tried to step backwards, but the man was holding her fast.

'We have nothing,' she breathed. 'Sir, please . . .'

It was only an invitation for the man to step closer still.

'You've got that fine shawl,' he said. 'That'd keep a man warm on a cold night.' He lifted his other hand, as if to stroke Nancy's cheek. 'Ladies dressed like this must be ladies of means. I'll wager you've got a few pennies hidden around your—'

Vivienne stepped backwards, her arm breaking from Nancy's. Whether she was looking for a weapon, some broom handle or stone to drive the man away, or simply resisting the temptation to turn and flee, Nancy had no time to work out – for in that same moment the headlamps of a motor car flared somewhere up Whitechapel Road, an engine roared into life, and in a screech of tyres, the taxicab slewed to a stop, banking around in the road.

In the next instant, the driver had emerged. With a flurry of wild invective, he floundered towards them.

Nancy took the chance and wrenched her arm free. Then, reaching once again for Vivienne, she hurried towards the waiting car.

141

'Get out of here!' the taxicab driver bawled at the vagrant – who was, even now, fading back into the night. 'You ought to be ashamed of yourself! Two innocent ladies like this, you ought to . . .'

In the back of the taxicab, Nancy and Vivienne caught their breath. Neither spoke a word, not until the driver reappeared and drove the taxicab back along Whitechapel Road.

'Just in the nick of time!' the driver declared. 'You ladies ought to know better than to go off wandering. You mightn't be so lucky next time!'

Nancy could feel Miss Edgerton trembling beside her. She put a hand on her knee, if only to steady her, and was surprised to find how much it steadied herself as well.

'Lucky?' Miss Edgerton exclaimed. 'Lucky!? Where on earth were you? You were told to—'

'I told you – I had to get myself some grub. I went back to the chapel, just like I said I would, but you two ladies was gone, weren't you? Didn't trust me, did you?' The driver shook his head. Outside the window, the open emptiness of the river had appeared between the buildings. Nancy could smell the water, with its faint tang of night soil. 'You Mayfair types just don't understand, do you? London isn't like it is in your beautiful hotels. There's a whole world out here. You want to do the world a favour, you stay where you are – safe up in those cloisters o' yours. Out here, miss, the rules you live by don't count for nothing. So you lovely ladies stay in your world, and let the rest of us stay in ours.'

July 1937

Chapter Fifteen

T EN DAYS AT SEA HAD turned into twelve. Such was the treachery of the North Atlantic. But, in those rare moments where he could stop himself thinking of Nancy and the moment he might see her again, every day had been a wonder. Even through the night, when the sea churned with ferocity, the journey seemed a magical fantasia.

Only a few generations ago, sailors believed great sea monsters lurked beneath these depths. They crossed these oceans in sailing ships, slaves to the wind. And now we cross them in luxury: the Veranda Café decorated with palm trees; the swimming pool on the uppermost deck; the Turkish baths; the dining saloon; the restaurant every bit as lavish as the Queen Mary at the Buckingham Hotel . . .

RMS *Othello* was even more luxurious than Raymond had been promised. He'd made the journey to America in a cruise ship half this size, but in the company of John Hastings, nothing would do but the uttermost luxury. Consequently, the twelve days had seen them dining each night in the liner's lavish À La Carte Restaurant, attending a show in the Captain's Auditorium and finally retiring to the Georgian smoking room to discuss the matters of the day. The band that played in the auditorium might not have had the pedigree of the Archie Adams Orchestra, but they were

as classy a substitute as Raymond had ever seen, turning effortlessly from a classical waltz to an Argentine tango – and, finally,
to Raymond's delight, to a song with such pace and rhythm that
it set the crowd of American tourists to jitterbug and jive. Just
watching the dance was infectious.

But they'll never stand for it in the Grand Ballroom, he thought.
It was with some regret that he realised he was going to have to
leave the jitterbug behind.

By the time the rugged coast of Ireland came into sight, the
darkness was settling upon the North Atlantic Ocean and the
Celtic Sea into which the *Othello* had turned. On the uppermost deck, where the last of the day's revellers were reclining at
the bar between the great potted palms, Raymond stood with a
martini in one hand, gazing at the horizon. At his side – still in the
double-breasted gabardine suit that he always wore, whatever the
weather – stood John Hastings Junior. Smaller than Raymond,
he was nevertheless an imposing presence. There was something about his quietness, Raymond had observed, something
about his studied air that gave the impression of a man of great
authority. His face was impassive, but he stood casually: one hand
dangling by his side, the other fiddling with a silver coin.

'The land of my forefathers,' John Hastings said. 'You been to
Ireland, de Guise?'

'I haven't had the pleasure, sir.'

'Nor me. But my grandfather told the most incredible stories
of his boyhood on the Emerald Isle. I intend to honour him while
I am on this side of the world. Well,' he added, 'this trip cannot
solely be about business now, can it? A man has to cut loose and
enjoy himself, or else all his years are squandered.'

Raymond had tried to help John Hastings 'cut loose and enjoy himself' ever since he'd arrived in New York. He'd found an ally in Hastings's wife Sarah, who clearly missed those days when John had worked hard to romance her – but the truth was that John Hastings was a man of business and, as such, seemed almost impervious to the charms Raymond de Guise had been dispatched to work upon him. He'd danced in the Sunset Lounge on Clinton Street, but here, aboard one of the most feted cruise liners the world had ever seen, he had been more interested in reading the financial news telegraphed to the vessel each morning, or writing memorandums in the smoking lounge, than joining Raymond de Guise in the Captain's Auditorium for music and dance.

'What I'll need,' John Hastings kept saying, 'is the books. All this talk of song and dance and kings and crown princesses – it's well enough, but only so far as it stokes up the books. What do the figures look like, cold, hard and simple. What's the engine room of that fine establishment. These are the things I'll need to look at, if I'm to come on board. Where can I add value? What can the future be? Glamour takes you only so far, de Guise. After that, it's all . . . mathematics.'

The following morning, when Raymond joined Hastings for smoked salmon and eggs *hollandaise* in the À La Carte Restaurant, the news was already out: they would be making landfall before noon, guided into the Liverpool Dock where the river Mersey gave way to the ocean. In his cabin, after breakfast, Raymond sat at his writing table, took out a leaf of RMS *Othello*-headed paper and began to write in his practised, cursive script across the top.

Dear Nancy,

This will be my very last letter, delivered to you by hand. In two hours' time, we will come to the Liverpool quay, and there I shall set foot on English soil for the first time since winter's end. And oh, how much has changed . . .

She had been in his thoughts every day – and now, as England drew near, his thoughts were more vivid still. Though he did not write it in his letter, the truth was he was beginning to feel nervous – yes, that was the right word – at the thought of seeing her again. Though he had written to her often, he had moved so frequently across America that only rarely had he been able to receive a letter in reply. Raymond was rarely given to doubts, but there was a little voice in the back of his head that dared him to wonder if she still cared, if she'd thought of him as often as he had of her. Sometimes it seemed that the world changed daily. How dreadful it would be if his world had changed without him even knowing . . .

Raymond had filled the page and moved on to another when the ship's horns sounded. Then, finally, a knock came at the door. Standing outside was one of the stewards, and beside him John Hastings Junior himself.

'Let's alight, de Guise. The captain's afforded us the "first foot" honour.'

In reply, Raymond folded his letter neatly into the pocket of his dinner jacket, and took his suitcase in hand.

Nancy, he thought, *I'm coming home.* He looked up at John Hastings, waiting impatiently in the hall. *And let us hope I'm bringing the Buckingham's saviour with me.*

Chapter Sixteen

'THEY'RE *LATE*,' CURSED MAYNARD CHARLES. 'Two days at sea, and now *this*.'

Two days ago, he had been ready. He had his composure. He had his balance. He'd anticipated John Hastings residing in the Crown Suite, taking dinner in the Queen Mary, attending the Grand Ballroom and seeing the lavish kind of show Hélène Marchmont and the returning Raymond de Guise could put on. But then had come the first telegram from the *Othello*. And then the second. Now they were two days late – and, apparently, delayed further still by the engine of the Rolls-Royce Maynard had dispatched to meet them at the quayside in Liverpool. The last he had heard, they were two hours from London, waiting in some provincial town for an engine component to arrive, courtesy of a local mechanic.

Two and a half days lost, when John Hastings ought to have been relaxing in style, soaking up the ambience of the Buckingham, falling in love with it before he'd even set foot inside the Imperial. Now, he'd stay here scarcely three nights in total. There'd be so little chance to indulge in the opulence of the place. And, worse still, the hotel board was gathering tomorrow – Lord Edgerton, Uriah Bell, the whole lot of them – to discuss business.

It was all so . . . *cheap*. So fast. There'd be no time for the romance Maynard had planned. No time for the subtle seduction.

All at once, the revolving doors began to spin. Frank Nettleton tumbled through, and scurried up to Billy Brogan. Then, puffed up with pride, Billy approached Maynard and said, in a conspiratorial whisper, 'They're here, Mr Charles.'

Maynard started. 'It's about time,' he snapped. 'Stay where you're needed, Brogan. Where's Bosanquet?'

The head concierge had been unwell for two days. He was always unwell, thought Maynard. *He's one of those who takes ill each time the wind changes.*

'I'll deputise, Mr Charles.'

Maynard dismissed the idea with a wave of his hand.

'Find somebody important,' he said, taking out a handkerchief and dabbing away the sweat beading on his brow. Then, without looking back, he marched out through the revolving bronze doors.

The sun was bright over Mayfair. The lime trees that bordered Berkeley Square were already in blossom and, between them, the crocuses and tulips were a dizzying array of colour.

The moment he felt the sun on his face, Maynard felt like a different man.

It's all of the waiting around. It can make a man start questioning himself. It can make a man crazy.

Now, at last, he was being called into action. At the bottom of the grand marble steps, the gleaming black Rolls-Royce was drawing to a halt. The hotel doorman was already in position and, as the Rolls-Royce stopped, he reached out and opened the door.

Raymond de Guise was the first to emerge. By God, the man looked as if he'd spent a season in the Sahara desert, so bright and tanned was his complexion. Raymond was naturally pale, and the new olive hue took Maynard quite by surprise.

He'd lost none of this showmanship, though. Maynard watched as, with practised ease, Raymond stepped back and allowed John Hastings Junior to emerge into the Mayfair light.

He was much less svelte than Maynard had been given to believe, but handsome in his own bookish way. Outside the car, he stopped and looked around like a mole coming out of its hole. Then, finding everything to his satisfaction, he started up the marble steps – and met Maynard Charles on the way down.

'Mr Hastings, it's my honour,' he said. 'Maynard Charles, director of the Buckingham Hotel, at your service.'

There was a moment of stillness. It lasted too long – long enough for Maynard to panic, to wonder at what else could possibly have gone wrong – before John Hastings nodded and took Maynard's hand in a handshake much firmer than his appearance suggested.

'Mr Charles!' he exclaimed. He was louder, too. His voice echoed out across the square. 'I'm tired, Mr Charles. Near two weeks at sea, and these legs of mine haven't got used to solid ground yet. That, and the unfortunate mishap with the car you sent . . .'

Maynard stepped back. 'May I tender my most sincere apologies for . . .'

John Hastings had been about to take off up the steps, but something made him halt.

'"Tender . . . your most . . . sincere . . ."' Then his face opened in a raucous guffaw. 'I forgot you spoke the King's English here!' He clapped Maynard on the back. 'No need to apologise, my man. The god of automobiles wasn't shining on us today. Nor were the gods of the sea. Let's put it down to happenstance and get me to my room. I've lost two days already. There's much to get through. Well, shall we?'

Maynard Charles nodded. Hurrying after John Hastings so that he might shepherd him personally through the door, he said, 'Your luggage and staff are on their way. I was sent word from the *Othello*.'

Together, they pushed through the revolving door. The water cascading down the obelisk made a soothing kind of music while, down in the Grand Ballroom, the afternoon demonstration dances were about to begin.

'I sent for one of our senior concierges,' Maynard began, 'to be at your service . . .'

But when his eyes roamed the reception hall, the only concierge he found waiting was Billy Brogan.

Inwardly, Maynard cringed.

Brogan isn't fit for this, he thought. *Brogan isn't . . .*

But already, Billy Brogan was hurrying over, plastered with one of his ridiculous smiles – so big it nearly obscured every other feature on his face.

'Mr Hastings, if I may.' He dropped into the most ostentatious bow Maynard Charles had ever seen – but, no matter how filthy a look Maynard gave him, Billy didn't seem to notice. 'I have your key right here,' he said, dangling one from his finger. 'Allow me to show you personally the way to your suite.'

John Hastings nodded, as if the appearance of this urchin in concierge's clothes was the most natural thing in the world.

'Mr Hastings, perhaps it would be better if I—'

'Oh, nonsense,' Hastings said, waving Maynard away. 'You're the hotel director, man. You've better things to be doing than chaperoning a guest. I'll be down presently, sir. Allow me to get

152

washed up, perhaps get a pot of coffee inside me. It's afternoon already and – your board, they're convening tomorrow?'

'That's correct,' breathed Maynard.

'Then we'll talk soon,' said John Hastings. Then, to Billy, he declared, 'Lead on, young man!' and they disappeared towards the guest lift, Billy chattering all the way.

Maynard stood by the obelisk, trying to control his rage, until he heard the footsteps behind him. In the corner of his eye, he saw the willowy figure of Raymond de Guise moving into view.

'My office,' Maynard snarled, '*now*.'

In the office, Maynard Charles poured them both deep glasses of brandy, and was on his second only moments after Raymond put the first to his lips.

'Well?' Maynard started. 'What news?'

Raymond had not been anticipating a hero's welcome upon his return, but nor had he been expecting to find Maynard – ordinarily so serene, even in the face of catastrophe – as animated as he did now.

'It hasn't been easy, Mr Charles. John Hastings is a particular sort of man. He's bookish and bright. He cares about logic and reason. When talk turns to spectacle and glamour, it doesn't fill him with longing like it might others. He's a man of facts. A man of detail.'

'A businessman,' spat Maynard. 'We'll have to show him, Raymond, what glamour is *worth*. There's no ledger book in the world that can truly account for the profits of glamour – but we have to make him *see*.' Maynard stopped. 'I'll need you in the ballroom tonight.'

'Tonight?' baulked Raymond. 'Mr Charles, I'm barely hours off the boat—'

'And I dare say you've been sunning yourself the whole way. It's time you were put to work again, Raymond. You're like a horse who's been indulged and can't race anymore. This is what I'm paying you for, isn't it?'

Raymond stepped back, putting his tumbler of brandy back onto Maynard's desk.

'Yes, Mr Charles.'

For a moment there was silence. Then, at last, something changed in Maynard's demeanour. When next he spoke, it was with a gentler, more forgiving tone.

'I'm sorry, Raymond. You catch me on a terrible day. There have been too many of those, in your absence. A new king. A new prime minister. The world is turning too quickly for me to keep up, and it's happening here in our hotel as well.'

'Has something . . . happened, Mr Charles?'

'Oh, only *everything*. A spate of thefts so bad I've been forced to hire a man I'd hoped never to set eyes on again. And, meanwhile, Mr Chamberlain's elevation is emboldening every fascist in this city. On Coronation Day we had Conte Grandi from the Italian embassy courting Europe's finest, right here in our ballroom, to choose sides in the war to come. And what can I do about it? Only funnel all of it, every last scrap of information I can find, back to Mr Moorcock and his spooks at MI5. I want to do more, Raymond. I want to *push back*, and yet all I can do is listen and gather information, while the hotel lurches towards ruin—'

'Ruin?' Raymond smiled. 'Why, we haven't started yet, Mr Charles. John Hastings is here. Perhaps he's late. Perhaps it isn't ideal. But we've got to put on a show!'

I've been putting on a show for years, thought Maynard, *and it's getting tired. But, even so, the show must go on.*

'I need John Hastings on side, Raymond. I appreciate what you did for me, curtailing your Californian sojourn to bring him to our door, but your work isn't finished yet. Tomorrow, the board are congregating in the Queen Mary. Afterwards, they'll take in the delights of the Grand Ballroom. Gene Sheldon has played his part well in your absence – but now you're back, you're to make it count. Show John Hastings what elegance and class *mean* to a place like this. Make him remember it, so that when he decamps to the Imperial, he sees what he's missing. Because one thing's certain. If the whispers I hear in this hotel, if the scheming of these Nazis and other fascists are anything close to the truth, then I was right all along. War really is on the horizon. And if the Buckingham is going to survive it, we *need* John Hastings to invest. We need the business he can bring. Without it, the Buckingham – and all those who depend on her – is going to fall.'

Chapter Seventeen

Emmeline Moffatt was not ordinarily flustered – it
had, she told her girls, been roundly trounced out of her
at boarding school – but today was different. Today, John
Hastings Junior was arriving at the Buckingham Hotel – and the
rest of her life might be decided by what he found.

As lunchtime approached, Mrs Moffatt returned to the housekeeping lounge. Lunch today would be a serious affair. She'd have
to lecture her girls about John Hastings, without quite letting on
why this easily overlooked American was of greater import than
any lord or lady the girls had ever attended. She was fussing with
teapots and crockery, mentally preparing the sermon she would
deliver, when there came a knocking at the open door. Turning, she discovered Raymond de Guise: his dark eyes twinkling
with the joy of his homecoming; his hair windswept and wild;
his skin more golden, more full of colour, than she had ever seen
it beneath the Grand Ballroom lights.

'Mrs Moffatt. You look as radiant as the day I left.'

Mrs Moffatt rolled her eyes, though in truth Raymond's
words had the very effect he desired: she felt warm, alive, her
worries about John Hastings momentarily dulled by Raymond's
honeyed tone.

He does it deliberately, she chided herself, and smiled. *But at least he knows how to make a woman feel good about the world.*

'Raymond de Guise,' she said, continuing to distribute bowls and plates around the breakfast table. 'Back from his odyssey in Hollywood.' She paused, because the import of Raymond's return was suddenly apparent. 'He's here, then? John Hastings?'

'He is,' breathed Raymond. Then, when the silence between them stretched on for too long, he strode into the room and began to help her set the table. 'Here, let me. I haven't forgotten the ways of the Buckingham, Emmeline. We're all in this together.'

You wouldn't catch Maynard Charles or any of the managers helping lay a table, thought Mrs Moffatt, *but as for Raymond de Guise . . . Well, upstairs or downstairs, wherever he lays his hat, that's Raymond's home.*

'She won't be here, you know.' Mrs Moffatt was wearing a sly smile. She looked at Raymond out of the corner of her eye. 'Nancy,' she went on. 'Well, you haven't stopped by here to give old Mrs Moffatt a present from your travels, have you?'

Raymond arched an eyebrow.

'Your Miss Nettleton's missed you. She hasn't said it, but I can tell. That girl gives herself away in the things she *doesn't* say, not the things that she does. Look, it's an important day for the Buckingham. You know that better than any. I've got work to attend to here and, Lord help me, I'd have Nancy here with me if I could. But she was summoned, you see. Summoned by young Miss Edgerton. And, even after everything she's done, it's a hotel rule – what Miss Edgerton wants, Miss Edgerton gets.'

'Vivienne?' Raymond breathed. 'And Nancy? What has Vivienne been up to, Mrs Moffatt? Is she . . . fallen on old ways?'

'Oh, quite the opposite!' Mrs Moffatt laughed. 'She's clean as a whistle, is young Miss Edgerton. But she's adopted our Nancy somehow. At some point, of course, I'll have to raise it with Mr Charles. We've been a chambermaid down on more occasions than I like, and all to indulge our lord's stepdaughter. But I've been turning a blind eye, you see. It's a vital talent in a job like mine.'

Mrs Moffatt stopped laying the table and gave Raymond a pointed look.

Good Lord, fresh off the boat, and already he's standing there like a lovesick puppy! If only I was young enough to have a love affair like theirs!

'She's with Miss Edgerton, in her suite. Don't ask me what they're plotting. I don't want to know. There's too many secrets in this hotel. Sometimes, you're better off in the dark.'

By the time Raymond had reached the fifth storey – where the Ethelred Suite had been paid for by Lord Edgerton himself for more than a year – his curiosity had turned to a kind of fear. It had been more than six months since the events of New Year. Six months since Vivienne had revealed the kind of petty, selfish, small-minded character she could be . . . and six months since Nancy, and Nancy alone, had seen the true goodness in her heart and resolved to help bring it out of her, no matter what. Even now, Raymond did not know where Nancy got such generosity of spirit from. It was something that could not be learned, and it was only one of the countless things that had made him fall in love. And yet the thought still remained: *where Vivienne Edgerton goes, trouble follows. What in the name of all that's holy has been happening while I've been away?*

The door to the Ethelred Suite was inches ajar, and Raymond paused outside it, if only to gather his thoughts. Reaching into his pocket, he fingered the tiny parcel of lilac crêpe paper, tied in silver ribbon, that he'd brought all the way from the jeweller's on Fifth Avenue, New York. Then, catching sight of himself in the reflective gold panels outside the guest lift, he ran a hand through his hair.

I've looked better, he thought. *When I step out into the Grand, perfectly manicured, perfectly coiffured . . . But this is me, Raymond de Guise. I hope she remembers.*

He knocked on the door, waited for Miss Edgerton's voice to call out, and then stepped through.

Vivienne's suite was not the grandest at the Buckingham, but Raymond had quite forgotten how lavish the suites here could be. A four-poster bed dominated the room, and beside it stood a vintage armoire and dresser, with Parisian curls around its gilt-edged mirror. A glass table sat at the foot of the bed, and upon it was a vase cast in a spiralling design, with streaks of aquamarine circling the single orchid set inside.

Over that table hunched Vivienne and Nancy, a chaos of papers spread out between them.

Raymond had never seen Vivienne so dressed down. Gone were the extravagant ball gowns with which he ordinarily associated her; gone, the formidable creations of chiffon, satin and lace. Now, she sat in a simple grey house dress, as dowdy as any of the thousands of female clerks who took the Underground to their offices each morning.

But Raymond's eyes did not linger on her long. They were drawn, as he had known they would be, to Nancy. She must have been working this morning, for there she was in her white chambermaid's uniform, with her sleeves rolled up and her navy blue apron folded neatly at her side. Her dark hair, which had always been full of curls, was big and buoyant. And her eyes . . . Raymond had forgotten how bewitching those eyes really were.

She saw him.

She stood.

Her mouth opened, but when no words came out, only actions were left. She flung herself across the room and he swept her up, into his arms.

Time slowed to a halt, for both Raymond de Guise and Nancy Nettleton. He buried his face in her neck, lifted his lips to her ear and whispered, 'I've missed you. Oh, Nancy, I've missed you.'

All of the world between us, he thought, *and yet . . . it's like I've never been away.*

He might have remained that way forever but, when Nancy shifted, he saw, over her shoulder, that Vivienne was still sitting there awkwardly, not knowing quite where to look. Gently, Raymond eased Nancy down.

She doesn't want to let go, he thought. *And neither do I. Neither will I ever.*

At once, Vivienne stood. 'I believe we're quite finished here, Nancy. Let's sleep on this. We'll continue our discussions tomorrow.'

Vivienne's words seemed to drag Nancy back into reality. She released her hold on Raymond, and realised how absurd it was that she had been standing here, in Miss Edgerton's own suite, lost in the arms of Raymond de Guise.

'Miss Edgerton, please, accept my apologies. I quite forgot myself.'

'Oh, do hush,' Vivienne said dismissively, waving her hand. 'I can recognise the look of love when I see it. You're no good to me now. Your mind's been addled.' Vivienne exhaled and added, 'Nancy, thank you. But, really, I'd rather not see *this*. My mind's on higher things.'

It was time, or so it seemed, for them to leave.

'Miss Edgerton,' Raymond ventured, 'I've interrupted. Accept my apologies as well. It is . . . nice to see you again.'

Vivienne gave the most extravagant eye roll Raymond had ever seen. 'Please,' she said, 'spare me, Raymond.' She shook her head, but could not help smiling. 'Begone.' She grinned. 'I have more than enough to keep myself entertained this afternoon.'

Raymond had chambers on the Buckingham's fourth storey, and for the first time in long months he slipped his key into the door and escorted Nancy through.

The room was dark. Motes of dust eddied in the air, illuminated by a single shaft of sunlight. Raymond took in his old bed, his chest of drawers, the wardrobe where hung his various dinner jackets and dress shirts for his nights in the Grand Ballroom. All of it so welcoming and familiar – but he cared for only one thing.

Nancy turned in his arms and lifted herself to meet his lips.

The taste, the smell, the touch: all of it set his body alight. She was *his*. He had quite forgotten what it felt like to know that somebody as unique and special as Nancy Nettleton was *his*.

'Raymond, when did you—?'

'A mere hour ago, Nancy. I would have come directly, but—'

'John Hastings?'

'He's here. It's going to work. I can feel it. Maynard Charles may have an air of panic about him, but some of us have to keep the faith.' He was about to say more, but the only thing that seemed to matter was, 'But enough about the hotel. Oh, Nancy, I've missed you. I wrote to you on board the liner, but . . . I'd forgotten your scent. It's the most foolish thing. I love you, Nancy.'

Nancy whispered, 'I love you, Ray.'

Together they sat at the foot of his bed, hands clasped.

'I've so much to tell you. Frank's here. He's working as a page. Mr Charles has him scurrying around on errands for Abner Grant – he's the hotel detective, poached from the Imperial. And . . .'

Nancy looked down. In Raymond's hands was a tiny parcel of lilac crêpe paper. He pressed it onto her palm. Gently, Nancy teased back the ribbon – and there, lying within, were two silver figurines: ballroom dancers, cast in the most precise detail.

'It's . . . you,' said Nancy, marvelling at a three-inch, sparkling Raymond de Guise.

'And you,' said Raymond, showing her the other. 'Georges de la Motte has shown me so much. He introduced me to agents and artistes and the head of the studio he's been signed to. By the end of my stay, they were courting me to appear in a movie they're shooting for Christmas, but . . . Georges advised that I decline, that I hold out for something bigger, a proper starring role. Well, Georges says I could make it there, if that were what I wanted – that it would all depend on if they could match me with the right partner. If that can be done, I'd be up on the silver screen, following Georges on another odyssey. So the studio were trying to romance me. They sent me this figurine' – he lifted the figure made in his own image – 'but it seemed so lonesome,

162

so *wrong*, on its own. So I had another made.' He paused, aware that – quite contrary to his character – he was growing sheepish. 'It isn't a perfect image of you. It's the artist's impression of what I have in my mind's eye.'

Nancy lifted both figurines to the light. 'They're perfect,' she breathed.

'As are you,' Raymond added, his dark eyes looking intensely into her own.

There was so much more to catch up on, more than Raymond had poured into the countless letters he'd sent. If only he hadn't been on a mission to escort John Hastings to English shores, perhaps he might have remained in California until the studio found the right leading lady to match him; but that would have kept him in Hollywood long into the summer, perhaps even beyond, and the thought of not seeing Nancy in all of that time would have been an open wound.

'The truth is, it was too long already. Too long away from you, Nancy. I've missed so much. You – you look different, somehow. Something's changed . . .'

Nancy kissed him. 'A few months older, that's all.'

'Mrs Moffatt directed me to Miss Edgerton's suite. She said Miss Edgerton's turning you into something of a . . . retainer?'

'Like at court!' Nancy laughed. To Raymond, it was the most wondrous sound. 'I'm not wholly sure Mrs Moffatt approves, but I'm keeping up with my duties and I haven't once let her down. Raymond, the most wonderful thing is happening to Miss Edgerton. I hardly know where to begin.'

She could see the deep lines of suspicion creasing Raymond's face, and she quite understood why. Raymond's last abiding memory of Vivienne Edgerton was the New Year Ball, when she was at her very nadir – and threatening to bring so many other members of the Buckingham down with her. The Vivienne he thought of was drunk and wild. The Vivienne he thought of was vain and spoilt and concerned only with herself – but, if elements of the Vivienne of old still remained, they were more than eclipsed by the woman she was striving to become.

And everyone deserves a second chance, don't they? thought Nancy. *Good Lord, everyone deserves a third and a fourth. People aren't born knowing how to get on in the world. They have to learn it, making all manner of mistakes along the way.*

'Miss Edgerton had been forsaking her allowance from her stepfather. She'd started to think money was the root of all her problems. Then Mr Charles challenged her on it, thought she was trying to cause more trouble at the hotel, just when we don't need it. Well, it got Miss Edgerton thinking. She's decided she wants to do some good in the world – to invest her allowance in a charitable enterprise. And that's where I've been helping her. She puts on a good show, but Miss Edgerton isn't as brave as she makes out. She wanted a chaperone, out there in the city. We visited the Rowton House in Camden Town. And then, a little while ago, she found a place in Whitechapel. They call it the Daughters of Salvation. Only, when we went there—'

Raymond blanched. 'Vivienne Edgerton dragged you into Whitechapel?'

'I'd hardly say dragged, Ray. I went of my own volition.' Nancy wasn't certain that she had, but it made her proud to say it. 'She's decided to invest in it, what little she can. But more than that – she wants to devote her time and energy. That's what we were discussing in her suite. We're making plans to go there and . . . volunteer, I think you'd say. But the last time – well, let's just say, there are unsavoury elements on those streets. As I think you know well.'

'Whitechapel at night isn't a place for the two of you,' Raymond breathed. 'Nancy, you mustn't – and neither must Vivienne. It's . . .' He stalled, for it was not his place to issue orders – and, anyway, the Nancy Nettleton he knew and loved would never accept them.

Nancy grinned. 'Not all adventures in life are about the glory and fame of the ballroom, nor the silver screen!'

Raymond was canny enough to know when he was being teased.

'I hear you, Nancy Nettleton.'

'I think I *want* to be there with her, to follow this journey however far it goes. You can understand that, can't you, Ray? After everything I've been through with her. It sounds silly, but I feel like the hand of *fate* is upon me!'

Raymond smiled. This – impassioned and obstinate, righteous and good – was the Nancy he had missed so very much.

'No, Nancy, it doesn't sound silly at all.'

Then his fingers were in her hair, and hers were in his, and all of the world – the Buckingham Hotel, Berkeley Square, thoughts of Whitechapel and the Daughters of Salvation – simply melted away.

Afterwards, as Nancy laid her head upon his shoulder, tracing the line of his collar with a single finger, a thought popped, quite unheralded, into Raymond's head.

'You sound so certain about this work with Miss Edgerton.'

'I am,' whispered Nancy. 'I've never seen her so purposeful. It's like the devotion to something else, it cures you of being devoted only to yourself. It's like being in love, I suppose. Caring about something that isn't you . . .'

'And you really do mean to follow her back into Whitechapel after dark?'

'Raymond,' Nancy said, sensing the fear in his voice, 'I couldn't leave her to it alone. Imagine what might become of her if—'

Raymond rolled over and placed a single finger over Nancy's lips.

'Then I have an idea. Because I know a man who's almost certain to be looking for work. A man who knows all the dark places of Whitechapel and even further beyond. A man who might be glad to stand guard and be of service – if, of course, he was being compensated for his time. Another person, Nancy, who needs a helping hand, if he's to start making something of himself again.'

Nancy was silent. She gazed up into Raymond's dark, almond eyes.

'Of course, we wouldn't be able to tell Vivienne who he really is, but, Nancy, what do you think about my asking Artie? What do you think about asking . . . my brother?'

Chapter Eighteen

BEHIND THE DOORS OF THE Grand Ballroom, Hélène Marchmont stooped to help one of the younger dancers into her gown. The girl's nerves were evident – but she was only nineteen, and had scarcely danced at the Buckingham for a full month yet. Hélène remembered the first time she had stepped into a classical hold with a scion of some royal family, how fiercely her heart had been beating the first time a king's arm had slipped around her – but they would all have to find their own courage tonight. Tonight was the night when *everything* mattered.

The knowledge that John Hastings had arrived at the Buckingham had not taken long to spread into all its many corners. Rumours were wild currency in a luxury hotel; they spread faster than any virus. Billy Brogan had played his part in that, but so had all the pages, who whispered to the porters, who whispered to the chambermaids. And if the lowliest members of staff did not know the real meaning of John Hastings's visit, Hélène knew it only too well – for only an hour ago, Maynard Charles had wandered into the dressing rooms behind the Grand and, taking her to one side, announced that she was to dance with him tonight, but to dance with him gently.

'He's not a dancing man, but if he should wish to waltz with you, you're to make him look like a star. Do you understand me, Miss Marchmont?'

Hélène did. She was used to making men feel better about themselves. Sometimes, she thought, that was what men thought women were for. *Just to make them feel good.* It was only real men – men like Sidney had been, like Louis Kildare was, like . . . Arthur Regan – who knew differently.

'Are we ready?' she said, whirling around to take in her girls. The Buckingham troupe was ten strong, and the other four girls all looked resplendent. 'We're to put on a show tonight, aren't we, Gene?'

Gene Sheldon, who was on the other side of the dressing room, styling his hair in one of the long, baroque mirrors, looked round.

'Tonight's the night,' he said in his soft, feathery voice, 'we've got a hotel to . . .'

At that moment, the dressing room doors opened – and Gene Sheldon fell quite silent. Every face turned at once to gaze at the figure who appeared in the doorway.

Hélène's face opened in the most uncontrollable smile.

The figure, long and lithe, already in his midnight-blue dinner jacket, loped into the room and allowed the door to fall shut behind him. Hélène hurried over and flung her arms around his shoulders.

'I'd heard you were back.' She beamed.

'Fresh off the boat' – Raymond grinned – 'and Maynard Charles is already sending me into battle. Don't worry, Gene,' he called over, 'we're both to take to the floor tonight. This has to be spectacular. Every soul out there has to feel overjoyed about the world. John Hastings is a particular character, but tonight, let's make the Grand Ballroom melt his heart.' He paused. Then, taking in the assembled dancers and the Archie Adams Orchestra, he lifted his arms. 'Shall we?'

The King of the Ballroom had returned.

To think, thought Maynard Charles, *that the ballroom I never truly wanted might be the thing that saves us all . . .*

It had been the Great Depression that gave birth to the Grand Ballroom. Maynard Charles had never characterised himself as a man of music and dance – and, indeed, not once had he turned a foxtrot or a waltz across the ballroom floor – but he had known a business opportunity when it presented itself. The Grand Ballroom had brought glitz and glamour. It had brought *reputation* – and reputation, Maynard had long known, was a hotel's principal currency. It was the Grand Ballroom that had brought the old King Edward to the hotel; tonight, he was banking on the Grand Ballroom winning them another man's favour. If it did not . . .

His heart started hammering at the prospect, so he clicked his fingers and had one of the ballroom waiters bring him a martini.

The lights dimmed. A spotlight turned to the stage doors at the back of the ballroom floor. Then, two by two, out marched the members of the Archie Adams Orchestra.

As the applause went up, the doors leading up through the garlanded archways to the reception hall opened too – and there stood John Hastings Junior. His staff had arrived late in the afternoon, bringing with them all of his luggage, and now he stood in a black evening suit, sporting a white bow tie. There was still something bookish about the way he sauntered through the doors, but he did look debonair tonight. Maynard approached. It wasn't just the dancers and musicians that had to shine tonight. So did he.

'Mr Hastings, the spectacle is about to begin.'

'I can see now what your Mr de Guise was saying,' Hastings said as they wandered in – and, behind his back, Maynard made a sign for waiters to rush to their side. 'He spoke at such length about the magnificence of this place. It's like a cathedral.'

The observation made Maynard's heart soar, but he checked himself, for nothing was certain yet. Besides, the way John Hastings said it was not with the reverence with which others had taken in the Grand; he remarked on it like a man might remark on a positive set of figures on a balance sheet.

A man after my own heart, in so many ways. And yet somehow I have to convince him in a matter of days what it took me years to fully believe: that glamour matters; that glitz is all . . .

'Mr Hastings, allow me.'

Maynard led the way across the ballroom, and approached a group of dignified gentleman standing separate from the rest. They looked, he thought, like a copse of trees in winter – stark and unforgiving – but there were few other people that filled him with this kind of fear. He had so rarely been afraid before. It was not in his nature. But now it was a constant feeling, gnawing at his innards.

It's as much to do with what's becoming of Aubrey as it is with what's becoming of my hotel. I can't control one, he admitted. *I can't stave off illness. But I can control the other. The Buckingham doesn't have to perish . . .*

One of the unforgiving figures turned, and Maynard Charles looked up into the imperious features of Lord Bartholomew

Edgerton. At his side were the others: Uriah Bell, the financier of the Limehouse Docks; Peter Merriweather, whose family farms dominated so much of the Yorkshire wolds. Sandwiched between them was Vivienne, wearing a dress so forgettable that it almost made Maynard mistake her for some other.

She's done this deliberately, he thought, and inwardly fumed. *She's proving a point to her father, when what we really need is—*

'Lord Edgerton,' Maynard began, 'might I introduce you to Mr John Hastings Junior, whose presence we have been so eagerly awaiting.'

Put on a show, Maynard urged him. *Put on a . . .*

Lord Edgerton loomed half a foot and more above John, and now he reached out and took the American's hand.

'Welcome to London,' he announced. 'We're pleased you could make it. Might I introduce you to my fellow members of the board? Uriah Bell, you've had correspondence with already. Lord Merriweather, here, will be eager to hear of New York. You'll meet the others at luncheon tomorrow, I'm sure. And this . . .' He stepped aside, revealing the lady who had been almost entirely obscured behind him. 'This is my wife, Madeleine.'

'Charmed,' said the lady in the blossom-pink ball gown.

'And this is my daughter, Vivienne.'

Maynard could see, from the way Vivienne's face was set, that she was bristling. And no wonder: Lord Edgerton had called her his 'daughter' without any qualification. He willed her to ignore it – and perhaps Vivienne was willing herself too, because suddenly she stepped forward, gave the daintiest curtsey, and took John's hand.

'Charmed, I'm sure.'

She'd pronounced her New York accent, thought Maynard. *She'd made it so strong.*

John Hastings grinned. 'Do I detect a fellow Yank?'

'You'll have to tell me about old New York, John,' Vivienne answered – and her use of his Christian name made her stepfather's eyes narrow. 'I've been away too long!'

Maynard was spared further embarrassment, for Archie Adams had taken his place on the stage – and, at once, the music began. No sooner had the first number – 'The Belle of Broadway', especially for their American guest – struck up, than the doors opened again, and the Buckingham dancers twirled out onto the floor.

Hélène Marchmont was everything Maynard had hoped she would be. Bedecked in the diamond necklace and earrings that he kept in the hotel safe, she carved a glittering parabola across the dance floor. There she hung, in the arms of Raymond de Guise – and to Maynard, it was as if those months he had been away had never happened. Together, he and Hélène owned the ballroom floor. The other dancers faded away, and in the eyes of those who watched there were no others.

As 'The Belle of Broadway' came to its climax, Maynard found himself feeling lighter than he had for days, weeks, perhaps even months. It was seeing Hélène and Raymond together, he was sure of it. Something in it made him feel as if there was still something to *hope* for.

The song exploded. Then, for a few brief moments, there was silence.

'He's our star,' Maynard said to John Hastings. 'California tried to tempt him from us, but here he remains. I dare say, one day, he'll be up on the silver screen – but the Buckingham will always be where he belongs. He's helped us cultivate such a reputation.

I'm hopeful that the good King George may even attend the New Year's Ball this year – and it's all because of the spectacles put on by Hélène Marchmont and Raymond de Guise.'

On the ballroom floor, the dancers were coming apart, leaving each other and seeking their allotted partners for the night. Raymond met the first guest who stepped down from the balustrade and, bowing in deference to her, took her into hold.

Hélène reached the edge of the ballroom floor. On its edges, John Hastings was locked in conversation with Maynard Charles and the members of the board. Poor Vivienne looked so lost, stranded between them. She wondered if she ought to approach.

Win him over, Maynard had instructed her. *Bewitch him if you have to.*

And perhaps she might even have dared to, if only a separate set of eyes had not been watching her from the dance floor's edge.

'Arthur?' she whispered.

Arthur Regan stepped out of the crowd, onto the dance floor, and took her hand.

'Miss Marchmont, you must think me terribly uncivil, not to have forewarned you. I have been in and out of London, and something possessed me. I decided I would take a chance. That I might find you here.'

'Arthur.' She smiled. 'Where else would I be?'

She looked around, as if to indicate this was where she belonged, and – in the corner of her eye – she saw the Archie Adams Orchestra preparing for their next number. Louis Kildare stood out among them. She might have been wrong, but he seemed to be looking at her and Arthur with an almost resentful look in his eyes.

'Might I have the pleasure of the dance?' Arthur asked.

'Arthur, I'm promised to another . . .'

As soon as Hélène said it, she regretted the words. It sounded so *dramatic*, so doomed and romantic. She'd only meant John Hastings, but it was the image of Sidney which popped into her head.

'One dance,' she said, daring to risk it, 'while they're still . . .'

She looked up, imagining she might find John Hastings still trapped in conversation with the board, but instead she saw Maynard Charles and John Hastings striding towards her. Something inside her sank. She had, she privately confessed, been suddenly piqued by the idea of dancing a tango with Arthur.

'Hélène Marchmont,' Maynard began, 'allow me to introduce our most honoured guest, John Hastings Junior.'

Hélène's eyes returned fractionally to Arthur, before she remembered the import of the evening.

You have a job to do, Hélène. Lie to them all. Lie through your teeth. Just like you've been lying to yourself . . .

'Mr Hastings,' she said, 'I'm so pleased to meet you.'

She took his hand, detected some resistance in him, and said, 'If you'd rather, we could take drinks instead . . .'

'No, no,' John Hastings began. From behind his spectacles, he peered up at the glittering chandeliers, then around at the ballroom, which had come to life with the strident beats of the tango. 'It's part of my research. I'm to partake in whatever delights the Buckingham has to offer. Well, how else am I to know? Don't treat me as anything special, Miss Marchmont. I'm just your common guest . . .'

As he stepped closer, meaning to be led out onto the dance floor, Hélène caught Maynard Charles's eye.

He's not just a common guest, Maynard seemed to be saying. *He's everything.*

Then they were gone, drawn into the tango, Hélène letting John Hastings lead – no matter how unpractised or ungainly he was. *Tonight*, she thought, *he shall feel like a king. He shall feel like Raymond de Guise.*

At the edge of the dance floor, Maynard shook Arthur's hand.

'You must forgive me, Mr Regan. You too are a cherished guest. Perhaps if I was to tell you who our feted Mr Hastings is, you might understand—'

'No need at all,' Arthur returned. 'Why, I'm not even a guest this evening. Just somebody who passed by, hoping for the hand of Miss Marchmont. There is one thing, though, Mr Charles. One question I might ask. As you know, I've become most fond of your hotel. I intend to use it as often as I can.'

Talk like this could make Maynard warm to a man. He nodded appreciatively.

'I believe I could even bring more business your way. But first, perhaps you could confirm a little rumour for me? I was flitting around the Grand Ballroom this evening, and I happened to overhear something you said to the charming Mr Hastings.' He paused. 'Is it really true that King George himself might appear at the Buckingham's famous ball this coming New Year?'

Chapter Nineteen

NO LIGHT EVER STOLE BENEATH the door of the Park Suite, for Maynard had sealed every crack in the days after he secreted Aubrey Higgins behind its walls; but it was nearing midnight as he rattled the key in the lock, and he expected to find only darkness on the other side.

The first sign that something was wrong was the lights still blazing. The second was Mrs Moffatt, waiting for him in the empty lounge.

'Emmeline,' Maynard gasped, a riot of catastrophic thoughts tumbling through his mind, 'what happened?'

Mrs Moffatt rushed to him. 'He's all right,' she promised. Then, on seeing Maynard's eyes darting, frenzied, into every corner of the room, she clasped his hand. 'Maynard, Aubrey's all right.'

Maynard attempted to conquer his panic. 'Then why are you here, Emmeline?'

She was still holding his hand, so she led him to the cusp of the bedroom, where Aubrey was sleeping in the dark, the oxygen tank by his side.

'He managed to call me on the housekeeping line,' she whispered gently. 'He'd been trying you in your office, but he couldn't get through.'

He knows never to call the office. If somebody else were there, if somebody else picked up, why, it would be the end of everything I built here. The end of Aubrey's sanctuary. And, if Lord Edgerton and the board were ever to find out, it would surely be the end of my tenure at the Buckingham . . .

'He was having trouble breathing again. It spooked him this time, Maynard. But I came up here and settled him and, whatever it was, it eased away. I wanted to call Dr Moore. I'd have done it two hours ago, if Aubrey hadn't begged me not to . . .'

Maynard's jaw was set, his face a rictus of anger. 'Somebody should have come for me.'

'Good Lord, Maynard, who could I send? I'd have come myself, but I couldn't possibly leave him.'

It took only a second for Maynard's rage to dissipate. He squeezed Mrs Moffatt's hand and whispered his thanks.

'Maynard, there's something else.'

'Yes?'

'It's Abner Grant. When Aubrey called and I hurtled up here, he was . . . snooping in the hallway outside. It isn't the first time. I've caught him prowling up and down the floor twice already. Heaven knows how many times he's been up here. Aubrey's heard knocking. Once earlier this evening. Who knows – perhaps that's what set him off? A panic like that can do terrible things. Grant – he knows there's something going on here.'

Inwardly, Maynard cursed.

I gave him the hotel plans, he remembered. *The original blueprints. But then, half the chambermaids know about the Park Suite.*

'Ignore Grant,' he said – though it flew against every instinct in his body. 'He's paid to prowl the hotel halls. That's why I poached him from the Imperial. If he comes again, I'll deal with him. I don't know how, but I'll . . .' Maynard's words petered out. 'Give me a few moments, would you, Emmeline?'

Mrs Moffatt nodded, and retreated back across the suite.

In the darkness of the bedroom, Maynard took Aubrey's hand. How papery and light it was – so unlike the hands that had once held Maynard through the long nights.

I used to do this when he was first ill. In the base hospital at Reims, before they sent him back to England. Just sit there with him. Hoping. Praying. How unlike those nights it is, here in Mayfair. And yet how similar it feels . . .

Aubrey had been getting progressively worse with the passing of each year. Winters were the worst. The cold months only seemed to intensify his daily anguishes. Three years ago there was the pneumonia. A year before that, the bronchitis that lasted from December's first snow until the crocuses blossomed in Berkeley Square. And in the last few months . . .

Maynard had not been there on the day the mustard gas came, thick and pungent, into the trenches where they were stationed. It was bad luck that Aubrey had been there in that foxhole, struggling to fit his gas mask, instead of Maynard himself. For two decades now, he'd seen what a ruin it had made of the man he loved. That the gas would claim Aubrey one day, Maynard had always known; that it might claim him tonight, tomorrow night, some time before summer's end, should not have been a surprise – and yet it caught him unawares.

On the bed, Aubrey opened his eyes.

'You old fool,' said Maynard, his voice trembling with affection. 'I'm so sorry I wasn't here.'

Aubrey lifted the mask from his lips and, in a dry, cracked voice said, 'You would have been, old boy, if you could. I know.'

His body was too weak, thought Maynard. That was what the gas had done. All of these years his body had had to strain to defeat the ravages of that gas, but now it was too weak to resist a simple cold. *Perhaps you're to be the very last victim of our Great War*, thought Maynard. *And just in time for another one to dawn . . .*

'How did it . . . go . . . tonight?' Aubrey whispered, stalling between breaths.

It was just like him to care about Maynard's world, even as his own moved towards its inevitable end.

'It went as well as I'd hoped. But it's tomorrow that matters.' Maynard hung his head. It felt good to tell somebody, not to have to keep it all inside. 'Tomorrow, the board are arriving. They'll take luncheon with John Hastings in the Queen Mary. I won't be privy to it. I'll have to rely on what gets overheard. I should never have promoted Billy Brogan – that boy was more useful flitting about as a page than he'll ever be as a concierge – but there's a new lad, Frank Nettleton, who might do. I can't rely on a briefing from Lord Edgerton. The man doesn't do nuance. And, Aubrey, I need this meeting to go well. Our future depends upon it. After his visit here, John Hastings is to stay at the Imperial. If he finds them more to his satisfaction than us—'

'How . . . could he . . . possibly?'

'After the Imperial, John Hastings is bound for the Continent. He's to tour his father's interests out there. No doubt they're planning for the same as we are – what to do when the world walks willingly back into Hell.'

'Mr Churchill was on the news tonight,' Aubrey interjected. 'He reminds me of you, Maynard, my dear. He's never wavering. He knows it's wrong, what Mr Chamberlain's doing.'

'I've started to wonder . . .' Maynard began, his words throbbing with guilt.

'Maynard?'

'What if there's a chance? What if there might not be war? What if—?'

'It's all *what if*s. Mr Churchill has the right of it. We have to stand up to what's happening on the Continent. We have to do what's right.'

Maynard nodded, feverishly. *I'm being weak*, he scolded himself. *Mr Churchill always has the right of it. The more you appease them, the stronger the Nazis grow. It isn't a matter of knowing where to draw the line or not. The line has already been crossed.*

'John Hastings knows it too. His father has stakes in hotels from Copenhagen to Milan. He'll be out there, shoring them up, protecting what he can. He's not due to return to London until it's almost Christmas. I was thinking . . . what if I could rely on old contacts, arrange for something spectacular? If the good King George might attend the hotel when John Hastings returns, why, that might tip the scales in our balance. I've already handed over the hotel accounts to his bookkeepers. Heaven knows what they'll make of them, of course. I'm yet to discover an American who understands that the cost of *class* is a cost worth bearing. But if I was to welcome the King – well, maybe it would make all the difference. The royal connection, it's saved us before.'

And here Maynard's voice broke, thick with phlegm. 'If it falls, Aubrey, if everything's just dust, all of my people are lost. *You*, Aubrey. *You* are lost . . .'

Aubrey tried to move, but found himself too weak. 'You won't need to worry about me, my love.'

Maynard could look at Aubrey no longer. He tore his gaze away, stared into the shadows instead.

'Please, Aubrey. Don't say it.'

'But I must. You must hear it. I'm not long for this hotel, Maynard, my dear. I've loved being your secret for so very long – but my days in the Park Suite, they're numbered. Do what you must for your people. Your obligation to me is almost done.'

'Obligation?' Maynard uttered. 'Love isn't an obligation, Aubrey. Love isn't even a choice. It's just there, it's always been there, hanging in the air between us, and by God, I've loved you, Aubrey. By God, I love you . . .'

It was only as Maynard's words petered out that he saw, through the dark, that Aubrey's eyes were already closed. The rising and falling of his breast was steady, but the rattle of his lungs was worse than ever. Slowly, Maynard disentangled his fingers from Aubrey's grasp.

Out in the suite, Mrs Moffatt was waiting. As Maynard emerged from Aubrey's bedside, he staggered across the thick burgundy carpet to meet her. He had not gone halfway before his legs gave out. He pitched forward – and, by some strange mercy, Mrs Moffatt caught him, bore him up, planted him back on his feet.

There, in her arms, Maynard Charles wept openly for the first time since he was a small boy, clinging onto his mother's arm.

He wept for the future of the Buckingham Hotel. He wept for a war that he saw coming. He wept for all of those he'd lost in the fields of Flanders, so many years before.

And he wept for Aubrey Higgins, growing worse every day, for what his life would be worth without him in it.

August 1937

Chapter Twenty

S UN SPILLED THROUGH THE DUSTY windows of the Dog
and Drake, illuminating the daytime denizens of the ram-
shackle Whitechapel alehouse. In one corner sat a pair of
stevedores from the Limehouse Dock. In another, a group of old
men from the seaman's mission played dominoes. And, alone
in the corner, nursing a pint of his favourite Greene King, sat
a black-haired rake of a man in a hand-me-down checked suit,
two sizes too big, a hole poked in his dead father's belt to tighten
the trousers.

The man's head was buried in the newspaper he'd picked
up out on the street, so he did not notice when a new figure
stalked into the bar. Only when the footsteps tolled louder did
he look up and, his face curdling, recognise the figure looming
over him.

'Ray Cohen!'

The new arrival pulled up a chair and sat down. Gone was
the midnight-blue dinner jacket that Raymond de Guise often
donned when in the Grand Ballroom. Now he was in a worn
jacket of brown leather, tan workman's boots, and his sensational
black hair – ordinarily tamed by a tidal wave of pomade – was as
wild as a forest on his head. He even seemed to speak differently;

gone were the rounded cadences he'd acquired after so much tutelage from Georges de la Motte, and in their place was the shorter, rougher, more jagged tone of his East End childhood.

'When did you get back then, Ray? Last I heard, you was sunnin' yourself on some California beach.'

'I've been back some weeks, Artie. I've been meaning to come.'

'Well, here you are.' Artie spread his arms wide as if in welcome, though there was something of a sneer about his tone. 'Welcome back, brother.'

The newspaper Artie Cohen had been reading fell open across the ale-stained table. Staring out of it was a grainy image of King George on the day of his coronation. That day had been joyous, even for the crowds of Whitechapel, who'd packed out Cable Street with tables and chairs and served up sausages from a griddle. Now, splashed in bold black letters across the top of the paper was a different sort of story altogether.

BELFAST BOMBER STRIKES AT GOOD KING GEORGE!

'You missed too much, brother. We got a new king now. He's been crowned. And, look, those Irish have already tried to do away with him! He goes to visit that Belfast backwater and what do they do? They throw a bomb at him. And they can't even get that right, can they?'

Artie crowed with laughter, but Raymond was unmoved. There were always assassination attempts. Only last year, a man had drawn a pistol on the old King Edward as his parade moved through Hyde Park. But tempestuousness in the royal family was not good for business at the Buckingham; for this, as well as everything else, he was grateful that King George had survived.

'Artie,' Raymond began, 'I won't beat about the bush. I hate to be the kind of brother who only drops in when he wants something.'

Artie grinned. 'At least you're dropping in this time. Years can pass without you dropping by, Ray. You get yourself a new name, a new job, a new reputation—'

'Artie, please—'

'I'm only taunting you. Good God, you've been up among princes and princesses too long, if you can't take a good joke.'

'The last I heard, you were out of work.'

Artie stiffened. 'I get by,' he said, folding his arms across his chest. 'You haven't been sending a penny home, not since this California sojourn o' yours. But I picked up what work I can. I been down on the docks, scrubbing up fish guts even. Ma's not starved yet, on account of me.'

Raymond took a deep breath. There had been a time, not so very long ago, when years had elapsed without him seeing his family. Since they had re-established a connection, Artie's attitude towards him had mellowed – he'd even set foot in the grand environs of the Buckingham – but there was something spikier in his voice today. Perhaps it was only the idea that, not for the first time in their lives, Raymond de Guise – or 'Ray Cohen' as his ma and pa had once called him – was drawing away from the very people and places that had made him: first to Mayfair, and now, if the stars aligned, to Hollywood itself.

'You got work for me, at that poxy hotel of yours? Is that it?'

'Not quite,' Raymond returned.

'Well, you can tell me about it' – Artie pitched forward, rubbing his palms together with glee – 'over a pint of Greene King, if you would.' Then he raised his voice, raised his hand and called out to the rest of the room, 'Here, boys! Prince Ray is paying!'

Calmly, Raymond reached up and brought his brother's hand back to the table.

'I'll buy you as many pints of Greene King as your body can handle, Artie. But first, I'd rather *show* you what I mean. Come on, I'll explain it on the way . . .'

There must have been something tempting in the way Raymond spoke – because, without question, Artie relented. Together they stood and crossed the taproom floor, stepping out into the bright sunshine of Cable Street at noon. Behind them, the door fell shut, a handwritten notice dangling from it on a length of rope:

NO IRISH, NO BLACKS, NO DOGS

Some way east along Cable Street, past Wilton's Music Hall – where the afternoon band was practising a swing – Raymond banked north. There, sandwiched between a haberdasher's and a boarded-up butcher's, sat a little tea room with Union Jack bunting still hanging in its window, a relic of Coronation Day slowly fading in the summer sun. Through the window – *Molly's Teas and Creams* stencilled on it in lurid red paint – ladies and children could be seen taking tea and scones and waiting for their loved ones.

Among them sat Raymond's very own Nancy Nettleton, along-side one of the most beautiful girls Artie thought he had ever seen. With elfin eyes and striking red hair, red rouge upon her cheeks and, yes, even *painted nails*, she seemed as out of place here as Artie had felt stepping through the big bronze doors of the Buckingham Hotel.

Before they went into the café, Raymond clasped his brother's shoulder tightly.

'Have a care, Artie. Nancy might know who you are, but this other – she mustn't know I'm your brother.'

If Artie was offended by the suggestion, he didn't show it. His lips turned upwards in a crooked smile.

'She's pretty,' he said, his eyes still on the striking girl at Nancy's side. 'A lord's daughter, you say?'

'Stepdaughter,' Raymond corrected, 'but Vivienne's had her troubles. She's dug her way out of them too. Now she's trying to do some good in this world. And . . .'

Raymond wasn't sure what he was going to say next. He was doing this for Nancy – because Nancy *needed* him to. He reached out and opened the door.

'In you go, Artie. And follow my lead . . .'

Nancy looked up from her teacup, her face beaded with steam – and there they were, weaving through the other customers who crowded the tables.

Raymond glided across the tea room, Artie stomping at his side, until finally they reached the table.

'Nancy, Miss Edgerton, allow me to introduce—'

'Artie!' Artie burst in. 'Artie Cohen!' Dropping with an almighty crash into the chair between Vivienne and Nancy, he helped himself to the uneaten currant bun on Vivienne's plate. 'If the lady doesn't mind, o' course.'

Raymond rolled his eyes theatrically – and, while Vivienne was busying herself looking aghast, he gave Nancy a look.

He's playing his part, Nancy realised, watching Artie smear the currant bun across his face. *Although that part's closer to the true Artie Cohen than he thinks.*

'Miss Edgerton, allow me to explain. In my younger days, I danced at Wilton's Music Hall. While I attended tea dances hosted by Lord Meeke, Artie, here, was a dancer too – of sorts.' Raymond leaned in, as if conspiratorial. 'Well, the truth is, once upon a time Artie made his living shining shoes at the dance halls. Nowadays, he's devoted to his elderly mother. So, when Nancy told me about your predicament, a flash of inspiration hit me.' Raymond paused. 'Why don't you introduce yourself, Artie?'

Artie's cheeks were so full of currant bun that, caught unawares, he spluttered and sent crumbs flying across the table.

'Well,' he stammered, 'it's like this . . .' Raymond was a better liar. Artie could barely find any words. 'It's like Raymond says. I shined his shoes for years,' he spat. 'And, like he says too, I'm look-ing for work. He reckons I might be a fit for what you're after.'

'I've explained a little,' Raymond interjected, sensing Artie's reluctance. 'But perhaps you might like to give Artie the particulars.'

Nancy saw a look like terror ghost across Vivienne's face. Leaning over the table, she allowed her fingers to rest on the back of her hand. She was about to venture some subtle words of encouragement when, all at once, Vivienne summoned up her composure and stood.

'Now,' she ventured – and there were nerves quavering in her voice. 'As Raymond may have told you, I am to become the bene-factor of a charitable concern not a stone's throw from where we're now sitting. The Daughters of Salvation. Perhaps you know of it?' When all she got was an insolent look in return, Vivienne ploughed on. 'They are committed to helping the lowest among the low. But they can do so little with what they have, and I intend to give them more. Not only that – I intend to be a part of it, and help Mary Burdett accomplish everything she can, so that, one day, the scourge of opiates might be driven from these streets. Only . . .'

Nancy could tell that Vivienne was faltering, losing what little courage she'd had, so softly she interjected, 'When we came to visit the Daughters, we were set upon. It was as if they could smell Mayfair all over us.'

'That's where you come in, Artie,' said Raymond.

Artie had been sitting slumped in his seat, but now he picked himself up.

'The hired muscle, is that it? The henchman? The guard?'

Nancy could not tell whether Artie was aghast or just amused.

He's playing with us, she thought, toying with us like a cat with a mouse. But Artie Cohen has a good, solid heart, doesn't he? Of course, he's a thief by trade. He's spent years of his life in Pentonville Prison, and all for the privilege of stealing a few railway sleepers, or robbing the town houses down by the river. But when the fascists marched down Cable Street, who was up on the barricades? When the blackshirts swarmed through, raising their flags in friendship with those Nazis over the Channel, which side was Artie Cohen on? No, Artie might be a ragged sort of man, but his heart's as true as his brother's . . .

'I need a guide,' Vivienne declared, coming back to her senses. 'A protector, if you will. Because the people who need help, the people who need the Daughters, they don't gravitate there of their own accord. They're in gutters. They're in abandoned houses. They're in whichever den they fall into. And I intend to go out there and find them.'

She said the last with a flourish, as if only just convincing herself of this fact.

191

Artie stared at her with incredulity. 'You mean to go trawling around every last disreputable place you can find . . . *deliberately*?' He shot a look at Raymond – who still stood, like a sentry, above his shoulder. 'Ray, surely you've tried to tell them. Night-times out here, they aren't like they are in Mayfair. Oh, it's the same moonlight glittering over us both but out here it's *real life*.'

Vivienne stood. Then, with what courage she had left, she announced, 'There'll be a fee, of course. For your services. I'm not asking you to do anything out of the goodness of your heart. I'm asking you to do it for payment, fair and square.'

For a few moments, Artie seemed to be weighing up his decision. Raymond's brother had long ago lost the last of his scruples – but, for a moment, the thought of venturing into Whitechapel's more shadowy corners after dark seemed to have spooked him. Now, however, the promise of coin was making his eyes glitter quite as brightly as the chandeliers that hung from the rafters in the Grand Ballroom.

'The shadowy places, you say?' Artie stood. 'Those corners where even the down-and-out won't go? Back rooms of boarding houses where the windows are all shuttered up. The places down by the canal, between the street lights, where even the Metropolitans think twice. Under the bridge at the Shadwell Basin.' He smiled. 'Yes, I'm certain I could take you there *for a fee*.' The smile blossomed, taking over his face, and Artie held out his hand, snatching hold of Vivienne's own. 'Why, Miss Edgerton,' he went on, 'if it's what you want, I could take you tonight . . .'

Chapter Twenty-one

NUMBER 5 PALACE GARDENS WAS every bit as lavish as Hélène Marchmont had dreamed.

The gleaming black Rolls-Royce that had ferried her from Mayfair, along the banks of the twisting river Thames and to the wide-open expanses south of the city, had drawn to a halt on a wide grass verge – and there, framed by gargantuan horse chestnut trees, sat a double-breasted mansion house, painted in perfect white. It had the air of a palace in miniature. Its upper storey was even crowned with turrets, and Hélène found herself wondering if there might even be a courtyard nestled inside.

The driver was ready to depart – but Hélène lingered, too long, in the back of the taxicab. Now that she was here, answering the invitation from Arthur Regan himself, she was uncertain if she could go through with it.

It's only a tea dance, she told herself sternly. *Why, you must have been to a hundred tea dances before the Grand Ballroom drew you in. So what's changed?*

What's changed, she thought, was everything. She wasn't here on the arm of some paramour she knew she was never going to marry, some older gentleman who wanted a glamorous starlet on his arm just to show off to his friends and family. That had been the Hélène Marchmont of old. As a young woman, she'd been only too happy to trot around events like this, learning to dance and being praised for her beauty. Ten years had changed her in ways she could hardly fathom.

Now beauty hardly matters. Being 'seen' in the right places just doesn't mean a thing. So why am I nervous?

Hélène climbed out. Through the mansion's parted curtains she could see men in black tail coats and women in their finery holding flutes of champagne while, from somewhere beyond them, there came the sound of a small orchestra playing. She was not certain, at this distance, but she fancied she could hear the particular swoon of 'A Californian Serenade'.

A figure was already approaching across the sweeping emerald lawn.

He looks handsome, dressed up in his frock coat and bow tie. He's even groomed that wild red beard for the occasion.

Arthur stopped a yard away and his face opened in a beam.

'Miss Marchmont, I feel honoured that you accepted my humble invitation . . .'

'Humble?' Hélène laughed, gazing at the house.

'Would that I was its owner. It belongs to an old compatriot of my late wife's, a Mr Michael Fitzgerald.' He paused. 'Might I take your arm?'

Hélène nodded. Sometimes, Arthur Regan could put on even more of a show than Raymond de Guise.

As they threaded arms together, they turned to cross the lawns.

'I remember my father taking me to the theatre in Leicester Square, when I was almost a woman grown. *No, No, Nanette* was on. We'd dressed up for the occasion. I didn't know, back then, that I'd fall in love with the ballroom – or that, soon, I'd be going to tea dances just like the girl in the show. Just like this one . . .'

Hélène had grown wistful. It was, she recalled now, one of the only truly good memories she had of her father. All the rest had been shattered into a thousand pieces when he'd disowned her. All because of Sidney. All because of their baby. And . . .

What would Arthur Regan think, if he were to know? A widowed mother in secret, and mother to a little black girl . . .

Then she remembered Arthur's words – *one day, equality will prevail* – and she remembered what she was here for.

This tea dance was being hosted by one of Arthur's philanthropist friends. He'd brought the charitable men and women of London together, not simply to entertain and indulge them, as they did at the Buckingham. No, through those doors were people who would open their wallets and purses at the end of proceedings – who, together, might make a difference to the lives of the disaffected on London's streets. Was it really such a fantasy to think that if, one day, she told Arthur everything, he might understand?

'Arthur,' she said, pausing just before they stepped through the door, 'I'm grateful for the invitation. I didn't expect it. Perhaps I didn't deserve it, after that night in the Grand Ballroom. But I want you to know – I *wanted* to dance with you. Mr Hastings might know his balance sheet from his books, but he doesn't know his left foot from his right. I *had* to dance with him. Mr Charles demanded it.'

Arthur laughed. It was the last thing Hélène had expected.

'My dear, it's business! Men of business are the same the world over, from the jungles of South America to the Emerald Isle, to right here in the boardrooms and ballrooms of London.'

'It wasn't always so urgent at the Buckingham. When King Edward used to grace us . . .'

Arthur's hand was poised at the door, ready to knock.

'I have heard that the new king is being courted for the Buckingham's New Year's Ball?' He had lifted his eyebrows. 'Is it so?'

Hélène did not know. Kings and queens, counts and countesses – all of it paled in comparison to Sybil. She felt a fresh stab of guilt.

An afternoon away from the Buckingham, and I'm here *instead of in Brixton with my daughter.*

Before she could reply, the door opened up, revealing a butler in black with a silver platter balanced on one hand.

'Mr Regan,' the man intoned, and his benevolent blue eyes landed on Hélène. 'And Miss Marchmont. Do come through. Mr Fitzgerald has been expecting you.'

The butler showed them through an opulent hallway, with marble figurines set on plinths and portraits of older generations hanging on the wall. At the back of the house, the doors were open to the lavish gardens beyond. A white marquee had been erected on the lawn, with flower beds bright in scarlet and pink sweeping by on either side. Inside a gazebo was a miniature stage – and, on that stage, a small quintet was playing versions of songs Hélène knew intimately from the Grand Ballroom. 'Do It Like This' was reaching its peak as Arthur led her, arm in arm, onto the grass where the guests were gathered.

Here was a multitude of women in splendid gowns, brighter than any she could imagine seeing in the Grand Ballroom, the men in evening wear despite the midday sun. Some couples were already dancing. Others milled around, glasses in hand. Hélène

196

was soon offered a champagne flute; a moment later, there were canapés on plates; soon, people were coming up and clasping Arthur's hand – and the whirlwind of introductions was too much for Hélène to keep up with.

'Arthur!'

The voice had hailed him from behind. Arthur and Hélène turned to see a giant of a man lumbering out of the dancing throng. The lady on his arm was as petite as he was massive. He dismissed her with a whisper and then threw his arms around Arthur. Arthur was no dwarf, but this man enveloped him.

When the embrace ended, the men reeled apart like pugilists at the end of their fiercest bout.

'Miss Hélène Marchmont, might I introduce one of my oldest compatriots – Mr Michael Fitzgerald, our host for the afternoon.

'Mr Fitzgerald,' she said, 'I'm charmed.'

'The pleasure is mine, Miss Marchmont!' Michael's Irish brogue was even stronger than Arthur's. 'I've known this rapscallion you're gadding about with since we were boys. When he told me about you, I was determined to meet you. I've seen your face before, of course. My wife used to subscribe to *Vogue*. And then – weren't there stories of you disappearing off to Hollywood, for a shot at real stardom?'

'Real stardom, Mr Fitzgerald? Why, you can't have visited our ballroom—'

Michael Fitzgerald guffawed. 'That sounds like an invitation!'

Before he could say more, somebody else caught his eye and he walked away, shoulders drooping like the great apes Hélène had once seen at the Regent's Park Zoo.

Arthur was looking around the garden. In the gazebo, the band were just starting up a rich, urgent tango.

'Would you care to take a little turn?'

Dance by day, dance by night, thought Hélène. Sometimes the thought of it exhausted her – but not now, not when Arthur was looking at her with such daring in his eye.

She took his hand. 'Lead on!'

And so, they danced. In this way, one hour passed, then two, until the sun – directly overhead – began to dip towards evening. It was strange, Hélène decided, to be dancing in the open air again. Out here, the magic was so very different from the magic of the ballroom.

Occasionally, she and Arthur took a break from the dance floor. While Arthur talked with his countrymen, Hélène listened intently. There was something so energising about eavesdropping on an entirely different world, the realisation that there was a world out here beyond the ballroom and babies – but no sooner had the thought occurred to her than she locked it away again. Sometimes, Arthur solicited an old acquaintance for a contribution to his cause.

'Your brethren need you, Sean,' he said.

To another he implored, 'A hundred pounds could change the world,' while, to another, he said, 'A few pennies, perhaps. You can make such noise with so little. All we need is for London to sit up and *notice* . . .'

Some time later, her head light with champagne, Hélène took Arthur to the edge of the garden and threw herself into one of the seats arrayed around the trestle tables there.

'And I still have to dance tonight, Arthur! Maynard Charles has me bonded to Major Cadogan for the evening. He's stiff as a board. It will take all my guile to make him think he's floating on air . . .'

198

She was about to go on when, from somewhere close to the house, there came the sound of shattering glass. Arthur wheeled around, in time to see two of the burly men in Mr Fitzgerald's employ coming lumbering out of the house.

The man who had caused the disturbance was standing on the patio, with fragments of shattered green glass eddying in the pool of spilled champagne at his feet. By the set of his face, Hélène knew this was no accident.

The man was dressed as smartly as any other at the tea dance, but the scowl on his face was not the expression of a man who had come here to waltz or tango the afternoon away. As Hélène watched, Michael Fitzgerald stepped out of the dancers and gestured for his henchmen to wait where they were. Then, slowly, he approached the snarling man.

'Hugh, you've had a little too much, wouldn't you say? Why don't we step inside?'

'Step inside?' the man roared, and Hélène noticed that he had a plummy English accent, quite unlike many of the wealthy Irishmen who abounded. 'No, not with you, Fitzgerald.'

'One wonders why you came at all, Hugh, if all you wanted was to cause a scene. You cause quite enough of those at your own home, or so I'm told—'

'Shut it, Fitzgerald! You're not fit to shine my shoes. None of you bog-brained Murphys are. Ah, you look half-decent in your suits, with your bow ties around your necks, but underneath it you're still the same drunk fools. Make a donation to help your lot get on in London? It's like making a donation to help the street dogs, or the sewer rats. The sooner you get back to that God-awful island of yours, the better. Leave England to the English!'

As the guests looked on, aghast, Mr Fitzgerald nodded to his men. Taking the snarling Englishman by each shoulder, they lifted him bodily off the ground – and all he could do to resist was wheel his legs around madly.

'You tried to kill the King!' he roared, half-wild. 'You halfwits! You scum! The sooner the lot of you are driven out of London, the better!'

The man's voice faded as Mr Fitzgerald's guards heaved him through the house. Their host turned to the crowd with a sanguine expression, made a gesture to the band, and commanded the music to begin.

'I'm afraid there's no accounting for a drunk Englishman.' He grinned. 'Perhaps he should be invited home, boys. Maybe then we could teach him how to hold his liquor.'

'What was that all about, Arthur?' asked Hélène.

'Some Englishmen aren't as charitable as they like to seem.' Arthur sighed. 'It's after what happened in Belfast. There are some among my countrymen who despise your king, Hélène – and men like our friend Hugh want to tar us all with the same brush. But would you think we were all the same, just because of where we come from? If we can't move past this, the London Irish are doomed forever. Some of my countrymen can't move with the times. Their fathers and their uncles won Home Rule for the Free State, but not for Northern Ireland.' Arthur shrugged. 'We came to dance, not talk politics. Can we . . . dance?'

'I'm sorry, Arthur. I feel so . . . ashamed. Ashamed of my own countrymen, that they could come here, where everyone is gathered to do a good thing, and castigate you – simply for who you are.'

Arthur brushed a stray curl out of her eyes.

200

'Not all English people are the same. Nor are all Irish, for that matter. Some of us only want to see our fellows rise up, give them the chances they deserve. That any one of us here would condone an attempt to kill the King! The very idea!'

At that precise moment, Michael Fitzgerald turned past them, his wife in his arms.

'I, for one, consider myself a royalist, Miss Marchmont. Oh, I was as much in favour of Home Rule as the rest of my clan – but that doesn't mean I don't see the glamour in the House of Windsor. Why' – and he brought his own dance to a halt – 'Arthur, didn't you say King George himself will be dancing at Miss Marchmont's hotel for New Year?'

Together, the two men laid their eyes on Hélène.

'I hope so.'

'You must let us know! I would attend that ball myself, were the King to be there. Well, it would make for quite the story, wouldn't it?'

Then Michael Fitzgerald and his wife rejoined the dance – and were gone.

'Hélène, may we?'

She smiled. 'Dance on, Arthur.'

Soon, Hélène was in another world. Arthur's hold on her was soft but assured. She felt as if she was both being held and yet not – his arms not directing her, as so many boorish men tried to do in the Grand Ballroom, but simply enveloping her as she let the music take her. Soon, there was so little way to measure where one body ended and another began. They revolved around each other, perfectly in time.

It feels so natural, she thought. *It can take so long to know how to dance properly with a partner. Even when I began dancing with*

Raymond, it wasn't like this. Somehow Arthur knows. He knows me. It's like dancing with a mirror image of myself.

A foxtrot turned effortlessly into a tango, the band suddenly breaking into an Argentine standard, 'São Paulo Rain', which seemed quite at odds with the delicate English surroundings. It brought the garden to new life. Arthur was as good at moving fast as he was slow. In short, staccato movements they crossed the garden, described an arc back the way they had come.

The garden was naught but a blur of greens and browns, yellows and blues. The only constant in it was Arthur. They belonged in a world of their own.

Oh, Hélène, she thought, *what are you doing? Why here? Why now?*

But there was another voice inside her, and this one drowned out the first.

Just dance.

Some time later, an old grandfather clock began to chime out the hour somewhere in the hall.

One . . .

Two . . .

Arthur looked at Hélène. There was another look in his eyes, one that she had only caught glimpses of in the past. It seemed, somehow, as if his eyes were looking straight through her – straight into the heart of who she was.

Three . . .

Four . . .

Her breath stilled. They had stepped out of hold, but Arthur's hand was still over hers. Hers nestled in his palm. It was the perfect size and shape. Somehow, it just fitted.

Five . . .

Six . . .

He stepped towards her, closing the gap from which they'd just drawn away. Hélène could see that his lips were parted. For a second the rest of the garden faded away, and Hélène and Arthur were all alone. He lifted his lips, as if they might meet hers.

Seven . . .

The seventh peal of the grandfather clock suddenly brought the garden back into focus. Was it only an hour until the doors of the Grand Ballroom opened? Was there really so little time? How had the afternoon disappeared so swiftly?

Reality hit Hélène squarely in the face. She reeled backwards, taking her hand from Arthur's and, lifting her gown, hurried across the garden, through the arch of blossoms and back into the house.

She was almost at the front door when Arthur caught up with her.

'Hélène, please!'

She'd already opened the door – and now she looked out across the front lawns, wondering how on earth she would make it back to the ballroom in time.

Hélène Marchmont, you fool! You're letting everyone down. Maynard Charles. Raymond de Guise. Maurice and Noelle . . . and Sybil. Good Lord, Hélène, you're letting yourself down.

She turned.

You're letting Arthur down too.

His face was the perfect opposite of what it had been only moments before. The dazzle in his eyes was gone. Now he was crestfallen, downcast.

Even sad he looks handsome, she thought. *Oh, Hélène, you fool!*

'I need to get back, Arthur, it's too late . . .'

She meant that the hour was late but, as she said the words, she wondered if it was more than that, if it was too late for her, too late after everything she'd been through with Sidney, to find love again . . .

But if that was true, what, then, was this terrible beating in her heart?

'There are things about me you don't know, Arthur. Things you really ought to know, if we're to see each other again.'

'Whatever it is, Hélène, I—'

'I know I come across as cold. But it isn't because I really *am* the Ice Queen of the Ballroom, like all the chambermaids say back at the hotel. It isn't because I don't care, or love, or . . .' She drew a deep breath, afraid that she might spill it all, yet knowing she must say *something*, give him a reason, a reason to hope. 'I was married once, Arthur. A widow by the age of thirty-one. It's been two years, but I haven't thought about love in all that time. I've just danced and danced on. It's like they say in the ballroom – even when you're in the depths of despair . . . *dance!*' She tried to gauge Arthur's reaction by the look upon his face. 'I wondered if I could ever feel, again, what I felt about Sidney. I wondered if . . . romance dies. What if you fall in love once and once only – and, after that, you're barren inside. That's how it's felt. And now I feel like a child again,' she said brokenly. 'I don't understand myself anymore. I don't *see* myself. And I do want to love again. I want to get to know you, a little more each day. But I need it to be slow. Falling in love as hard as I'm falling *right now*, right now in this moment, it frightens me. If it goes on like this, I'm going to run – run and hide like I always do, and . . . I don't want to have to run, Arthur. Can you bear to understand?'

The silence engulfed them. It was thick and treacly and dark.

Then Arthur smiled. 'I remember the year after my Agatha died. And the year after, and the year after that. The desert inside me. The drought. But here's a secret it took me many long years to figure out.' He hesitated before taking her hand, as if she really might take flight. 'The rains do come again, Hélène. And I should like it so very much if I was there, perhaps with a parasol, at your side when they finally come down.' Though Hélène said nothing, for the moment the lightness returning to her face was enough. 'Come, Miss Marchmont. I'll have Mr Fitzgerald's butler summon one of the drivers. We'll get you to the Grand on time – you can rest assured of that!'

Chapter Twenty-two

RAYMOND DE GUISE'S ARMS WERE soft and strong and so achingly familiar. Hélène spent the night in and out of them. When she was not dancing with Raymond, she was dancing with Major Cadogan, or the shipping magnate Irons – who stood to make as much from any coming war as the Buckingham did to lose – but, no matter whose arms she found herself in, she was thinking of Arthur Regan.

She'd arrived at the ballroom only moments before the doors opened and the Archie Adams Orchestra marched out. Raymond had been contemplating dancing the opening number with one of the other girls, and perhaps he ought to have – for Hélène's heart had been somewhere else from the first number to the last. Now, as the last number ended and the dancers all disappeared to a round of stirring applause, the exhaustion of the evening caught up with her. She said barely a word as she allowed one of the girls to help her out of her ball gown – a creation of lace so intricate that it gave the impression of a butterfly's wings – and remained silent still as she sat in front of a mirror and rubbed the rouge from her face.

On the other side of the dressing room, Raymond's eyes lingered on her. Soon, he was aware of Louis Kildare at his side.

'There's something wrong, isn't there, Louis?' Raymond asked.

Louis looked at Hélène. She was staring, inscrutable, into the mirror. That face, that expression, that was why the chambermaids and kitchen porters, anyone who didn't know her, called her the Ice Queen. But Louis fancied he could see something beyond it; that brittle exterior was something Hélène had had to learn, a way to keep a secret of both her motherhood and her grief.

'It's the uncertainty, isn't it?' Raymond began. 'But I know, in my heart, what John Hastings is going to do. He's going to provide for us. I know it.'

He was about to stride across and tell Hélène the very same thing, when Louis said, 'Raymond, let me. You have a guest . . .'

And, looking up, Raymond saw that Nancy was waiting for him. Dressed in a simple grey pinafore, she looked so much more elegant and beautiful than the guests in the Grand had all night. He floated across to her, drawn like a moth to a flame.

By the time Louis pulled up a chair at Hélène's side, he had lost all words. Then, finally, he said, 'Hélène, what's wrong? You haven't been yourself all evening.'

She would look at him only through the mirror, as if to look him directly in the eye might break her resolve, but one of her hands darted out sideways and fumbled for Louis.

'I didn't go to Brixton today.'

Louis was still. 'Oh?'

'Arthur Regan took me to a tea dance. Some of his countrymen and a charitable foundation. They were raising funds, so they hosted a dance. I believe I was . . . one of the attractions.'

Louis seemed as if he wanted to say one thing – but then something stiffened in him, and he said quite another.

'You'll see Sybil again soon. She misses her mama, but it doesn't mean you can't—'

'I told him, Louis. I told Arthur how I felt.'

Louis's eyes widened. He did not mean to, but he drew his hand away – and, as he did so, the magic that was rooting Hélène in place seemed to vanish. She turned to face him, but Louis was shuffling backwards, as if he did not want to be faced.

'I told him I was falling in love.' The tears that welled in her eyes had turned Louis into an indistinct smudge. 'And I told him . . . about Sidney. About how I'd been married before. Oh, I left out the details – details he'd have to know if, one day . . .' She turned her hands into claws, tore at her own legs as her frustration mounted. 'What am I doing, Louis? I'm betraying him, aren't I? Every promise we made. I'm betraying Sybil, Maurice and Noelle, and everything they've done for us. It's all such a mess!'

Louis found himself trembling in his chair.

'You . . . love him, Hélène?'

There was panic in Hélène's eyes. 'Oh, Louis, you think it too – that I'm the worst person on this earth, that—'

'I didn't realise you were in love.'

Hélène saw the way he was shaking, as if trying to expel some thought he desperately did not want to believe. Louis Kildare, her dearest friend – and even *he* thought she was a traitor.

'I didn't mean it, Louis. I won't . . . I'll stop it. I won't see Arthur Regan ever again.'

Louis shook himself one final time. At last, something in him changed.

'Sidney wouldn't want that,' he uttered, though it seemed to pain him to give it voice. 'He'd want you happy and free – and, yes, in *love*, if that's what life throws at you. He was the best man I know. He'd want you with somebody – somebody who *cares*.'

The way he stressed the last word gave Hélène pause of her own.

'Louis,' she ventured, 'don't you trust Arthur Regan?'

'It isn't that, Hélène. I don't know the man. I don't know anything about him.'

He stood, as if to leave.

'Louis?'

Louis rocked from foot to foot. 'You should follow your heart, Hélène. We should all follow our hearts.'

Before Hélène could say another word, Louis took off. Soon, he was heading out of the dressing rooms, up and away from the Grand Ballroom itself, out through the reception hall and through the staff entrance into the Mayfair night.

He was not aware, until the chill of the clear evening hit him, how much he'd broken into a sweat. It was a sweat of panic. It was a sweat of fear. He stopped to dry himself on a red silk handkerchief, and then he walked on, on past the opulent town houses, on until he reached the broad thoroughfare of Regent Street. He was too late to the bus stop – the omnibus hurtling past even as he reached his hand out – and so, for a long time that night, Louis sat and looked up at the stars, trying to understand why his heart was beating out of rhythm, trying to understand why he hadn't put his arms around one of his oldest friends and told her that everything was going to be all right.

So lost in those thoughts was he that, when the next omnibus finally arrived, he barely got to the open door before it closed. On the empty top deck, he cradled his saxophone and heard Hélène's words spinning through his mind.

I told him I was in love, she had said. *Is that a betrayal?*

Tears of Louis's own came to his eyes.

No, Hélène, he thought, *to be in love with Arthur Regan isn't a betrayal. But for me to be in love with you, for me to feel it like a knife in the side when I think of you with him, for me to remember your scent, remember your laugh, to close my eyes and yet still picture your own eyes staring into mine – and all while Sidney was as close to a brother as I ever had? That, Hélène, that's the real betrayal. And I don't know how I could ever hope to extinguish this flame, how I could ever hope to make it right . . .*

Through the window, the shops and streets of London whistled past.

September 1937

Chapter Twenty-three

RAYMOND PUT HIS HAND ON Hélène's waist and said, 'Shall we?'

In the corner of the little dance studio behind the Grand Ballroom, the gramophone player crackled with a fast swing number.

'I found it in a record store in the Bowery,' Raymond explained. 'I brought so many back with me on the *Othello*. Music, Hélène, like you wouldn't believe. And it goes a little something like *this . . .*'

He lifted his hands, took hold of her own and, slowly at first, rocked back and forth. When Raymond stepped back with his left foot, he directed Hélène to step back with her right. When he pulled forward with one clasped hand, he directed her to step forward with the opposite foot. Their bodies seemed to work against each other – and yet, somehow, it was all fluid and alive.

After a little while, Raymond felt the rhythm of the new dance ripple from his body and into Hélène. Soon, she was dancing without direction. She'd got it, he realised, just as he had known she would. If only she'd been there, in the clubs of New York with him. Hélène Marchmont may have been known as the Ice

Queen of the Ballroom, but wild, untamed music could infect her as easily as it did any other dancer. They ducked and kicked and wove together, until at last the music sputtered out.

'And they call it the jitterbug,' said Raymond.

'It's so very . . . American!' Hélène laughed. 'And you think you can take this out there?' Her eyes turned in the direction of the ballroom itself.

'Don't you ever get the feeling that you've danced every dance? That there's nothing left to learn? Well, maybe a dance that starts out in the dance halls and clubs, maybe it can be refined and cultivated, made fit for the ballroom as well. By God, isn't that what the tango is? Wasn't there an age when a simple foxtrot was too risqué for civilised society?'

Hélène threw her head back and laughed. The very act made Raymond furrow his brow. There and then, he realised that there had been something different about her in the passing weeks. Something lighter. Something freer. He looked her up and down. He'd seen a look like that before. He'd seen it in the mirror in the days and weeks after Nancy first came into his life. Was it, he wondered, possible that Hélène was . . . in love?

'I've got to go, Raymond. I'm . . .'

'You're what?' Raymond asked with a twinkle in his eye.

'Late!' she announced, and whirled across the room.

Before she reached the door, it opened of its own accord – and there stood the rangy page, Frank Nettleton. Hélène pirouetted past him, as Frank tottered hesitantly within.

'Mr de Guise,' he stammered, 'a letter . . .'

The envelope he produced was eggshell blue and marked with myriad stamps. Nervously, Frank crossed the studio floor and handed it to Raymond. He was about to leave when Raymond said,

'Frank, thank you. I fear we haven't seen enough of each other, you and I. Why don't you—?'

Frank had started blushing. 'I'm on duties, sir. I'm meant to—'

'You mustn't call me "sir", Frank. I'm practically your brother.'

As Raymond spoke, he looked down at the letter and recognised the elaborate, florid handwriting in an instant. This missive hailed from Georges de la Motte. As Frank waited anxiously, uncertain whether to stay or to leave, Raymond let his eyes course over Georges's delicately written words.

Disaster, my boy. Fate has kept me and my body safe for so many years, but I write to you from my bed in the Hollywood Hills — where, alas, I must remain for the following four weeks. The fates have betrayed me at last. My foot is broken in three places, my leg just below the knee, and I have near brought down A Ballroom on Broadway with me. Two days ago, I was performing the final dance with Laurana St Clair, when I tripped and staggered, and the scaffold into which I crashed came down upon me. No other was hurt, but the pain in my foot was like nothing I can describe.

By good fortune, the director of A Ballroom on Broadway has been able to find footage enough to build the final scene of the picture. Movie directors are masterminds, Raymond, and can weave stories out of smoke and thin air. My foot will take many weeks to heal; my leg, it is feared, may heal crookedly — and the studio can take no more risks. Consequently, I have been told that they must replace me for my next picture, the upcoming shoot of Stairway to the Stars. The movie must be recast.

Raymond, do you begin to detect why I am writing to you?

I have spoken to Mr Meyer, and he is in agreement: they remember you well from your sojourn with us this spring, and there is something in your sad, dark Englishness that appeals to the casting directors here. If you are able to return to Hollywood in the New Year so that rehearsals can get under way, your own journey to silver screen stardom might finally begin! More exciting still: Mr Meyer believes he has identified the perfect leading lady to become your partner. Ivy Archembeau is a Midwest girl with a beautiful Italianate look: eyes of the most vivid green I have ever seen, and hair as black as pitch. Alongside you, she will be staggering: the dark dancers, mysterious and tragic and romantic. I find myself envious, even as I write!

Write back swiftly, and make arrangements – if you will – for the end of your days as a hotel dancer, and the start of your silver screen odyssey.

Raymond's eyes shot up. He had quite forgotten Frank was still standing there. Something in the sight panicked him. Raymond knew too well what the pages did in this hotel.

'Have you read this letter, Frankie?'

Frank shook his head. 'It was sealed, Mr de Guise. I'd never read private c-correspondence.'

Raymond's heart stopped beating as wildly in his breast. The thought that Frank might have read the letter, that he might even relay its contents to Nancy, had been more frightening than he anticipated. He would speak to Nancy about the letter – but how to describe the flurry of wonder, of excitement, of joy that had reared up inside him on seeing Georges's words? How to describe the passion that took hold of him – a passion he hadn't felt in his professional life since those early Buckingham days?

Raymond de Guise and Ivy Archembeau: their names spelled out for the ages on celluloid . . .

Hurriedly, Raymond pushed the letter in his back pocket.

'Frankie,' he said, 'is there something else?'

'Actually, Mr de Guise, there is.' Frank straightened himself. It seemed to be taking all the courage in the world, just to get the words onto his lips. 'There's a . . . girl. We were at the coronation together, earlier this s-summer.'

Inwardly, Raymond beamed. 'Oh yes, Frank?'

'I don't want you to th-think I'm foolish, sir. Only, I would like to invite her to a dance. Oh, nothing as fancy as you in your b-ballroom. I couldn't imagine setting foot in the Grand! But to a club. A dance hall.'

'Frank,' Raymond began, and he put his arm around the younger man's shoulder, 'the one thing you must remember about the fairer sex is that . . . they're people too. You might think they're not having the same doubts as you are, the same fears, but don't underestimate – in the world of romance, everyone is as anxious as everybody else.'

Frank spluttered, 'It isn't that, Mr de Guise. I'm afraid, but not *so* afraid. No, it's that, if I g-go to a dance hall, well, I'll need to know how to—'

'Dance?'

Frank looked downcast. 'They don't teach miners' sons how to foxtrot, sir.'

'Do you know, Frank, I taught your sister how to dance, last year. Right here, in this room. I should think I could show you a few steps, if that might suit you?'

Raymond stepped forward, but the boy suddenly stiffened and, with his arms by his sides, staggered back.

'Frank, relax. Let me show you a little box step, just something to get you started . . .'

'I thought you might just tell me?'

'Tell you?' Raymond laughed. 'Can a man learn to swim on dry land? Oh, Frank, loosen yourself! If you're going to dance, you'll have to *enjoy* it!'

The gramophone was silent now, so Raymond strolled over, placed a new record on the turntable and started it running.

'Archie Adams himself,' said Raymond as he came back across the studio. '"I'd Do Anything Twice". Now, Frank, stand right . . . here.'

Frank did as he was told.

'I'm going to lead,' Raymond began, 'and, once you're familiar with the steps, we'll turn things around. Then, *you'll* be the one leading *me*.'

Frank took a deep breath.

If this is what I've got to do, he thought, *it's what I'll do. It's for Rosa, isn't it?*

There was something so awkward about clasping Raymond's hand, or laying his own on Raymond's shoulder. It was only as Raymond started moving, describing a simple square across the studio floor, that some of the embarrassment floated away. And, even then, it was only because he was concentrating so hard on not letting one leg get entangled with the other that there wasn't space in his head for humiliation.

'No slouching, Frank. Think of yourself as a king on Coronation Day. Hold yourself with that bearing!'

'I'd Do Anything Twice' ended and another song began. Archie Adams and his 'Mayfair Magic'. After that came a song with a more strident rhythm, so that Raymond soon had Frank box-stepping at an urgent pace, so urgent that, more than once, he floundered over his own feet.

As they danced, Raymond's thoughts returned to the letter in his pocket. Perhaps it was the memory of dancing, right here, with Nancy – but, suddenly, the idea of abandoning the Buckingham for Hollywood seemed obscene. What good was California, what good the silver screen, if Nancy was not there beside him?

Something moved in the edges of Raymond's vision. He danced on, looking over Frank's head. Just thinking of her must have willed her into existence, because Nancy herself had appeared in the studio door. She stood there watching, and the smile on her face was the deepest, most childlike Raymond had ever seen. What joy it must have been, he thought, to see Raymond dancing with her brother – and how absurd!

I'll burn the letter. Never think of it again. Life is here, isn't it? Life is her.

It was at that moment that Frank's eyes lit on his sister. Horrified, he wrenched himself out of Raymond's hold.

'Nance! I was only . . . so I can take Rosa dancing. I mean, if she'll have me . . .'

'Frankie,' she said, rushing to him. 'You looked wonderful. I didn't know you had it in you! You're a natural. If my leg wasn't playing up today, I'd get out here with you—'

Frank wriggled back. 'Get off me, Nance!'

Rising onto her tiptoes, feeling the twinge in her leg, Nancy placed a kiss on Raymond's cheek.

'I'll be out with Vivienne tonight. I'll be late, but look for me before midnight.'

Raymond tensed. He wanted to tell her how scared he was for her, going out there into the Whitechapel night, but he held his tongue. He'd have gone out there himself if the Grand Ballroom hadn't been calling.

'Make sure that brother of mine brings you back.'

'You worry too much.' She put her lips to his ear. 'It's one of the things I love you for.'

After Nancy was gone, Raymond turned back to Frank. He still seemed to be squirming.

'Frank Nettleton, you're not . . . ashamed, are you?'

'Of course not!'

Raymond moved to the gramophone, turned the record, and braced Frank by each shoulder.

'Now, Frank, listen to me and listen well. No, don't go shy on me. I can sense, already, how embarrassed you feel – to be standing here, with me and the music. But be bold! Be strong! In the town from which you hail, they might claim differently – but if you're to win the heart of a lady, you have to push this from your mind – there isn't anything *soft* about dancing. You might be a miner's son, but not one of the miners you grew up with is as strong or agile as the best ballroom dancers. Not one of them could glide across the Grand in a perfect waltz. Not one of them could take his partner in his arms, lift her off the ground and turn on his heels, over and again, until all the world is a blur. Yes' – Raymond took hold of Frank's arm playfully, as if judging its weight – 'you might have been strong and lean enough to ferry coal up and down the mine, Frank, but you've got a lot of work to do if you want to really impress . . . Rosa, is it?'

In spite of himself, Frank nodded.

'Come, Frank Nettleton, I'll make a dancer of you yet!'

October 1937

Chapter Twenty-four

THE LIME TREES IN BERKELEY Square were losing their colour and the great willow that dominated the square was shedding its leaves.

Midnight was but an hour away, and the skies above Mayfair were banked in cloud. The sounds of the Archie Adams Orchestra had fallen silent, and those revellers who were not resident at the Buckingham Hotel were dropping down the marble steps to where the flotilla of taxicabs awaited.

And here, on the tail of the lords and ladies, came a solitary musician, wrapped up against the autumn cold, with his saxophone case in his hand.

There was no taxicab waiting for Louis Kildare, but tonight he would not wait for the omnibus either. Instead, he made haste through the town houses of Mayfair, and through the Regent Street arcades, crossing at last into the warren of streets on the other side.

Soho was later to bed than Mayfair. As Louis hurried down Carnaby Street, the music was still raucous at the Tatty Bogle. He met nobody's eye as he wound his way to the empty cobbles of the Berwick Street Market, and from there to the hidden doorway at its furthest end. From here, a narrow black stair led down into a basement from which the raucous sounds of a rumba spilled out. The legend above the doorway read THE MIDNIGHT ROOMS.

Louis Kildare had come looking for a new life.

Inside, dancers thronged the floor. The orchestra – barely six men and their leader – were cramped together on a stage set into the deepest, cavernous wall. Down here, the walls were black as coal, and the only light came from the buzzing electric lanterns balanced in every alcove. The air was a thick haze of sweet-smelling smoke, the floor sticky wherever Louis trod. At the bar, he ordered himself a rum and took a seat in one of the alcoves. On the dance floor, black and white danced together – and the image gave him a joy he was dearly needing this evening.

I've never seen a black man dance at the Buckingham Hotel . . .

Louis had nursed three glasses of rum by the time the orchestra came to its final flourish and announced they would return in half an hour for yet more revelry. As they took their bows, Louis stepped out of the alcove and caught the bandleader's eye.

Jack Oliver was the best groomed man in the Midnight Rooms. Sixty years old, in the subterranean dark he might easily have passed for forty. He had a wave of silver hair and the face of a matinee idol. There was something so warm in his face – he had the air of a benevolent English schoolmaster – only, when he sat down at his piano, he turned into an untamed young man, inspiring his orchestra to some of the greatest feats of showmanship Louis had ever seen.

He smiled at Louis and beckoned him forward.

Some time later, having followed Jack Oliver through a tiny door at the back of the club, Louis sat in a cramped changing room, where black dinner jackets and frock coats hung above the detritus of old instruments, fit only for spare parts. Most of the rest of the Jack Oliver Band were taking drinks out at the bar – but Louis sat, with his saxophone on his lap, and his feet nervously kicking.

'Jack, I've left Archie Adams. I resigned my post with the Buckingham.'

Jack Oliver had seen and heard many strange things in his time playing the clubs and dance halls of Soho, but this one struck him as particularly peculiar.

'I've known you a long time, Louis. I remember you and that friend of yours, Sidney Archer, when you first tumbled into London, looking for work. A couple of chancers, I thought, but I'm a man who always liked a chancer. You two proved yourself, time and time again. When Archie Adams came knocking and you signed up with him, well, I was disappointed, but hardly surprised. You and Sidney were the best. You were *going places*.' He paused. 'What changed? A safe, warm life like that? The promise of work every week for the seasons to come? What's going on, Louis?'

Louis shook his head, as if he could not say. 'I heard you were in the market for a saxophonist, Jack. I didn't see one up on stage tonight.'

'Harlan's given up the game. Gone to work at his father's tannery.' Jack Oliver smiled. 'A choice I wouldn't have made, but his wife's with child—'

'So what do you think? Might I audition?'

Jack threw back his head and laughed. That crowing laugh: Louis remembered it from days of old.

'Audition? Louis Kildare, you're not a man who needs to audition! You're the king, Louis! The absolute king!' His laughter ebbed away. 'But I want to know why. You and Sidney, you wanted to take it as far as you could take it. Clubs like the Midnight

Room were never big enough for you. Never grand enough.' Jack leaned forward. 'I *know* you, and I *know* something isn't right.'

'The Buckingham was everything I wanted, for a while. I don't know. Maybe it's since Sidney died. Maybe it's just the same old lords and ladies and bowing and kneeling you have to do, just to fit in. It constrains me, Jack. It isn't like it is down here. I want to play the wild rumbas. I want to play the new polkas. I want to . . .' He stopped. 'Raymond de Guise came back from America, filled with life because he'd discovered the jitterbug. The jive. But at the Buckingham, nothing changes. The truth is, it feels stale. It feels old. And I want to be back where the action is.'

Jack looked him up and down. 'You're lying, Louis.'

There was nothing severe about Jack's voice, but still Louis felt like a runaway schoolboy.

'Tell me, Louis. Tell me what it is . . .'

Louis wanted to tear his eyes away, but something would not let him.

'There's a . . .'

Jack's eyes widened, as he began to understand. 'Louis, you have . . . romantic trouble?'

Louis froze. Was it really so obvious?

His voice was broken when he next spoke.

'Can I play tonight?' he breathed. 'At least for one night?'

And Jack, who dared not back his old friend even further into a corner, said with a smile, 'And for all the nights to come. Welcome home, Louis. I couldn't be more pleased to have you.'

As midnight approached, Hélène stood at the entrance of the Candlelight Club. Tonight, the garden terrace was closed to the early winter cold, but the air still smelled like summer. Only moments before she'd left the dressing rooms behind the Grand Ballroom, Frank had pressed a hurriedly written note into her hands. Now, she slipped it into a pocket. She would face it another time – for there, seated at a table in the very middle of the room, was Arthur Regan.

She sank into the seat opposite him and, in a moment, the waiter brought her a vermouth.

'The club's about to close,' Hélène said, breathless. 'I'm sorry I couldn't come sooner.'

Arthur smiled. 'I'll take every second with you I can find. You are quite a wonder, Hélène.'

They'd seen each other several times as summer gave way to autumn. Arthur's work had taken him back and forth between London and Dublin, but every time he stayed in London he gravitated to the Buckingham. Two weeks ago, they'd spent a perfect autumnal morning walking through the green of Hyde Park, up and down Rotten Row. The week before that, Arthur had procured tickets to the Theatre Royal on Drury Lane to see Ivor Novello's *Crest of the Wave*.

'You're not yourself, Hélène. Can I detect some sadness in you?'

Uneasily, she reached into a pocket and produced the note Frank had delivered:

Hélène, I'm sorry for such haste. I shall see you soon. Louis

'He left without a word,' Hélène began. 'My dearest friend in the hotel and . . .'

Arthur grinned. 'Am I not your dearest friend, Hélène?'

He was teasing her and, for a little while, it worked, lifting her up and out of her unease. Then she imagined how it must have

227

been: Louis picking up his saxophone, donning his coat, and slipping away into the Mayfair night, unable to even say good-bye face to face.

'He told Archie right after the last number. Just upped and left. I've never seen Archie angry before. How's he to find another saxophonist at such short notice? And how am I—?'

'To find another friend?'

Hélène's frustration flared up. 'He's been a part of my life for so long.'

Arthur reached across the table and took her hand. 'The world changes. People come and go. Sometimes, I think, all we can truly do is abide.' He paused, his fingers dancing over Hélène's. 'I'm to go back to Dublin, to the family estate. If you could spare the time, beg Maynard Charles, perhaps you could . . .'

Hélène whispered, 'No such luck. Not with Christmas already on the horizon.'

In truth, she was not thinking of Christmas. She was thinking of Sybil, all her stolen visits, everything she missed out on.

But how to tell Arthur all this? When should I tell him I have a daughter? Too soon and perhaps he'll run away. Too late and it turns me into a liar.

'I'll be back by December, and in London for the Christmas season. Perhaps we could . . . spend it together?'

I'll never spend a Christmas with another, not unless they know about Sybil, about Sidney, every last thing about me.

'Perhaps,' she whispered.

'And I could dance with you, perhaps, at the New Year Ball? I should like that, Hélène. I should like it very much indeed.'

Her hand tightened on his. There was a moment when Hélène thought she might draw away. *But no*, she told herself, *you've*

228

been drawing away too long. She felt his hands on hers, drawing her towards him – and, this time, she did not resist. Her lips met his. She had been trembling as she leaned in, but as soon as they touched she was trembling no more. She had been expecting to think of the last time she kissed a man, the touch of Sidney's lips on hers, but she was relieved to discover it was . . . different, that no two kisses were alike, that kissing Arthur did not need to compare with kissing Sidney for her to melt into it. Every first kiss, she realised, was the very first time – and, when she drew back, she looked into Arthur's eyes and realised she was lost. This, right here, was the moment when she finally accepted it.

I have fallen in love.

And at the Midnight Rooms, not so very distant from the Buckingham Hotel, Louis Kildare put his saxophone to his lips, and sent a melody sailing out to enrapture the dancing throng.

For Louis, the Buckingham Hotel and all its heartbreaks were over. He had found his new home.

November 1937

Chapter Twenty-five

ARTIE COHEN BREATHED IN THE scents of the Whitechapel night. If it wasn't for the mug of piping hot cocoa in his hands, all he might have smelled was the horse dung in the middle of the thoroughfare, the soot and the smoke. But to Artie, everything seemed right in the world.

He'd come on 'shift', as he'd started calling it, at 4 p.m., just as the daytime was hardening to dark. Ordinarily, work began out on Whitechapel Road – where, twice a week, a taxicab stopped and out stepped Miss Vivienne Edgerton. After that, depending on the tone of the night, Artie might lead Vivienne – and perhaps her stalwart companion, Nancy – out to any one of a dozen different dosshouses he knew, to hand out the pamphlets they'd had printed, anything to spread the news of the work they were doing; or he might simply stand guard out here, while Vivienne and Nancy performed their 'ministrations' within. In return, at the end of each week, Miss Edgerton gave him an envelope, and inside it was his pay for services rendered. There were perks, as well: hot cocoa, hot soup, and as many barley sugars as he could suck his way through on a shift.

'It beats working for a living,' Artie had often joked.

The doors to the Daughters of Salvation former chapel were left ajar, so that a crack of electric lantern light spilled out into the night. In its thin shaft, snowflakes eddied.

Winter is coming, Artie thought. *It's bound to bring more desperate ones to the Daughters*. Then he turned around, and looked through the door . . .

Inside, beds were laid out in rows of six, army issue tent rolls or mattresses and, beyond them, a partition wall behind which two double beds – purchased courtesy of Vivienne Edgerton, and patched together by Artie Cohen's own hands – housed the hall's worst cases. Most of these men had gravitated to the Daughters of their own accord, following the rumour of a rumour from some dosshouse or back room opium den, but others had been hustled in under Artie's watchful eye. There was a taphouse on the Limehouse docks where, if you spoke the right words, you could walk out with whatever you desired. Beyond that lay the Limehouse Causeway, the heart of Chinatown; there were dens enough there, if you knew where to look. Sometimes, you'd find people comatose by the canal, or under the awnings of shops. One man had sunk to his knees outside a haberdashery and awoken in the Daughters of Salvation. He'd fled at once, then returned two nights later, begging for help – and that, so Mary Burdett said, was one of the greatest triumphs she had ever seen.

Through the crack in the door, Artie saw Vivienne Edgerton – dressed not in an elegant chiffon gown, but wearing an apron of hard, starched fabric – kneeling at one of the mattresses, while Mary Burdett fluttered behind a counter, ladling hot soup into bowls. Mary was a queer old girl. Artie thought he understood what was driving Miss Edgerton to do it – spiting her stepfather was a motive he could really get behind – but what propelled somebody like Mary Burdett was beyond him.

If it doesn't profit, then what's the point?

On the other side of the doors, Vivienne scrubbed her hands with carbolic soap in a tin pail by the open fire, then found Nancy at the desk in the corner. Nancy, who had run her father's household finances when she was scarcely nine years old, had proven herself adept at totting up the outgoings of the Daughters. Every penny counted, that was what Mary Burdett kept saying, and a penny looked after could do so much more than a penny squandered.

'The laundry costs are astronomical,' Nancy piped up. 'Perhaps there's a way we could use the Buckingham's load? Don't you recall – Mr Charles closed the laundry on site and farmed it out to an industrial cleaner. Well, there's bound to be a way, isn't there?'

'My stepfather would *loathe* it, were he to find out. Nancy, it's perfect.'

On a side table by the desk, a little wireless buzzed. There was more news out of Europe. Hardly a month had gone by since Italy's foreign ministry declared that they were entering the same Anti-Comintern Pact that the German and Japanese empires had already agreed. Now – or so the BBC newsreader reported – they had announced their withdrawal from the League of Nations itself.

The whole of the Continent fracturing, Nancy thought, *but there are wars even closer to home . . .*

Between the recumbent souls at the Daughters of Salvation, other volunteers flitted backwards and forwards. On the furthest side of the hall, one of them crouched over a bedroll and taking its inhabitant by the arm, tried to heave him aloft – but the man, a dead weight in his arms, plunged back to the floor.

'Get on up!' the man looming over the bedroll hissed.

Nancy started up. *This* was no volunteer, no familiar face. The man was young and shabby – his face an unshaven fuzz, dark bags around his eyes – and agitated. As Nancy lifted her eyes to follow the commotion, she thought he looked more like he deserved a bed in the Daughters of Salvation than he did a job.

'Get up and out of here, Pat, you dark horse. This soup they're serving, it's slop, anyway. There's better swill down at the Charlie Brown's. And, anyway, I got what you need. Come on, I can sort you out.'

After that, everything happened in an instant. Mary Burdett was out from behind her counter and with a broom in her hand in a second. Then, as if it was a thing she'd done many times before, she stalked across the room to brandish the broom at the man. As the bristles hit him, he staggered backwards, releasing his grasp on the sleeping man. But, seconds later – by which time Nancy and Vivienne were themselves striding across the room – the man had seized the brush head, heaving the broom out of Mary's hands.

Nancy and Vivienne joined her, as the eyes of everyone still awake in the chapel turned towards them. The two other volunteers – women of Mary Burdett's vintage, though not, perhaps, of her steel – shrank away, eyes open in horror.

'He's my brother, you old *bitch*!' the assailant screamed. 'What business have you got keeping him here? I can very well take care of him myself—'

'He isn't your brother,' Mary Burdett returned. *She has the benevolence of Mrs Moffatt when she's calm*, thought Nancy, *and something of her severity when she's angry as well*. 'I know what you are.'

'Oh yeah, and what's that?' he snarled.

'A dead man . . .'

The voice came from across the hall – where Artie Cohen, his cocoa mug still in his hands, was suddenly framed in the open doors with the snow turning a foxtrot behind him. Calmly, Artie stepped forward, and bent down to place his mug on the ground. In that moment, he was serenity personified. He even smiled graciously.

Then he threw himself forward.

Artie had to cross half the chapel before he reached the intruder, but he did it so quickly that the man had little chance to react. A moment later, Artie had wrestled the broom handle away, locked his arms around the man's breast and brought his hands behind his back.

'I'm sorry, ma'am,' he said, nodding in mock chivalry, first at the shell-shocked Mary Burdett, and then – with the slyest wink – at Vivienne Edgerton. 'He must have crept past. I thought he was one of these dossers . . .'

Mary Burdett's eyes flared – she had already warned Artie twice about referring to those who needed the Daughters of Salvation in such a way – but Artie could see the deep relief behind her eyes.

'I'll take this one out, shall I? It's always nice to earn my keep.'

Artie began to march the man to the doors. With eyes agog, Nancy watched him go; the man seemed to be little more than a marionette under Artie's direction. And was that *whistling* that she heard? Was Artie trilling a *merry tune*?

Mary picked up the broom from where it had landed on the floor, prompting the volunteers back to action. Nancy began to sweep away the snow that had chased Artie in through the doors. As she worked, Vivienne joined her.

'That's the third time this month.'

Nancy nodded. 'Miss Edgerton, it's getting so that Artie Cohen isn't nearly enough.'

Mary Burdett had explained the very peculiar predicament in which they now found themselves. Two months of Vivienne's allowance had allowed them to buy new mattresses, build new bed frames, supply the chapel with more tinctures and syrups, vegetables for making soup, loaves of bread, tea and sugar – all of the things lost souls needed to sustain their bodies while they fought their demons away. It had also allowed the volunteers, including Miss Edgerton herself, to venture out, under the stewardship of Artie Cohen, and find lost souls to bring back.

But the stories of the good work the Daughters of Salvation were doing did not only reach the ears of those desperate to break the shackles of their addictions. Other, more nefarious types heard those stories too. And, in the litany of men who came to the Daughters seeking help, some found a steady supply of customers for the opiates they brought in off the docks . . .

'Money makes the world go round,' Mary Burdett had explained. 'And there's a profit to be made, even out of the destitute. It's a clientele, just like all of the rest.'

'We have do something about it,' Nancy whispered into Vivienne's ear. 'We hadn't considered it before, but the better the work we do here, the more we need to protect it. And the more we need to protect it, the more—'

'Money we need,' Vivienne interjected, finishing Nancy's thought. She gazed around. The volunteers were back to their ministrations; Mary was chopping fresh potatoes into the soup. Even the peel, broken down, added thickness the men in here would slurp up. 'One day, more men like that will come – and Artie's only one man. And this place – why, it's a hospital now, but all it would take is the wrong sort of man, and it would be an opium den itself. All the clientele in one place . . .'

'It's like the Buckingham Hotel itself, isn't it? The more you spend, the more you have to spend.'

At that moment, one of the men in the beds on the other side of the partition started groaning – and Vivienne, seizing the moment, tramped across the hall, Nancy on her tail.

The figure in the bed was deep in the grip of some fever dream. Vivienne dipped a rag into the bowl of water on the bedside stand and began mopping at his brow. Sweat beaded his every feature – and it was only as she sponged it away that Nancy realised he was quite the youngest figure she'd ever seen in the Daughters of Salvation. His hair was the yellow of a cornfield in summer, and his face – cheeks like a cherubic little boy, turned-up nose like a mischievous imp – had not even a whisper of downy fluff.

He's younger than Billy Brogan, thought Nancy. *He's barely as old as Frank . . .*

They were soothing him back into his fitful slumber when Mary Burdett appeared. As she peeled the sweat-sodden sheet off him, she took a thermometer and slipped it between his lips.

'He'll be right as rain,' she began. 'He always is . . .'

'Always?' asked Nancy. 'He's been here before?'

'Warren here is a regular patron of ours.' Mary brushed the silken hair out of his eyes, as if he was a babe. 'Aren't you, Warren?' Then she turned on her heel. 'Maybe you might sit with him, Miss Edgerton. Tell him stories. He likes that. He's still a child, after all.'

Mary was about to depart when Vivienne said, 'Mrs Burdett, who is he? He hardly looks . . .'

Mary's lips twitched, as if suppressing a smile – and Vivienne, who looked suddenly at Nancy, had the terrible feeling she had been caught in a trap.

'Hardly looks what, Miss Edgerton?'

Vivienne flushed crimson.

'Hardly looks like one of those vagabonds on the other side of the screen, is that it? Well, no, I should think not. This young man is Warren Peel. Perhaps you know of his father, George? George Peel is a noteworthy man. A railway man. His family once owned the blacking factory down in Charing Cross. Those days are gone, of course, but money goes to money in this world – and Warren, here, is the result . . . When a lad like Warren, a dreamer you understand, gets plied with money, well, he finds ways to spend it. I'm afraid Warren winds up here all too often. His father, I'm told, barely knows. It's the family "staff" who deposit Warren on our steps every time they drag him out of one of the dosshouses where he thinks he's made friends. We've set him right many times before, only for him to do it all over again. And not a soul dares tell his father . . .'

Mary left the bedside, but stopped before she left the partition. 'Addiction obeys no divides, Miss Edgerton. The rich, the poor, the working man, the men of means – the scourge of opiates affects them all. But then, I think you knew that already, didn't you, miss?'

Vivienne looked down. Warren Peel was fast asleep, whatever nightmare had racked him ebbing away. She took his hand in her own and, in spite of every belief she thought that she had, she whispered a prayer.

Chapter Twenty-six

THE SOUND OF BIG BEN, pealing out the midnight hour, could be heard across the rooftops of Mayfair when a taxicab pulled across Berkeley Square, disgorging Nancy and Vivienne to the snowy steps of the Buckingham Hotel. As they parted ways – Vivienne through the revolving bronze doors, Nancy limping into the narrow darkness towards the staff entrance – the last bell tolled, and one day turned into the next.

At the Daughters of Salvation, Nancy thought, *we're one and the same. Equals, almost. Down there among the destitute, Vivienne and I stand side by side. But here at the Buckingham, she's not Vivienne; she's Miss Edgerton, and I'm just the chambermaid who changes her sheets. What a difference a few miles can make . . .*

Just inside the staff entrance, Frank was snoozing in a chair. Nancy stirred him gently, kissed him on the cheek and said, 'You ought to have gone home, you silly dear.'

'I swapped shifts, Nance. Said I'd keep an eye on the door.'

'And a fine job you're doing.' She grinned. 'You been dancing the whole night with Raymond, have you?'

'Just a little.'

Nancy pulled a ragged blanket around him and said, 'You mustn't let Mr Charles catch you sleeping on the job. You'll be out on your ear.'

'I shouldn't worry, Nance,' said Frank as she left. It was funny, but he never stuttered when it was Nancy at his side. 'Mr Charles hasn't been around all night. He's been locking himself away somewhere. Billy Brogan, he says it must be because of John Hastings. Mr Charles has too many worries, so he's hiding away . . .'

It doesn't sound like Mr Charles, thought Nancy as she left, *but the years change us all. Just look at Vivienne . . .*

As she rode the service lift upwards, exhaustion hit. It wasn't just her leg that ached – though it throbbed more than ever, now that she was on her feet night and day – it was her whole body. In less than six hours she would have to be down in the housekeeping lounge for breakfast with Mrs Moffatt. But the day had been long, the night had been hard, and she needed something more. So, moments later, she was outside Raymond's quarters, tapping gently on the door.

It was a wearied Raymond who put his arms around her as she stepped within.

'I've missed you, Nancy,' he whispered – and, for some time, they simply lay together in the dark. It was what they both needed.

'I need more time with you,' he finally said. 'Nancy, I squandered half my year in California. I missed you then and' – it was difficult to admit it, because she was right here in his arms – 'I'm missing you now.'

Nancy laughed. 'I'm right here, you old fool . . .'

In the dark, they kissed. All the aches and pains of Nancy's day melted away in that kiss. And Raymond knew, suddenly, that he could keep it in no longer.

He drew back, but his arms were still around her when he said, 'Nancy, there's something I need to tell you. A few weeks ago, I received a letter. A letter from Georges de la Motte. I've been meaning to talk about it, but there never seems the time. He's . . .' It was fortunate it was dark in his bedchamber; if there had been light enough to see her by, his courage would have deserted him. 'They want me, back in California. Georges had an accident. There's a place for me, and a partner, a Midwest dancer named Ivy Archembeau. She's . . .'

Raymond felt Nancy disentangle herself from his arms. A moment later, the light at his bedside flared as she reached out for the cord and pulled it.

Her face was a mask, deep with lines.

'Raymond?'

'I can't go without you, Nancy. Not again. One time is an adventure. Twice would be torture.'

His face had opened with a smile – but, if he had expected it to be returned, he was sorely mistaken. Nancy had pulled the bed-clothes up around herself, as if trying to hide, and she trembled with words she did not say.

'You can come, Nancy. I want you to come. They'll find us a house in the Hollywood Hills. You can meet Georges. I've told him so much about you. And they'll take us to parties and you'll meet . . .'

For the first time, Raymond saw the expression hardening on Nancy's face.

'What is it? Nancy, did something happen tonight?'

'Tonight?' she said, hardly able to say the word. 'Raymond, it's happening right now. Tell me, please tell me, that you haven't said yes to—'

'It could be perfect. Driving through the orange groves with you. You there, on my arm, when we attend the premiere. Don't you see what life could be?'

His eyes were alive with it, but Nancy only narrowed hers.

'I love you, Raymond, but . . .'

This time, it was Raymond's turn to be affronted. His eyes brimmed with delight, with confusion, with fear.

'I love you too, Nancy. That's what I'm saying. Here,' he said, and scrabbled for his dinner jacket, 'read what Georges said. It could change our lives . . .'

Nancy breathed, 'I don't want to change my life.'

'The Buckingham Hotel, it's been fine for now, but there's a world out there. I've seen it.'

I've seen it too, thought Nancy. *I've seen it in Whitechapel.*

'I don't need to go to California to know there's a world out there, Raymond. *This. This* is my world.' She opened her arms, but she didn't just mean Raymond's chamber. She meant the hotel. She meant Miss Edgerton. She meant Mrs Moffatt. She meant the Daughters of Salvation. And she meant Frank. 'Frank's only just arrived. All my life I dreamed of London – London for us both. I can't abandon him again. And—'

'Nancy . . .' Raymond implored. Wearing his most devilish smile, he shuffled across the mattress towards her. 'You're not thinking. It might be the thing that defines our lives!'

Nancy's face turned ashen. 'Defines my life?' she uttered. 'Defines my life, Raymond?' She dropped the bedsheets, marched to the door. 'It's my life. I want to *define* it myself!'

There was an anger in her voice that Raymond had never heard before. He felt himself falling, falling to the earth. He crossed the room to meet her, but stopped before he got to her side. She was holding herself, rigidly.

If I try to put my arms around her now, he thought, *I'll never hold her again.*

'Nancy, talk to me. What did I—?'

'Haven't you been listening, ever since you got back? I'm making something here. Something for me and something for Frank and . . . something for the world. Yes, the whole world. I know it sounds foolish to you, Raymond, but you don't see it. Those people in Whitechapel – I'm helping them. It counts for something. It *matters*. And I love you, Raymond, I do, but that I'd come to California with you, on a whim, without so much as a by-your-leave? The very idea! I'm not one of your debutantes, desperate to take a turn through the ballroom with you, with nothing else to say for myself. I'm . . . me. I'm Nancy. And what if *this* is what *I* want? What if California and Hollywood – what if that would ruin me, here, deep inside, where I need to be alive?' She held her hand over her heart, her words petering into silence.

'Nancy, I . . .'

She shook herself, as if trying to rid herself of the terrible feeling.

'I need to sleep, Raymond,' she said coldly.

'Yes,' he said, with urgency in his voice, 'sleep on it. You may think differently in the morning.'

Nancy's eyes flared. 'Raymond de Guise – *Ray Cohen!* – you haven't been listening to me at all!'

And with that, she was gone, out into the hallway and the Buckingham Hotel beyond.

246

Chapter Twenty-seven

I N THE LOUNGE AREA OF the Park Suite, the wireless crackled with news from the Continent. All over the world, from
Japan to Germany, leaders stood on podiums and preached
peace, while secretly harbouring the lust for war. But in the
lounge area of the Park Suite, not a soul was there to hear it.

The room was still.

Some time later, the newscaster announced the end of the
evening service, and for long hours silence reigned in the Park
Suite. Through curtains left undrawn, glittering stars arced over
the night sky. The moon rose and fell, shedding its light on the
frosted rooftops of Mayfair. At last, the sun began to shed its
weak, half-light.

Then, slowly, the door to the bedroom inched open and a
drawn, dejected figure emerged to face the day. Not a soul was
there to see Maynard Charles as he tramped across the lounge
and sat down by the telephone stand. For the briefest moment,
he turned his face to the light streaming in through the window.
It was bitter and cold in London today, but the bitterness did
not penetrate the Park Suite. He watched as the winter sun burst
up above Mayfair and felt a presence all around him. Maynard
had lost his God long ago, snuffed Him out in the barbed wire

and avalanche of earth that was Flanders, so it was not God that came across him today.

But perhaps, he decided, *it is something near.*

He picked up the telephone and dialled a number.

Mrs Moffatt was presiding over breakfast in the housekeeping lounge when Rosa handed her the telephone receiver. To the chambermaids, Mrs Moffatt was a bastion of composure. Not one of them had ever seen the colour drain out of her face as it did when she picked up that phone.

'I'll be there directly,' she said.

Placing the receiver back in its cradle, she took a moment to find her breath. Then all of the girls watched, their faces creasing in concern, as she hurried away, leaving the chambermaids – for the first time that they could remember – to fend for themselves.

Maynard was waiting, in the same seat by the telephone stand, when Mrs Moffatt arrived.

'Emmeline,' he said, 'he's through here.'

His face was impassive, his tone even. It was as if he was dictating to her the location of an unmade bed, or a housekeeping trolley accidentally knocked over. He was so matter-of-fact, so respectable – every terrible emotion he must have been feeling locked somewhere inside – and it shocked her to her core.

Maynard stepped back into the twin bedroom of the suite, with Mrs Moffatt following a few steps behind. In the dark, they stood abreast of one another, and gazed down at the bed where Aubrey lay.

'I was holding his hand when it happened,' Maynard said. 'I told him I loved him, and that I would see him soon. I do believe

248

he rediscovered his God in the end.' It was only now that his voice cracked. His hand darted out sideways and, though he did not take his eyes off the man he had loved, he grappled nevertheless for Mrs Moffatt's own hand. 'I hope He comes back to me, in the end. Emmeline, I . . . want to believe.'

Then the tears came. They came out of him in great, fitful explosions. They came out in a hot, urgent cascade. They came out with such violence that his body quaked, his knees buckled underneath him, and it took all the strength in Mrs Moffatt's body to keep him aloft.

She held on to him like a little child.

Some time later, Maynard Charles stood in his slate-grey suit, fixing his tie in front of the mirror, while Mrs Moffatt fussed with his shoes, polishing them so fiercely that she could see the reflection of her face.

'You don't need to do this, Maynard. The hotel's survived without you, while you've been tending to Aubrey. It can survive without you one more day. On this day, of all days, Maynard . . .'

Maynard lifted a comb and drew it through his hair. He'd sobbed in Mrs Moffatt's arms until his body was dry and aching – but, as quickly as the cascade had started, it had all dried up.

It's as if he rebuilt a wall around himself, as soon as his crying was done, thought Mrs Moffatt – and only rarely had she imagined anything as sad.

'John Hastings returns in less than ten days,' Maynard began. His voice did not quaver. It was as if there were two versions of Maynard Charles: the first, lost to grief; the second, an automaton, marching forward. 'It can't be in vain, Emmeline. And . . .' He allowed her to slip on his polished shoes. 'Elias Schillinger and Dr Haring – Eckard Haring – are taking luncheon in the Queen Mary today, with that slippery fellow from the Italian Embassy. You know what that means.'

Mrs Moffatt had heard the names before. They were Berliners from the Ministry for Public Enlightenment – which had always seemed, to Mrs Moffatt (who held little truck with such things), the most 'Nazi' department of all. *The Ministry of Lies*, Aubrey had called it. They'd stayed in the Buckingham on so many of their London soirées. Maynard Charles had reported on their conversations to his paymasters at MI5 before, and he would want to do so again.

'Maynard,' she said, with a hint of motherly concern.

'Mr Moorcock will pay me a visit before long. I must have intelligence to share. I must be down there. My responsibilities in this hotel don't end. They never end.' His voice faded into silence as he marched to the door. 'I'll make the calls, Emmeline. I'll . . .'

She rushed to him. 'Maynard, it's one day—'

'So are they all, Emmeline,' he said sadly, 'and yet the world keeps turning.'

He was grateful that he could reach the hotel director's office without being accosted. Maynard was only too aware of what the pages and porters had been whispering since the dying days of summer. It wasn't like him, they all said, to vanish from the hotel without a trace. Maynard Charles was all-seeing. Maynard Charles was all-knowing.

My absence has been felt, he thought, *and perhaps that's a good thing. But now it can be felt no more.*

Nevertheless, he gave silent thanks when he reached the office and, closing the door behind him, poured a tumbler of brandy from the decanter on his desk. The brandy set his body on fire more than it had in years; perhaps that was merely the effect of having sobbed so much of the moisture out of his body. He would call one of the pages to bring him a jug of iced water, but there was another call he had to make first.

His fingers knew Dr Evelyn Moore's number by heart. He trembled as he dialled it. There would be much to do, but at least he could lose himself in the logistics of it. It wouldn't be the first time he'd removed a dead body from the hotel without being seen. Men – especially wealthy men, whose doctors kept them alive far past their prime – died in their sleep. Then there had been Annalise Hesse-Darmstadt, the 'foundling princess' who could trace her line back to some long lost Prussian dynasty. *She'd* choked on her own tongue after a night consorting with an unlikely paramour. Other guests took fright when they saw a corpse being borne out of a room. Rumours could begin. Whole rooms could become stained with the stigma. And for those reasons, it was of paramount importance that these things were dealt with subtly.

I'll close the back stairs, when the undertakers come. I'll summon a carpenter and a joiner, find them some spurious work to do. Draw the eye, while I do what has to be done. But first – the doctor.

Aubrey's death was going to need to be formally pronounced, by one of the only other people in the world who knew where he'd lived.

He was dialling the last number when a knock came at the door. Not wanting to be overhead saying what he had to say, he slammed down the phone. The room was a blur. He focused on the ink pot in front of him, the only thing currently sitting on his desk, and called out, 'Enter!'

It was Abner Grant who lumbered through, carrying a mug of that bitter, stewed tea he always drank. Maynard closed his eyes, reaching down deep inside himself for what reserves of patience he might yet have.

'Come in, Abner.'

'Don't mind if I do, Maynard.'

The chair groaned when Abner dropped into it, as if it might suddenly splinter.

'You been hard to find, old son. I've owed you a report on the state of this hotel for days. Well, John Hastings is about done on the Continent, isn't he? They say he'll be on a boat again this week – and, after that . . .'

Abner's face had lit up, as if something in the idea pleased him, but Maynard was too washed out to care. He was staring at Abner Grant, but in his mind's eye all he saw was the cold form of Aubrey Higgins lying upstairs. The eyes he would never see again. The voice he would never hear.

'I'm dealing with it,' Maynard uttered, and poured the burning brandy back into his throat. 'Abner, how can I help you?'

'I'm closing in,' Abner said.

'On what?'

'On your thief. I've got them in my—'

Maynard waved his hand. 'You've been here six months and more. The burglaries ended as soon as you arrived. That's your use in this hotel, Abner. You're my scarecrow, not my thief-taker.' It was only after the words had come out that Maynard realised with what bile he'd spat them out. 'If that's all, Abner, you'll forgive me, but—'

'Actually,' said Abner, propping his elbows up on the desk, 'that isn't all. You see, I've got to know this hotel pretty well over

252

the year. I've had my thinking cap on, looking for ways you might be exploited. Well, that's the way of hotels like this, isn't it? Your thieves come from within more than they come from without. You've got to worm them out. It can take time. You need . . . clues. And I found one, Maynard. I found a big fat one, just hidden in plain sight.' His piggy eyes opened, and his whiskers twitched with a smile. 'It's called . . . the Park Suite.'

Maynard's hand trembled over his glass. With the other, he reached for the decanter, poured another measure of brandy, drank it at once. The fire gave him steel. It ripped him out of his thoughts of the Park Suite – where he wanted, more than anything else on this earth, to be, just curled around Aubrey one last time – and planted him, squarely, across the desk from Abner Grant.

'Oh yes, Maynard. A big fat secret. The Park Suite's up there, locked up, but it hasn't had a guest for fifteen years. That strikes me as odd. Doesn't it, you? That a hotel as luxurious and over-subscribed as this hasn't got all its suites opened up? That the hotel master keys don't fit its lock? That . . .'

Maynard reeled. The brandy had gone to his head, but it was certainly much more than this that sent his mind spinning.

'Why so surprised, Maynard? I told you, once before, that there was more to stealing in a hotel than lifting a few pearls out of some dowager aunt's bedside cabinet. There are bigger crimes. Like . . . embezzlement. One of your concierges might be cooking the books. One of your cocktail waiters might be pocketing loose change. Or . . . one of your heads of department might have quietly decided one of your suites doesn't exist, so that he has it for his own personal enjoyment. Do you see what I'm getting at? There are gradations to these things.'

Maynard seethed. 'Are you threatening me, Abner? You're here, in my hotel, on my forbearance. You're here because I needed a task performed – one for which you were suitably able – and if it hung the Imperial out to dry in the process, well, so much the better. But threaten me, and I'll have no compunctions about ejecting you from this hotel.'

'Steady yourself!' Abner crowed. 'Who said anything about threatening *you*? Unless – you don't know anything about the Park Suite *personally*, do you, Maynard? And here I was, simply trying to bring it to your attention—'

There was a sudden shattering of glass. Maynard looked down, to find the brandy glass in a million pieces where he had slammed it onto the desk. His hand was a chaos of brandy and blood and broken glass, but he felt not a thing.

'The Park Suite is empty,' he quaked.

He took a handkerchief from his breast pocket and wrapped it around his lacerated palm. By the way Abner looked, it was clear he was quite stunned at the image. But Maynard remembered him in France – the fool hadn't been able to take a minor injury, even as a young man; the sight of blood made him shiver.

'It's been empty for years. It was a private suite, you fool, for our investors. For the board to take advantage of – before Lord Edgerton bought half of them out. Have we neglected to refurnish and repopulate it? I dare say we have, Abner – but it's far from the only thing falling to ruin in this hotel. Glamour *costs*. Keeping the Buckingham alive *costs*.' Maynard raised himself out of his seat. 'I'll take you there, if you don't believe me. I'll walk you up to the Park Suite this afternoon and *show you*. It's empty, Abner. It's empty, empty, empty! It's all gone!'

Abner picked himself up. 'You invited me to the Buckingham to do you a job, Maynard. I'm trying to do it.'

Sit in your chair, thought Maynard. *Keep your eyes and ears to the ground. Look surly, so the staff know you mean business. You're my scarecrow, Abner – that's all you are to me. But if you're planning to blackmail me, well, you're too late . . .*

All of this he meant to say. All of this and more. And yet, when Maynard Charles next looked up, the hotel detective was gone. All that was left was the great emptiness, the great loneliness of life. He cried and cried and cried.

He was crying still, the decanter of brandy virtually drained, when another knock came at the door and Billy Brogan dared to peer around.

'Mr Charles, is everything all right?'

There was a moment's pause. Then Maynard lifted his hand to shoo Billy away – and Billy, who had never confronted a scene as perplexing as this, quickly obeyed.

Hurrying back to the reception desks, Billy's heart stilled. Mr Charles missing for days on end was strange enough – but Mr Charles sitting anguished at his desk?

Think deep on this, Billy Brogan. You've got a smart head on your shoulders. You're a concierge now! You're moving on and up in the world! If something's happened to Mr Charles, isn't it your responsibility to make it better?

He racked his brain.

John Hastings, he thought. *It has to be Hastings. Maybe Mr Charles has heard from him already. Maybe he's written from the Continent. Maybe he's already made up his mind – it's the Imperial he'll invest in, and hang the Buckingham out to dry . . .*

255

Billy's thoughts were leading him deeper into this labyrinth when, across the reception hall, the bronze revolving doors disgorged a familiar face, framed in slick black hair. Conte Dino Grandi had not made an appearance at the Buckingham Hotel since the eve of King George's coronation – but his implacable mask of a face, with its piercing eyes and dominating stare, had often appeared in Billy's recollections. He watched, nervously, as Conte Grandi was welcomed by one of the other concierges. And he remembered, all of a sudden, the reason he had been hunting Mr Charles down in the first place: the conference was about to begin.

Herr Schillinger and Dr Haring had taken their table in the Queen Mary half an hour ago, enjoying a pre-luncheon aperitif – courtesy of the house, as it always was when Mr Charles wanted to get tongues wagging – before their guest arrived.

Mr Charles ought to be here, Billy thought, *to welcome them, to grease the wheels, to gather what intelligence he can. But . . .* The image of the hotel director weeping at his desk came back to his mind. And Billy thought: *you know what he'd have you do, anyway, Brogan. You just need to do it.*

Some minutes later, Billy stood with Frank at the entrance to the Queen Mary. Through the double swing doors, the restaurant was buzzing. Waiters described complex arcs across the floor, balancing trays and plates with the skill of acrobats in a travelling circus.

'I don't know, Billy. How can I?'

'You did it once before – you can do it again. This isn't just for the good of the hotel, Frank! It's for the good of the country!'

Moments ago, Frank had been happily going about his duties – and now here he stood, contemplating the very thing he'd promised he'd never do again.

'Wasn't Mr Charles pleased with you last time?'

Frank nodded.

'And didn't he give you a special bonus, because you'd done so well?'

Frank nodded.

'And wouldn't you like one again, so that you might . . . take Rosa out dancing, perhaps? Come on, Frankie, you can't hide it from me! I know Raymond de Guise has been showing you some tricks. I know you're sweet on her . . .'

As Frank marvelled at how quickly rumours travelled in the Buckingham, the restaurant doors flapped open again and he caught sight of Conte Grandi sitting at one of the nearest tables, hunched in conversation with two imperious-looking men in dark grey suits. One was dark as night, the other blond and blue-eyed – but both loomed over the ambassador.

'Why don't *you* do it, Billy?'

Billy said, 'I've just shown them through to the restaurant, Frank. They already know *me* . . .'

Then, with his hand in the small of Frank's back, he propelled the poor lad onwards.

So, thought Frank, *this was it*. There was no turning back now.

It was not difficult to find a perch where he might stand sentry, as if he was awaiting the instruction of some other patron, or waiting to deliver a message. As long as he stayed out of the eye lines of the Germans and the Italian ambassador, perhaps it would be all right. If only he could control the hammering of his heart . . .

What would Nancy think of me, if she knew what I was doing, right here, right now? Oh, Nancy, he thought, *I wouldn't have got on that train at all if I'd known that this is what life is like at the Buckingham.*

The conversation on the table was hushed, but occasionally it flared up and Frank was able to catch snippets of what was being said. Halifax, one of the English lords, had visited his associates in Germany – and his visit had been both pilloried in the press and debated in the House of Commons itself. This seemed significant to Frank, though he couldn't say why.

At the start of this year, the House of Commons might just as well have been imaginary, for all it mattered to me. The world looks so different from a Lancashire village . . .

There was talk of the war in Spain. There was talk of the war being waged between China and Japan.

'One folly leads to another,' said Conte Grandi, with a sneer, 'and so, here we are—'

'There is, of course, the *other* matter,' the man Billy had pointed out as Herr Schillinger ventured.

'The other matter, gentlemen?' asked the Italian.

Herr Schillinger and Dr Haring shared a pointed look.

'The Irishman,' Herr Schillinger began.

Conte Grandi arched an eyebrow, inviting him to go on.

'The Irishman, Russell, he's long been making it clear that an alliance, of sorts, might be useful. Well, these Irish, they've been looking for ways to make war on the English for generations. They have plans of their own.' Schillinger's thin lips smiled. 'Russell thinks he may soon become chief of their organisation, this . . . Republican Army of theirs. The IRA. Should it happen, he'll escalate his war on the English. You heard about Somerville last year?'

Conte Grandi nodded. 'The Vice-Admiral. They killed him in County Cork.'

'And they tried to kill King George.'

Conte Grandi waved his hand dismissively. 'A botched attempt. I don't believe that was the work of true Irish Republicans – just some hero with a bomb—'

'Regardless, they're making movements,' Dr Haring interjected. 'They petition us for arms. In the event that the British declare against the Reich, things could become ... interesting between us. Plans are being laid. Sean Russell's compatriots are in London, even now, raising funds. Oh, it's dreamer stuff right now, but they call it their Sabotage Plan. The *S-Plan*. That they might bring London to a standstill with shows of force. That they might show their English oppressors of what they're truly capable.'

'It's true that they're raising the stakes. They have one of their rising stars in London right now, mustering funds. An interesting man. He has, what they call, the "Irish charm". I would not let him alone with my lady wife, if you catch my meaning. His pretence is that he raises funds for the benefit of his countrymen in England – the London Irish, as they say. Well, these Englanders, they think the Irish are little better than dogs – worse, even, than blacks. This Arthur Regan does a good impression of somebody who cares – a man of charity, even – with his stories of his dead wife, and all the tragedy of his past. All horse shit, of course, but he plays it so well! Conte Grandi, you should go to one of his soirées one day – he hosts them with that old boor, Michael Fitzgerald. Go there. Drink their wine. Pretend you care about the plight of the poor. Arthur Regan will have you eating out of his hand. You wouldn't think, for a second, what he's really after ...'

'And that is?' asked Conte Grandi, with the slyest of smiles.

'Why, like all of his compatriots, he's waiting – waiting for Britain's eyes to be on the Continent, so that finally, they might

259

make their very own war . . . and retake the land that is theirs by right of blood.'

Frank's blood was running cold. He heard no more – for louder even than the din of the dining room was the hammering of his heart. He wasn't made for work like this. He turned one way, then the next – and remembering his footing at the very last instant he scurried to the Queen Mary doors.

Out there, he crashed headlong into Billy Brogan.

'Woah, Frank! Slow down!'

'Not here, B-Billy,' stammered Frank, with desperate eyes. 'Come on . . .'

Soon, they were hidden around the corner, in the corridor that led to the hotel director's office.

'Frank, what happened in there?'

Frank was still shaking. 'I'm s-sorry, Billy. I had to get out. I—'

'What did they say? Is it war, Frankie? Were they talking about . . . war?'

'No,' said Frank, 'it isn't that. It's . . .' He looked into Billy's eyes, as if he still could not believe. 'It's Arthur Regan, Billy. They were talking about Miss Marchmont's friend, Arthur Regan.'

December 1937

Chapter Twenty-eight

As November lurched into December, and the London skies grew heavy with the promise of snow, all talk at the Buckingham turned to the second coming of Mr John Hastings Junior.

Nancy heard it in the chambermaids' kitchenette. Her brother Frank – tormented with what he'd learned of Hélène Marchmont's new friend – heard the other pages gossip about the American businessman who'd returned in a flotilla of Rolls-Royces and assumed control of the conference chamber where only the hotel board ever went. In the Candlelight Club, Diego, the head cocktail waiter, had taken delivery of a shipment of Tennessee bourbon, reputed to be John Hastings's tipple of choice. The head concierge sat his team down, one by one, and impressed upon them the importance of first impressions. The second coming of John Hastings escaped no kitchen porter, no caretaker, no lift attendant or maître d'.

But on the day John Hastings's boat came in, Maynard Charles stood in a suit of charcoal grey, his red raw eyes hidden beneath the brim of his bowler hat, in the cemetery at Highgate.

The funeral of Aubrey Higgins was a lonely thing. Maynard stood at the graveside and cast a handful of frozen earth onto the coffin as the undertaker's assistants lowered him into the ground, but the only souls at his side were Mrs Moffatt and Marianne Christie, a second cousin from Bournemouth who, on being notified of Aubrey's passing, had caught a train at dawn. The only other figure was Dr Evelyn Moore.

The priest spoke the saddest, most beautiful words to see Aubrey on his way, but aside from that there was no service to remember – which was just as Aubrey had wanted it. Then, before the graveside attendants prepared to fill in the grave, Mrs Moffatt, Marianne Christie and Dr Moore stepped aside – leaving only Maynard to whisper his words of love to the dead.

Mrs Moffatt watched Maynard from a distance. She had excused herself from breakfast in the housekeeping lounge by claiming a family emergency (which was itself enough to propel rumours of the most fanciful sort). The rippling snow was a veil between them, so that it seemed, for a moment, as if Maynard himself was on the other side – joining Aubrey in whatever came next.

Maynard might have lost his faith in the Lord, Mrs Moffatt thought, wringing her hands, *but I know they'll meet again. Let us hope it isn't soon – for the Buckingham needs Mr Charles more than ever. But one day, when his time is done, I know he'll see Aubrey again . . .*

She tried to tell him as much as they climbed back into the taxicab that had been waiting at the cemetery gates. As the bare trees of Highgate flickered past, Maynard sat with his hands in his lap, his bowler hat occupying the seat between him and Mrs Moffatt. It might as well have been an ocean that divided them. Every time she tried to speak, he barely moved.

'He wouldn't want you to lose yourself in grief, Maynard. That wasn't Aubrey's way.'

He liked the way she said his name. It reminded him he was real. Sometimes, it was too easy to imagine Aubrey had been a figment of his imagination: the man in the tower, to whom he returned each night.

It's too easy to pretend, thought Maynard, *he never existed. Now that the Park Suite has workmen in it. Now that the walls are being stripped. Now that the beds where Aubrey and I slept are gone to scrap. Now that, each and every night, I eat dinner alone . . .*

'I went to see the work yesterday evening,' Maynard whispered. 'I summoned the joiners and the carpenters, the carpet layers and decorators only two days after he died. By God, Emmeline, he was hardly cold . . . If it wasn't for Abner Grant, perhaps I'd have kept it, if only for a little while. But what good's a mausoleum? A museum to a man that only you or I know lived among us.' He exhaled, long and hard. 'We must remember him, you and I.'

'We will. Oh, Maynard, we will.'

Maynard suddenly began to tremble. They had reached the conflux of roads at King's Cross now; the traffic was stuttering around the tangle of junctions, but Mayfair – and everything that was waiting for them – was not so very far away.

'Abner Grant knows, Emmeline. He knows what manner of man I am.'

Mrs Moffatt detected the old distress in Maynard's voice, and reached out for his hand.

'Maynard, you're the very best man.'

'You know what I mean. The Buckingham needed a man like Abner Grant, and I was able to deliver a wound to the Imperial in the process. And yet . . .' Maynard paused. 'Abner has served his purpose, but I fear his presence in our hotel. Were Aubrey still with us, he would wield it against me. I'm quite certain he was close to discovering the secret of the Park Suite. He would have blackmailed me with it – I see that now. But now Aubrey's gone, and I have been saved in the most unwelcome of fashions.'

For a time, Mrs Moffatt was silent.

'What's the story of Abner Grant, Maynard?'

'He served with Aubrey and me, back during the Great War. Oh, he was an oaf then, just as he's an oaf now – but that was an age when oafs had their uses. There was one night, deep into that dreadful year of 1917, when he discovered the love Aubrey and I bore for each other. He stumbled on us in our dugout three nights before the battle at Arras, and he—' Maynard breathed heavily. 'He understood what we were. Emmeline, he thought to hold it against us. Some men loathe what they do not understand. And I do not believe Abner Grant has ever known love. He would have used what he knew to curry favour with the other men, or to advance his own cause with the NCOs. He was ever a scheming, ambitious sort of a man. But on the eve of the battle, something happened to Grant. It happened to men, sometimes. They suddenly saw the folly of it all. Oh, they knew it, in their heads, of course. But then, suddenly, they knew it in their hearts.

'Abner Grant ran, Emmeline. He sloped out of the dugout, made as if he was ferrying a message down the line and he . . . ran.'

They had come, at last, into Berkeley Square, where the boughs of trees hung heavy with snow and roaring fires crackled behind every one of the town house windows. Up above them loomed the Buckingham Hotel, its large copper crown dusted in white.

'It was Aubrey who stopped him. Call it serendipity. Call it fate. But Aubrey happened across Grant as he tried to disappear into the dark, and somehow he coaxed him to the dugouts, where we waited, all three of us, until the whistles went off that morning.

If Aubrey hadn't intervened, he would surely have been caught and shot for cowardice. So, you see, Abner Grant owed his life to Aubrey.'

'It seems, to me, that you both hold secrets about each other, Maynard.'

'Perhaps,' whispered Maynard. 'But my secret was worth so much more. Nobody would put Abner Grant against a wall and shoot him for cowardice, not now it's twenty years in the past. But what do you think would become of me, were Lord Edgerton to find out who I am, or who I'd been hiding in the Park Suite? Men like Aubrey and me, we're tolerated, of course. We are not alone. But Lord Edgerton and his allies, the men in his Union, the fascists he courts and entertains at our hotel, do you truly think they'd suffer me for long, Emmeline?'

Maynard stopped as, at last, the taxicab came to a halt outside the hotel's simple white colonnade.

'You're safe now, Maynard.'

'Perhaps,' said Maynard as he stepped out into the bite of the winter wind, 'but is the Buckingham?' He looked up at its grand façade. 'Its fate is in another's hands now, Emmeline. I fear, with all I have dealt with this year, it may already be too late.'

Frank had felt the hole his secret was burning inside him for days. Unburdening himself to Billy hadn't been enough. He'd gone to bed at night with the secret coiled up in his belly. He'd woken, in the dark, to feel it sitting – like some hag out of a nightmare – upon his chest. At breakfast with the gaggle of younger Brogans, it had whispered in his ear. He'd gone up to the chambermaids' kitchenette, meaning to tell Nancy, but Nancy had been nowhere to be found. The truth was, he hadn't seen her for a week or

267

more. When she wasn't with Raymond, she was out there, with Vivienne Edgerton – out on their crusade, whether the sun or the snow beat down.

I used to go to Nancy with almost any problem I had, he thought. *Whatever happened, Nancy would be there, and Nancy would know what to do. But now . . .*

He'd paused, last night, on the threshold of the chambermaids' kitchenette. Frank had stared too long, watching Rosa and Ruth make tea. He'd still been staring when Rosa looked up. Then, as always, he flushed crimson and reeled away.

Not now, Frank, he'd told himself. He still needed to practise his dance technique. He still needed to find the courage, if he was ever going to really ask Rosa to step out with him one night.

Now he sat in the storeroom just inside the staff entrance, wrapped up in a blanket, watching through the open door as the snow grew deeper on Michaelmas Mews. Nancy would be back soon. It wasn't the first night she'd spent at the Daughters of Salvation – Frank knew that they had beds there – and if he could keep his eyes open, he would catch her as she came in.

'Nancy,' he'd say, 'I don't know what to do. It's about Arthur Regan. It's about Hélène Marchmont . . .'

And Nancy would sit him down with a cup of hot cocoa and make it all go away, because that was what she always did.

All of a sudden, there were voices out on Michaelmas Mews. Frank readied himself. It was only as the voices grew near that he realised they didn't belong to Nancy and Miss Edgerton at all.

Then his heart stopped beating.

Two figures had appeared. First came Mrs Moffatt, wrapped in a brown fur coat to ward off the winter chill. Then, shuffling behind her – his shoulders hunched over and his hat so low that it almost obscured his eyes – came none other than Maynard Charles.

It made no sense. Mr Charles had no need to come in through the staff entrance – not unless he didn't want to be seen. He was wearing a smart charcoal suit and its cuffs were lined with salt where he'd been tramping in the snow. And – no, Frank wasn't mistaken – he had a handkerchief in his hands and he was using it to dab at his eyes.

Something was amiss here. Frank could feel it deep in his bones.

But then ... something else was wrong at the Buckingham, wasn't it? All the spying Billy Brogan did for Mr Charles.

'Mr Charles must see and hear all,' Billy had said. 'He's got his reasons. This is his hotel ...'

Well, wasn't *this* something Mr Charles should know as well? Arthur Regan – and who he really was?

It seemed, to Frank, that Mrs Moffatt was almost *leading* Mr Charles – as if it was she who was the hotel director, and he merely her valet. As they passed, they barely noticed the figure swaddled in the little wicker chair.

But I have *to do this*, Frank thought. *It's Mr Charles's hotel. If not him, who else?*

'Mr Charles!' Frank cried out.

Almost as soon as he heard himself, he was mortified. *What right do I, Frank Nettleton, have to speak to Mr Charles like this?*

'Mr Charles?' he ventured again.

This time, Maynard Charles seemed to notice – but it was only in the same way that a horse flicks its mane at an irritating fly.

'You're the Nettleton boy, aren't you?' Mrs Moffatt began. 'Nancy's brother.'

Frank nodded. Mrs Moffatt had taken a shine to Nancy. Perhaps she'd . . .

'Come now, Frank.' She reached into a coat pocket, produced a handful of barley sugars, and palmed them at him. 'Here, take these. It's a big day in the Buckingham, Frank, dear. We really must be getting on! Don't you know who's returned?'

Frank stammered, 'J-John Hastings.'

'There's so much to be done!'

Mr Charles had been plodding ahead all this time, and now Mrs Moffatt heaved herself after him. With the barley sugars raining out of his hands, Frank watched them disappear deeper into the hotel.

'We'll get you cleaned up,' Mrs Moffatt was saying. 'A new shirt, a new tie, you'll feel a different man. You can still do this . . .'

'There's nothing to be done, Emmeline. The die is already cast.'

But whatever Mr Charles said next faded into silence as they rounded another corner, leaving Frank alone with his secret.

The conference room, formally known as the Benefactors' Study, was a grand meeting hall dominated by a single oak table, perfectly round so that, when the hotel board assembled here, no individual member could be said to be sitting at its head. Even so, there was no doubt to anyone in that room who would be dominating the discussion today. John Hastings had been the first to arrive, with his personal secretary, his two bookkeepers, and Mr Marshall, who appeared to be nothing other than a bodyguard. Confronted by this expanse of papers and ink, diagrams and charts, blank contracts and copies of the old hotel ledgers, all seven members of the hotel board had shrunk back onto the table's second side. The effect, Maynard Charles thought, was to

270

make them seem a class of overdressed schoolchildren lined up in front of their house master.

Maynard stepped into the room, closing the door behind him.

Just let me get through this moment, he thought, *and then . . . well, then, we'll see what comes next.*

Maynard had quite forgotten what an inconsiderable kind of man John Hastings first appeared. Less than half Maynard's age, he did not impose himself on the room. He did not have the physical stature of somebody like Lord Edgerton, nor even Raymond de Guise – who, for all his effortless grace, towered over the rest of the dancers in the ballroom. It was not that John Hastings was diminutive; it was just that he was entirely . . . unremarkable.

And therein lies the danger, thought Maynard as he stepped forward. *A man who goes unnoticed is a man who can slip a dagger into a rival's side and walk away unblemished. A young man is easily overlooked.*

Maynard reached out his hand and accepted John Hastings's own. Both men looked the other in the eye.

This is 1937, he thought. *The heart of the twentieth century. It isn't men of brawn who decide the future anymore. It's men of brains.*

'Mr Hastings, welcome back to the Buckingham Hotel,' Maynard began. 'I shall look forward to hearing about your Continental endeavours.'

'Indeed,' said John Hastings. Even his voice, Maynard remarked, was entirely uncommanding. Then he shuffled to the other side of the table, clasping the hands of each member of the hotel board in turn.

'Gentleman,' John Hastings began, 'we need just a few moments further. Do excuse us.'

As John Hastings and his team formed a huddle around their papers, Maynard reached Lord Edgerton.

'Maynard, after all this is done, I'll need a word – whatever the result . . .'

'Of course, sir.'

'It's my stepdaughter, Maynard. Where is she? This is the second time I've visited the hotel to find her *in absentia.*'

Inwardly, Maynard bristled.

She isn't our prisoner. You married her mother; you didn't take her as a hostage. She can come and go as she damn well pleases.

But he was shocked at his own ire. Ordinarily, all he wanted was to limit Vivienne's capacity for causing scandal at his hotel.

Something's changed in me, he thought. *A whole year watching everything I love die and it's changing what I care about the most.*

'I'll identify the problem, sir.'

At the head of the room, John Hastings's huddle came apart and resumed their places at the board table. At last, only John Hastings remained standing.

'Sirs, I appreciate your time. I'll keep this as swift and precise as I can – not only because that, gentlemen, is my way, but because I'm aware how long I have already kept you waiting. Yet, the months I have spent investigating the best course of action for the corporation my grandfather founded have been invaluable. As some of you are already aware, I have spent the last season on the Continent, overseeing our operations in Munich and Berlin, in Paris and Nice, in Milan and Rome. The European interests of the Hastings family holdings pale into insignificance compared to our North American interests – but this does not mean they are not held in the highest esteem, nor that they do not make up

272

a considerable part of our profits. Accordingly, we are as worried as any righteous men would be at the slow slide of Europe back towards disunity and war. The effect of the war in Spain is already being seen across our balance sheets. Our hotel in Madrid will see no profit for the foreseeable future, if ever again.' John Hastings paused. 'Accordingly, my mission has been to expand upon the Hastings family assets in your proud island nation – and shore us up against whatever calamities might come to the Continent. We have already taken a leading stake in the East Essex Railway Company. We have a leading stake in a number of north country shooting estates. But the prize has always been London, and it is on this front that I appear before you today.

'My team and I have spent the past months building intimate profiles of the two hotels we've identified as possible investments. Both the Buckingham and the Imperial have achieved great things in their times – both have the scope to achieve so much more.'

John Hastings slammed his palms directly down on the table – and, for the first time, it seemed to Maynard that the words he spoke had not been endlessly rewritten and rehearsed.

'Gentlemen, I like this place. I do. But I find it wanting as well. I find it indulgent. The Imperial, it runs a tighter ship. Does it generate the turnover of the Buckingham? Hell, no! But does it generate the tidal wave of expenses? Does it need the same avalanche of money to keep its wheels greased? Not a chance! Gentlemen, my investigation of the Buckingham has revealed, to me, some elementary errors that require immediate rectification . . .'

An abyss had opened up inside Maynard's stomach. Just when he thought there were no depths further to drop into, here it was.

He felt himself falling, falling, falling. Only Lord Edgerton, still holding himself with unfathomable pride beside him, made him keep listening.

'My team has been making projections, based on any one of a number of future conditions. The collapse of mainland Europe will bring with it a cessation of European incomes. Gentlemen, the fact of the matter is that the Imperial Hotel is less dependent on foreign dignitaries than the Buckingham. The Buckingham invests much to draw those dignitaries from overseas, while the Imperial requires only the business of English financiers, industrialists and bankers to make sure its balance sheets tally . . .'

Maynard felt his hands curling into fists under the table. All his concentration was focused on keeping his face an unreadable mask.

John Hastings did not understand glamour. John Hastings did not understand elegance and grace. He did not know what advantages they brought. But it was too late – too late to make him see . . .

'Gentlemen, every instinct in me, every lesson from my fathers and forefathers, has been driving me to invest in the Imperial Hotel. It is the course of action that makes cold and clinical sense.'

The world, which had been turning too fast for so long already, seemed to spiral even further out of Maynard Charles's grasp. This time, he let it go. What use was there in holding on? Aubrey was gone. The Buckingham too. He'd done everything he could. The future would have to take care of itself.

'And yet . . .'

The faces of the hotel board had been twisted into astonished grimaces. Uriah Bell seemed ready to leap to his feet and remonstrate with the young American. And yet, for the first time, John

Hastings had started to smile. It was such a peculiar sight that it hardly suited him at all.

'There is one thing' – he grinned – 'that sets the Buckingham apart from the Imperial. I did not appreciate it for what it was when I was last here. It was only when I decamped to the Imperial, to go through my processes with *them*, that I began to get an inkling of what it all might mean. Gentlemen, I do not know if you have ever graced the ballroom at the Imperial – I do not know if you can even call it a ballroom at all, for it pales into insignificance when set beside the Grand. This I noted the last time I was in England. But then, on the Continent . . .'

All of a sudden, Maynard was back in the room. The world had slowed its turning again – and somehow, John Hastings's words were coming at him out of the mist.

'Well, let me tell you a story. When I was in New York City last, a certain dancer of yours named Raymond de Guise conspired with my wife to take me to a dance club, where I was further cajoled into "jitterbugging" and "jiving" the night away. I confess – I am no dancer. My wife, on the other hand, has her very heart open to it. So, when I was on the Continent – and missing my wife, as all good men do – I decided I would take it upon myself to investigate the Thè Dansant Magnifique in Nice, the Stella in Rome, the Thè Dansant de Notre Dame. All so that I could write to Sarah, and fill her with tales of the things I had seen.

'Perhaps it was just how much I missed Sarah. Or perhaps it was the excitement I saw in the letters she sent back and forth – all the things she wanted to know about the Italian dancing, the French dancing, the crowds at the Folies Bergère . . . But I know that, the moment I set foot back in New York, I am taking my wife to the Sunset Lounge. I'm taking her dancing. I think

275

I understand, now, what Raymond de Guise was trying to tell me – that a good ballroom can *connect* people. That it can deepen the bonds between them. My father would think me a sentimental young pup, but this seems, to me, to be worth more than all the gold in the world.

'I am not a dancing man,' John Hastings confessed. 'It is not how I was ever brought up. Good sense trumped *fun* in the Hastings household – and it is on these precepts that lasting civilisations are built. And yet, there is something else your Raymond de Guise said to me, when we were on the *Othello* crossing the treacherous Atlantic. He was proclaiming, for the hundredth time, the glory of the Grand Ballroom – and he looked at me and he said, "Mr Hastings, when you feel it, you feel it." I didn't know, until a few short days ago, what lasting impact those words had had on me. Ever since I came of age, I have directed the decisions of my life by tallies of numbers, one column matched against the next. Well, am I to believe, all of a sudden, that there can be other reasons for existing? Am I to believe that decisions can be made on *other* grounds?' He beamed. 'Gentlemen, when you feel it, you feel it. And, Heaven knows why, but I am feeling it now . . .'

Maynard Charles felt himself rising from his seat. He hovered, on the tips of his toes, as if he might at any moment explode forth and shake John Hastings by the hand. But something held him there. Could it really be that something as ephemeral as a *feeling* had convinced John Hastings, the bona fide man of business, to choose the Buckingham Hotel? Could it be that a man of numbers and reason was casting all that aside because of some unimaginable spark that had suddenly come alive inside him? He needed to hear the words, before he believed them.

A verbal contract is still a contract, he found himself thinking. *A gentleman's word is his bond. So say it, Mr Hastings. Put us out of our misery and—*

Then, a sudden great wailing came from beyond the doors of the Benefactors' Study.

At the head of the table, John Hastings stilled. Lord Edgerton and the other members of the board looked from one to another, and then finally to Maynard Charles.

The noise was deafening: the constant, turning cry of air being forced through a bellows.

Maynard knew the sound of that wailing. He'd tested the device himself, though he'd never had cause to use it. The drone of the siren rose and fell, rose and fell, rose and fell – but whoever was pumping it seemed to be doing it with increasing urgency.

'Mr Charles?'

In a second, he was up and across the room, bursting through the doors of the Benefactors' Study and, clinging to his braces, pounding the hallway to the reception desks.

Maynard looked around. A dozen guests were standing in huddles around the great Norwegian fir, bedecked in baubles and glittering crystal stars, that had been brought in for Christmas, their faces etched in consternation. Behind them, at the second check-in counter, Billy Brogan was turning a crank hidden behind a panel in the wall. When Maynard caught his eye, they turned together to the ornate archway that led down, down into the Grand.

The clock on the wall read 1 p.m. The afternoon demonstration dances were about to begin.

Maynard pounded through the arch and down the hall. Halfway there he saw the ballroom doors open up. Two hotel patrons scurried up the hall, staggering past him, with half a dozen more on their tail. He reached out for one, tried to take him by the arm – but the man was already rushing past.

'Out of my way, man!' he bawled.

Maynard continued onwards, but soon more guests were pouring out of the doors. He asked one what the emergency was, what was going on.

No one answered him, but now that he was near Maynard didn't need to ask another soul. He ploughed into the Grand, where patrons were either fleeing or gathered in huddles at the edge of the hall, and his eyes turned to the stage.

The doors at the back of the dance floor were open, and from their maw came a roiling vortex of thick black smoke.

Chapter Twenty-nine

MAYNARD HAD TO FIGHT HIS way through fleeing hotel patrons to get to the edge of the dance floor. Yet more guests were trying to force the wide glass doors that, during summer, opened up onto Berkeley Square itself – but the snow had fallen thick and wild last night and the doors were held fast. Maynard cried out, summoning one of the bartenders from where he was hastily locking down the bar.

'Leave it!' he roared. 'Get them away from the doors! Up and out of the main entrance, before anyone gets killed. What in God's name—?'

A fresh explosion tore through the ballroom – and a great gout of fire erupted somewhere on the other side of the dressing room doors.

Screaming.

He heard screaming from beyond the flames.

Maynard's eyes flickered into every corner. Guests who had tarried too long were streaming out of the reception entrance, battling against a tide of porters and chambermaids coming the other way. Marshalling them all came Mrs Moffatt. She caught Maynard's eye across the dance floor. Only a few scant hours ago: the peace of a cemetery in winter. Now: Hell itself was being unleashed.

Maynard ripped off his jacket, straightened his braces, turned and bellowed with all the authority of a commanding officer in the depths of Flanders itself, 'Form a line! Form a line!'

Somebody had fallen in the entrance to the ballroom. Somebody else stopped to pick them up. As they did, others stumbled or toppled behind them.

They'll get trampled. It's the panic that kills you before the smoke, he thought. *Or the gas . . .*

For a second he was back in the field outside Arras, waiting for the whistle to sound, trying to control the fearful hammering in his breast.

Pull yourself together, Maynard! These people need you now!

He rushed into the fray himself, bodily forcing the patrons taking flight away from the fallen lady and helping her to her feet. Only when he was certain she was all right did he snap his fingers at one of the chambermaids and order her to get the woman to safety.

'Get them all out!' he ordered, and the look on Mrs Moffatt's face betrayed the fact that not even she had seen Maynard Charles look as statesmanlike and kingly as he did right now. 'You, boy!' He reached out, and snagged Frank by the collar. Frank – who had followed the train of porters rushing in to confront the madness – found himself careering around. 'Get out onto the square. Direct the fire engines when they come. And . . . *you!*' he snapped, commanding the attention of Mr Bosanquet, the head concierge. 'Make sure the guests are all accounted for. Take them out onto the square. Send attendants up onto every floor. Vacate the Queen Mary, the bistro, the Candelight Club—'

A great geyser of black smoke erupted from the dressing room doors – and, in that same second, the first figures started to emerge. First came Archie Adams himself, followed by his band. One after another they came, faces black with soot.

'It was the back door,' Archie gasped, his voice barely audible behind the snap and crackle of fire. 'The explosion came at the ballroom doors, so we tried to get out the back. But . . . Mr Charles, it was locked!'

When the taxicab turned the corner into Berkeley Square, its passengers immediately knew that something was amiss.

Nancy had wanted to sleep all the way back from the Daughters of Salvation – there was something hypnotic about the way the snow was gently falling that could lull a person – but, as soon as they came upon Berkeley Square and saw the crowds spilling down the marble steps, any thoughts of the comfort of her nice, warm bed left her. The window glass was misted, so she wound the window down to look out. Snow streamed in, half-blinding her, but still she could see Rosa and Ruth, an army of kitchen porters and pages, shepherding hotel guests out into the white.

'Stop!' she cried. 'Stop here!'

The driver slammed on the brakes. The taxicab slewed in the snow, turning in the road. It was still sliding when Nancy leaped out, trailing Vivienne behind her. As Nancy landed, her bad leg screamed out. Why did it always complain most bitterly when she needed it most? She gritted her teeth and pounded across the snow.

'Frank!' she called out – for there was her brother, darting between the frozen guests in only his shirtsleeves and trousers.

He raced to her, feet flailing in snow that reached beyond the line of his knees.

When he reached her, she gripped him by the shoulders.

'What's happened?'

'There's a fire in the ballroom! Mr Charles sent me to . . .'

Nancy's face turned as white as the snows that eddied around them. Too late, Frank realised it was the word 'ballroom' that had drained all the colour from her skin.

Nancy lifted her skirts and made, as quickly as she could, for the marble steps. Twice her bad leg betrayed her and she plunged to her knees, ungainly in the snow. Twice she picked herself up and, ignoring the cries of her brother hurrying after, plunged onwards. The old injury slowed her – but she battled against both it and the snow until she was past the white colonnade. Entering the Buckingham by its main doors was a crime almost unforgivable for a mere chambermaid, but today Nancy thought nothing of it as she staggered into the reception hall. In one direction lay the Queen Mary, where the lunch service had been abruptly cancelled, meals abandoned and champagne still fizzing. In the other, through the ornate arch, lay the Grand Ballroom itself.

The ballroom was emptying out. She recognised waiters and service staff, porters and caretakers, all holding guests in check to manage the flight from the inferno raging beyond the dressing room doors. Plumes of smoke billowed out of those doors, rising into the rafters at the top of the ballroom itself. Perhaps the fire would not be far behind.

In a huddle at the back of the room, untouched as yet by the smoke, stood a collection of men in dark black winter cloaks. Among them, Nancy was surprised to see Lord Edgerton himself.

She thought, fleetingly, of Vivienne stumbling up behind her – but her eyes were quickly drawn to something else.

Dancers were still staggering out of the flaming dressing rooms. Each was a silhouette, formed out of smoke. Each was hunched over, racked with wild, animal coughs as they finally came to clean air.

Last of all, came Raymond de Guise.

Nancy lost all reason. She forced her way forward, ignoring her brother's cries, until she was at the heart of the dance floor, where Maynard Charles himself was standing, barking orders at the staff lined up behind him. The musicians and dancers who'd already fought their way out of the smoke were sitting on the dance floor itself or propped up by the balustrade, Maynard organising chambermaids and porters to get them away. Nancy ignored them all, trying to battle through the last figures in front of her.

She could feel the heat.

She could taste the smoke.

What it must have been like, to be trapped inside that dressing room when the inferno began . . . How it must have felt, to be enveloped by driving flames . . .

How could a fire start so quickly? she thought.

She'd known fires at the Buckingham before. Kitchen fires, when figgy pudding went up in flames, or a tea towel left in the wrong place suddenly went up in smoke. But those were little things, and easily quenched.

How can this happen?

A voice came out of the roiling blackness beyond the doors.

'Raymond!' it cried.

Nancy thought she knew that voice. Her eyes darted around. There was no sign of Hélène Marchmont anywhere.

283

'Raymond!' the voice screamed again.

Raymond had drawn himself up to his full height. Even smeared in ash, he looked handsome. His eyes panned around, taking in the full sweep of the room. Past Maynard Charles they came, past Archie as he crouched down to tend to his trombonist – until, finally, they hovered over Nancy.

What's he thinking? thought Nancy.

They'd argued too much in the past weeks. Ever since that morning in Raymond's rooms, when he'd tried to tell her what her future held: orange groves in California, wide-open beaches, the Hollywood Hills. She'd wanted to tell him: come back to Whitechapel with me; let me *show* you what it means.

But in his eyes – oh, in his eyes, the love was still there.

Her lips pursed to tell him it, but the chance never came. Raymond turned on the spot, took in the black maelstrom through the dressing room doors, and – without missing a beat – hurried back into the storm.

'Raymond!' she screamed. 'Raymond, no!'

She meant to take off after him. She meant to tackle him to the ground and tell him to his face, that it was not worth it; that she needed him to be safe, here and now, and to hang the consequences. But something was holding her fast. She thought, at first, that it might have been fear. But then she heard his voice.

'Please, Nancy,' Frank was saying.

She realised, then, that he had his arms wrapped around her, locking her in place. She had never known her Frank could be so strong. Maybe it was all those months he'd spent working in the mine – or maybe it was just how fiercely he loved her.

'Frank!' she screamed. '*Raymond!*'

But he didn't let go, and Raymond had already been swallowed by the smoke.

Raymond cupped his hand around his eyes, but there was so little point. The smoke was already in them. They were already streaming. He dropped down to his haunches, inched his way forward. Somewhere, timbers were creaking. He heard the shattering of glass.

'Hélène!' he called out. She'd been screaming, only seconds ago. That *had* to mean she was still alive. 'Hélène, where are you?'

She'd been right at his side when it happened, he was certain of it. He tried to cast his mind back, but the smoke was in his eyes, in his nose, in his throat, and to even concentrate on putting one foot in front of another was almost too much.

He'd come into the dressing rooms only moments before it started. The place had been crowded, as it always was in the moments before the orchestra began: Archie Adams and his musicians in their own huddle; Gene Sheldon preening himself in front of the mirror; Hélène Marchmont helping the other dancers into their ball gowns. The drinks had already been flowing. It was not, of course, condoned by the hotel director, but a drink before a dance helped to loosen the body; it helped dissolve the inhibitions.

Raymond had glided through the dancers, waiting for that old feeling of anticipation to flood through his veins. He'd been missing it, of late. Ever since he'd come back from California, something wasn't quite right. The old excitement somehow seemed harder to come by.

'A drink, Raymond?' Hélène had asked, suddenly appearing at his side.

Raymond's eyes roamed the cluttered dressers and found the teapot sitting between the empty glasses where the musicians had been taking their Scotch whisky and ice.

'I don't need wine to dance, Hélène. But something warm . . .'

Hélène rolled her eyes. 'That tea's been brewing too long. Old Abner Grant had Frank Nettleton brew it – deep and black, just the way he likes it. He treats that poor boy like he's his squire!' Hélène saw the distasteful look on Raymond's face. 'This is the third night he's been down here this month. Always asking the same questions. He wants to know where Sofía LaPegna went, if anyone's heard from her. Lord knows why.'

Raymond said, 'I've told Mr Charles before – the dressing rooms ought to be sacrosanct, the hour before the ballroom opens—'

'Maybe when Hell freezes over! We've had the whole hotel floating through here tonight. Diego delivered drinks from the cocktail lounge stores. Billy Brogan was looking for you – said he had a message from Nancy.'

'It will only be to tell me she's with Miss Edgerton tonight. He might have saved himself the visit.'

'Good Lord, even Mrs Moffatt came through. We're losing the seamstress, so she's volunteering to keep the ball gowns in check herself. She sent one of the porters – Ashton, I think – to pick up ones we're not using.'

Raymond stopped. He knew Hélène too well. The way she was speaking at a thousand miles an hour, he was quite sure it meant there was something important that she *didn't* want to speak about.

286

'Everyone rushing through here, but ... Arthur Regan, Hélène? Is he in the ballroom tonight?'

Hélène's eyes told a whole odyssey.

'He was going to be, but he was called away. One of his philanthropist friends, demanding an audience. But he came earlier . . .' Raymond followed her eyes and saw the great bouquet of flowers by the ballroom doors. 'I wasn't here when they came, but the girls say he delivered them by hand. He stayed for a drink, charmed them – each and every one – but then . . .'

Raymond dared open his eyes. Black coils of smoke turned like seething dragons in the air.

He inched forward where the air was at its clearest – but he had not advanced another yard into the dressing rooms when he pressed his palms to the floor and whipped them back, covered in blood. All around him was shattered glass – pieces of green wine bottle, scoring jagged lines into his flesh.

He thought he could smell petrol. Petrol and ... aniseed liqueur?

It was the least of his problems. He couldn't get on top of his breathing. Each breath he took only demanded another.

It was then that he realised he was running out of time.

He cried out for Hélène again – and this time, she returned his call. By following her voice, somehow he found his way to the back of the dressing room. Here crouched Hélène, pressed up against the door to the rehearsal studio. He could barely see her through the shifting smoke, but there she was, the hem of her gown lifted up and wrapped around her mouth.

'Raymond?' she gasped.

'Hélène, we have to—'

'It's locked,' she said, hammering her other first on the door. 'I thought . . .' She had to stop talking, for there was not enough breath left in her lungs.

Something exploded. Timbers crashed. Raymond turned back the way he had come, but all he could see was the churning darkness. It was getting thicker.

'We have to go. Hélène, we . . .'

It was then that he realised she had gone limp – slumped, a dead weight, against his shoulder.

At last, Nancy tore herself free. Around them, porters were ferrying the last of the musicians and dancers away. Maynard was still bawling out orders – but, at last, the ballroom was emptying through the main doors.

'Frank Nettleton!' she screamed. 'Don't you ever tell me what to do again!'

Nancy lurched forward, but Frank had not finished yet. He leaped forward.

'Nancy, please. You're all I have in the whole world . . . Nancy, please!'

The desperation in Frank's voice gave her pause. It lasted only instants – but it was enough, for no sooner had he spoken, the smoke still pouring out of the dressing room doors parted, and there, framed by tongues of orange and red, staggered Raymond de Guise.

At first he seemed a shadow man, a figure made entirely out of smoke. Then, as he stumbled forward, they saw that he was labouring under the weight of another. The long, lithe figure of Hélène Marchmont was cradled in his arms.

By sheer determination, Raymond strode into the heart of the dance floor. Others rushed to his side. First, Diego the cocktail waiter. Then, Maynard Charles himself. As they helped him lay Hélène down, Nancy and Frank reached him. Nancy threw her arms around him, grappled him tightly, letting go only when he began to splutter. He took great gulps of the air, the noises that came out of him animal and unearthly. His eyes rolled feverishly.

'Raymond?' Nancy whispered.

'Get him out of here,' Maynard whispered. 'Frank, Diego, get her out of here too.'

Together, they stooped to lift up Hélène. Soon, others were at their side, helping to form a human stretcher to bear Miss Marchmont away.

'Everyone away!' Maynard roared.

He turned, like a madman, on the spot. The ballroom had emptied itself of guests, but at the very back of the hall, Lord Edgerton was still there. So was Uriah Bell. Between them: Hastings himself. The bespectacled little American – he'd been so full of *zing* just a few short moments ago, about to proclaim his investment in the Buckingham Hotel. Now, his face was unreadable. *A feeling*, he'd said. *When you feel it, you know . . .*

Well, what might he be feeling now?

'Everyone, out!' Maynard thundered.

Out in the snow of Berkeley Square, where a hundred guests stood beneath the gently falling flakes, sirens could be heard. Soon, scarlet fire engines were appearing. Behind them came the first ambulance. Billy Brogan, who had abandoned the crank behind reception, was waving madly at them, shepherding them into the parking bays behind the white colonnade. Others were brandishing shovels, desperately clearing the snow banks by the Grand Ballroom's outer doors so that the fire brigade could sweep straight in.

It was remarkable how everyone came together in a time of crisis. Porters and kitchen hands were working with maître d's and head chefs to make sure the guests out in the snow were not too cold. Somebody had already organised trolleys of hot beverages to be handed around. Somebody else was bringing out blankets from the stores. Yet more were simply milling around, diverting attention from the calamity unfolding inside. It made one think there was hope for humanity . . . but, standing alone in the middle of the Grand Ballroom, watching the wall of flames advance out of the dressing rooms to devour the stage, the balustrade, the dance floor itself, Maynard could not keep himself from thinking that all hope for the Buckingham Hotel was already gone.

Chapter Thirty

FRANK HAD ALWAYS LOVED CHRISTMAS. He remembered waking early, creeping into Nancy's bed with his stocking, while their father – too often in his laudanum haze – snored on. Today would be different. For a start, it was not his sister that he slept alongside, but Billy Brogan, who had kicked and grumbled all night long. And the dinner would not be a turkey or goose, but a pair of huge baked salmon. Even so, as Frank had helped to put the Brogan children to bed on Christmas Eve, the familiar feelings of childhood had flooded through him. Mrs Brogan had even let him eat the mince pies the children had left out for Father Christmas – and to Frank, that seemed the most magical thing of all.

He woke early. Some of the Brogan children were already awake, and he could hear them through the walls, debating loudly whether or not it was time to go and rouse their parents. In the end, it was Roisin who broke first. Frank heard scampering out of the girls' room and down the hall, four-year-old Gracie May toddling behind. He rolled over and gently pushed Billy in the back. It wasn't often that Billy slept at home anymore – he was so proud of his Buckingham quarters that he only rarely passed up the opportunity to use them – but Christmas, Frank thought, would always draw him home. Besides, what Christmas cheer there was at the Buckingham Hotel this year was in short supply. The Norwegian fir still stood in the heart of the reception hall, twelve feet tall and shimmering with stars, and the smells that had been wafting up from the Queen Mary for days were of cinnamon and cranberry, crackling duck fat and sage. But the doors of the Grand Ballroom remained closed. Music did not drift through the Buckingham's halls. Nancy had told him about last year, her first London Christmas, and how, after the dinners were served, the housekeeping lounge had become a Grand Ballroom in miniature. He would, he thought, like to have seen that. After everything Raymond had been showing him – those exotic American dances, the jitterbug, the jive, with all their kicks and flicks – he fancied he might even, finally, have the courage to ask Rosa to dance with him.

But there would be none of that in the Buckingham this Christmas. Only the snow hardening into icy mounds out on Berkeley Square. Only the taxicabs that came to take the guests somewhere else for the night. The fire behind the ballroom had devastated the dressing rooms, advanced out into the ballroom itself to destroy the stage and portions of the dance floor, but it had done so much more than that. The French bistro, directly above the dance studio, could no longer be used, for fear its floor – charred from beneath – might cave in. There was smoke damage in storerooms, and six of the first floor rooms had been put out of commission. It was, Billy had described, like a cancer in the hotel: the fire had been brought under control, but the damage had already been done. No Christmas dances this year. No Jingle Bells at all.

Frank crept to the bedroom door, just as Billy opened his eyes.

'Come on, Billy!' he begged. 'They're going downstairs. They're going to open their presents!'

Billy rolled out of bed, rubbing his weary eyes.

'Frank Nettleton, you're acting like you're eight years old!'

Some time later, as the Brogan children hurtled around the room with new wooden trains, or fed imaginary porridge to new dolls, Frank grinned, delighted, as Mrs Brogan presented him with a steaming mug of cocoa. *Chocolate for breakfast!* Frank was unsure if he'd ever been quite as indulged, no matter how hard Nancy had always worked to make his Christmases so magical. In the kitchen, Billy was proudly presenting his mother with all of the many things he'd managed to rescue from being thrown away at the hotel – three venison steaks wrapped in grease-proof paper; pomegranates deemed too sour; a whole pot of greengage jam – and taking particular pride in the pink champagne one of the kitchen porters had offered him.

'It's a bounty every Christmas, Ma!' Billy proudly declared. 'But this year more than any – well, the Queen Mary's still open, but guests have been cancelling in droves. It's like the hotel's been cursed, and all because of that fire!'

And, sad as she was for the Buckingham, Mrs Brogan could not have been better pleased with how her boy provided.

Frank was dying to get down on the ground and play toy trains with Patrick, but as he slurped up his cocoa, Mr Brogan came to sit beside him, a steaming cup of his wife's famous soup in his hands. It was what he had every morning – a lovely, thick, vegetable broth cooked with her own rich chicken stock.

'Hard times at your Buckingham then, son?'

Frank nodded. 'They've cancelled the New Year Ball. Mr Charles had to write to King George *personally*. That's what Raymond told Nancy, and he ought to know.'

'And he's all right, is he, your Raymond?'

Frank nodded. 'Dr Moore came and looked over all the dancers. He said it's a good job the ballroom's had to be closed, because none of them ought to be dancing for a while. Well, they need to let their lungs recover. But Raymond's all right. It's Hélène who was shaken up the most.'

'A delicate flower, if what Billy says is to be believed.'

What Billy said, Frank was slowly learning, was never to be *entirely* believed – and the idea that Billy described Miss Marchmont as a 'delicate flower' made Frank furrow his brow, bewildered. Delicate? Hélène had always struck him as composed, elegant and graceful – but, more than anything, as *strong*.

'It could have been so much worse,' said Frank, 'if it hadn't been for Raymond—'

'You told him yet?' interjected Billy.

Frank turned, to find Billy coming out of the kitchen with a big slab of his mother's apple pie on a plate.

'Well, it's Christmas, isn't it?' Billy added, tucking in as he sat down.

'Told me what?' Mr Brogan interjected.

Frank looked between the two of them, panic stirring in his eyes. 'It's n-nothing.'

'Sure it is,' said Billy. 'Go on, Frank. My old man won't bite you. It's like I said – he's a worldly sort. He'll know what to do.'

Frank felt himself trapped – but then, the same feeling had been stealing up on him for weeks, ever since Billy sent him

294

eavesdropping in the Queen Mary. A big part of him thought he ought to walk straight up to Hélène Marchmont and tell her what he'd heard, but it all seemed so preposterous, and he'd never quite found the courage.

I never had worries like this back in Lancashire . . .

'Well?' Mr Brogan intoned.

'The th-thing is, Mr Brogan, I'm not sure where to . . . start. A little while ago, B-Billy here asked me to—'

'Frank here had to do a little job for me in the Queen Mary, Pa. That's the finest of all the Buckingham restaurants.'

'And I heard some guests talking.'

'Nazi types, Pa. Fascists.'

Mr Brogan's face creased up in anger.

'They were talking about a man we know. A man named Arthur Regan. He's been coming to the Buckingham – all on account of Hélène Marchmont.'

'I see,' mused Mr Brogan, letting his wife's soup steam up his face. 'He and Miss Marchmont are—'

'He takes her for dinner,' Billy chipped in. 'She comes back . . . buoyant.'

Mr Brogan considered this carefully. Then, only too aware that he was speaking to two young men yet to truly understand the meaning of the word, he whispered, 'Love?'

Frank nodded. 'I think so.'

'This Regan, what was his connection to your guests?'

'See, Pa, that's where I thought you could come in. Arthur Regan swans around, telling everyone he's a man of charity. He's raising wealth, he says, to help folks like us – the London Irish. But these guests of ours, they had him down as a Republican man. They were talking about Republicans petitioning the Reich!

An alliance, in case there's a war. And, Pa, they were talking about sabotage . . . against London!'

Mr Brogan put down his soup. 'Boys, this is a very serious charge.'

'We're just saying it how Frank heard it. Aren't we, Frankie?'

Frank nodded, feverish.

'You lads are too young to remember the war, of course.' Mr Brogan saw the way they were looking at him and went on. 'I don't speak of the Great War, of course. I mean the War for Independence. In 1916, before either of you scamps was born, the Irish rose up, did what they'd been hankering after for generations – to cast off the English. Well, it was bloody, boys, but – after a little while – they got what they wanted. Almost . . . The year after you was born, Billy, Ireland got its Home Rule. Or, most of it did. The folks in the north, they stayed with the king. They stayed with Britain. And ever since that moment, there's been *elements* fighting the war, as if we never came to terms. Blowing things up. Killings, where there shouldn't be any. Shooting at English lords, and all because of who they are and what they stand for.' Mr Brogan paused. 'It makes me ashamed. Ashamed of my countrymen. Ashamed of the blight they visit on the rest of us.' He stopped again, managing to rein in his anger. 'It's Christmas, boys. We must think of kinder things. But if this Arthur Regan truly is who you think he is, if he really is involved with the Irish Republican Army, with men who'd kill and maim, well, you boys know better than to keep it to yourselves. Your hotel's been through enough lately.'

'Arthur Regan was meant to be coming back at New Year,' said Billy, 'but now that the ball's not happening.'

'Well, when's he due?'

Billy shrugged, but his father's face remained impassive.

'You boys need to tell somebody, before he comes back – before he steals Miss Marchmont's heart away. She needs to hear it from somebody who cares about her, so don't go bouldering up to her and announcing it in front of everyone. But, boys, she *does* need to know. Miss Marchmont, she's one of the good people. There's too few of them in this world. They need protecting, boys. So I think you know what to do . . .'

At the exact same moment that Mr Brogan was proclaiming Hélène Marchmont's good name, Hélène herself sat cross-legged beneath the boughs of a tiny Christmas tree in a Brixton terrace, while Maurice Archer coaxed last night's embers back into flames in the hearth. In her lap, Sybil strained at the crêpe paper wrapping and ribbon of yet another present. The wasteland of paper and string around them was a testament to how much she was loved. Presents had come from Maurice and Noelle, from her uncles and aunts – and, last of all, from Hélène herself. She'd been anticipating Christmas morning for so many weeks, making quick trips to Hamleys on Regent Street. But the one thing she hadn't anticipated was being here herself.

She had the ballroom fire to thank for that. *To every cloud, a silver lining.* Even though days had passed, she could still feel the ache in her lungs – could even, sometimes, taste the smoke in the back of her throat. But at least she was here, and it was Christmas morning, and Sybil's presents were scattered around. She could be grateful for that.

The Archer household was always so full of light at Christmas. It was not only the flames that leaped and danced in the hearth.

It was not only the lights they strung up. Hélène believed the place simply radiated with love and warmth. It had been some years since she last ventured back to her parents' country estate outside Rye, but none of her memories of it were as vivid and homely as this.

I feel like a different person when I'm here. I feel like . . . me.

Noelle was in the kitchen, busy preparing a feast in anticipation of the rest of her family's arrival. Hélène had offered, more than once, to go and help her – but Noelle would hear nothing of it.

'You have so little time with Sybil, Hélène. Make every second of it count.'

'Here,' said Maurice, lifting a package of brown paper and ribbon, 'there's one you missed, young lady!'

Hélène took the present in her lap and, as Sybil crawled inquisitively near, looked at the tag.

For Sybil Archer
All the love in this world and many others
Louis Kildare

Hélène had a feeling she could not articulate ghosting through her. Her heart was buoyed to see Louis's name, to know she and Sybil were not forgotten. And yet . . . it had been two months since Louis vanished from the Buckingham. The boys in the orchestra said he'd turned up at the Midnight Rooms. But Hélène had heard not a word, and somehow it continued to sting.

'Sybil.' She grinned. 'Let's see what Uncle Louis sent, shall we?'

Hélène helped her tease back the corners, but Sybil brushed her hands aside and tore eagerly at the packaging herself. In the end, Hélène had to sneak her hands in and help wherever she could – until, at last, the paper unfurled.

'A parrot?' Hélène wondered, squinting at the embroidered bird that had been wrapped up. 'An . . . eagle?'

'Chicken!' Sybil announced. 'Chicken!'

Hélène had never seen a chicken with scarlet plumage and green zigzags on its wings, but the delight on Sybil's face was absolute.

'Let's call her Chicken, shall we?' Hélène began – and then, suddenly up on her feet, she began to squawk around the room like a chicken.

'Even as a chicken you're graceful!' Maurice roared as, replacing the fireguard, he tramped out of the living room to help Noelle in the kitchen.

Hélène danced around, turning on the spot, to shrieks of delight from Sybil. Soon, she had tempted Sybil up on to the tips of her toes, and twirled her around – just like she might some unconfident dancer on the floor of the Grand. It was only later, as Sybil demanded more and more dance, that Hélène began feeling the tightness in her chest. Dr Evelyn Moore had warned her of this; the effects of the smoke that had blackened her insides would not easily be driven away.

So, 'I'm sorry, Sybil,' she said – and, helping Sybil back to the deep pile of the rug, she sank into one of the armchairs, closed her eyes and recovered her breath.

Some time later, she was not sure how long – it might have been mere seconds – she opened her eyes . . . and there was Sybil, her face pressed up against the fireguard, head bobbing in fascination to the dancing flames.

'No!' Hélène shrieked.

The tightness was still in her chest, but she threw herself across the room, and scooped Sybil into her arms. In a fever, she checked the girl's face, her naked arms, her naked legs – and, though there was not a mark on her, Hélène's heart beat wildly.

What if . . . ?

She'd been keeping the thought at bay, but now it thundered down upon her. She'd first felt it in the chaos backstage, as she beat her fists at the door and screamed out Raymond's name.

If I die here, she'd thought, *what then? What happens to Sybil? If I'm not alive to send money back into Brixton . . .*

She cradled Sybil, swallowed down the urge to reprimand her. She was only a toddler. She had no idea.

'Maurice,' she called out. 'Noelle? Has Sybil . . . ?'

With Sybil in her arms, she headed past the glittering tree and down the hallway towards the narrow, galley kitchen at its end. Strange, how there was so little conversation coming from beyond the kitchen door.

In the kitchen, where the air was heavy with sage and onion, Maurice and Noelle stood together.

'Noelle, she's started playing with the fire. Maybe . . .'

Hélène stopped. There was something wrong. She saw, now, that Maurice and Noelle were deep in contemplation, lingering over a single piece of paper between them.

A letter.

Hélène's heart imploded.

Before she knew what she was doing, she reached out and plucked the letter directly from Noelle's hand. There was no need to read it; Hélène had read it a dozen times before. She'd been gazing over it in the taxicab that brought her to Maurice and Noelle's front door. By the way it was folded, they'd only read the first page. She let her eyes gaze back over it now.

Dearest Hélène,

News has reached me of the devastation wreaked at the Buck-ingham Hotel. Please know that my heart goes out to you and your fellows. Know, too, how devastated I am that there is to be no New Year's Ball — and that you are not to introduce me, humble Irish peasant that I am, to the good King George! In light of these events, I will remain on the Emerald Isle to ring in the New Year with friends from the older days. But my business will bring me back to London early in the New Year — Michael Fitzgerald and I have such big things planned, things London society will never forget! — and I should be honoured if I could dance with you again. If the Grand is to remain out of commission, perhaps the silver lining for us is that you, too, remain out of work? Might an expedition to the ballroom at the Savoy be in order? Or might you even know of some more magical corner where we can . . .

She stepped back. She'd already seen the looks on their faces. They'd read enough, she was certain, to know what was happening in her life.

'Maurice moved your fur,' Noelle began, mortified. 'Hélène, it fell from your pocket . . .'

Hélène strained at the page. 'Noelle, you had no right.'

'Hélène . . .'

She held the squirming Sybil in her arms and marched back into the living room. Here the fire still flickered. Here the tree still glittered, reflecting the orange light. Here the table was laid: not just for the four of them, but for six, seven, eight – all of Sybil's aunts and uncles coming for Christmas Day. Hélène turned. She wanted to walk straight out of the door. She wanted to feel the snow upon her face.

She wanted the time and space to breathe.

She could hear footsteps behind her. Maurice and Noelle were lingering in the kitchen passage. She could almost *hear* how nervous they were of approaching.

A hundred thoughts cascaded through her.

Why are you so angry, Hélène?

No, she thought, *it isn't anger, it's . . .*

It's shame.

You're ashamed.

But, Hélène, you've no need to be ashamed.

What must they think of me? she asked herself. Slowly, by degrees, she turned around. *What are you going to do now, Hélène? Walk out of here? Leave Sybil behind? Or . . . take her with you? Take her away from the only true home she's known, on Christmas Day?*

Life was never supposed to be like this. It was supposed to be Hélène and Sidney and Sybil and . . .

No, she thought – and found herself being as stern with herself as any of her dance tutors had ever been with her – *life's about looking forward, not back. And, no matter what's next, Maurice and Noelle, they're your family. So whatever they're feeling, whatever you're feeling, this is it. This is Christmas Day. And it mustn't be ruined. For Sybil . . .*

She turned. Maurice and Noelle were standing there with their eyes wide open. But they were not about to admonish her. They were, she thought, *scared*.

'Come on, Sybil,' Hélène said, though her lips were tight, 'shall we help Grandma and Grandpa set the table?'

Later that day, as Hélène laid her daughter down in the crib she was getting too big for, and sang a lullaby to coax her into a nap, Noelle appeared in the doorway.

'Noelle,' Hélène whispered sadly, when Sybil was finally asleep. 'I didn't want you to see that. I'm sorry that I overreacted. It's only that . . .'

There was a moment when Noelle might have either turned and fled or broken down and cried. Instead she very gently, and very deliberately, folded her arms around Hélène.

'Shush, dear,' she said, 'shush, now.'

At first Hélène was brittle but, moments later, she melted into Noelle's arms.

Still clasping her, Noelle whispered, 'You're the most beautiful girl, Hélène, inside and out. One day, somebody else was going to fall in love with you. One day, you were going to fall in love again.'

'I don't know what's right,' Hélène said. 'I don't know what life looks like for her if I'm alone, and I don't know what life looks like for her if I'm . . . not.'

Noelle's breath was warm in her ear. Though Hélène couldn't see, she was certain she was smiling.

'That's life, my precious girl. That's what you have to find out. It's all just life, Hélène. All the good and the bad and the grey bits in between. We're all born. We all die. And we have to colour the bit in the middle with the brightest colours we can. Sybil's fine. She's always going to be fine. But she deserves a mother who's happy and . . . yes, even in love!'

Hélène drew back, so that she might look in Noelle's eyes. 'Would he hate me, Noelle, if he's up there, looking down?'

'Hate?' Noelle smiled. 'My beautiful Hélène, he'd be beaming from ear to ear, egging you on! Just promise me one thing.'

'Anything.'

'Promise me he's a good man.'

Hélène traced the line of Noelle's cheek with her finger.

'I believe he's one of the very best . . .'

Chapter Thirty-one

I T WAS GROWING DARK AS Raymond and Nancy walked arm in arm through the streets of Lambeth.

By the time they reached the Brogans' terrace, the snow was falling once more. The streets sparkled with crystals of white, the lamplight spilling perfect circles onto the ice. The rippling snowflakes made even Lambeth look like a dream.

'We could just carry on walking.' Raymond grinned. 'Just you and me.'

Nancy had to admit it was tempting. They'd walked down through St James's Park, around the palaces at Westminster, where every tree was wearing its own crown of white, and as they'd come they hadn't spoken of Georges de la Motte and the Hollywood Hills; they hadn't spoken of Vivienne Edgerton and the Daughters of Salvation; they'd spoken only of Frank and Billy, of a house full of children, of the strange opportunity the decimation at the hotel had granted them – to spend a Christmas together, like this: a glimpse – or so Nancy hoped – of things to come.

'I always wished Frank and I had had some more brothers and sisters,' Nancy admitted, as they reached the Brogan house. Lights were lit in all of its many windows, and from within they could hear the raucous sounds of play. 'Frank would have been an excellent big brother.'

'I think he already is,' said Raymond.

Nancy followed his finger and saw, played out in silhouette in one of the lower windows, Frank chasing a line of children, a toy aeroplane in his hand.

'He'll always be nine years old in my heart!'

They had to knock three times to be heard over the high jinks. When the door finally did draw back, Nancy saw a lady with her red hair tied back in a ribbon, her apron smeared in gravy and grease. She had kind eyes, Nancy thought – just like Billy Brogan.

'Nancy!' she beamed – though they had not once laid eyes on each other before. 'And you must be – why, yes, Mr Raymond de Guise! Oh, come in, come in! We've heard so much about you!'

Nancy looked at Raymond. Raymond looked at Nancy. The sparkle in their eyes told it all: this, they both understood, was going to be a treat as magnificent as any Christmas Day spent at the Buckingham Hotel. So, clasping hands, they walked inside.

They had barely taken off their coats, when a rabble of miniature Billy Brogans – some in pigtails, some with hair that steadfastly refused to be tidied – poured out of the living room. Behind them was Frank.

'Hey, Nance!' he cried out. 'Children, gather round! This is Nancy, my big sister, the best sister in all the world!'

At this, the children went wild. One of them grabbed Nancy by the hand.

'Come and see my new pony!' she cried, heaving Nancy bodily into the living room – where a tree was decorated with home-made paper stars and tinsel, and two mismatched tables had been pushed together and laid out with crockery, ready for dinner. A great fire spat in the hearth, and toys and books were scattered across the floorboards.

Yes, this was Christmas, thought Nancy – just the way it was supposed to be.

Dinner was served, and never was a finer meal had – not even in the Queen Mary. Nancy thought she had never tasted a finer roast potato, dripping in duck fat and salt, and if sage and onion stuffing was not a regular accompaniment to two fat baked salmon, she still judged it a taste sensation. At first, the Brogan children had better manners than most of the lords and ladies who stayed at the Buckingham. They folded their hands to say grace, and politely passed buttered parsnips and carrots back and forth. Only when the sausages wrapped in bacon, with a sage leaf tucked inside each, came out of the oven did the squabbling begin. Nancy was proud to see Frank leap to attention at Mrs Brogan's request, and soon, whatever squabbling had begun was over as faces were lowered to plates, or forks were used like shovels: the Brogan children enjoying the cast-offs from the Buckingham like it was the finest meal on earth. Nancy and Raymond had brought crackers with them, and soon miniature explosions were happening all around the table, and trinkets being exchanged.

At last, conversation turned to darker things.

'We were devastated to hear about the fire at your hotel,' Mr Brogan said, picking a salmon bone out of his teeth.

'The whole of the backstage destroyed,' Raymond said, 'and it reached out into the ballroom itself before the firemen could fight it back. There's smoke damage in the restaurant above as well. But Mr Charles is holding things together, you can be sure of that.'

Perhaps Billy thought he was being defensive, because suddenly he chirruped up, 'Mr Charles could hold things together if there was an earthquake, Pa. A little fire isn't anything, not to Mr Charles. See, he might have had to cancel the New Year Ball, but it's not as if plans aren't afoot. It's the Buckingham! Plans are *always* afoot!'

'What kind of plans?' asked Mrs Brogan, stopping only to slap Roisin's hand with the back of a spoon as it darted for the very last roast potato – which she duly offered up to Raymond.

'We won't have the ballroom, so we'll have to make do,' said Raymond, accepting the potato and secretly passing it back to Roisin under the table. 'Yesterday morning, Mr Charles called the heads of department together. The ballroom's lost, for three months we think, and we can't use the French bistro, but there's still the Candlelight Club, the Queen Mary, the reading room, the smoking room ... Anywhere that's not a room or a suite, anywhere guests might gather, we'll be putting on a show. There'll be singers and harpists. Hélène and I, we'll drink and dine with the guests. We'll do whatever we can to make it a night to remember.'

'But all your guests ... they'll decamp for the Savoy, the Ritz, the Imperial, won't they?'

At mention of the Imperial Hotel, Raymond flinched.

'Some of them have,' he admitted. 'But there are only six rooms out of commission. We can cope with that. It's the damage to our reputation that hits us hardest. People don't like to think of the Buckingham as being unsafe – or, worse, cursed.'

There'd been little heard of John Hastings since the flames had devastated the ballroom. Word was his people had gone directly to the Imperial, to sift back through its finances and decide upon

308

the value of the offer they would be making to its board – but, after that, there had only been silence.

'Sometimes,' said Raymond, with a suddenly serious tone, 'I feel like that fire has been coming all year. It's like the whole of the Buckingham's been on borrowed time, ever since I set foot back on English soil.'

'What do you mean, Raymond?' asked Nancy.

'Well, those burglaries earlier in the year. Abner Grant, the hotel detective, lurking on every corner. The new financier. All this talk of wars to come. Doesn't it feel like . . . fate?'

For a time, there was silence around the dining table. Then, Mr Brogan pitched forward.

'That fire, Mr de Guise, that wasn't fate. That was—'

At that moment, there came an almighty crash. Every eye at the table turned to Billy's sister, Gracie May, who – in the attempt to snatch the last carrots from the bowl – had stumbled back, bringing the gravy boat with her. Now, mired in a flood of luke-warm brown liquid, she sank, sobbing, to the floor.

'Well,' said Nancy, as Mrs Brogan scooped Gracie May up and began to sponge her clean, 'that's that. I've had quite enough of all this doom and gloom! It's Christmas! So . . .' Her eyes had found the fiddle propped up in the corner. 'Mr Brogan?' she said. 'Yours?'

'My old man's, from back in the day. I can scratch out a tune or two.'

'And, look,' Nancy said, seeing one of the children's tambour-ines on the floor by the tree, 'there's music in this house, if you know where to look. And we've got the best, most handsome dancer in London at our side!'

Raymond grinned. 'I'm not sure I deserve quite that accolade, Nancy.'

Nancy flashed her eyes at him. 'I was talking about Frank.'

All around the table, faces opened in laughter – or flushed with embarrassment – or both, in equal measure.

Then the festivities truly began.

Mr Brogan was no slouch at the fiddle, and soon he had found a melody that he remembered. Frank worked hard to line up the Brogan children and instruct them in the melody of 'I Told Santa Claus To Bring You Me', which the Archie Adams Orchestra had been playing every Christmas since Bernie Cummins first recorded it in 1931. After that, there was 'Good King Wenceslas' and 'God Rest Ye Merry Gentlemen' – until, a little while later (and after Raymond had taken Mr Brogan into the corner for a secret conference) a strange string version of last Christmas's 'Swingin' Them Jingle Bells' began.

'Watch me for the changes, Frank!' said Raymond – and heaved him bodily into the square of carpet around the hearth, where the tables and chairs had been cleared away.

As Raymond and Frank jived, bodies bumping up and down, Nancy gathered the Brogan children around her, clapping in time and singing along.

Jingle bells, jingle bells.
Jingle all the way!
O what fun it is to ride
In a one-horse open sleigh!

Raymond turned to Nancy, holding out his hand, and whispered, 'Shall we?' – and before she knew it, she too was on the makeshift dance floor. There was hardly enough room to move, but she swept up one of the girls and twirled her around. Probably this was not the jive. Probably this was not the jitterbug.

Whatever it is, Nancy thought, *it's . . . joy! Pure and unadulterated Christmas joy. The joy we've been crying out for all year. And here it is. Right here. Right now.*

There came a knocking at the door. Vaguely, Nancy wondered if it was one of the neighbours, determined to come and join in the raucous family fun. Mrs Brogan slipped away to answer it, while in the living room the song wailed on.

Nancy felt a tapping on her shoulder and turned. At first she could not hear what Mrs Brogan was saying, but then Mrs Brogan cupped her hands around her lips and called out, 'It's a taxicab! He says it's for you.'

The music stopped.

Nancy turned, her eyes searching out the clock on the wall. The hour hand was inching towards nine o'clock. She spun around, gripped Raymond by the shoulders.

'Raymond, I've got to . . .'

She was scurrying towards the hallway when Raymond tore himself out of the song and hurried to join her.

'Nancy, what's happening?'

'It's the taxicab. I didn't see the time!'

'The taxicab? The—'

'You remember,' she said, only going on when she saw his crestfallen face. In the hallway, the front door was hanging ajar, letting stray flakes of snow flutter in. She reached for her scarf, tightened it hurriedly around her neck. 'I'm due at the Daughters. The taxicab, he's one of the Buckingham regulars. You won't believe how hard I had to fight to get him to come out on Christmas Day. Well, Miss Edgerton's paying, of course.'

Raymond's mind reeled back. So much of what Nancy had said this year was about her work in Whitechapel. He felt a prickling, somewhere behind his eyes. Couldn't there be one day, just one, when they might laugh and dance together like they used to? Suddenly, his mind went back to last Christmas – how they'd danced together, down below stairs at the Buckingham, and he'd taken her in his arms and known she was his, his alone. That feeling of having her and loving her and being loved in return – why did it suddenly feel it had slipped out of his grasp?

He put the thought away, swallowed it down, forced out a laugh.

'You do know, we haven't even had dessert.'

'Figgy pudding can wait!' She laughed. 'Save me a slice, won't you? Or, on second thoughts, don't worry – you'll never keep a slice safe from that lot in there.'

She was almost skipping, Raymond thought, as she reached the door. She was halfway out, into the cascading snow, when he tried to take her hand.

'Nancy, it's . . . Christmas.'

'I know,' she said, only half turning. 'They need *somebody*, Raymond. Miss Edgerton's out in Suffolk with her stepfather – well, she could hardly go down, could she? Not if her stepfather might find out. And . . . all the volunteers, they've got Christmases too. It's only Mary Burdett, and Artie standing on the door.'

'Nancy,' he repeated, 'it's Christmas. *Our* Christmas . . .'

She pulled her hand away, tightened her coat at the collar. In the street outside, the taxicab's engine guttered.

'Those people deserve a Christmas too, Raymond. Look at us – we've got it all. And they—'

312

'Got it all?' Raymond breathed. 'I haven't got *you* . . .'

'Oh, Raymond, you're doing it again! You just don't understand, do you? I was patient with you, wasn't I? You were off, gallivanting all over California, and I sat and waited for your letters. I was *thrilled* you were doing something you needed to do. For *you*. For your . . . soul! I knew why it mattered.' She had said too much; her words were coming apart. 'Oh, Raymond, you've half a heart if you can't see what matters to me!'

In an instant, she was at the bottom of the steps, waving to the taxi driver. As she disappeared into the curtain of white, Raymond cried out, 'Nancy, wait! I could . . . I could come!'

She looked back once, her face illuminated in the street lamp hanging overhead.

'I don't want you to, Raymond!' she cried back. 'If you don't understand, there's nothing else to say.'

Raymond stood there in the doorway as the taxicab drove away. He stood until the tip of his nose felt as if it was turning blue, until Mrs Brogan implored him, from behind, to close the door and keep the warmth within. As he stepped back, he reached for the letter in his pocket.

Dear Raymond,

I am afraid of your silence, my boy! I have put myself in a precarious position, having promised your presence. Am I to understand that you will be with us come the New Year? Pre-production has begun on Stairway to the Stars. I pray that you are, even now, organising your prolonged absence from the Buckingham Hotel, preparing for this next glorious phase of your career . . .

Your loving friend and ally

Georges de la Motte

313

He'd received it the day after the fire. A part of him wished it too had gone up in smoke. But . . . Georges deserved his answer.

'Mr de Guise?' came a voice from behind. Raymond turned, to see Frank standing there. 'Is everything all right?'

Raymond was silent, so into the vacuum Frank went on.

'They're still singing, Mr de Guise. If we find the right song, we could sh-show them our jive!'

This, at least, brought a smile to Raymond's face: the thought of him and Frank jitterbugging about the living room, being careful not to collide with the table, Christmas tree, hearth or any one of the restless Brogan children.

'You need to try that jive out in the world now, Frankie boy. You need to get up the courage, finally ask Rosa out for the night . . .'

Frank's face turned a shameful shade of scarlet. 'I know,' he said. 'One day, Mr de Guise.'

An image flashed into Raymond's face: Nancy, in the back of the taxicab, bound for her own destination; Raymond, boarding an aeroplane and soaring into the sun, bound for quite another. He shook himself; he wasn't ready to deal with it yet. Her words had cut him to the bone.

'Come on, Frank,' he said, forcing himself to smile. 'It's a jitterbug Christmas. Let's show them what we've got!'

Chapter Thirty-two

HE'D BEEN THINKING ABOUT IT for weeks. Months, even. But thinking and doing, Frank was about to find out, are two completely different things.

He felt almost overcome as he approached the chambermaids' kitchenette and rapped his knuckles on the open door. As always, Nancy was nowhere to be found. She was probably out there in Whitechapel. Wherever she was, she was certainly not joining in with the New Year festivities about to begin in the kitchenette. With the New Year Ball cancelled, countless other little soirées were being planned, down in the housekeeping lounge, the Queen Mary larder and the bookkeeper's office. And, throughout the last week, Maynard Charles had been rallying his troops. Plans were afoot for an evening of songs and laughter in the Candlelight Club; Archie Adams, against doctor's orders, was to play the piano while a roster of guest singers crooned out the hits. The smoking room was to become a starlit buffet for the evening – with the stars of the ballroom bedecked in their finery and sashaying around, entertaining the crowd. Hélène Marchmont, Gene Sheldon and Raymond de Guise were already down there, charming their way from guest to guest. It was imperative, Maynard had declared, that the Buckingham be seen to soldier on.

'We might not have a ballroom tonight,' Mr Charles had declared, 'and the king himself might have forsaken us. But we, dear friends, will not forsake our guests. Let's make it a New Year to remember . . .'

A New Year to remember. Well, that was what Frank intended too. He reached into his pocket and fingered the two stubs lying there. It was Billy Brogan who'd given him the idea, Billy who'd got him the tickets too.

'Off one of the other concierges, who owed me a favour. These are rare as gold – I could've sold them for a pretty penny. But you got a job to do, don't you, Frank? And why not have a little fun with it at the same time?'

Fun, thought Frank. *Well, maybe I could have some fun tonight. If only I can get up the courage.*

There she was. In the kitchenette, Vera and Edie were lighting some candles, Ruth was filling a tin basin with water for apple bobbing – and Rosa was putting a record onto the gramophone player. Frank readied himself.

'Rosa,' he said. And, when nobody seemed to hear, he piped up again, 'Rosa?'

Perhaps he'd spoken too loudly – for, on this second 'Rosa', all eyes in the kitchenette turned and found him. His heart itself seemed to still. He fumbled in his pocket and brandished the two tickets towards her.

'I was w-wondering . . .' he stammered. 'That is to say . . .' He stopped. All of the blood in his body seemed to be rushing to his ears. 'I had such a n-nice time with you, on the day of the coronation—'

'Frank Nettleton!' one of the other girls shrieked. 'That was six months ago! Half a lifetime!'

316

'Nevertheless,' stuttered Frank, and held out the tickets.

To save him any further embarrassment, Rosa plucked the tickets out of his hand and studied them. Soon, the other girls had come to scrutinise them too.

'The Midnight Rooms!' Ruth exclaimed. 'Frankie, where'd you get these?'

Frank shrugged.

'They for us, are they?' Vera asked. 'Rosa, who're you gonna take? Me, Ruth or Edie?'

Rosa pressed the tickets back into his hand. Then, with a smile that gave even Frank courage, she said, 'I think they're Frank's tickets, to do with as he wants. Now, was there something you wanted to ask me, Frank?'

Frank whispered, 'Would you do me the—'

'A bit louder!' Vera chortled.

Frank's face felt so hot he was certain he'd start burning up. Rosa seemed to sense it too.

'I'd love to, Frank. I'd be honoured.' Then she turned to beam at the other girls. 'No apple bobbing for me tonight, girls! I'm going dancing!'

'It's not as *stately* as the Grand Ballroom in here, is it, Frank?'

'I don't think it's meant to be,' blushed Frank. 'That's the j-joy!'

It was scarcely six o'clock, and already the Midnight Rooms was alive. Frank and Rosa stood at the bottom of the black staircase and looked out at the couples cavorting on the dance floor. The tango was coming from a gramophone player, whose music could hardly be heard above the chatter.

The band must be starting soon, thought Frank. *Louis Kildare will be up there, with all of the rest. Somehow I just need to catch his eye.*

He looked sidelong at Rosa, who was still taking in the beautiful chaos.

'Come on, Rosa, let's get a seat before they're all taken!'

The Midnight Rooms was edged with a multitude of cubbyholes where lovers might sit, secluded from the dance floor, and Frank left Rosa hidden in one while he battled his way to the bar and came back with two glasses of spiced rum. Rosa looked impressed, but Frank saw her trying hard not to wince as she took her first sip. Frank smiled to himself; the truth was, he still hadn't acquired a taste for alcohol, either.

'You been here before, have you, Frank?'

'I can't say I have . . .'

'I shouldn't think you've been living the London high life, have you?'

'I've been busy.'

'Busy?'

Frank could hardly tell her that what he *really* enjoyed was rushing back to the Brogans' after his day at the Buckingham, tucking the children up in bed. Somehow, this seemed too unexciting. So instead he told her about his after-hours lessons with Raymond.

'I didn't think I'd get the hang of it at all. So at first it was just simple stuff – just a little box-stepping, a little footwork. Well, then things got a little adventurous. Mr de Guise, he discovered things in the clubs in America that even he hadn't danced before. So he showed me a little of those things too. The . . . the jitterbug, you see, it's freer, it's looser than the waltzes they perform in the Grand. It doesn't have the same kind of hold. Raymond said you just have to close your eyes and let it happen. That's the part I found most difficult. Just *believing*, I suppose. But, well, Raymond taught Nance to dance, didn't he?'

'I should think he wishes he was still teaching her! Your Nancy, she's had her head in other things since Mr de Guise got back from America, hasn't she? I should think dancing with you's nice enough, Frankie, but I'll bet he'd rather be dancing with your sister!'

'What about you?' Frank ventured. 'You must have done some dancing?'

'Well, there's a proper little dance hall where I'm from. Bell's, they call it. When I was sixteen, I used to go there with my sister. The finest place in all of Southend-on-Sea – right up on the cliff, looking down on the seafront.' Rosa grinned. 'But then London was calling, wasn't it? Adventures in the big city. Only, so far, my big adventure's turned out to be changing the sheets for dukes and earls and Heaven knows who else, so I haven't been dancing much, Frank. You'll have to show me what you got—'

Outside the alcove, an almighty cheer engulfed the Midnight Rooms. At the side of the tiny stage, a hidden door had opened and the bandleader – Jack Oliver, they called him – had stepped out to run his fingers up and down the upright piano. Next came his percussionist. Next, his trumpeters. A great, burly black musician tramped out next, waving his trombone to the crowd, and receiving rapturous applause in return. Then, last of all, came the face Frank had been eager to see: Louis Kildare.

'Ladies and gentlemen!' Jack Oliver cried out. 'Welcome to the Midnight Rooms! Your New Year extravaganza is about to begin!'

Her face wide with delight, Rosa squeezed past him, jumped down the step to the edge of the dance floor and looked back expectantly.

This is what you came for, Frank told himself. *If it was only about Mr Kildare, you could have come alone. But this is what*

you've been daring yourself to do ever since you crash-landed at
the Buckingham Hotel! You're here . . . with Rosa!

'Come on, Frank! You can show me what you've been learning!'

Rosa had extended her hand. Frank knew he ought to take it. He knew that Rosa even *wanted* him to. But something made him hesitate. It was that same little voice he'd had since he was tiny, telling him it was all a big joke, that the world was teasing him, that it would all be so much safer if he just stayed in his room and lined up his tin soldiers. It was Nancy who had always told him not to listen to that voice. So he plucked up the courage, took Rosa's hand, and together they stepped out onto the dance floor.

'And it goes something a little like this!'

The band had started the night sedately, charting a path from quickstep to foxtrot, and then sliding into a quieter waltz so that the dancers could catch their breath.

But they were only just getting started.

The first sign of how wild the Midnight Rooms could be came when the band broke into 'I Stole the Gal (Who Was Stolen From Me)', which Jack Oliver introduced with a wicked smile. This quickstep, which had the dance floor turning and spinning with carefree abandon, morphed into something even more dramatic with the first rumba of the evening. Frank and Rosa shared a speechless look when the girl next to them wrapped her legs around her partner's waist. They called this song 'Dance Delores', and – between the bobbing heads of the crowd – Frank saw Louis weaving back and forth, his saxophone leading the melody, then beating a retreat, then bursting forth to dominate the song all over again.

It took Frank a few songs to find his feet. It took Rosa even longer – but she didn't seem to mind. Perhaps, he thought, just being here was enough. It was only when he closed his eyes that his body truly remembered what to do. He kept them firmly shut as he tried to inhabit the moves Raymond had shown him.

'Frank, what's *that*?'

Frank opened his eyes and laughed. 'It's what Raymond showed me!'

'The jive?'

Frank grinned.

'Is it a jiving song, Frank?'

'I don't know.' He shrugged. 'But . . . I think anything *can* be a jive. You've just got to want to do it.'

He took Rosa's hands and closed his eyes.

'Try not to focus, that's what Raymond said. He said the perfect moment is when you're in time and not thinking about it at all.' That's *heaven*, he had said. The dancer's heaven, right there. 'Come on, Rosa, let's go!'

Rosa was game, so Frank took her in an open hold and, closing his eyes to the music, leaned into the dance. At first, they started gently. Then, something took hold of Frank and he stepped it up. With his eyes closed, he could never be certain if Rosa was keeping up – but he led the dance as well as he could and, by the touch and feel of it, everything seemed to be working. He dared to spin Rosa round – and nobody ended up in a tangle of arms and legs on the floor, so that had to count for something. And . . .

I'm enjoying it! he thought, with ridiculous relief. *I'm actually enjoying myself!*

They danced on. He'd been practising the moves alone in Billy's bedroom for months. It seemed such a short step to dance it in the Midnight Rooms as couples frolicked on every side. And, at last, he truly understood what Raymond had meant: there really was a heaven of sorts; somewhere between the music and the dance, there existed a whole other world. He was soaring through it now.

The song came to its explosive finale, but Frank was so swept up that he hardly noticed – not even after the last note was finished, and he and Rosa were still dancing. It was only when the silence overcame him that he opened his eyes. Somewhere in the middle of the dance, the whole dance floor had cleared. Now, it was only Frank and Rosa alone in the middle of the floor – and every eye in the Midnight Rooms was upon them.

Frank whirled around, mortified. But every face that he took in was open in pure, unadulterated joy. Smiles stretched from ear to ear. Then, all of a sudden, hands were raised in applause. Whistles screeched out. Up on the stage, Louis Kildare beamed – and then the band leader, Jack Oliver, got to his feet, peered down into the crowd, and said, 'If you liked that one, young man, we've another that's going to blow a hole in your world! Midnight Rooms, let's see if you can dance until you drop, like . . . What's your name, son?'

Frank felt petrified.

If only the music would start again. Then I can pretend I'm Raymond de Guise, jitterbugging and jiving in a Harlem club.

'I'm Frank,' he finally piped up. 'F-Frank Nettleton.'

'Not tonight, Frank!' announced Jack. 'Tonight you're the . . . King of the Midnight Rooms! Now, everybody, dance on!'

The next song began thundering: 'Dance Until You Drop'. By now, Rosa seemed to understand the basics that Raymond had spent so long teaching him. All you really had to do was let the rhythm infect your feet, and the rest took care of itself. She was a much more talented student than Frank himself had been. The trick, Frank decided, was just *letting go* . . .

Rosa beamed. 'Frankie, look at them all!'

Frank dared to look up. This time, the Midnight Rooms had not come to a standstill. This time, couples filled the dance floor – and not a classical ballroom hold among them. Palm to palm, lovers faced each other. Somebody twirled somebody else around.

'It's a real jive!' Frank laughed. 'If only Raymond could see us now!'

At last, the song came to an end – and the applause that went up was not only for the band up on stage. Even the musicians were on their feet and cheering. Rosa threw her arms around Frank's neck.

'It's all for you, Frankie!' she laughed, and Frank thought he had never heard a more glorious sound. It was so glorious he didn't even feel embarrassed. 'King of the Midnight Rooms indeed! They'll have you in the Grand Ballroom next!'

'Oh, give over!' he said, wriggling out of her embrace. 'Come on, Rosa, it looks like the band are taking a break. Let's get ourselves a drink.'

In the end, neither Frank nor Rosa were quick enough to reach the bar. As soon as the musicians took their bows, the entire dance floor descended on the poor bartenders. Frank couldn't help cringing every time some other reveller clapped him on the back and implored him to show them what he'd learned.

I can't be that good! he told himself. *A few months ago, why, I could hardly box-step!* But a little part of him, he realised, was thrilling with pride. *Wait until I tell Nance! It feels good to be a natural at something.*

He was enjoying the thought when a familiar voice boomed out.

'Frank Nettleton, as I live and breathe. What's possessing you tonight, boy?'

There, looking as if he couldn't stop smiling, stood Louis Kildare.

'Mr Kildare,' he stammered, 'I'm so p-p-pleased to see you. You must know Rosa—'

'Charmed!' Rosa exclaimed, grabbing Louis by the hand.

'Happy New Year to you, Frank. You look like you've been learning a few tricks from Raymond de Guise. How's the Buckingham faring without me? I heard Archie Adams found a new saxophonist . . .'

Frank nodded, more meekly than any King of the Midnight Rooms should have been allowed.

'They all say he's not a patch on you, sir.'

Louis's face turned stern. 'I heard about the fire, Frank. I was glad that no one was hurt.'

'Well, see, that's one of the reasons I came—'

Rosa looked wounded. '*One* of the reasons, Frankie?'

'Well, I wanted to take Rosa dancing. I been wanting to for months! But . . .' Frank screwed his eyes up, looking puzzled at Louis. 'How long have you got until the band's back on? I think I need to buy you a drink, Mr Kildare.'

There was no quiet area in the Midnight Rooms, not tonight – so, after he'd forced his way to the bar and bought three glasses of sweet, sticky rum, Frank followed Louis into the small room behind the stage, where the rest of the musicians were catching their breath.

'Backstage!' Rosa gasped, taking in the posters of older musicians on the walls. 'Frank, you know how to give a girl a memorable New Year.'

Louis pulled up a chair and Frank was grateful to sit down.

'It's aw-awfully good of you, Mr Kildare. You see, I didn't know who else to come to. And Billy, he said you were the man.'

Louis tapped the rim of Frank's glass. 'Drink up, Frank. It sounds like you need it.'

The rum burned as it went down, but once he'd stopped wincing, Frank had to admit that it did fill him with new strength.

'Louis, it's about Miss Marchmont.'

Louis froze, his glass halfway to his lips.

'If Hélène sent you—'

'No!' Frank exclaimed. 'Miss Marchmont doesn't know I'm here. I didn't dare speak to her, Mr Kildare. She's too *grand* for the likes of me. But . . .'

Louis still had not taken a drink. 'Spit it out, Frank. You're worrying me now.'

'Miss Marchmont, she's been spending time with a gentleman by the name of—'

'Arthur Regan,' said Louis, with a distant kind of sadness that Frank did not fully understand.

'Well, the thing is, Mr Kildare, Arthur Regan isn't the kind of man he says he is. He says he's a charitable man, a benefactor. But he's not that kind of man at all.'

'What kind of man *is* he?'

'He's a . . . soldier, of sorts. He raises funds and plots with the Irish Republican Army.'

Louis was still for a few moments.

'Frank,' he said, 'you need to tell me everything you know.'

Frank took a deep breath.

This is it, Frank. This is what you came here to do.

At that moment, he felt Rosa – who had been idling at the edges of the room, staring at the posters up on the walls – drop her arms around his shoulders, bend in low and whisper in his ear, 'The band are getting ready again, Frank. Come on, I want to see more of your dancing.'

Frank looked around. The rest of the band did seem to be getting ready. One of them called out for Louis, as they hurriedly finished their drinks – but Louis was still staring directly at Frank.

'He'll be with you shortly, Rosa.' Then he called out, 'I'll be with you shortly, gentlemen. There'll be no music until we're finished here.'

Jack Oliver and the rest of the band shared quizzical looks, but seemed happy to wait.

'Rosa, please,' Louis uttered – and she drifted back off, plucking up the courage to speak to the rest of the band.

'Go on, Frank.'

'It's like this, Mr Kildare. There were men in the Queen Mary. German men. *Nazi* men. And they were talking with the Italian ambassador, all about how the Irish Republicans want to make war on England again, just like it was twenty years ago. And how, if there's war in Europe, that's the moment the Irish Republican Army will strike. They're calling it their "Sabotage Plan". And that's when they mentioned Mr Regan. How he and a Mr Fitzgerald are like scouts. Raising funds, getting things ready, and all for something catastrophic—'

'Catastrophic like what?' Louis uttered.

'Well, the Irish Republicans tried to kill the king, didn't they? In Belfast, last year.' Frank paused. 'And—'

'And?' Louis reached out for Frank and gently angled his face so that he had to look Louis directly in the eye. 'It's important, Frank. Miss Marchmont, she's one of the world's most special people. She's one of the treasures – not just of the Buckingham Hotel, but . . .' Now it was Louis's turn to clam up. In the end he had to force the words out. '. . . of God's green earth. So whatever it is, you'd better—'

'It's just an idea, but . . . the fire, Mr Kildare. The fire that ripped through the ballroom, that might even have brought down the Buckingham. A fire can start by accident in a kitchen, can't it? But in a ballroom? Somebody had to start that fire. And somebody had locked the back dressing room doors. It's a miracle everyone came out of it alive. What if that's what Arthur Regan has been planning all along, a little something to get their Sabotage Plan started? To choke a few lords and ladies in a ballroom fire? To . . . send a message to all the English gentry?'

The stage door opened, and the raucous cheering from outside rose to a deafening roar.

'Louis!' one of the other musicians called back. 'Our glory awaits!'

Louis looked up at a clock hanging on the wall. The hands were inching towards eleven. One more hour and they'd ring in the New Year together, the Midnight Rooms erupting into a glorious, ragtime 'Auld Lang Syne'.

'Frank, go and dance with your girl.' At this, Rosa – who was standing impatiently by the door – suddenly perked up. 'You did the right thing tonight. Never forget that.'

Then Frank was up on his feet, reaching out and taking Rosa's hand. This time, he realised, he wasn't nervous at all.

'What are you going to do, Mr Kildare?'

Louis swallowed hard. 'I'm going to do what I should have done before I left the Buckingham,' he said, with a sad, faraway look in his eyes. 'I'm going to speak to Hélène Marchmont.'

January 1938

Chapter Thirty-three

THE DOORS TO THE GRAND Ballroom opened, and in the rush of air that erupted out came all the smells of smoke and devastation that Maynard Charles had come to despise.

With his hands folded behind his back, Maynard guided Lord Edgerton through, and down onto the dance floor – where Raymond de Guise stood, surveying the wreckage alone.

A photographer could have made a mystery of this. Were someone to train their camera lens in one direction, they might have seen only a ballroom in its prime. But, if they were to turn around, to face the stage and the dressing room doors, they would have seen a charred, black ruin. It was into this deathly portal that Raymond now stared.

He hardly shifted as Maynard and Lord Edgerton passed him, heading to that frontier where the dance floor turned to pitted black holes. He hardly noticed as they crossed the frontier and disappeared into the black cavern.

In the ruin of the dressing room, Lord Edgerton tried to hold his breath.

'Royal Insurance have already sent their loss adjusters, sir – but, of course, you know our problem.'

Lord Edgerton seethed. 'They dare to call it *arson* in my hotel. I've dealt with these people before, Mr Charles. Renegades, every last one. They're happy to take your money and make you promises – but, when the very thing they've insured you against happens, they do almost anything within their power not to live up to their responsibilities.'

'Indeed, sir.'

'Arson, in *my* hotel!'

Maynard stopped himself from replying: there was little doubt that this had been a deliberate act. Only the loss adjusters could tell the full story: how a small cask of Pernod anise, perhaps purloined from the Candlelight Club, had been sitting at the dressing room door; how a single lit cigarette, dropped into it, had ignited the curtains; how the three explosions that rocked the dressing rooms were caused by the canisters of gas brought up from the Queen Mary kitchens . . .

Less an arson, Maynard mused, *than an attempted murder. Here. In* my *hotel.*

'I need it open, Maynard, and soon.'

'I understand, sir. And yet . . .'

Lord Edgerton's eyes widened in fury. Against the charred landscape of the dressing rooms, he seemed almost demonic.

'We are at the mercy of the loss adjusters, my lord. We are but men. We cannot move mountains.'

Lord Edgerton loomed close, so that Maynard could see the crooked set of his long, Roman nose.

'*I've* moved mountains, Maynard. So must you. We need to rebuild our reputation, and fast. There has to be a Spring Ball. Don't forget – we still haven't had the official ruling from our Yankee friend Mr Hastings. He's yet to announce for the

332

Imperial either.' He said it with such bile it was a wonder he thirsted for John Hastings's investment at all; but Maynard Charles understood a pact with the devil when he saw one. 'Sort this out, Maynard. *Solve* it. That's what you're paid for.'

In the ballroom, Raymond sensed a new presence on his shoulder, and looked up from the letter he was holding to see that Hélène Marchmont had entered the Grand Ballroom. It had been some days since he last saw her. She'd disappeared moments after the stroke of midnight on New Year's Eve – perhaps, Raymond thought, to see that new beau of hers, the dashing Irishman with the flaming red hair – and, judging by the fur coat in which she was draped, dusted with snow, she was only just returning.

Raymond wasn't sure why Hélène shook as he put his welcoming arms around her. The weeks had passed, the body healed – but something, it seemed, in the mind remained an open wound.

Hélène found her composure, rocked back out of his arms and gripped him by the shoulders.

'Thank you,' she said.

'For what?'

'For being a hero.' Hélène laughed. 'A genuine hero, Raymond.'

'Rushing back into a burning building is all a part of the job. Especially for my leading lady ...'

It was the final two words that made him falter. He reached, again, for the latest missive from Georges de la Motte.

'What is it, Raymond?'

Raymond hesitated before he handed Hélène the letter. Part of him still thought he should pretend it didn't exist. Another part of him wondered if she'd look at him with the same mix of disappointment and horror that he saw etched on Nancy's features whenever he dared speak of the Hollywood Hills. He wanted, more than anything else, for Nancy's face to open up with the same wonder as it did when she first took in the sights of the Grand Ballroom, or when she first touched her lips to his.

But then he looked around, at what had become of the Grand. Times changed, didn't they? People changed. Lives went in any one of a hundred different directions. Just look at him and Artie: two brothers, carousing up and down the terraces of Whitechapel together. Then, ten years later, Artie in prison and Raymond a champion at the Hammersmith Palais. Lives torn asunder, just like the ballroom in which they now stood.

Inside the envelope were two notes. The first, short and to the point, simply said, '*Raymond, I await you . . . and so does Miss Archembeau!*' The second was in an altogether more delicate hand. Hélène's eyes only scanned the words – '*I have heard so much about you that I have even begun to see you in my dreams. I fancy I can even feel how you might dance!*' – for, folded inside the note, was a signed photograph of a girl who called herself 'Ivy Archembeau'. She was, Hélène had to admit, a revelation: jet-black hair, luminous eyes, her lips full. Not even the diamonds in her ears could distract from the beauty of those eyes.

'Raymond,' she whispered, 'what's happening?'

'There's a part for me,' he admitted. 'Georges had an accident. It opened a place in production. His studio, they're shooting a movie called *Stairway to the Stars*. They're expecting me, Hélène.'

'And this girl?'

'To be my leading lady. The new Fred and Ginger, that's what Georges is saying. One of his producers, they said I was like . . . Fred Astaire, with better hair.' Raymond laughed, though there was so little merriment in it. 'It's what I wanted, Hélène. And last year, being out there, in Hollywood with them, it made me want it more. Only . . .'

Hélène thought that she understood. Her mind flitted back to that night at Simpson's with Arthur. From there she flashed forward to the garden party at Richmond, and all the times in between. Love could anchor a person. Love could divert a life. But sometimes life strained against love in the most unimaginable ways.

'You turned down Hollywood once upon a time, Hélène. Tell me – did you ever—?'

'Regret it?'

Raymond nodded.

Hélène knew not what to say. 'It was different for me. I'd already fallen in love with the ballroom by the time they tried to coax me out there. Perhaps I *would* have loved Hollywood. I've often looked at pictures and thought that I would. But, for me, it was the choice between one great love I absolutely *knew* I had . . . and one I just wondered about.' She paused. 'I chose the love I knew. The ballroom.'

'Maybe it's the same for me. It's . . .'

She touched the back of his hand. 'It's Nancy, isn't it?'

'I've been a fool, Hélène. A bloody fool. I got swept up in the idea of Nancy and me being out there in the Hollywood Hills together. The sun beating down. The pool in the back garden. The days on the studio lot and . . .' He closed his eyes in a silent curse. 'I didn't, for a second, think of what she would want. I didn't even ask her. Now she's . . .'

Angry with me? thought Raymond. *Disappointed?*

The memory of her leaving the Brogans' on Christmas Day was still vivid. The pain he'd felt in his side as the taxicab drove away. He'd seen her since. On Boxing Day they'd taken tea. Three days later, he'd taken her to the picture house on Leicester Square, where *Top Hat* was playing – and maybe it had been the images of Fred Astaire and Ginger Rogers dancing across the enormous screen that had soured the evening, because neither had dared speak of Hollywood or what the future might hold. Then, when New Year's Eve came around, she was back at the Daughters of Salvation – this time with Vivienne Edgerton in tow – while Raymond sashayed around the Candlelight Club.

I'd go out there for her, stand with Artie outside, act like a bodyguard for them all – if only she wanted it. But it's as if she doesn't want me near. The Daughters of Salvation – it's hers and me, I'm . . .

'You need to talk to her, Raymond. *Really* talk. No more dances. No more soirées and stepping out. No more romance. Real, honest-to-goodness partnership.' Hélène laughed, cutting it quickly short when – in the corner of her eye – she saw Lord Edgerton stooping out of the obliterated dressing room. 'Goodness, Raymond, how did you get to be the dancer you are without really, *truly* knowing the value of a good partnership? Conversation, it's like a dance. You have to do it together. Listening is a dance too. You have to *learn* how to do it.'

'I love her, Hélène. I'd take her with me, if that was what she wanted. But she has her place now and . . . what if that's what life is? What if that's love? Just two people pulling in harness for a time. Until they just . . . don't.'

'If I knew the answer . . .'

'I know.'

'Life or love – which is it? And can you really have one without the other?' Hélène paused. 'I'll tell you one thing I've learned,

Raymond. There are different types of destiny. And make of that what you will.'

Raymond folded the notes back into the envelope.

'I can almost see it, almost taste it . . . The two of us, on billboards from Los Angeles to Monte Carlo. Me – and the beautiful Miss Archembeau.'

Hélène rolled her eyes. 'You men, even the best of you, are too blinkered to see it.' She turned, as if to leave. 'Beauty's just the same as stardom. It all fades, in the end. So, she's beautiful – so are you, Raymond. After it's gone, all that's left is the love. Whatever you do, just make sure you have it.'

As Hélène left, Raymond watched Maynard Charles and Lord Edgerton approaching. There was something portentous about the way Lord Edgerton moved. He seemed to cross the dance floor in only a few brief strides, stepping over the frontier that separated the ruined from the rest – while Maynard shuffled in his wake.

'De Guise,' Lord Edgerton intoned in his deep, baritone voice. 'We need this place open. We need you back dancing. I've told Mr Charles, here, he's to do whatever it takes.'

Raymond gazed around, and declined to say that it would take a miracle.

'Well?' Lord Edgerton continued.

'Sir, if you'll excuse me, I don't—'

Lord Edgerton's face turned into a monstrous rictus. 'Not you as well, de Guise. None of you could succeed in the City. I don't need "no" men. I need men who know how to get a job done! This ballroom, I'm told it needs gutting. Well, we'll gut it. We'll make it bigger and better and . . . then we'll see who's flocking to the Imperial. Then we'll see what those braggarts at the Savoy have to say. Our Spring Ball – King George in attendance. The Bucking-ham, rising from the ashes. Don't any of you here have any *guts*?'

'Courage is a quite separate matter from economics,' came Maynard's whispery voice.

Raymond saw the rage building in Lord Edgerton's features. Maynard Charles had always been a blunt man, unafraid of saying what he felt – but never, in Raymond's recollection, to his superiors.

Before Lord Edgerton erupted, Raymond said, 'We could make changes, sir. Disasters like this, they can be opportunities as well. There are new dances, ones I discovered in America. The jitterbug. The jive. Were we to bring them here, we might start something truly—'

Lord Edgerton's face creased – but this time with laughter, not rage.

'They're not the kind of changes I had in mind, Mr de Guise. Rather – does this ballroom really *need* a sprung floor? Does it need an orchestra quite as large as Archie Adams insists? Can't we achieve the same effect with half as many dancers? *Real* changes! Ones that transform our balance sheets. Ones that can get this ballroom open by the equinox.' Lord Edgerton turned to stalk away. 'American dances, indeed! Jives and jitterbugs won't rebuild our reputation, Mr de Guise. People want tradition. No, we'll get this place open – swiftly and cheaply. And we'll do what we do best.'

Lord Edgerton took two strides away, then stopped. 'I'll need to see my stepdaughter, Mr Charles. Have her sent directly to the Benefactors' Study. I'll speak with her there.'

Raymond heard the suppressed sigh in Maynard's voice when he answered, 'I don't believe Miss Edgerton is on the premises today, sir.'

Lord Edgerton seethed. 'Was she made aware I was coming?'

'A message was left, sir.'

'Well,' he uttered, 'where is she?'

'I'm afraid I don't know, sir.'

Lord Edgerton turned his dark eyes on Raymond.

'Have you seen her, Mr de Guise?'

'I'm afraid not, sir.'

'You can be assured, Lord Edgerton, that Vivienne's stay with us has been uneventful of late. She is keeping herself out of almost every sort of nuisance—'

'That, Mr Charles, is why I am suspicious.'

Raymond felt Maynard draw close to his side as, together, they watched Lord Edgerton go.

'It's madness, Mr Charles. If we're to rebuild the ballroom, if there's even a hope, we should move it onwards. Think of the future. But we're determined, aren't we, to stay in the past . . . ?'

'America has corrupted you, Raymond.' Maynard fell as silent and seething as Lord Edgerton, before he caught himself and added, 'I'm sorry. My ire is not aimed at you. Well, we find ourselves in something of a predicament, do we not?'

'I'm not sure I've been in a deeper one, sir.'

'Nor I.' Maynard smiled wanly. 'You do know where Miss Edgerton is, don't you?'

In Raymond's eye, he saw the doors of the Daughters of Salvation, just as Nancy had painted it: the destitute milling around inside; the desperate begging for help in the corners.

'I may have been preoccupied these past months, Raymond, but I haven't lost my sense of it yet. I know where Miss Edgerton goes. I know she takes your young Miss Nettleton with her . . .'

Billy Brogan! Raymond swore, inwardly. *Maynard Charles's eyes and ears . . .*

'I haven't formed an opinion of this little charitable mission of hers. I've had bigger concerns. But I've detected the change in Miss Edgerton, just like everybody else. Why, I haven't seen her sprawled drunk in this ballroom once in the past twelve months. I'd wager she hasn't thrown herself at you either. But she's drawing attention nevertheless. And if Lord Edgerton were to discover how she's using the allowance *he* provides on this kind of endeavour – well, I'd wager he'll wreak more hell down on our poor, beleaguered hotel. Raymond, I'm' – here Maynard's voice took on a new inflection, as if his air of despondency might even have been an act – 'not finished yet. What Lord Edgerton said is true – John Mr Hastings hasn't announced himself for the Imperial yet. There's still hope. It grows more distant by the day, but I have to believe it's still there. I need Lord Edgerton now. He mustn't be diverted. So if he ever finds out . . .'

Raymond lifted his hands. 'I hear what you say, Mr Charles.'

'Talk to your Miss Nettleton. Make her understand.'

As Maynard Charles departed, Raymond was left in the middle of the dance floor.

Bring her in line? he thought. *Mr Charles, you've evidently never spoken with my wonderful fiery, impassioned Nancy Nettleton . . .*

No, there isn't a hope of diverting them from their cause. And – to Hell with it – why should there be? Nancy's got her passion. She has her life's purpose at last . . .

His fingers reached again for the letter from Georges de la Motte, and the picture of Ivy Archembeau hidden inside.

And, maybe – just maybe – so do I . . .

Chapter Thirty-four

U P AHEAD, WHERE THE SNOW banks grew deepest outside the haberdasher's, the grocer's, the butcher's of
Whitechapel Road, a group of children scattered as
the taxicab approached. From the back seat, Vivienne Edgerton
watched through the window as they took flight for the alleys
between the shopfronts. Then, in a series of juddering fits and
starts, the taxicab came to an unexpected halt.

A snowball exploded against the window.

'Why have we stopped?' There had once been a time, Vivienne
was ashamed to admit, when she would have treated this taxi
driver with something only a little short of contempt. Now, she
tapped him on the shoulder gently and smiled. 'Reg?'

'See for yourself, Miss Edgerton. It's the frontier out here . . .'

Vivienne wrapped her coat and shawl around herself as she
opened the door and stepped out onto Whitechapel Road. Thin
flakes of snow still eddied in the wind, but the real snowfall had
come during the night. Up and down Whitechapel Road it rose
in high banks against the shopfronts – but here the road seemed
to have been shovelled clean, and all of the snow had been built
into the most enormous wall, complete with turrets four feet
high, across the middle of the thoroughfare.

Reg, the cab driver, wound down his window.

'Crikey, just look at those barricades! It makes you want to be a boy again, don't it? Building snowmen and igloos, and castles out of snow!'

Vivienne was aware of tiny faces peering at her from the ends of every alley.

'We'll just have to go around.'

'Around, Miss Edgerton? *Around?*' He looked, deliberately, in every direction, as if to say that it would have been easier to thread a tree trunk through the eye of a needle. 'No, I'm sorry, miss. The fare ends here.'

Vivienne looked at him, trying hard to hide the uncertainty in her eyes.

'You can get to the Daughters if you walk that way. Up the lane to your left, just follow it round. You'll be there in five minutes. And don't worry, miss' – here Reg gave a gleefully boyish grin, and levered himself out of the cab – 'I'll give those street kids hell while you make your getaway!'

Moments later, he was down on his knees, scrabbling together a mountain of snowballs – and the children, sensing some great adventure about to begin, began to emerge from the alleys in force.

Five minutes, Vivienne thought, *that's all he said. And . . . it isn't yet midday. What is there really to fear?*

But, even so, her heart was thundering as she crossed the barricade and took off up the thoroughfare as the war for Whitechapel Road broke out behind her.

The street kids were waging their battles as far north as the St Bartholomew Gardens, where a multitude of fortresses each manned by snowmen had been assembled. Vivienne had thought she knew the way to the Daughters of Salvation, but it was strange how the world became so different when seen through a shifting curtain of snow. Indeed, by the time five minutes had passed, she had got to thinking that she had somehow stumbled into a different part of London altogether.

At least when it snows in Manhattan, you can find your way. Walk east or west and, sooner or later, you hit the Broadway – or else one of the rivers. But London? London's older. London likes to set snares . . .

Vivienne stopped on a corner where two streets flowed together, an open square of parkland behind. Across the way, one of the taprooms was just opening its doors, and a motley collection of vagrants picked themselves up to go through the doors. As they reached the threshold, they were met by a man coming out. Vivienne saw a tussle, the man who'd been within buffeted back and forth as he floundered out into the snow.

She stopped. She knew that face.

The man was young, boyish, and wearing a black felt coat. At first, Vivienne could not be certain, for the swirling snow obscured his face – but then a memory of one night at the Daughters of Salvation burst into her thoughts.

Warren Peel, she thought. *Mary Burdett called him Warren Peel.* One of the Daughters' most unlikely visitors – the son of some industrialist, an heir in waiting. *But what was he doing in the –* she looked at the taproom sign – *Beggar of Shadwell before its doors even opened?*

She watched as Warren Peel reeled away down the street. Certainly, he was drunk, for he staggered from side to side, and twice had to catch hold of a lamppost to keep himself from falling.

Vivienne did not know why she did what she did next. Perhaps it was only the sudden thought that, at the end of everything, Warren Peel was not so dissimilar to what she had once been: spoilt and pandered to, having everything, wanting nothing – nothing except some way, *any way*, to fill that desperate, yawning chasm inside. She'd found it in opiates too.

So she decided to follow him as he took off through the deepening drifts and turned back towards Whitechapel Road. The streets grew more narrow. The houses more cramped. Warren Peel had to stop and catch his breath more than once, Vivienne lingering some distance behind, and only when he had crossed to the southern side of Whitechapel Road did he seem to find the place he was looking for. In the backyard of another public house – its windows dark and boarded – he climbed a rickety set of wooden stairs. Vivienne, watching from the corner of the yard, saw, for the first time, how cold and drawn Warren looked. In his features he was seventeen, but in his eyes he was ten, twenty, thirty years older. He knocked on a door, and waited.

You know what kind of place this is. You know what Warren Peel's here for. He spent the night on the floor of some taproom, and now he's looking for something else, something to see him through the day. Well, it's now or never, isn't it?

She stepped out, into the frozen icescape of the yard. A simple wooden trap, with two missing wheels, sat in the middle of the square.

'Warren!' she called out.

His eyes scanned around to find her. They narrowed as he tried to figure out who had called his name.

But then the door opened up behind him, and all that Vivienne saw was the dark figure of a man, his hand stretched outwards, beckoning Warren Peel to step in.

'Yeah,' said Artie Cohen, 'I know that place all right.'

It was late in the afternoon, the sky darkening as it turned towards night. Artie had been standing sentry outside the Daughters of Salvation since Vivienne had arrived at noon, and already he'd had to run off some ne'er-do-well who'd tried to set up camp outside the chapel steps. After such a long day, Archie had been grateful for the cocoa, thick with sugar. He'd been even more grateful that Vivienne had brought it; she made the best cocoa in the whole organisation. And, besides, he was getting to admire the scent of her perfume.

'Round the back of the old Coach House, right? I knew a lad from the Limehouse dock. He'd go up those stairs on a Friday night and not come out again until Monday morning. Damn stupid way to spend your time, if you ask me – but, here I am, profiting from their misfortune myself. It's funny how the world works, ain't it?'

Vivienne screwed up her eyes. Artie Cohen's logic was as non-sensical as it was infallible.

Inside, the Daughters of Salvation was heaving. Some of these people had come looking only for shelter – and, though the Daughters liked to preserve its beds for those whom the other hostelries and church floors turned away, since the snows had started falling it had been too difficult to say no. Consequently, even the spaces between the beds were full. People huddled against every wall, shared bedrolls and blankets – and

Mary Burdett was a whirling dervish, trying to keep them all fed.

The day had been spent in what Vivienne had come to call the Daughters of Salvation's 'daily toil'. Feeding those who needed to be fed. Bathing those who needed to be bathed. And, most of all, *listening* to the stories that poured out of each and every person who came into the chapel. It was the listening, Vivienne had decided, that truly mattered. It was her idea, but the truth was, she wouldn't have been able to do it without Nancy spurring her on. It had been Nancy who'd talked Vivienne down, last Christmas. Nancy who saw what she really was, behind the nastiness and deceit and self-loathing – all of those things that the opiates propelled her towards – and helped guide her back to the light.

The last year's changed me. I didn't just find purpose. I found . . . myself. And now . . . the chapel, it's getting too small. The addicts and all the rest, there are just too many. And it could all come crashing down. One whisper to my stepfather – and all of this vanishes in a puff of smoke.

Sometimes, she woke at night, haunted by the thought of it. If her allowance was cut off . . .

All of these people, sent back onto the streets. Back into the snow. And me . . .

She fancied she would follow them, if it came to that. Ask them where they were going, traipse after them up some derelict back stair, and lie down in the dark with the old, familiar bliss running through her veins.

'I want to go there,' Vivienne announced.

Artie Cohen opened his eyes wide. 'Now, Miss Edgerton, I know you had the devil yourself. You can't mean—'

346

'No,' she said, resolute. 'I mean – he's only a boy. He's younger than I am. I want to—'

'You're looking to be Whitechapel's first saint, ain't you?' Artie said, slurping up the last of his cocoa. 'Well, it's you who's paying my way, Miss Edgerton, so I'll do what you say. Left to me, though, I'd let him rot. Spoilt little rich kids, well, they get what they deserve, don't they?'

'Spoilt little rich kids?' she breathed. In truth, she was more wounded than she was angry, though she didn't dare show it.

'I didn't mean nothing of it, miss. See, rich you might be – and little you certainly are – but I've never counted you as spoilt. A spoilt girl doesn't do what you're doing in here. And, look, if you're truly spoilt, you never learn how to make cocoa like *that*. You have maids to help you do it. So I'll have one more, miss, and then we can be off – into the night.'

Vivienne eyed him coolly. Then, with a wicked look in her eyes, she ripped the mug out of his hands.

'You can drink it on the way.'

The old Coach House taproom had been closed for two winters already – at least, that was what Artie said, and he seemed to know almost everything about the streets from Spitalfields to Stepney Green.

'Want me to knock?'

Vivienne looked at Artie. She could sense an eagerness in him – though whether that was an eagerness to please, or just to look into the opium den at the top of the stairs, she had no idea.

'I thought we might just wait.'

'Wait?' Artie baulked. 'Out here? In this snow? For how long? And . . . how do you even know he's still in there? Nah, I'm not

347

waiting, miss. I done enough standing around in the cold today.'
Artie was already off, across the yard. 'Well, are you coming
or not?'

He was loping up the stairs by the time Vivienne had flailed
her way after him.

Lord, if my stepfather could only see me now!

Artie was already at the top of the stairs. Vivienne heaved herself up the rickety wooden steps. Though her fur coat was keeping her body warm, something of the night's chill was working
its way into her legs.

'Artie,' she said, 'what if he's . . .'

'Let's just find out, miss. We'll deal with the rest later.'

The door drew back.

All that Vivienne could see was the darkness beyond. That's
all it was: a measly narrow hallway, the paper peeling off its walls
revealing plasterwork and bare brick underneath.

Then a face appeared. Vivienne did not see the curtains hanging at the end of the hallway until they rippled and came apart.
A man, carrying a paraffin lamp, was shuffling towards them.

'I'm looking for a friend,' Artie said. 'Warren Peel.'

'No friend here!' snapped the man, and reached out to slam
the door in Artie's face.

Artie looked, sidelong, at Vivienne and gave her a mild shrug.

Then he kicked out with his boot, blocking the door.

He was stronger than the other man. Though he strained to
close the door, all Artie had to do was keep his boot in place to
make sure it stayed open.

'I'm not going to hurt anyone,' Artie said – and, behind him,
Vivienne felt a strange thrill of terror. Artie Cohen – surely he
was not a violent man? Nobody whom Raymond de Guise knew

could really be violent . . . could they? 'But you're going to show me your den now. I want to see Warren Peel.'

The man's eyes were full of fear. 'Warren Peel's not here! You're too late. Warren had nothing left to give. So he's gone.'

Artie muscled forward. 'I'm going to want to see that for myself.'

He bustled past the man and, ignoring the shrieks of alarm, hurried to the end of the hall, the patron following close behind. All Vivienne could do was watch as they disappeared.

It was unnerving, being alone. Mere seconds passed before she could stand it no longer. She stepped over the threshold – and it was only then that she realised how dark and dank the place smelled. She knew these smells from the Daughters of Salvation on its most desperate nights. The smell of fever. The smell of night soil. Part of her wanted to go back into the yard, where the purity of snow made everything feel clean. But another part of her drew her on, further down the hall.

It's only a year of your life since you were like them, she thought. *Thank goodness for Nancy Nettleton . . .*

She parted the curtains and dared to step through.

It was just the upper storey of the derelict public house below. It reminded her, almost, of the Daughters of Salvation – only, here, the smell in the air was not of coal tar and carbolic soap. It was the sweet, ripe scent of the smoke that collected above the beds. The beds where men lay in simmering states of consciousness. The beds where men muttered their way through fever dreams . . .

Artie burst around a corner, the patron still yapping at his heels. 'He's not here.'

'I told you this!' the man crowed. 'Out! Out!'

Artie turned back to face the man.

'Tell me where he is.'

'I don't care where he is. Warren Peel is not my concern.'

'He'll be your concern if you don't tell me where he is,' Artie snapped. 'When the Old Bill come to tear this place down, then he'll be your concern.'

The man exploded in unspeakable vitriol, his words running together in a torrent of hate. And then came something Artie and Vivienne could understand.

'He goes where he always goes. His taproom, where his friends lock in every night. Food and ale there and back here for more. That's little Warren Peel. Now out! Out, out, out!'

Artie ushered Vivienne outside, and refused to flinch even as the slammed door shook behind him.

'You shouldn't have come in there, miss.'

'I've seen enough at the Daughters of Salvation,' Vivienne shivered. 'It's not the first time you've taken me out on the streets.'

Artie nodded. 'Are you all right?'

It's the smell, she thought, as Artie helped her down the stairs. *I haven't tasted it in a year and more. But the rush – you never forget the rush . . .*

'Where now, miss?' asked Artie. 'Back to the Daughters?'

But Vivienne was shaking her head. 'The den keeper might not know which taproom Warren Peel goes to, but I do. Artie, it's the place I followed him from. It's called the Beggar of Shadwell.'

They were not yet halfway to the Beggar of Shadwell when they found him.

Warren Peel was sitting between two rubbish bins underneath the awning of a cobbler's shop. At least, here, he was safe from the Arctic wind that whipped its way between the tumbledown

350

terraces. But that was his only good fortune. The first thing Vivienne saw was that he was wearing no coat. The second thing was that he was wearing no boots.

'He's traded 'em in,' said Artie, gently slapping him about the face in an attempt to wake him up. 'Can't leave him here, miss. He'll be dead inside the hour.'

Vivienne gave him a glare as if to say he didn't need to state the obvious.

'Traded his coat? And his boots? They'd *take* them?'

'Anything of value, miss. Look, I know you had your struggles – but you always had the means to buy your powders. Some folks don't. So when the need gets strong, they sell what they got.'

Vivienne was already unbuttoning the front of her fur coat when Artie realised what she was doing.

'Miss Edgerton! You'll catch your own death—'

'I haven't been out in it for as long . . .'

Artie grunted. 'Put it back on,' he said, and in a flash had ripped off his own patched felt overcoat. 'You'll have to help me get him into it, too. Good God!' he cried, as he heaved him aloft. 'He's made a mess of himself as well!'

'I did tell you, once upon a time, that this was dirty work.'

'Yeah,' grunted Artie, 'but my ma has to launder this coat. She's going to kill me.'

It took both of them to lever Warren Peel into Artie's coat. By the time they were done, the snow was coming down heavily.

Now that he was wrapped in Artie's felt, something seemed to have stirred in Warren. One eye opened, promptly closing again as it took in the white whirlwind all around. Then his lips parted and, out of the chaos of grunts and curses, there came the three words, 'Where am I?'

351

'Warren,' Vivienne said, 'it's Miss Edgerton, from the Daughters of Salvation. We found you right here in the snow. We . . .'

'He's gone again, miss.'

Artie was right. Warren's head was lolled against Vivienne's own shoulder. It was only the frigid air that was stopping him drooling all down her fur.

'See if you can wake him, Artie. We can't stay out here.'

Artie levered himself around. Then, still bearing the majority of Warren's weight, he used his spare hand to prise open one of Warren's eyes.

Artie grinned. 'He's in there somewhere, miss.'

'Warren,' Vivienne ventured, 'you have to listen to me. Where do you live?'

He grunted something unutterable.

'Warren, I'm going to get you somewhere safe, but you need to tell me – where is home? Not the Beggar of Shadwell. I know you were going to spend the night there, but where's home, Warren? Where are there people who love you?'

On hearing the word 'love', Warren seemed to hold more of his own weight.

'The mansion house,' he slurred, 'on St Luke's Field.'

Artie shook his head. 'That's bloody Old Street! We won't be walking there, miss, not with him slumped between us. Back to the Daughters, is it?'

Vivienne stared one way up Whitechapel Road, then back the other. The Daughters of Salvation was not so very far.

But what's the point? she thought. *Take him back there. Find him a bed. Hold his hand and read him a story while he sweats it all out of his system. Change his sheets, empty the bucket at the side of his bed, then cast him out into the streets until the next time, and the next time, and the time after that. What if,* she began to think, *there's another way . . . ?*

'He's out cold again, miss. We got to get him somewhere warm . . .'

'I know,' said Vivienne. And then, with a decisive flourish: 'Artie, we're going to need a taxicab.'

Old Street was a pristine valley of white, and the taxicab that careered along it kept slipping from one side of the thoroughfare to another. In the back seat, Vivienne and Artie held Warren Peel between them, rubbing his hands as if to knead some warmth back into his body.

'You ought to be rubbing my hands,' Artie grunted. 'It's me who's got no coat.'

'You're a regular Sir Galahad,' Vivienne replied.

'Sir . . . what?'

Finding a taxicab in this snow had been the first miracle of the evening. Getting to St Luke's Field without crashing into either lamppost or shopfront was the second. Some God up there was smiling on them, of that Vivienne was quite sure. And, by the time they'd reached the grand gardens at St Luke's – where the magnificent church spire seemed to be made out of pure ice – they'd been granted a third miracle too: Warren Peel had woken three times, but he didn't start retching until they were out on the street.

'Retching is fine,' Artie insisted. 'Retching is good.'

'This way, Warren,' Vivienne whispered. 'We're nearly there.'

The town houses here may not have been as magnificent as the ones that crowded Berkeley Square – but, between the less opulent ones, one loomed more magnificent than all of the rest.

A grand Victorian mansion house, as wide as the Buckingham Hotel, occupied one corner of St Luke's Field. Behind iron railings, the gardens were a fantasia of white and a pathway snaked up to a three-storey house. Separate outhouses – stables, perhaps, or simply pleasure rooms for summer garden parties – formed a horseshoe in front of the grand double doors.

Warren came out of his stupor long enough to know where he was.

'No!' he cried, and tried to kick his way backwards. 'No!'

'What is it, Warren?'

'Not my father. If he sees me like this . . .'

Then his head slumped, and he slipped out of consciousness once again.

'The brat thinks he'll be in trouble,' said Artie as, together, they heaved Warren through the iron gates. 'Are you sure about this, miss?'

'Artie, trust me,' Vivienne replied. 'The Daughters of Salvation are living on borrowed time. I've known it for months. The longer this goes on, the closer we get to my stepfather finding out what I'm doing with my allowance. Once he finds that out, he'll cut me off – you can be certain of that. So . . .' She looked up at the grand house. 'We need new benefactors.'

'And you think you can trade Warren Peel for . . .'

It's just like you, Artie, to think of everything as a trade.

'No,' Vivienne answered. 'I'm hoping for common decency. We saved the life of his son. We're doing it over and over. Maybe he'll . . . want to help.'

You sound like Nancy Nettleton, thought Vivienne – and she was surprised to discover how much the thought pleased her. *Looking for the good in someone you've never even met . . . Standing up for someone you barely even know . . . When I tell Nancy what we've done tonight, why, she'll hardly believe her own ears . . .*

At the top of the pathway, Artie rapped his knuckles on the door. As they waited, Vivienne was distinctly aware of how nervous he seemed. His eyes, which were already roaming the shadows in the garden, seemed to spook at every noise.

He's almost . . . sweet when he's nervous, Vivienne thought. *All of that bluster, all of that anger, maybe it's just a disguise . . .*

'Are you all right, Artie?'

'I think I robbed here once, miss. Well, not robbed, but definitely stood guard while some other fellas smashed their way in. Years ago, o' course, but . . .'

Before Artie could go on, the door opened up, revealing a diminutive woman of middle years in a white lace apron. At first, she took in the three figures on her doorstep with something approaching surprise. It was only when her eyes really took in the frigid form of Warren Peel that her surprise turned to horror.

'You blinkin' fools!' she crowed. 'You can't bring 'im in by the front gate! The master'll have one of his outbursts! He'll get rid of us all! Here, bring him round the side. I'll open the scullery door.'

'Madam,' Vivienne began, ignoring the tirade, 'if you would be so kind, I would like to see Mr George Peel.'

'Mr Peel?' she screeched. 'If he sees what you done to Warren, he'll go after you with the full force of everything he's got. And I don't mean the law!' She stopped, for something was just occurring to her. 'You new friends of Warren's, are you? Haven't seen you two before.'

'Just two people trying to do some good in this world,' Artie butted in. 'Is Mr Peel here or not?'

The maid barrelled forward, pulling the door closed behind her.

'Get him round here,' she said, making as if she could sweep them round the side of the building. 'This is what comes of Warren having no companion anymore. Mr Peel should never have got rid of Jacob. He'd see Warren right, whatever mischief the lad got up to. But then, of course, Jacob falls foul of Mr Peel hisself, so he's got to go. And now poor Warren's left with … What did you say your names was?'

As if breaking the surface of water in which he'd been drowning, Warren opened his eyes. It took a few moments for him to recognise where he was. His eyes landed on the maid, he cried out 'Duckie!' and no sooner had the word left his mouth, he doubled up and opened his guts out into the snow.

The maid rushed to him, held his hair back, dabbed at his face with the hem of her apron.

'Warren, Warren, you stupid boy,' she said – and, in spite of what she was saying, Vivienne felt the deep affection in her voice. 'Oh, you'll be the death of me!'

Artie looked at Vivienne. 'I don't know about you, miss, but I've had enough of this. That lad's just chucked up green bile all down my lovely winter coat.'

He turned on his heel. He tramped back to the doorstep. He hammered on the door.

'No!' the maid, whom Warren was now cuddling as he muttered 'Mrs Duckworth', cried out.

But it was too late. Lights were already coming on all across the front of the house.

'Whoever you two are, you don't understand. Warren here, he's a good boy really. He's got his weaknesses – just like us all. Lord above, not one of us is perfect. And the boy never did have a mother, not even when she was alive – the old harridan! He's just got friends in the wrong places. That's all. And the rest of us, the staff as it were, we look out for him when we can. All so's his old man doesn't find out what he's—'

The front door opened – and there, in its frame, stood a man in a long navy blue cardigan, with dark, mahogany hair and a fat brown moustache perched on his upper lip. Jowly around his face, but lean of body, his blue eyes narrowed as he took in the scene.

'Mrs Duckworth!' Though his voice had a quality of grace, it nevertheless shook Vivienne to her core. 'What is the meaning of this?'

Vivienne saw Mrs Duckworth's face fall. She tried to lift Warren back to his feet, but the boy was too heavy. Vivienne clicked her fingers and – throwing her an odd look, as if to say 'you might have just asked' – Artie staggered across to help.

It was now or never, so Vivienne cast her mind back, tried to remember what life had been like when she simply *knew* she was better than everyone else, and approached the front door again.

'Mr Peel?'

George Peel looked directly through her.

'Mrs Duckworth – an answer!'

'It's Warren, sir! He's . . . unwell.'

'Unwell, is it? Your behaviour, Warren, is intolerable!' George Peel's eyes swivelled, to find Vivienne. 'And who, pray tell, are you?'

Before waiting for an answer, he turned and bellowed back into the house. Immediately thereafter, two sheepish look-ing footmen barrelled out and helped pick Warren off Artie's shoulder.

'Good God!' George Peel exclaimed as they carried him past. 'What happened to his shoes?'

'Mr Peel!'

George Peel would have closed the door already, if Mrs Duckworth hadn't been hesitant about slipping past and into the house. As it was, he was compelled to look, again, at Vivienne.

'What is it you want, girl? Thanks? For turning my boy into some . . . *degenerate*? If I see you or your husband here again, I shall have no other choice but to—'

Husband? Vivienne thought. Then she sensed that Artie was back at her side.

'Mr Peel, I'm a director of the Daughters of Salvation. We're a charitable concern off Whitechapel Road . . .'

To George Peel, nothing seemed as distasteful as the word 'charity'. His face turned sour, as if he'd detected a bad smell.

He's just like my stepfather, Vivienne thought. *Men of money, they're all the same . . .*

'Your son, Warren, has had cause to rely on us on multiple occasions. I'm given to believe your staff bring him to us, every time he indulges too far. We've set him back on his feet a dozen times before. Mr Peel, tonight we saved Warren's life. If we hadn't found him, he might have frozen to death.' She thought she saw George Peel's face soften. 'I'm glad we found him, but I fear this won't be the last time I meet Warren – not unless . . . Well, I mean to say, the work we do at the Daughters, it's valuable – for Warren, and everyone else like him.'

'Warren?' Mr Peel seethed. 'He's a weak-minded little whelp. When I was a lad, there wasn't time for gallivanting and indulging. When I was younger than Warren, I was working for a living – and supporting my mother, all for the privilege of being her son.'

'Be that as it may, Mr Peel, Warren needs help. So I wanted to ask – what might a man of your means be willing to do, to help people like Warren live their good lives?'

George Peel looked Vivienne up and down, as realisation hit him squarely between the eyes.

'Oh, I see. Yes, I see this for what it is. Just another beggar, come looking for funds. Well, let me tell you, miss, I'm a self-made man. This house – every brick of it, bought with my own sweat and blood. I'll not be manipulated into—'

Vivienne was letting the words wash over her, when suddenly Artie spoke up.

'You big men ought to just *listen* sometimes.'

George Peel blanched.

'Yeah, you heard me,' Artie grunted. 'Miss Edgerton here, she's the only one who's been telling the truth about your boy in there. Everyone else, even dear old Mrs Duckworth there, they've been filling you full o' horse shit for years.' Artie saw Mr Peel's face and cackled. 'Yeah, that's right! Horse shit! Don't like the word, do you? A man of too many sensitivities, are you? That staff of yours, all those footmen, they been letting Warren get stoked up, most likely profiting off him, and covering it up along the way – all to save their own skins. Well, Miss Edgerton, she's not one of your "yes, sir, no sir, how's-your-father-sir" sort o' people. She's trying to do some good for the world.' Artie glared. 'The question is – what do you men of means do to help? What, apart from sit up there in your counting houses counting all your money? And you, with a son just crying out to be saved—'

George Peel said, 'If you're quite finished, I'll give you ten seconds to vacate my property.'

'We're already done, aren't we, Viv?'

Viv? Vivienne thought. *Viv?*

Then she felt Artie putting his arm through hers, wrenching her around to follow the garden path back to the gates.

'That told him,' Artie whispered when they were back at the road. 'That put the wind up the rich ol' bastard. Speak to you like that—'

'Artie,' Vivienne said, 'you really shouldn't have given him my name. If my stepfather—'

'To hell with your stepfather! You're a better man than either o' them.'

Vivienne was not sure if this was a compliment or not.

'We'll see Warren Peel again, won't we?'

'I should think he'll be dead by the time he's twenty,' said Artie.

As they set off into the dark, Vivienne looked back, once, at the grand building. One by one, the lights in its face were being snuffed – until, at last, only one window remained illuminated. In that frame, there hung the figure of Mr George Peel: staring, just staring into the winter darkness – whether lost in despair, fear, or anger, Vivienne did not know.

Chapter Thirty-five

THE WORK HAD ALREADY STARTED in the Grand Ballroom. Hélène could hear the carpenters through the ballroom doors as she crossed reception, where Billy was busily pontificating to one of the Lebreton-Whites about the magnificent Park Suite that was due to be opened at the very top of the Buckingham. She paused at the obelisk, as if to imagine what the ballroom might be like when it reopened. There would be a ball, of course. Maynard Charles would send out all the formal invitations – but the secret truth was that, no matter what a song and dance they conspired to make of it, the ballroom would be slightly less 'grand' when it reopened. The dance floor would still be sprung, but not as masterfully as it had once been – and the light from the chandeliers would fall upon a temporary stage, varnished so that it looked new, with a lacquered pine balustrade where once it had been pure mahogany. The Grand, which had once been the very height of opulence, would be an imitation of its former self. Hélène thought she knew how that felt.

But then had come Arthur Regan . . .

He'd sent word, the second week after New Year, that he was due to return to London – and that, though he planned on staying at Michael Fitzgerald's Richmond estate, nothing would bring his heart greater pleasure than the chance to spend time with Hélène. It was the boost she had needed. With the ballroom closed, her duties at the Buckingham consisted of sashaying around the Candlelight Club after dark or joining diners with the board in the Queen Mary. The devastation of the Grand might have given her more chance to potter around Brixton with Sybil – but the thought of an evening with Arthur was something else entirely. She'd felt his absence more than she'd thought she would. It was startling, terrifying, *enlivening*, to realise how keenly she felt it when he wasn't there.

I need this, she told herself. Images of Sybil kept popping into her mind, but she tried to keep them at bay. *Remember what Noelle said? 'Sybil's fine. She's always going to be fine. But she deserves a mother who's happy and . . . yes, even in love!'*

Was it bad to be so excited? It would have been wrong to say she felt like a girl again. Being a mother changed you in some irrefutable way, and you could never go back. But she did feel lighter. She did feel . . .

Ready. Yes, that's the word. Ready to step out and see what life is like.

There was still snow on Berkeley Square. As Hélène came down the marble steps, she could still see the colonnade was frozen, and the white field at the heart of the square entirely untouched. The doorman nodded graciously as she passed, and she smiled back. That smile – it was growing on her face, because she could already see Arthur Regan's Rolls-Royce waiting for her on the other side of the hotel approach. Its window was wound down, and there in its frame Arthur was staring at her with the most enchanting eyes she had ever seen.

As she walked out onto Berkeley Square, she was so fixed on Arthur – so bursting with the possibilities of what her day had in store – that she did not see the other figure who approached. She saw nothing at all until she heard her name and, startled, turned to see Louis Kildare.

It had been four months since she last saw him. Four months since he vanished from the Buckingham Hotel, leaving only that paltry note. All of those years, every secret they shared, and that was all she had deserved. By rights, she ought to have been furious. But Louis had not changed a bit. By God, he was even carrying his saxophone. He was dressed in his evening jacket, as if he was about to take to the stage in the Grand, and, suddenly, Hélène was being wrenched back in time – to last summer, to the winter before, to all the hundreds of nights she'd taken a drink with him after the final dance, and talked about Sidney, and talked about life.

Then Hélène stopped dead. There was *one* thing different about Louis.

He wasn't smiling.

'Louis?'

'Hélène,' he began, nervously, 'I was coming to . . .'

Her eyes flashed across the road, at Arthur Regan through the Rolls-Royce window. His face had assumed a puzzled air, but it was still beckoning her forward.

'Hélène, can I speak with you? Just five minutes of your time?'

Hélène said, 'You might have spoken to me months ago, Louis.' It was harsher than she'd meant. Surely Louis had had reasons of his own for taking such sudden flight.

He's your friend, Hélène. Remember . . .

'Louis, I'm sorry. I didn't mean to be so abrupt. It's only that' – she looked over her shoulder – 'I have an engagement.'

Louis followed her gaze. It had been months since he last set eyes on Arthur, but the charming Irishman had been, for too long, on his mind. He did not look like much. He did not, Louis thought, look like a man to fall in love with. And yet, the way Hélène's eyes lingered on him told him everything he needed to know.

This was going to be the most difficult thing he'd ever done.

'Don't get in that car, Hélène.'

Hélène stared.

'There are things you don't know about that man. Things you need to know . . .'

'Louis!' she cried – and both she and Louis were shocked at the vitriol in her voice. 'I know what you're thinking. But if that's the reason you left the Buckingham then shame on you! Shame on you, Louis!'

'Hélène?'

'You're the one who told me Sidney wouldn't want me growing into an old maid. You're the one who set me on the road to thinking, well, maybe there *could* be a second life. Then, as soon as I dare to find one, you walk out on me? You abandon me after all the years we spent together? You, me and Sidney? Louis, I'd never expect you to befriend him. You have your loyalties, just like me. But, to come out here and try to *forbid* me from following my own heart . . .'

Louis stood, shell-shocked, listening to the full force of Hélène's anger. The only thing that brought him back to his senses was the sound of the Rolls-Royce door opening, and Arthur Regan unfolding himself from the back seat.

'You have me wrong, Hélène. Sidney *would* want you to fall in love again. *I* want you to fall in love again. But . . .' There was no

364

other way to say it. He looked her squarely in the face. 'Arthur Regan isn't a charitable man. He spins a pretty story. He tells the world he's hell-bent on helping the London Irish. But it's all a fairy tale, designed to make him look safe. Hélène, he's a leader in the Irish Republican Army. He's one of its financiers. The same men who tried to kill King George in Belfast last year. And they're planning something. Something big. That's the reason he's been at the hotel so much this year . . .'

Hélène twisted, as if to call out across the square, but Louis risked it all: stepping forward, he took hold of her hand.

He knew, within moments, that he'd made a mistake. Hélène snatched back her hand, stepped back to widen the distance between them.

'It isn't just me, Hélène. I—'

'Louis,' she said – and it seemed to Louis as if her entire body was rejecting his words, 'I know how much you've cared for me. I know you think you owe it to Sidney – to be there for me and for Sybil. But I'm a grown woman. I have to trust what's here, in my heart – not some scurrilous rumour you've been digging up just to—'

'Frank Nettleton heard.'

Hélène stopped.

'There were two envoys from Berlin, meeting the Italian ambassador – right there in the Queen Mary, and they talked about him. Frank didn't mean to hear it. But thank God that he did. It isn't just rumour. It's stone-cold fact. Arthur Regan and his men are planning attacks right here in London. They're petitioning fascists to turn them into allies, if there's a war to come. You need to be careful, Hélène. You're walking into a trap—'

'Louis,' Hélène quaked, 'you're frightening me.'

'You should be frightened. He almost killed you, Hélène. The fire in the Grand Ballroom – it was never an accident. It's all down to these Irish Republicans and their Sabotage Plan . . .'

Silence.

Then, as if to shatter it, came the voice of Arthur Regan himself.

As Louis had been pleading with Hélène, Arthur had swept across the snow between them. Suddenly, he was at Hélène's side, linking his arm with hers.

'Who is this man, Hélène ? Perhaps we might—'

'Oh yes,' Louis snapped, 'you're as much of a snake as I feared.' He turned to the doorman, who stood at the top of the hotel steps and cried out, 'Bring me Frank! Frank Nettleton, the page!' Then he looked back at Hélène, pointedly ignoring the man who was trying to lead her away. 'Hélène, you know me – inside and out. I'm an honourable man. Tell me I'm not an honourable man . . .'

'Louis,' she breathed, 'why are you doing this?'

'Because he isn't worthy of touching a hair on your head, Hélène. He isn't—'

'Hélène, your friend has gone quite mad,' said Arthur, bringing his lips close to her ear. 'It's like I said once before – all men want to tar we Irish with the same brush. Well, it simply isn't so. Please, let's not let this ruin our day. I have such things planned—'

'Always planning, aren't you, Arthur? Or is "plotting" is a better word? You can't deny it, can you? Nazis in the Queen Mary, sitting with other fascists, talking about *you*. Is it nice to keep that kind of company, Mr Regan? Do you like your name being whispered in the very worst circles on this good green earth?' He shifted slightly, so that his next words were directed at Hélène. 'He doesn't even deny it, Hélène. His hands are all over you and he doesn't even—'

'I have to insist that you desist, sir,' Arthur said. 'One more word of this slander and you'll feel the full force of my organisation's lawyers. My *charitable* organisation, Kildare, you—'

Louis was about to bite back when a smaller, less vengeful voice piped up:

'It's all true, Miss Marchmont.'

Louis, Hélène and Arthur turned as one to see Frank Nettleton coming, nervously, down the Buckingham steps.

As he reached the bottom, he wrapped his arms around himself, as if fearful of the late winter cold.

'It's just like Mr Kildare said. I was there, in the Queen Mary. I know I shouldn't have been. But Conte Grandi was there, from the Italian embassy. He was meeting two envoys from Berlin. They were talking about war, Miss Marchmont. The war Mr Charles thinks is going to come. Then their conversation changed. They started talking about a different kind of war. The IRA, sabotage, right here in London. A man named Russell, begging them for weapons. And . . . Arthur Regan, raising funds to make it all happen.'

Arthur slipped his arm out of Hélène's and took a great stride in Frank's direction.

'Kildare paid you to say this, did he, boy?'

Louis stared. There was a moment when Frank might have turned tail and fled – but not now. Now he unfolded his arms from his chest. Now he took a deep breath, and glared down the steps at the advancing Arthur Regan.

Frank Nettleton – King of the Midnight Rooms! thought Louis. Never had he looked more noble.

'Nobody's paid me a thing, *sir*. I don't want a part of this. I didn't come to the Buckingham looking for adventure. I came to be with my sister. Not to spy on Nazis or find out secrets about . . . about you, sir! But I am not a liar. My sister Nancy, she taught me the importance of truth. At the end of the day, it's all we have. And I did hear it, sir. All about you and Sean Russell and Michael Fitzgerald.'

The final name seemed to work a magic on Hélène. Louis saw her face blanch.

'Frank,' she called out, 'what did you say?'

'Sean Russell and Michael Fitzgerald. I heard them in the same breath as Mr Regan, like they were his friends . . .'

'Arthur,' Hélène said, 'how would Frank know Michael Fitzgerald's name if he wasn't telling the truth?'

'Hélène?'

A thousand thoughts were tumbling through Hélène's mind, but suddenly one of them eclipsed all the others.

'Michael Fitzgerald said he'd never been a guest at the Buckingham. Why would he, when he has his estate down in Richmond? I know Frank. He's a good boy. He has no reason to lie. He's—'

'It's finished, Mr Regan!' Louis exclaimed. 'What you did here, it's over. And you'll pay for it. I'll make certain of that. The Buckingham might not be my home anymore, but I'll still stand up for what that place means. And you and your murderous friends can—'

Louis never finished the sentence. Arthur Regan stepped suddenly forward, bringing his clenched fist back, and drove it with all the force of his body into Louis Kildare's chin.

Louis's head snapped back. His body reeled. One moment he had been standing tall; the next, he was crashing into the snow, his saxophone case flying out of his hand.

Hélène's scream filled Berkeley Square, but it did not stop Arthur from striding to where Louis had fallen and standing above him, with both fists raised.

'You think *I* set that fire?' he roared. 'Do you truly think that the sort of man you are accusing me of being would care about a fire in your little ballroom? The world is *bigger* than a few lords and ladies dancing a foxtrot. There are *bigger* things at stake than the survival of your hotel. By God, you don't see a thing, do you? You fools, with your music and your dancing, you don't really live in the world! Do you think *I'd* set that petty fire, just to choke out a few dancing girls? No, Mr Kildare, it's that fire that ruined my plans. I had a much bigger ambition in mind . . .'

His fists were raised. Beneath them, Louis cringed.

Out of nowhere, Frank appeared. Hélène watched as the gangly page threw himself forward from the last of the marble steps, landing with his arms entangled around Arthur's neck. There he hung, flailing madly – but it was enough to stop Arthur's punches.

Beneath them, Louis scrabbled back to his feet.

Arthur Regan roared, 'Get off me, you English pig!'

He flung himself backwards, sending Frank flying. In the same moment that Frank hit the ice, Arthur wheeled around, brought back his boot and drove it into Frank's ribs. Frank doubled up in pain, would have screamed out if only he had the breath.

The second kick was to his face.

'Arthur!' Hélène screamed.

She dived for Frank, but she was too late. Arthur had already brought his boot back to kick the page again – and this time, instead of Frank, he caught Hélène full in the face.

Louis charged forward – but he was not the only one. The outer doors of the Grand Ballroom opened, and out of them poured the carpenters and joiners who had been hard at work rebuilding the dance floor. Down the marble steps streamed Billy Brogan and two of his fellow concierges, the doorman and a gang of porters tumbling behind, each of them moving in on the place where Arthur Regan stood, trembling and alone.

'What are you looking at?' he thundered. 'You bastards in there, serving your English lords. You'll be the first,' he seethed. 'When this war comes, you'll be the first against the wall!'

He turned, snapping his fingers at the driver still waiting in the Rolls-Royce. As he stalked away, Louis rushed to where Hélène lay and took her in his arms, hoisting her up from the glacial ground of Berkeley Square. Billy and his concierges were already at Frank's side, helping him to the marble steps.

Arthur was already clambering into the Rolls-Royce when Louis screamed out, 'I know you, Arthur Regan! I know who you are!'

After that, there was only silence in Berkeley Square.

Louis held on to Hélène until she had stopped shaking. At some point, he became aware that everybody else had drifted back into the hotel. He looked up at the steps, and the only figure he saw was Maynard Charles, his hands planted squarely on his hips as he took in yet more devastation.

'Come on, Hélène,' he whispered, 'let's get you inside. You need hot cocoa, or a stiff drink'

Louis had already helped her to her feet but, when he tried to steer her towards the marble steps, she froze. He tried, again, to ease her forward – until the idea that he was just as bad as Arthur Regan, forcing her against her will, took hold of him and he let go of her arms.

'Hélène, none of it is your fault. He—'

'Oh, keep it, Louis Kildare!'

Louis was shaken.

'Hélène?'

Hélène looked up at the great white façade of the hotel.

'No,' she whispered. Then, she repeated it, over and over again: 'No, no, no,' until she had almost run out of breath. She turned on the spot, wheeling around, as if she had little idea where she was, where she would go, what time of day it might have been. 'Not now, Louis. Not here. I need to be where it matters. I need to be where *I* matter.'

The mark where Arthur Regan's boot had caught her was already purpling. She took one last look at the hotel that had, for so long, been her home, then turned, and took flight across Berkeley Square. Instinct told Louis to follow – but he had not taken three steps when something even greater told him to stop.

Hélène Marchmont disappeared among the town houses – and Louis Kildare was left alone, wondering if what he'd done was right, if what he'd done was wrong, and if he'd just lost the person he loved most in all the world.

As the clock tower in Westminster struck midday, an omnibus carved its way south. Over the river at Lambeth, down through the town houses of Kennington Road, and at last through the teeming railway square at Brixton. Hélène alighted at the new Marks & Spencer and, with her fur drawn tightly about her, walked the final furlong up the Brixton Hill. Some time later, the

371

bruise on her cheek finally in full colour, she stood in front of the Archers' front door. Ordinarily, she knocked, but today she simply reached out and opened the door. Inside, in front of a roaring fire, Noelle sat with Sybil sleeping on her lap.

'Hélène!' Noelle exclaimed. 'We had no idea . . .'

'No,' she whispered.

Then she was in through the doors, a sleeping Sybil pressed into her arms, and being guided down into the chair where Noelle had, until moments ago, been sitting.

'I tried,' she said. 'I really did try.'

And soon she was spilling it out: all about Arthur Regan, who he was and what he'd done.

'Was I a fool, Noelle, to think love might strike twice?'

Noelle stroked her face. 'Oh, Hélène,' she whispered, and together they watched Sybil starting to stir, 'I should think you'd be a fool if you didn't believe it. I should call you a fool if you thought it couldn't strike three times, four times, five times and more. It's . . . love, Hélène. It isn't a puddle. It doesn't run dry.'

On Hélène's lap, Sybil opened her eyes.

'Mama! Mama here! Mama!'

And this, Hélène thought, *this right here is the most perfect love there ever is.*

Chapter Thirty-six

'I'VE MISSED THIS.'

Dawn had not yet broken, and Raymond rolled over to see Nancy lying beside him. She nestled closer, up against the curve of Raymond's arm.

It ought to have been easier, in the days since the Grand was set aflame, for Raymond to spend time with Nancy – but the truth was that this had been the first night in ten that he had seen her. And God, how beautiful she looked, just lying there, the steady rise and fall of her chest, the moonlight spilling down. He hadn't quite forgotten it, but they'd been apart enough, this winter, for it to catch him unawares.

He'd spent more time showing Frank the jitterbug and jive than he had doing this, just lying here in the dark with Nancy. Frank was learning fast.

Some of us have talents we don't even know about. Frank's about the unlikeliest dancer I know, but you can't deny how the boy moves.

He brought his lips down to kiss Nancy.

They'd spent last night at the Palladium, where the Crazy Gang were putting on an extra performance of their London Rhapsody. Raymond had always liked the Palladium – it was here he'd first seen Duke Ellington himself – but tonight was not about the music. Tonight had been about seeing Nancy laugh for what felt the first time in an age. And what a joy it had been: all their talk of the future forgotten for a few brief hours as, together, they watched the men cavorting on stage, making fools of themselves to the delight of all around.

Afterwards, they had walked a cold London night together, from the wide empty thoroughfare of Oxford Circus down to the great lights and billboards of Piccadilly. There, by the frozen fountain, Raymond had reached inside his coat and produced a slim package, wrapped in brown paper and ribbon. As Nancy unwrapped it, Raymond waited nervously at her side. The truth was, he was not certain how she might take this. He'd been itching to give it to her for days, but the moments when he saw her were so fleeting that he never took the chance.

He watched as Nancy peeled back the layers of brown paper, and there, inside, discovered the crest he'd had commissioned. In a beautiful silver frame there was a copper shield, and on it inscribed the words: THE DAUGHTERS OF SALVATION.

'I thought you could display it outside the hall – so that everybody might know what kind of work you're doing out there.'

For a moment, Nancy was silent. Something hardened deep inside Raymond – he was certain he'd done something wrong, made another terrible mistake – but then she looked up at him, her eyes dazzling with the bright lights of Piccadilly, and she smiled.

'Raymond, it's beautiful. I don't know what to say.'

He felt charged. He felt alive. Just the way she had spoken, the way she was looking at him now, reminded him of how it had been before California – that first flush of love between them.

Perhaps he should have been content with this feeling, but something compelled him to close the gap between them. He rested his hand on her shoulders.

'I should like to come out there with you,' he said. 'Out to the Daughters of Salvation – and not only to visit that disreputable brother of mine.'

Nancy grinned. 'Hardly disreputable any longer! The way he treats Miss Edgerton – your ne'er-do-well brother's turning into a saint.'

'Even so, I should like to come there one night – to see you in action, Nancy. To see this thing you love so much.' He hesitated. It was most unusual to see Raymond de Guise unsure of himself – but true love unmade even the strongest of men. 'Nancy, I'm sorry.'

It poured out of him, then, everything he'd been thinking since Christmas. How he'd watched her leave, in that taxicab, and ached to go with her. How he hadn't meant her to think badly of him. How all he wanted for Christmas was the few hours he had with her. And how, every time he tried to put it into words, they came out all wrong.

'I feel it too, Raymond,' she said, and his heart soared when he felt her slip her arm into his and, together, they took off up the long sweep of Regent Street, bound back for Berkeley Square. 'When you talk about California and stardom and ... Ivy Archembeau.' At least she was smiling at the final name, teasing him even – for, no matter what the future held, both of them knew their eyes would never wander to another. 'I think of all those things you dream about and I wonder – where do I, little Nancy Nettleton, fit into any of it?'

'Right at my side,' said Raymond, with an involuntary tremble.

'But do I? Do I, Raymond, if what you want is orange groves and open Californian skies . . . and what I want is right here, doing the good work, out in the slums of Whitechapel?'

For a time, they walked in silence. Up above, the clouds were parting, revealing a night blanketed in stars. The perfect night, Raymond thought, for walking with the one you loved. If only he could take this moment and keep it forever, then perhaps he would be happy. There seemed something almost criminal in the fact that time had to keep marching on.

'By summer, the Daughters of Salvation will be twice as big again.'

'*If* we can find the support.'

'It's like Maynard Charles says,' began Raymond – and then, together, they finished in chorus, 'Money makes the world go round.'

'But there's a chance, Raymond.' Suddenly, Nancy seemed energised – as if there was news she was desperate to impart. 'If things go well, we could survive into spring. We could be thriving by summer. If you did come, Raymond, you might see an empire of Miss Edgerton's very own design.' She fell silent. 'But we're not allowed to speak of spring, are we? And summer, it's just a dream . . .'

They had reached the centre of Regent Street. An omnibus went past them and, after it was gone, all around them was silence.

'Have you heard from Georges?' Nancy whispered.

'I have,' Raymond returned.

'And?'

'They need my answer, Nancy. They've been waiting too long. Georges says I'd be a fool to pass it up – and I have, through all the years of my dancing life, trusted him above all else. Only now . . .' His words were faltering. 'Now there's you.'

Raymond thought of the Buckingham. There'd be a Grand Ballroom again. Oh, it wouldn't be quite as grand, but it would still be here, drawing the good and the great of London. The dancers would waltz and twirl, the Archie Adams Orchestra would play sublime music, and all would go on as before.

But maybe that was the problem. Maybe that was the thing still gnawing at his heart. Maybe going on as before wasn't enough – in love, or in life. Maybe you had to keep changing, just to keep feeling like *you*.

A sense of something lost had settled in Raymond de Guise. A sense of something that had slipped through his fingers. A feeling, as fleeting and transitory as the *hesitation* in one of his beloved waltzes.

He wanted to feel the magic again.

'I'd never stand in the way of your dreams, Raymond,' Nancy whispered. 'You must know that about me. If your dreams take you away from me, well . . .' The thought was too much to bear, so she stifled it, there and then. 'Raymond,' she finally went on, 'what do you want? In your heart, where it matters the most . . . what is your heart telling you?'

'It's telling me to spend every second of every day with you. It's telling me we've both been swept up in adventures of our own, adventures we both need, but the spare moments, the moments in between, we've been squandering them, lost in our fears for each other. It's telling me, Nancy, that all this talk of the future – of wars to come – is dragging us down. You and I, we used to live in the moment.' He paused, and took a deep breath. 'My heart is telling me we should go out dancing – you and me, and Frank and Rosa. We should dance together – and, for now, that's all that I know.'

After that, they had slipped in through the staff entrance together. Now, Raymond watched her in the predawn darkness, held her hand under the covers, and she in turn watched him.

He dared not tell her about the letter he'd received from Georges de la Motte. He dared not tell her about the ticket Georges had sent him, his last desperate attempt to tempt Raymond into setting sail for adventures unknown. He dared not think of anything further than this moment, and the wonderful girl in his arms.

Some time later, they were taking breakfast in the chambermaids' kitchenette – where the other girls had slowly been getting used to the occasional appearance of the debonair Mr de Guise. Vera and Edie had even made an extra large pot of tea, before they scurried off for the housekeeping lounge. First, however, there was time for the gossip of the day – and no gossip had been more savoured in the history of the Buckingham Hotel than Hélène Marchmont's doomed affair with that brigand Arthur Regan.

'They say the police were too late. He was in the middle of the Irish Sea by the time they caught up with him.'

'There's nothing anyone can do, is there?'

'Someone'll have to pay for it! I heard Royal Insurance won't pay a pretty penny—'

'No insurance for a broken heart, is there now?'

'I meant for the arson attack!'

'More than arson!' Ruth chimed in, arriving from her chamber. 'That's an act of war, if what Frank heard is true. Hey, Rosa, how's our Frank?'

The girls tittered.

'Hey, Nance,' said Ruth, 'you won't mind Rosa as a sister-in-law, will you?'

Nancy rolled her eyes, even as Rosa flushed crimson. Frank and Rosa had stepped out twice more since New Year, each time to one of the dance halls in Soho, and though she could not help fearing for him on those dark London streets, nothing gave her greater pleasure than the few moments she'd been able to see him dance. *Her* nervous little Frank, giving himself to the music.

'Raymond had the most wonderful idea last night. He thinks we should go dancing, Rosa – you, me, Raymond and Frank.'

'Grand!' Rosa enthused. 'Back to the Midnight Rooms? Or . . . there's got to be somewhere more posh – well, if we *are* dancing with Raymond de Guise . . .'

'I'll hardly be the star of the show,' Raymond laughed, 'not if Frank's there.'

'Taught him everything you know, have you?'

'He'll be taking your place with Miss Marchmont, I shouldn't wonder,' said Ruth. '*If* she ever comes home to the Buckingham, that is.'

It had been two days since Arthur Regan was exposed and the mystery of the fire in the ballroom apparently solved, and Hélène had not set foot in the Buckingham since. Maynard Charles was being lenient. There was no doubt, Raymond thought, that something had changed in him this year; not so very long ago, he would have been incandescent at the thought of her absence.

Perhaps Mr Charles was too consumed in plotting the future of the Buckingham to waste time worrying over a few days without Hélène Marchmont. Budgets were being slashed. The most expensive items were disappearing from the menus in the Queen Mary. Rumour had it, he was plotting laying off some of the staff.

'Who knows who'll be the first for the chop?' Ruth said, when conversation turned that way. 'Well, you dancers are probably all right, but . . . what does a hotel need more? Extra chamber-maids or extra porters? Billy Brogan had better watch out. So had you, Nance! All that time you're spending away with Miss Edgerton. Mr Charles is liable to think you're not committed. And you'll be spending even more time away if this Mr Peel of yours comes good!'

Raymond turned to ask Nancy what Ruth had meant, who 'Mr Peel' might have been, but in the corner an alarm clock started trilling and, all at once, the girls picked themselves up and hurried for the door.

'Come on, Nance!'

But Nancy remained behind.

'I didn't get a chance to tell you last night,' she said, and Raymond was caught up, suddenly, in the excitement in her voice. 'It's the most wonderful thing . . .'

And she began to tell him all about Warren Peel, whose life Vivienne and Artie had saved when they returned him to his father's mansion house overlooking St Luke's Field. Whose father knew nothing about his son's indulgences, nor how many times he had come close to killing himself, and all because his household staff were too afraid.

'He sent them away, didn't even seem grateful for what they'd done – and that was the end of it. Until . . .' She smiled. 'A letter came. It turned up at the Daughters yesterday morning. Miss Edgerton had it when she came back last night . . .'

Nancy could remember the words almost exactly. *I shall be attending the Daughters of Salvation with my reformed son Warren on the evening of 12th February. I should see for myself this place that transforms him.*

'Well, don't you see? Why else would he want to see it, if what Miss Edgerton said didn't . . . break through, in some way?'

'You think he's your Hastings,' Raymond said.

'That's exactly it! I only hope we have more good fortune than Mr Charles did . . .' Nancy's eyes suddenly landed on the clock. 'Raymond, I've got to go!'

She scuttled across the room, thought twice, dashed back to plant a kiss on Raymond's lips, and turned again.

He stood and kissed Nancy on the brow. 'Good luck,' he whispered. 'I'll see you at shift's end, won't I?'

And when Nancy whispered, 'I promise. I have three hours before I have to be at the Daughters, and they're all yours. No,' she added, 'they're *ours*. I'm sorry, too, Raymond. I want you to know – the Daughters matters to me, but it never, ever meant that you didn't.'

Raymond hushed her with a kiss.

'Of course,' said Nancy, breaking away, 'I have to survive dusting down the Atlantic Suite first. Mr Brechenmacher's been in town. Last time he was here . . .' Nancy shook her head, as if it was the grisliest of thoughts. 'I love you, Raymond.'

'I love you, Nancy.'

After she was gone, leaving the kitchenette empty, Raymond drew Georges's letter from his pocket.

My boy, enough of the dallying! Destiny calls! Raymond, trust in me as you trusted once before — and permit yourself a new, fresher future.

Raymond, I both know and love you dearly. I can tell when you are lost. And, my boy, you are lost now. Were you not lost, you would have written to me already and dismissed this opportunity out of hand. But the time for a decision has come. And to gee you on your way, I have asked the Royal Transatlantic to forward to you, post haste, a first-class berth on RMS Othello, leaving Liverpool on 13th February. It is your last chance to fulfil the promises I have made and become the star you were born to become!

13th February, he thought. *The morning after Nancy and Miss Edgerton meet with their mysterious benefactor, Mr Peel.* It was with a sinking feeling that he realised that, on that night, two dreams might be being fulfilled, two life's ambitions realised: Nancy celebrating the birth of Miss Edgerton's charitable empire, and Raymond taking the overnight train to Liverpool, setting sail for his own adventure in the sun.

What a bitter irony it was that for two dreams to be fulfilled, one love had to be broken.

Not for the first time, he thought back to Hélène Marchmont and her words: what was more important, to live a life or to live a love?

Thoughts like this could send him into a spiral, so he picked himself up, pocketed Georges's letter, and walked to the kitchenette counter. One more cup of tea and he would be ready to face the day.

The pot was still warm, so he poured what was left into his cup and sipped. Instantly, he winced. There was not enough milk and sugar in the world to rescue tea as stewed as this. Only one man in the world would have been happy to drink this: that great bear, Abner Grant, dragging his way into every corner of the Buckingham all year, poking around in people's private affairs, making everything *his* business, leaving a trail of teacups behind him.

He'd tasted tea this bitter before. In the dressing room, moments before the explosion and geysers of flame.

Yes, he remembered now, the tea had been there, sitting on the side, still warm to the touch.

Then had come the chaos.

Tea, he thought, *bitter and overbrewed.*

Because Grant had been there, hadn't he? Asking all those questions – those questions about the long gone Sofía LaPegna . . .

Raymond picked himself up, because a terrible idea was beginning to take root inside him.

He hurtled from the room.

Chapter Thirty-seven

BILLY WAS IN RECEPTION WHEN Raymond crashed out of the service lift and floundered up the hall.

'Billy, I need to see Mr Charles. *Now.*'

Billy leaped to attention, summoning one of the other concierges to deal with the retired colonel who was currently checking in.

'The last I saw of Mr Charles,' he announced, guiding Raymond behind the reception desks, 'he was in his office, hosting meetings. It looks like we'll be losing a night manager. Well, if what I heard is true, Mr Charles thinks he can take the role himself – double up and save a salary.'

'How did you hear that, Billy?'

Billy shrugged. 'Same way I always do. I had my ear to a door. He's finally decided to get rid of Abner Grant as well. Well, a hotel detective – that's a luxury, isn't it? We haven't had a robbery in months. And old Grant never did solve the last spate—'

By now, they were halfway towards Maynard's office.

'No, Billy,' breathed Raymond, 'I think there's every chance Grant solved that mystery many moons ago. But that's not what he's been doing in this hotel.'

Billy looked furtively, up and down the corridor. 'Mr de Guise?'

'Tell me what you know about Abner Grant, Billy.'

'He's been snooping, but that's his job, isn't it?'

Raymond strode down the corridor until, at last, he reached Mr Charles's door, Billy still by his side.

The door opened beneath his touch.

There was Maynard Charles, sitting at his desk as if he'd been up all night. The circles had deepened around his eyes, the stubble was growing in deep lines along his jaw; he looked old, thought Raymond, older than he truly was.

'Raymond, what the devil . . . ?'

'Mr Charles, forgive me. I know you have much to do.' Raymond paused. 'Sir, we have to talk.'

Maynard hung his head even lower, so low that Billy thought it might soon collide with the surface of his desk.

'Can it wait, Raymond? However passionate you are about bringing the jitterbug to our ballroom, it's hardly high on my list of priorities.' He shrugged his big, round shoulders and laughed. 'They've been talking about war in my hotel for years. European dignitaries coming and going, discussing wars gone by and wars yet to come. But for an Irishman to try and *start* a war, right here, under my nose?' Here his laughter turned, almost, to a sob. 'It's the crowning glory to my year.'

Raymond stepped further into the room, closing the door behind him.

'Sir, that's precisely why I need to speak with you. What Frank Nettleton unearthed about Arthur Regan – it's abhorrent. It's shocked everyone to the core. Hand on heart, I'll never understand how a man could do that to someone as perfect as Hélène. But . . . sir, I believe it's clouding our judgement.'

'What the devil are you talking about? The police have a nationwide manhunt going on. If he sets foot on British soil, they'll have him for what he did here. It doesn't help me clear up the mess it left behind, but—'

'*Sir!*'

The ferocity of Raymond's voice sent a tremor across the room. Billy reeled back, as if under a blow.

Maynard stood. 'You'd better have a damn good reason for coming into my office and speaking to me like this, de Guise. Don't you know the decisions I have to make to buttress the Buckingham for the year to come? Don't think you're above the cut. Gene Sheldon coped admirably while you were gallivanting around California – and for almost a fifth of the price—'

'Sir,' Raymond interjected, heedless of Maynard's rising anger. 'I'm glad Regan's exposed as the warmonger he is. I hope to hell he never sets foot in this hotel again. Should he do so, I'll run him down myself. But Regan wasn't responsible for the ballroom fire, sir. I'm certain of it.' He stopped. 'Sir, come with me. Please.'

The old audit room sat sandwiched between the hotel archive and the head concierge's study. As Raymond stole close, Billy clinging to his side, Maynard trudged behind. Only as they drew near, and he realised where they were going, did his mask begin to slip. He set his shoulders, as something approaching his old steeliness set in.

'Arthur Regan's a scoundrel,' Raymond said. 'It's satisfying to think that he set that fire. Somehow, it *fits*. But then . . . Well, then you start asking *why* and you start asking *how*. Because it wasn't just a fire in the dressing rooms, was it? Somebody had locked those back doors. If I hadn't gone back in there, Hélène might have perished, and that wasn't Arthur Regan, sir. He might be a blackguard. He might have been plotting atrocities here at

386

the Buckingham, but he's an Irish Republican – his anger's with the king and his ministers, not with Hélène. Whatever else he wanted her for, there had to be love in it too. She's still Hélène Marchmont. What man wouldn't fall for her?' Raymond paused. 'No, Regan didn't lock those doors. He would no more want to choke Hélène than the three of us would. And, besides, the door wasn't just barred, Mr Charles. It was locked. Well, it got me thinking – somebody had a key to those doors, and they used it to cause panic and chaos and to rip the very heart out of our hotel.'

Billy said, 'Mrs Moffatt has a master key to the rooms and suites. The caretakers have keys. Mr Charles, you have the master set . . .'

'No,' said Maynard. 'I have *one* of the master sets.'

'Precisely,' Raymond went on. 'Because somebody else has a master set, don't they, Mr Charles? Somebody who needs them for his role at our hotel. Somebody whose very business is to snoop and pry behind locked doors . . .'

Raymond pressed the flat of his hand onto the door in front of them and gently pushed. There was a soft click, and the door glided inwards.

'And somebody who had already been there, snooping around the dressing rooms, on the night of the fire . . .'

In the darkness of the office, there sat Abner Grant.

The hotel detective looked up, to find three pairs of eyes staring at him. Dumbly, he grunted and lumbered up to his feet.

'You needn't go through the spiel with me, Maynard. I know when the writing's on the wall.' There was an open envelope on the desk, with a letter already pressed inside. Abner picked it up, and tossed it to Maynard. 'It's my resignation. I know the corners you have to cut now, old son. I know I'm for the chop. I'd rather get out with my dignity intact, that's all. Besides, my old job's waiting for me.' It seemed to give him enormous pleasure to be able to say, 'I'm off back to the Imperial. The winner takes it all, eh? Hastings's investment – and *me!*'

He was cackling as he tried to move towards the door; but neither Raymond, Billy nor Maynard moved.

'Can't keep me here by sheer will,' Abner grunted. 'My mind's made up.'

'The thing is, Mr Grant,' Raymond de Guise announced, 'to say you're going *back* to the Imperial's all bluster, isn't it? The fact is, you never truly left.'

'Put your dancing shoes back on, de Guise. You're making no sense.'

'It's the silliest thing, but it was a pot of tea that did it for me. It made me remember what the girls had said – that you'd been in the dressing rooms before the fire began. And—'

Grant's face twisted. 'Am I really hearing an *accusation*, de Guise? Arthur Regan planned that fire. You don't need a hotel detective to prove that. The Metropolitan Police have already got Nettleton's sworn statement . . .'

'He didn't plan that fire, Mr Grant. *You* did.'

Grant reached out, as if to paw his way through to the door, but the line held firm.

'I don't know why I didn't see it before,' Maynard interjected, and fleetingly Raymond remembered: long before he was a hotel director, Maynard Charles had been a soldier with a soldier's steel. 'I brought you in from the Imperial to undermine them, but instead *you* undermined *me*. That was the intention all along, wasn't it, Abner? How did it happen? When I had Frank Nettleton bring you that message, did you go straight to the Imperial board? Did they come up with the idea . . . or did you?'

'I don't know what you're talking about,' Grant railed, 'but if you're accusing me of arson, Maynard, well, I've got some pretty stories to tell about *you* and the Park Suite!'

Raymond and Billy each turned, fractionally, to see Maynard more fully, but Maynard himself remained unbowed.

'I see that now,' he said. He stepped forward, closing the chasm between himself and Abner Grant. 'That was your first line of attack. The moment you were here in my hotel, you set about unearthing its every secret. That's the very thing I invited you here to do. But instead of focusing on who was stealing from my guests, you started digging for secrets – something that you might pass back to the Imperial, something you might expose to John Hastings, something that might undermine his belief that we were right for his investment—'

'You old fool!' Grant barked. 'I knew who'd been robbing your rooms within weeks of getting here. I'm *Abner Grant*. I know what it's my business to know. There was a dancing girl. A Spaniard. Sofía LaPegna, they called her. She ran away to look for her brother, bombed out of Guernica. But she was never going to get far, not on the pittance you paid her. So she started to steal . . .'

Maynard nodded. Abner Grant was no fool, but pride had been many a lesser man's downfall.

'It wasn't enough for you, was it, to do the job I asked you for? You came here with one mission in mind: to unearth a secret, any secret, and use it to wrench John Hastings away from the Buckingham Hotel. And God help me, I almost gave it to you, didn't I? The Park Suite . . .'

Raymond said, 'The suite that's just reopened?'

'He was snooping around it all year,' Billy interjected. 'Frank said he saw him poring over the plans.'

'Well, go on,' said Grant, with a wolfish grin. 'Tell them what I found.'

Maynard stared him down. 'What you found,' he said, 'was that it was already too late. You thought you'd struck gold, didn't you? All you'd have to do was let Hastings know that the very director of the Buckingham was stealing from under the noses of the board, and the Imperial would win the investment – just like *that*! But, you sorry fool, you were too late. The secret evaporated . . .'

Billy and Raymond exchanged a bewildered look.

'I could have told them anyway,' uttered Grant. 'I thought about it. How delicious it would be. But, by that point, I had so little evidence to show what you'd *really* been doing with that suite.'

'You were running out of ideas,' Maynard seethed. 'Without a secret to string us up with, all you had left was destruction, wanton destruction! You're the one who set the fire in the dressing rooms behind the Grand, Abner. And, by God, it almost worked. But as soon as John Hastings understands what you did here, as soon as he understands how he's being manipulated by your masters at the Imperial, well, things are going to—'

'You're not going to say a thing, Maynard.'

The three of them stared.

'You breathe a word of any of this, and I'll tell them who was living in the Park Suite all these years. Once I learned about the black hole at the middle of this hotel, it didn't take long to put the rest together. I remember you, Maynard. The looks the pair of you threw each other in the dugout at night. In the base hospital at Riems, and Aubrey muttering your name in his sleep . . .' Grant stopped. His eyes took in the blank, empty looks of Billy Brogan and Raymond de Guise. 'I can see, by their dumb faces, that your fellows, here, have only the vaguest idea of what you've been up to in this hotel. Well, let's start with this one, shall we? Your precious hotel director, boys, he's had a dirty secret hidden here in this hotel. His name was Aubrey Higgins. He was Maynard's . . . *wife*, shall we say?'

Maynard quaked. 'I kept your secret all these years, Abner. Lord help me, on the night you ran away from the trenches, my heart even went out to you. I knew that same fear. I knew how it could take hold of a man, compel him to things of which he didn't know he was capable. But Aubrey saved your life that night. If he hadn't have brought you back, if the NCOs had known you were gone – why, you'd have been found by morning. You'd have been dead by the fall of the next night – dead at our own hands, no doubt. Aubrey *saved* your life, Abner. *I* saved your life. And now—'

'Rather a coward,' Abner spat, 'than a *fairy*.'

Maynard opened his mouth to retort, but never got the chance. Already, Raymond was stepping forward. All that Maynard really saw was his closed fist whistling past. It connected with the side of Grant's face with a sickening crunch.

Grant's head flew back, he lost his footing, and in the next instant he crashed to the cluttered office floor. Not a soul in the room knew whether it was the might of Raymond's punch that knocked him out cold, or the way his head ricocheted off the edge of his desk as he tumbled. But not a soul cared. Abner Grant lay, breathing but unconscious, on the audit room floor.

The punch had been thrown in anger, but seconds later Raymond was on his knees, making sure Grant still had a pulse. Billy, who did nothing but stand there gawking, was quickly instructed to go and summon an ambulance – 'and the police, Billy!' – and only after he was gone did Raymond look up at Maynard Charles.

'Sir,' he said, 'forgive me. I couldn't stand for this man to . . .'

Maynard touched Raymond's shoulder, as tender a gesture as the old man had ever shown.

'Make no apologies to me, Raymond. Though I'll remind you – and not for the first time – that this body of yours is insured by this hotel. Never put it in a position of such flagrant danger again. Good God, Raymond – rushing into burning buildings, felling men with one punch . . . You're a dancer, not a hero!'

Raymond stood. 'Sir, about what Abner Grant said . . .'

Maynard was quite still. He gathered himself.

'It's all true, Mr de Guise. Every last thing. It's been the defining factor of my life. It's the reason I'm in thrall to those spooks who have us eavesdrop on every fascist and foreign dignitary who passes through our hotel. It's the reason I . . .' Maynard paused. 'You're looking at me oddly. If this new knowledge of me is something you have a problem with . . .'

'We all have secrets, don't we, Mr Charles? And' – Raymond reached out and clasped Maynard by the hand – 'you've long been my boss, Mr Charles, but I consider you my friend, as well.'

Maynard flushed crimson. 'Yes,' he breathed. 'Well, that's quite . . . That is, to say, that this is something I could . . . tolerate.' *Tolerate* – such a strange word, to be imbued with such positive feeling. But Raymond felt the warmth emanating out of Maynard. 'It doesn't change anything, you know. The ballroom's

392

still closed. I still have to scythe through the next year's budget to save it. John Hastings will see that. His accountants will know it. The Buckingham's adrift at sea. There's nothing I can do to steer it.'

Billy crashed back into the room.

'The ambulances are in Berkeley Square. The Old Bill isn't far behind . . .'

Maynard crouched down and stared, long and hard, into his old friend's lined face.

Some men are born rotten, he thought, *but some of them choose it.*

'What were they paying you, Abner? By God, if it was about the money, I would have doubled it . . .'

'Whatever it was,' Raymond added, 'it wasn't enough. That night he was in the dressing rooms, he was asking about Sofía. Where she went, where she might be . . . It wasn't just you he was trying to blackmail this year. If he found Sofía, why, he could blackmail her too . . .'

Maynard looked at Abner Grant's prostrate form.

A poison, he thought, *and I let him into my hotel.*

'Mr Charles,' Raymond ventured, 'what if he does . . . betray your secret?'

There were footsteps pounding up the hall. Maynard stood.

'Then I'll face it as I've faced every other scandal in this hotel. I'll find a way to spirit it away. And if I can't—'

The door opened, revealing two ambulance men, who stepped quickly through. The footsteps pounding up the hallway behind them must have been the Metropolitan Police.

'Billy,' Maynard said, 'prepare a way to the staff entrance. Let's keep this as private as possible, shall we?'

Raymond looked Maynard up and down. It was funny, he thought, but the past half an hour seemed to have wrought a change in the man. He was holding his head up high. Nothing had changed for the Buckingham, that much was true – but a burden seemed to have lifted from Maynard Charles; some private war had been resolved. In the midst of chaos and confusion, of betrayal and heartache, he seemed more like himself than he had done since Raymond first set foot back on English soil. You could trust a man like Maynard Charles, thought Raymond. You could put yourself in his hands. All the hundreds of people who worked at the Buckingham Hotel had done exactly that.

It was, Raymond thought, as the ambulance men laid out a stretcher and started to hoist Abner Grant aboard, the most magical thing.

February 1938

Chapter Thirty-eight

T HE NEWS OF ABNER GRANT'S arrest spread through the Buckingham Hotel more wildly than the fire he had started. By the second week in February, not a soul in the hotel was not talking about the traitor who'd been among them. It was said that old Abner was sitting in a remand cell in Pentonville Prison, where the slop they got served would never be enough to fill the bottomless pit of his stomach, and that he might even go on trial by the spring. Maynard Charles would be called to testify, and so too would all the dancers at the hotel.

But that, thought Raymond de Guise, *is for another day . . .*

In the little corridor that opened out, through the storerooms, into the staff entrance on Michaelmas Mews, Raymond put his arms around Nancy and breathed her in.

'Raymond,' she whispered, 'I'll be back. You have my word.'

'The night's still young,' he said.

'And it'll be young for some time yet. But I . . . can't leave Miss Edgerton to it alone. She needs me. You understand, don't you?'

He kissed her, gently, on the cheek. 'Be safe, Nancy.'

'I have your brother for that!' She grinned.

'Frank's so excited about tonight. He'll show you his stuff, Nancy.'

'I can't believe the wonder he's turning into, Raymond. To think, my Frank, my little man, actually *dancing*. If only the miners could see him now!'

Perhaps she would have said more, but at that moment Vivienne appeared and took her by the arm.

'I'll bring her back to you, Mr de Guise. Have no fear on that account.'

Raymond stood alone as Vivienne led Nancy down through the staff entrance. At the door, on the edge of Michaelmas Mews, Nancy looked back and threw him a smile.

'I promise,' were the words she mouthed. Then she shuffled her feet, weaving her hips in imitation of the dances she'd seen him teaching Frank. 'We're going dancing!'

After she was gone, Raymond stood there alone. That smile she'd given him – something in it reminded him of those earliest days, back before California, back when he and Nancy were only just beginning to dance around the edges of their future relationship. And now, tonight, they were going out dancing. It made his heart soar.

As he turned to leave, a familiar face was bowling over to him. Billy Brogan seemed to grow taller with the seasons – or perhaps it was only the concierge uniform in which he now dressed himself. It smartened him up, made him seem more grown-up than ever before. But nothing could change that overeager, irrepressible grin he always wore.

He was brandishing an envelope.

'It came for you express, Mr de Guise. A courier's delivery! Well, all your friends in high places, it's a wonder you don't get more private mail.'

Raymond took the envelope gracefully – and surreptitiously checked it for any signs that Billy was up to his old ways, snooping inside envelopes that didn't belong to him. Even though there were no signs of Billy's fingers sneaking inside, his heart gave a skip – for there, stamped onto the back of the envelope, were the words ROYAL TRANSATLANTIC.

He dismissed Billy with a single sharp nod – ignoring the boy's eager eyes and hand virtually outstretched, asking for a tip – and retreated to the solitude of the dance studio. Only here, breathing in the scent of the freshly whitewashed walls and lacquer on the new flooring, did he open the envelope.

The ticket inside was one way: straight to New York City.

RMS *Othello* left in twenty-four hours.

He'd been keeping the letter from Georges in his pocket. A part of him had meant to burn it, but a part of him clung on to it too – this totem from a life he might yet have.

His eyes glazed over so much of it, but a single sentence still called out.

Destiny calls! Georges had written.

He smiled – because, not for the first time, Hélène Marchmont's wise words came back to mind.

There are different types of destiny, she'd told him. And how right she was.

Later, as the work was ending in the Grand, as the skies above Berkeley Square turned towards night and all the enchantment of the stars, Raymond waited in the dance studio.

He was listening to his old Cab Calloway recordings, wishing the hours away so that the dancing might begin, when the door opened and Frank appeared with Rosa – both of them in long woollen coats.

Frank took in the emptiness of the room, then said, 'Where's Nancy?'

Raymond looked at the clock on the wall, its hands inching towards seven o'clock.

'She'll be here soon. She did promise.'

'We'll hang on, shall we?'

Raymond's eyes lingered on the clock. Seven o' clock seemed perilously near.

'Let's show Rosa some jive, shall we, Frank?'

Raymond had grown to cherish the lessons he was giving Frank. Sometimes they danced in the old hotel laundry, when the other pages were lost in their duties; sometimes they danced in the chambermaids' kitchenette, where there was barely enough room to perform; but now that the studio was back in operation, they had the perfect seclusion for their routines. To perform the jive tonight with Frank in one of Soho's dance halls would be sublime – but, more than that, the chance to step out again with Nancy, to take her dancing, to see her in the Midnight Rooms or the Nest, or even the Ambergris, that little dance hall underneath Charing Cross where they planned on going tonight, would have meant *everything*.

But the clock moved past seven, and drew inexorably towards eight.

It did not matter, not for the moment. Raymond set the gramophone to playing another of his Cab Calloway recordings and ostentatiously bowed, as if to welcome Rosa to the ballroom floor.

Frank roared with delight.

One song turned into the next. Sometimes Raymond danced with Rosa; sometimes Raymond danced with Frank; sometimes Frank and Rosa kicked and turned and eddied together, slipping in and out of hold.

And still there was no sign of Nancy.

The clock on the wall had already passed 8.30.

'Frank, Rosa,' Raymond began, 'the night is getting old. May I suggest that you . . . go on without us?'

'But Mr de Guise!' Frank protested. 'This is *our* night. All four of us . . .'

Raymond smiled wanly. 'And yet, there are only three of us here.' He composed himself. 'Dance a jive for me, Frank. You're a master of the art. I'll wait for Nancy. If she comes . . .'

If, thought Raymond. How quickly 'when' turned into 'if'.

It was with a great sadness that he watched Frank and Rosa disappear off into the night. It was only one dance, he told himself. It was only one night. Stacked against what Nancy was doing tonight, what hopes and dreams she had pinned on Mr George Peel, one dance surely did not matter. Well, did it?

And suddenly he was back there, on Christmas Day, watching Nancy walk away. Suddenly, in his mind, they were at loggerheads again, each trying to tell the other about their dreams, but neither truly listening to the other.

Tonight was meant to be the night when none of that mattered. But instead . . .

The last of the Cab Calloway recordings came to its triumphant conclusion. If only, Raymond thought, the same sense of victory was in his own heart tonight. With a great sigh – the sigh of some decision being reached that could never be taken back – he snuffed the lights in the dance studio, closed the door, and left it behind.

He did not notice the letter that had rucked up out of his pocket and drifted down to the floor as he left. He did not notice it as it landed, face turned upwards, on the new lacquered flooring. He simply left it there, in the dark, and set out to do the thing that finally, in his heart, he knew must be done.

Chapter Thirty-nine

As Frank and Rosa slipped towards the staff entrance, Maynard Charles was emerging from behind the reception desks and breathing deeply to steady his nerves. By the time he reached the doors of the Queen Mary, he had found some of his old resolve, and he stepped inside to the smells of roast venison, sage and thyme and rosemary potatoes.

Lord Edgerton was easy to distinguish, holding court at the table in the restaurant's very centre, Uriah Bell and the other members of the hotel board around him.

Half of me still thinks he's about to round on me and dismiss me from service, Maynard realised as he approached. *But Abner Grant hasn't breathed a word yet – or, if he has, nobody pays it any attention; a man facing the rest of his life in a stone-cold cell will say almost anything . . .*

Sometimes, the Metropolitan Police would come back to Maynard with more news of the case being built against Grant. Though he'd confessed little, dogged police work had begun to piece a story together. There was even talk of one of the day managers at the Imperial being charged with aiding and abetting the crime. One of the detectives wondered if Grant had learned the art of explosives digging the tunnels into the no-man's-land of

Flanders, but the fact was his crime had been so much more prosaic: gas canisters and liquor, all of them stolen from right under Maynard's nose.

Maynard reached the table and announced his presence with a cough. As one, the eyes of the board turned to study him.

'Sirs, if you'll excuse the change of plans, I must ask you to accompany me into the Grand.'

'The Grand?' Uriah Bell looked aghast at his plate. 'Mr Charles, my scallops will hardly eat themselves . . .'

'Be that as it may, sir, it is requested.'

'Up!' Lord Edgerton announced, directing the rest of the board like Archie Adams did his orchestra. Then, as the other six disgruntled board members forked the remnants of their starters into their mouths and rose, Lord Edgerton muttered, out of the side of his mouth, 'What word, Maynard?'

Maynard Charles was impassive. 'I know as little as you do, sir.'

'The man plays us like marionettes. It won't do.'

'As you say, sir.'

As the board trooped out of the Queen Mary, Lord Edgerton added, 'My stepdaughter. She's absent again, isn't she?'

'I believe so, sir.'

'It's almost eight, Maynard.'

I'm not her keeper! Maynard wanted to snap. *This little endeavour of hers, out in the East End, is just another one of the secrets I'll have to keep. As soon as you shed one, three more rise up to take its place.*

'Sir,' said Maynard, and led the way.

The doors to the Grand Ballroom were already open. Inside, the contours of the refashioned ballroom could be seen. A frame

404

of timbers stood where the new orchestra stage would one day stand – and, although the new dance floor had not yet been laid, the cavity beneath it had been stripped bare and its charred panelling replaced. The struts of the new balustrade were in place, and great portions of the walls scraped back to bare brick. The bar, which had survived the fire intact, was almost the only thing that remained of the old Grand – and there, standing at it, flanked by a multitude of men in slick suits, stood the bespectacled figure of John Hastings Junior.

At a nod from Maynard, Billy closed the doors behind them.

Look at John Hastings, Maynard thought, *a mere pup compared to Lord Edgerton, Uriah Bell and the rest – and yet he holds us all in the palm of his hand.*

'Sirs,' John Hastings said, 'shall we begin? I'm sorry to have kept you waiting. I'm sorry, too, for the last-minute change in plans. I assure you, you shall be back in the Queen Mary before long – and, I dare say, I shall be joining you . . .'

Maynard saw the backs of the board stiffen. He'd seen this before, too. It all stank of *hope*. Joyful, desperate, urgent *hope*.

'I thought it more apposite that we speak of these things here in the Grand Ballroom, the once and future glory of the Buckingham Hotel. Would that all your dancers and musicians could be here as well – but I am a man of decorum in all things, and in business most of all.

'As you must be aware, I have been poised, since Christmas, to announce my investment in the Imperial Hotel. The Imperial offers many things: stout, reliable business, with scope for development beyond the imaginations of its current board. My business associates had always believed the Imperial the sounder choice for our investment. In short, the Buckingham relies on variables far too flighty for men of economics and science. Reputation. Glamour. The uncontrollable delights . . . Before Christmas, I was able to sway them – for, in spite of myself, I had come to under- stand the importance of the *feeling* of a place. You gentlemen had the efforts of Raymond de Guise, your own star dancer, in seeking to convert me to the cause. The cause of *joy*!' He paused. 'But then came the calamity.'

He turned to the gaping hole at the back of the ballroom.

'When fire tore through those dressing rooms, out into this ballroom, no feeling in the world could change the economics of the matter. The Imperial Hotel was the more robust investment by far. I retired to New York for the Christmas season. On New Year's Eve, my wife and I returned to the Cotton Club to dance – and there, though I admit to my two left feet, I remembered everything that I had learned last year. About music. About joy. About the things to which we can't ascribe dollar signs, nor ster- ling. But the fact remained – love cannot change mathematics. I would have to return to London and sign my name to the Imperial. And then . . .

'Well,' said John Hastings, 'then came Raymond de Guise once more. Then came the revelation. Gentlemen, you have been the victims of a most egregious act.'

He looked at each of the board in turn – and it seemed to Maynard Charles, then, that some understanding was being reached between them.

'I know I may appear less steely than most. But know this – I am not a man who likes being pushed around. I am not a man who likes being manipulated or hoodwinked. What the Imperial commissioned against you – well, let us just say, Abner Grant may be the one to languish in a prison cell for what he did, but

406

the whole of the Imperial will suffer in return.' He broke into a smile. 'Those snakes at the Imperial Hotel can go to hell. I'm a Buckingham man, gentlemen.'

Maynard had not thought it possible, but all of a sudden the dour old men of the board were beaming. Lord Edgerton's eyes were fixed, momentarily, on Maynard Charles, before he turned to John Hastings, strode towards him and . . .

He's going to kneel! thought Maynard. *Like a medieval knight to his king – he's going to kneel!*

But Lord Edgerton simply held out his hand.

'A Buckingham man!' he announced. 'I like the sound of that, Mr Hastings. I like the sound of it very much indeed.'

Then the rest of the board were gathered around – and, not for the first time, Maynard's mind turned to Raymond, and all of the good the man had done for the hotel.

We'd be a lesser place without him, he thought. *I must remember to issue a new contract. A new contract, for a new Grand Ballroom . . .*

As hands were shaken and champagne corks popped in the Grand Ballroom, all was quiet in the chambermaids' kitchenette. Vera and Edie were playing backgammon over a big pot of tea, but neither of them looked up as Raymond approached Nancy's room.

There was no use in knocking. He knew she was not here. He reached up and, taking a little pin out of his pocket, fastened an envelope to the door. Then, for a moment, he simply stood there, breathing it all in. He closed his eyes and remembered the first day he'd seen her: the spirited chambermaid who had dressed herself up to the nines and dared to venture into the Grand Ballroom, risking her very role at the hotel. Scarcely eighteen months had passed since that day, and yet the world had turned.

Raymond crept back out of the chambermaids' quarters and rode the service lift to the ground floor. There was something of a tumult coming from the Grand Ballroom as he approached the reception desks – where Billy Brogan was just getting ready for the end of his shift. Taking out a second envelope from his evening jacket, he passed it into Billy's waiting hands.

Billy looked at the address. His eyes were agog.

'I'll take it to the post room straight away, Mr de Guise!' He paused. 'Oh, and Mr de Guise, there's a car waiting for you out on Berkeley Square. Courtesy of Georges de la Motte?'

Raymond nodded. The old man had thought of everything.

He turned, just in time to see a stream of men in long black dinner jackets filing up and out of the Grand. Looming among them stood Lord Edgerton, whose gaze landed on Raymond. It was the strangest sight, something Raymond had never seen before, for at this moment Lord Edgerton himself was smiling. Then, flanked by the other members of the hotel board, he vanished through the Queen Mary's doors.

Last of all came Maynard Charles – and, beside him, John Hastings Junior.

John Hastings's eyes lit up when he saw Raymond.

'Quite a ballroom you're going to have in there, old friend. Quite a ballroom!'

Raymond's face must have betrayed his bewilderment, because presently Maynard joined them.

'Let it be you, Raymond, who hears the good news first. Mr Hastings here is to join the board of the Buckingham

Hotel. His American patrons will begin staying with us by the equinox – just in time for the Spring Ball, and the reopening of the Grand.'

'Which will be more elegant and refined than it ever was before!'

Maynard's head bobbed. 'No corners cut. No expense spared. It will be the envy of London town again, Raymond – and there you'll be, leading the way.'

Raymond was aware, in the corner of his vision, of Billy cantering back to the reception desk, having delivered his letter to the hotel post room. He let Mr Charles's words sink in.

'Oh, yes, I'm looking forward to that!' John Hastings beamed. 'Sarah talks non-stop about our visit to the Cotton Club, Mr de Guise. Now, as I'll be the first to attest, I was something of a spoilsport. Well, no more! I'll have my dancing shoes on, the moment I come home. And, by spring, Sarah and I will be back along with the children – and she'll be dancing with you at the Spring Ball.' He paused. 'Do you know, Mr Charles, I often wonder why I make the decisions I do. But this time I *know* why. A little less than a year ago, Mr de Guise here and I spent some time together at sea. For days and days, he talked about the Grand Ballroom and what I'd find when I got here – and did I care? Not one jot! But something changed – and I believe it all began with this man . . .'

Maynard looked Raymond up and down.

'Yes,' he said, remembering a single punch thrown in anger – and in honour. 'Our own Mr de Guise is among the best of men.'

'We'll be seeing a lot more of each other, Mr de Guise!' John Hastings exclaimed, and shook Raymond enthusiastically by the hand. 'From now on, you're my own leading man!'

After that, Maynard and John Hastings drifted on, off to the hotel director's office to look at ledgers and charts, profits and disbursements. But Raymond de Guise stood alone.

'Billy,' he whispered, 'did you deliver my letter?'

'Just like you told me to, Mr de Guise!'

Then it's done, thought Raymond, and closed his eyes.

Chapter Forty

T HE LAST TIME I SET *foot in here*, thought Hélène Marchmont, *I got caught in the middle of a brawl on the dance floor.* She paused on the threshold of the Midnight Rooms. *Let's hope it's nothing so insalubrious this time round.*

The winter was finally in thaw, and the snow banks between the stalls of the Berwick Street Market were turning to rivers of grey slush. Hélène looked back at the closing stalls, and thought, momentarily, about taking flight. She did not *have* to do this. But for days there had been a feeling in the pit of her stomach, a feeling so much worse than the realisation of who Arthur Regan really was.

It was a feeling called Louis Kildare.

The Midnight Rooms didn't look like much without any of its patrons. Without the revellers on the dance floor or the musicians up on stage it was just a cellar with jet-black walls and innumerable little alcoves and cubbyholes studded around. The acoustics in here, Hélène remembered, were terrible – and yet, when the place came alive, none of that seemed to matter. She'd danced, once, with Raymond de Guise right here. She'd come here, too, with Louis.

And there he was. Louis was in a huddle of other musicians on the floor in front of the club's tiny stage, while their bandleader ran through the set list for the evening's performances.

Hélène waited.

It was the band's percussionist, an older gentleman with a wilderness of white hair, who saw her first. He nudged Louis in the ribs, and only then did Louis turn around.

For too long, silence stretched out between them. It seemed to widen the distance, so that the cramped surroundings of the Midnight Rooms became a ballroom more vast than the Hammersmith Palais.

'Come on, boys, let's leave Louis to it,' said the percussionist – and, in pairs, the band disappeared through the backstage door.

Finally, only Hélène Marchmont and Louis Kildare remained on the dance floor. Even the cleaner had waltzed away with her mop.

'Louis,' she said, 'my Louis. I believe I owe you an apology. And . . . my thanks.'

Louis said nothing.

The cat has caught his tongue, Hélène thought, *and why not, after everything I said?*

She waited. Then, after her heart had started pounding and her lips had turned bone dry with nerves, he said, 'Hélène.'

That was all. He stepped towards one of the cubbyholes, and there they settled in the comforting darkness.

Louis produced a book of matches and lit the candle between them. The scent of beeswax rose up.

'Is he gone, Miss Marchmont?'

Hélène's jaw was set. 'I won't speak to you at all, if you don't call me Hélène.'

'Is he gone . . . Hélène?'

'I haven't seen nor heard from him. He cancelled all the reservations he had at the hotel. He hasn't written, or even tried to explain. Louis, I've been having dreams. Nightmares, you'd call them. And every time, there he is, grinning. Those last words he said . . .'

'"Do you think *I'd* set that fire, just to choke out a few dancing girls?"' Louis whispered.

'I've been going back over it all, racking my brain, and . . . It was all about the King, Louis. Arthur had been asking about it ever since I met him. The royal patronage of the Buckingham. When was the King coming to grace us? Was King George truly going to be there for the New Year's Ball?'

'Hélène, you can't—'

'Well, they'd tried it already, hadn't they? They went after the King in Belfast last year. So why not . . . ?'

'He'd have gone down in glory,' Louis said slowly. 'Arthur Regan – a king slayer—'

'And our Buckingham the scene of the assassination. Louis, he—' She started to tremble as the realisation moved through her body for the hundredth time; it still did not seem real. 'He was using me all along. He knew, from the start, that the Buckingham had royal patronage. He turned me into his fountain of knowledge. He even took me to a tea dance, just to meet his colleagues – the men he was plotting it with. They asked me about the King that day as well. They were making me *help* them.'

For the first time, Louis reached across the table. Something stopped him from taking her hand, no matter how much he wanted to. He patted it gently, then withdrew – and hated himself for the fact. A real friend would have put his arms around her.

413

'It was the fire that stopped him,' Louis breathed. 'He didn't set it at all.'

'They arrested Abner Grant.'

'The hotel detective?'

'A saboteur, for the Imperial Hotel . . .'

Louis let out a deep, melodic whistle. 'A saboteur he may be, but perhaps he saved the King's life. If the Grand hadn't closed, if the New Year's Ball had gone ahead – if Regan and his fellows had done everything they set out to do . . . Why, Grant is almost a hero!'

Hélène betrayed herself with a smile. 'Don't let Mr Charles hear you speak of him like that.'

She didn't tell him the rest, not about what Raymond had told her about the secret Abner Grant carried on Maynard Charles's behalf, nor about how Sofía LaPegna had been the one, creeping from room to room, taking whatever she could, just so that she might have a hope of crossing the Continent and finding her lost brother. Instead, she whispered the very thing she'd come here to say.

'Why, Louis? Why did you . . . leave?'

Louis thought: *she must know.*

'I couldn't stay, Hélène. Not once I saw him with you. Not once I knew the way you felt. I . . .'

'You were angry with me, because of Sidney.'

Louis's face fell. 'No, Hélène,' he said sadly, 'not angry. I was lonely. I . . .'

The change in her face was so subtle that a stranger might not have noticed. But Louis was no stranger.

Now she knows, he thought. *She knows and yet . . . she isn't running . . .*

'I'm sorry, Hélène. I didn't mean for it to happen. I didn't truly know it had, not until Regan . . .'

Hélène had only one word to say: 'Louis,' she whispered.

'I'm a fool, Hélène. And a fool in love is the most foolish fool there is. Sidney, he was my best friend. He was my *brother*.'

As Louis's words vanished into silence, Hélène filled the void.

'If love's made a fool out of either of us, Louis, it's me. I dared to think I could love Arthur. I wanted to so very, very much.' She hesitated, if only to make sure the tears that were threatening to come did not eclipse all her words. 'Here's the thing that bruises me most: I *could* love him. It wasn't quite real, not yet, but I could feel it bubbling up inside me. I could feel something I hadn't felt for years. And now . . .'

Louis's eyes darted away, unable to hold her gaze. 'You'll find it again, Hélène.'

'You understand, don't you? I want to feel it again. I do. But I chanced my heart again and—' Why were words such damnable things? She wanted to say so much, but everything came out sounding like the tortured scribblings she'd made in her diary when she was a girl. 'I do love you, Louis Kildare. Only . . . as a brother. As a friend.'

Louis nodded, still unable to hold her gaze.

'I want to be in love,' Hélène went on, trying to take his hand. 'If Arthur Regan taught me anything, it's that I'm not dead, not yet. He was wrong for me. He was using me. But there's love left to give in me – I have to hold on to that. But, Louis—'

'It's all right. I understand. It isn't me. It's an age-old story, isn't it, Hélène?' He smiled, took her hand, forced himself to meet her eyes. 'I knew it already, deep inside. That, Hélène, *that's* why I left the Buckingham.'

Hélène said, 'I want you to come back.'

Louis was silent.

'The Buckingham needs you. It needs all of us. There's such change coming, Louis. I don't even know if, by this time next week, we'll have Raymond de Guise.' At this, Louis's face creased. 'But we won John Hastings's investment, in spite of everything that happened last year. There'll be a new Grand Ballroom, and it will be better than ever. There'll be a Summer Ball, and a Masque for next winter. The world keeps turning, Louis, and I need you in my life. You're the only one who knows who I am. Oh, there are others who know tiny fragments of my life. But not like you. You're the one who knew Sidney. You're the one who plays saxophone at his grave, or takes Sybil in his arms and tells her who her mother and father truly were, in those days before she was born. The hotel needs you, Louis, and I need you too. I'm' – her voice cracked – 'sorry it isn't in the way you dreamed it might be, but I do love you, Louis. You're my family. You're the Buckingham's family. Just listen to the wireless: there are such testing times to come. If the world's to go to Hell, let it do it while I'm dancing to the sound of your saxophone rising out of the band.'

Out on the dance floor, the musicians had reassembled. There was just enough time to run through a couple of songs before the evening's patrons would start flooding down the stairs.

'I'm needed here—'

'But, Louis . . .'

Louis found the courage to fix her with his eyes – and in them there was no pleading; there was no sadness; but nor was there any hope. There was just a curious kind of peace.

Acceptance, Hélène thought. She was beginning to know that feeling well.

'I'll treasure everything you've said tonight, Hélène. I'm grateful you came. I just need more time. I need to know what's right. For me,' he added, 'and for what happens next in my life. I hope you can understand.'

Louis teased his fingers out of hers and stepped out of the alcove.

Hélène snuffed out the candle and sat there in the dark. Some moments later, she heard the sound of Louis's saxophone soar up to join the rest of the band. She wanted him back at the Buckingham more than anything else, but she had heard the wisdom in his voice. Everyone had to find their own way back to love, in the end. And she wanted that for him too – wherever it might lead him.

Chapter Forty-one

A S THE CHAMPAGNE CORKS ARCED up and over the Grand Ballroom, thin rags of snow tumbled over the streets of Whitechapel, lightly dusting the steps where Artie Cohen stood, guarding the doorway to the Daughters of Salvation.

Inside, as the volunteers moved between the partitions, Nancy and Vivienne waited patiently with Mary Burdett. Occasionally, Artie looked over his shoulder and saw the worried looks on their faces, the way their eyes kept darting towards the door, as if expecting it to open. Through the thin crack he watched as they paced the edges of the room. It put him in mind of nothing more than his own stay in Pentonville Prison – where he was given to believe Abner Grant, the Great Arsonist of the Buckingham, was languishing.

The night was getting colder.

When the bells of some distant church tower tolled out eight times, Nancy quietly picked her way through the sleeping bodies, until she slipped out of the chapel. Artie turned expectantly, anticipating the hot drink about to be pressed into his hands, but all that Nancy had brought was herself.

'No sign of him?'

'I'm not hiding him, miss,' Artie said, turning out his pockets. 'A man like George Peel doesn't go for being hidden.'

She came down the steps, looking up and down the street – but the only movement was a street fox, scavenging for some food.

'He should have been here two hours ago.'

'I know, miss.'

'Raymond and I, we were meant to go dancing. I promised him, Artie. I'm getting good at breaking my promises.'

'Seems to me it's promises you been keeping,' said Artie, 'to that lot in there.'

Nancy nodded. 'It meant a lot to Raymond. And—'

'I reckon he'll understand.'

And Nancy thought: *Perhaps. But there's still California out there. There's still Hollywood and Havelock Meyer and* Stairway to the Stars. *There's still a different future, if that's what Raymond wants . . .*

'It's useless,' Nancy said. 'He was never really coming, was he? So we'll just go on, using whatever Miss Edgerton can pull together until her stepfather finds out. Lord help us then, Artie. He won't be able to send Vivienne away, so he'll . . .' She shook her head, as if she might be able to shake away the thought. 'Artie, I shouldn't be there.'

'That doesn't sound like you, Nance.'

She looked up, into the twirling snow. Winter, she thought, had gone on too long.

'There's too many people. Too many to help. And the Daughters, it should grow and spread – and it's all I've been thinking about, isn't it? It's been in my every waking thought. But really, life's a hundred different things and . . . Oh, hang it, Artie, I want to dance. The Daughters will be here tomorrow, George Peel or . . .'

419

Nancy didn't finish the sentence, because in that moment Artie's gaze shifted further along the road. Headlights were approaching, the purr of an engine growing louder. Soon, the headlights loomed large, dazzling Nancy as the creamy white Jaguar they were leading came to a halt. She had seen cars as ostentatious before, but only lined up in Berkeley Square for the valets at the Buckingham to attend to. Here on the streets of Whitechapel it seemed an aberration.

So too did the man who stepped out of its passenger side, with a look so imperious he might have come out of one of Frank's books about the great British Men of Empire. This man ought surely to have been taking tea on the lawn of some palatial estate, playing croquet while his manservants milled around him. Instead, he waited as a burly man in a long brown trenchcoat emerged from the back of the car, bringing Warren Peel with him.

The last time Nancy had seen Warren, he'd been reclining in the chapel, half-awake and happy to take sugary tea out of a chipped china cup. The last time Artie had seen him, he'd been so much worse. He looked healthier, thought Artie, but if a grown man had ever looked more like a sheepish, scolded child, Artie had never seen it.

So, thought Nancy, *this is George Peel.*

She tried to take him in. She'd changed the sheets and plumped the pillows for a hundred men as wealthy, but never had she felt the same nerves rising in her as she did now.

'Mr Peel,' she ventured – but George Peel was already addressing the man in brown.

'Stay with the car, Mr Slade. Not a single scratch, you hear?'

When the burly man nodded, he seemed strangely chastened.

'Come on, Warren, you can lead.'

Warren Peel shuffled forward.

'And don't delay. We're late already because of you. A Peel is *never* late!'

George barely noticed Nancy as Warren shuffled past and entered the alley, but his eyes *did* land on Artie Cohen. A single nod was his only acknowledgement, and then he strode on.

As Nancy and Artie turned to follow, Artie muttered, 'He's still got my coat. I'm never going to get it back, am I?'

By the time they caught up, George and Warren Peel were standing in the open doorway of the Daughters of Salvation. As Nancy and Artie slipped through behind them, Vivienne Edgerton and Mary Burdett crossed the hall. Mary stopped to take in the sight of Warren.

'Young man,' she announced, 'I've never seen you look as well!'

Nancy sensed Vivienne's hand squeezing her own.

'Remember everything we said,' Nancy whispered. 'It's you who moved him enough to come here, Miss Edgerton . . . even if he is two hours too late. So it's you who'll have to show him.'

'This is it, then? This is the place, Warren?'

Warren whispered, 'Yes, Father.'

'Well, speak up, boy! What have you got to say?'

George Peel's voice boomed so loudly that it echoed in the chapel rafters.

Warren's voice was much smaller, but it echoed still.

'Thank you.'

'Louder, boy!'

'Thank you!' said Warren.

George's hand around the back of Warren's head prompted him to say it one last time, this time with his head held high.

'Thank you,' he said, 'for everything you've done for me. For putting me right.'

'And?' uttered George.

'I'm sorry,' said Warren.

The look that came across Mary's face was one of disgust – that anyone should make such a fool of the boy – but somehow she managed to keep it buried inside.

'Warren, seeing you on your feet, it's all the thanks we need. But to see you here again—'

'Oh, he'll be here again,' said George.

Mary's face twisted. 'A little faith, Mr Peel. Young men in Warren's predicament need support to—'

'No,' said George, craning around as if to inspect the building, 'you misunderstand me. Warren will be returning here – because he is to be your new volunteer. Explain, Warren.'

'My father says I have to make recompense for what I put you through.'

'What you put us *all* through,' George added. Then he reached up and snatched the top hat from his head. 'Miss Edgerton, Mr Cohen. Since we last met, I have undertaken an investigation of my own. I was rash, the night you arrived at my door. There were many things I could scarcely believe that night, but the one thing I could not disbelieve was the evidence of my own eyes. My son, turning up bedraggled and half-dead, strung up between two strangers – and owing them his very life. Well, you were right, Miss Edgerton. My household staff have been helping Warren here hide his every mistake for a number of years. Ever since his mother passed away, in fact, Warren has had a damaging amount of freedom. And you have seen the result. Well, no more. Warren is to become a man. He has been looked after for too long. So I trust you will accept him here. He will work often and he will work hard – and expect nothing in return. Isn't that right, Warren?'

Warren nodded. As he lifted his head, Vivienne caught his eye.

He's handsome, she thought, *when he's not in his stupor. But the shame in his eyes – it's palpable. It's almost physical.* She imagined crossing the room to console him, but remained where she was.

'A Peel always makes good on his debts, ladies. You can be certain of that. And . . .' He stopped. 'You made me a proposition, when you turned up on my doorstep, Miss Edgerton.'

Vivienne found her voice. 'Mr Peel, I have been working with the Daughters of Salvation for nine months and more. Were I to describe to you the changes we have made to this chapel, you would think we had been operating with many more resources than we have. I have brought to the Daughters what little money I can. We have brought in more volunteers. We have built more partitions and put up more beds. We feed and clothe whoever we can. We pay for a doctor to make visits, and I am quite certain it is saving lives.'

This was it, she thought. This was the moment that counted. She could feel every eye in the room upon her – but, among them, she felt George Peel most of all. She tried not to think of him. She stared at Warren instead. And there it was: a life set back on the straight and narrow, just as Nancy had once done for her. It had been worth it, after all.

'And yet we are limited, Mr Peel. There are others out there – others we can't help. And—'

George Peel lifted his hand, silencing her in one gesture.

'Money makes the world go round, Miss Edgerton. I should know – I've seen enough of it run through these fingers. I've sat in many meetings like this. Men asking me for their investment, so that they might brew new ales or open old factories, or bring new silks in from the Orient. And do you know the one thing – the *only* thing – that ever makes me acquiesce?'

Vivienne wanted to form words, but not one of them would come.

And then Nancy fixed her with a look, and she steeled herself.

'I confess I do not,' Vivienne found the courage to say. Then, her voice changing in tone, she went on, 'Mr Peel, if you don't mind, there's something I must say. Your son, Warren, is not a bad man. You might think him a man of weak will, sir, but that is not the case. The men and women we're trying to help here at the Daughters of Salvation – they're not the degenerates society may think they are. And I should know, sir, because I . . .' Her eyes roamed around, landing first on Artie Cohen, then Mary Burdett – and finally Nancy herself. 'Because I was one of them.'

George's eyes widened.

'I've been ashamed of myself for too long, sir, but I'm strong enough to say it tonight – I was like Warren. My family have means. I want for nothing. Nothing material, that is. But there has always been a part of me that . . . *longed*, I suppose is the word, without really understanding what I was *longing* for. And into that space came my "indulgences" – my addiction.' She paused. 'I was fortunate. I had no need for the Daughters – because I had a friend' – here she lifted Nancy's hand – 'to guide the way. I am proud to have been that person for Warren. Perhaps, some day soon, Warren will be proud to be that person for somebody else. But, sir, from there on it gets more complicated. There are too many to help. It cannot simply be one after another. There are things we can do. Not just more beds – though, Lord knows, that would be a beginning. But there are people we can reach out to before they fall into the dens. There are ways we might . . . educate. A story we might spread, so that we can reach troubled young minds before they fall prey to things that might destroy them. And it is not the will nor the energy that is stopping us pursuing these ambitions already. Sir, it is the *means*.'

'I'll stop you there, Miss Edgerton.' George Peel's voice was stone cold. 'I'll repeat what I said just now. There is one reason, and one only, that has ever swayed me to an investment. And it is not, as you might expect, the prospects of a return on my investment. It is the people I see in front of me.'

Vivienne felt something curdling in her stomach. She squeezed Nancy's hand tight.

'I like what I see, Miss Edgerton. And I will do what I can to help you achieve what you have locked in there.' He pointed first at her head, and then in her heart. 'And my son Warren can watch and learn exactly how it's done – so that, one day, he might have the wherewithal to make something of himself as well. Now!' he announced. 'I trust this is no place for champagne. And yet, an agreement of this magnitude demands celebration. So, what will it be? Earl Grey . . . or Assam, the finest tea in all the Empire?'

Mary Burdett looked as if she herself had been caught in the headlights out on Whitechapel Road.

'We have soup, sir. Chicken broth, with butter beans.'

'Hearty stuff!' roared George. 'Warren, you can serve. Hop to it!'

Nine o'clock had turned into ten by the time Nancy extricated herself from the Daughters of Salvation. It was the distant striking of the clock that had snatched her up from the celebration

425

and sent her scurrying out into the snow, Artie Cohen close on
her heels. Where that hour had disappeared, she did not know –
but, as she tumbled onto Whitechapel Road, vainly searching for
a taxicab, the image that remained, emblazoned across the backs
of her eyelids whenever she closed her eyes, was of the look on
Vivienne's face.

It isn't just triumph, thought Nancy. *It isn't just pride. It's . . .
validation. It's feeling worthy at last.* Seeing it, she thought, was
almost as intoxicating as love.

Love . . .

'Nance!' Artie called after her. 'Nance, where are you—?'

The clock tower had stopped tolling.

'He's been waiting, Artie. Waiting too long.'

She didn't only mean since eight o'clock, when they were supposed to set out for the music and lights at the Ambergris. She
meant all year, ever since he'd come back. She meant all the nights
she was here at the Daughters. She meant Christmas Day . . .

'He'll be waiting even longer if you freeze to death out here.'

Artie marched over to the creamy white Jaguar George Peel
had left behind, its burly minder still prowling around.

'Orders of Mr Peel,' he announced. 'You're to ferry this
young lady to Berkeley Square and return immediately after.
You hear me?'

The driver looked as if he wanted to snarl back, but instead he
nodded glumly.

He's one of those who was protecting Warren, Nancy realised.
He probably counts himself fortunate to have his job.

As she climbed into the back seat, Artie leaned in and whispered, 'You give that brother of mine a kick from me, and tell
him Ma wants him to visit again soon.'

'Artie,' she said, 'thank you.'

Then the engine was roaring and the Jaguar turning around to take her home.

It was a desperate Nancy Nettleton who arrived in style upon Berkeley Square and, gushing thanks, scrabbled up Michaelmas Mews, through the staff entrance and, by the back stairs, to the little studio behind the Grand. When she crashed through the doors, the studio was as dark as it was empty. She stood there, cloaked in the blackness for a moment, then reached out for the lights. As they buzzed into life, she had the foolish idea that she could see ghosts dancing across the new lacquered floor – the after-images of Raymond, Frank and Rosa, who had danced here while they waited.

The clock on the wall had climbed past ten. Two hours, she'd left them waiting.

Two hours and now – only the darkness.

She sank down to her haunches, and listened to the beating of her heart. She'd made a promise, hadn't she? Promises were meant to be kept. But what if keeping one promise meant breaking another? How could you do the right thing, then? As one hope blossomed, another died away, like a rose left to wither on the bush.

She'd make it up to him. She would. This time, she'd be there. Vivienne had George and Warren Peel now. Between them, with Artie and Mary Burdett in tow, they could bring the Daughters of Salvation to life. If they missed little Nancy Nettleton while she was out dancing a tango with the man she loved, well, after everything she'd done for them, they could put up with that.

427

She was feeling the fire of that decision in her heart when she looked down and saw the scrap of paper lying on the floor at her feet.

At first, something told her not to pick it up. It was the sense an animal gets before a storm, the sense of something coming, of something that might change the world. And, like that animal before the storm, the need to run away came suddenly upon her.

But she swallowed the feeling, bent down, and picked it up.

My boy, enough of the dallying! Destiny calls! Raymond, trust in me as you trusted once before – and permit yourself a new, fresher future.

Her eyes scanned the rest of the letter.

Raymond, I both know and love you dearly. I can tell when you are lost. And, my boy, you are lost now.

Each word was a body blow.

The time for a decision has come. I have asked the Royal Transatlantic to forward to you, post haste, a first-class berth on RMS Othello, leaving Liverpool on 13th February. It is your last chance to fulfil the promises I have made and become the star you were born to become!

Nancy had known, ever since the height of summer, that Georges de la Motte's letters reached the Buckingham Hotel, filled with words of entreaty, filled with the vision of a brighter, sunnier future in California climes. But there was an urgency about this letter that she'd not known before. And the fact that Raymond hadn't dared share it with her was itself a kind of poison.

She let her eyes, watery now, scan back over Georges's words. *The star you were born to become.* The idea hurt her more than she had known it would – because it was true, wasn't it? Dreams were there to be fulfilled. She was fulfilling a dream of her own. Why shouldn't Raymond? He wouldn't be Raymond de Guise if he didn't have his dreams. Who was she to stand in his way?

Something struck her.

13th February.

She looked at the clock.

It was less than two hours away. RMS *Othello*, that had brought him back to her, would be the very same vessel taking him away. And, if it left from Liverpool, there was every chance he was already gone.

So she took off, back to the service lift and up, up, up, until she reached the Buckingham's uppermost storey.

There was no light on in Raymond's quarters. Perhaps that meant he was out dancing with Frank and Rosa, missing her the same as she missed him, but in her heart she knew this was not so. She knocked once, knocked twice, knocked in vain a third time, and when there was no answer she hurried away.

In the chambermaids' kitchenette, Vera was asleep in a chair. At her side, the wireless still crackled. Nancy heard snippets as she stole past, the BBC broadcast coming to its nightly end. Mr Eden, the Foreign Secretary, had announced his resignation, and Lord Halifax was to take his place.

The world keeps turning, Nancy thought.

All those days and nights she'd spent at the Daughters of Salvation, it changed lives – but it did not keep the world from spinning on its axis. Kings were still crowned and dethroned. Men like Arthur Regan still plotted their dirty little wars.

429

Government ministers still resigned and rose again. And as for Raymond de Guise . . .

She came past the kitchenette and, finally, to her own bedroom door.

There she stopped dead.

Secured by a single pin to the paintwork was an envelope. Across the front, in Raymond's familiar florid hand, were inscribed the words 'My Dear Nancy'.

She stared. How long had it been since Raymond last wrote to her? Nine months? Ten? All of a sudden, she could vividly recall the feeling of those moments, waiting for Billy Brogan to make an appearance, envelope in hand. The explosion of feeling when she'd opened one of those missives and let his voice wash over her from three, four, five thousand miles away. The very idea that his words had been able to reach out and touch her, when she could no longer touch his skin, nor breathe in his scent . . .

It took Nancy too long to pluck the letter from the door. Even then, she could not open it. She began to dwell on those three words inscribed upon the front.

Why would he write to her, now? Why, if not because he'd made some decision she couldn't bear thinking about? Maybe there'd be a hundred more letters, now. Maybe that was what was left: the two of them, off on their own adventures, and only words to connect them.

A little piece of her said: it was only two hours; it was only one night.

But it was so much more, wasn't it? It was the question she'd been avoiding all year: was it life, or was it love, and could you have one without the other?

Destiny calls! The words of Georges de la Motte himself.

She returned to the kitchenette. Vera slept on, but Nancy sank into one of the other armchairs and let the letter lie, unopened, on her lap. She tried to imagine how it must have been: four hours ago, Raymond waiting for her in the dance studio. Perhaps he'd sent Frank and Rosa off into the night. Perhaps he'd waited there still. Perhaps, when he was done with waiting, he'd written her this note as a way of explaining why he was doing what he had to do.

The next time I'll see him, she thought, *it will be up on the billboards at Piccadilly Circus. Or his giant image strobing on the silver screen. In the arms of somebody else . . .*

A hundred curses filled her. Why had she waited for George Peel? Why not just leave Miss Edgerton to it? Why had she walked out on Christmas Day? Why . . . ?

The recriminations were too much.

He hadn't even said goodbye.

She did not want to open the letter. It seemed a kind of punishment. But still her fingers slipped under its seal. She wanted to see the words. She wanted to know that she was holding the page across which his fingers had danced. She wanted to hear the goodbye washing over her, even if he wasn't here.

Nancy, I choose you every time. X

She had to look at the letter twice to make sense of the words. At first, it seemed just a mixed-up assortment of letters. Then, when the words came into focus, she was up and on her feet. She turned around the kitchenette, as if she might have missed something . . . or *somebody*.

Her feet led the way. She was drawn, inexorably, back to her bedroom door.

431

She opened it.

There stood Raymond.

He was waiting patiently at the end of her bed, decked out in his finest black evening wear, starched white collar and black bow tie. She saw, too, that her wardrobe door was open – and there, hanging on the back of it, was an elegant ball gown of golden silk, bows on its shoulders, bows on its waist.

'Nancy . . .' She sensed the tremor in his voice. 'I thought you'd never . . .'

The letter still clutched in her hand, Nancy threw herself at Raymond and was whirled around in his arms.

After some time, she tried to disentangle herself, but Raymond was holding her fast. She realised, then, that he was as desperate as her; he didn't want to – no, *couldn't* – let go. His face was buried in her hair and he was breathing her in. She and Raymond, they were exactly the same.

'I thought you'd gone,' she whispered into his ear. 'The *Othello*, doesn't it leave . . . ?'

'On the morrow,' Raymond said.

'And yet . . .'

His lips touched her ear. 'I sent another letter. One to Georges de la Motte. They'll need a new star for their picture, Nancy. They'll need a new leading man. Georges, he'll be disappointed in me. And yet . . .' He drew back, because he wanted more than anything else to be able to look her in the eyes as he said the next words. 'If I were to board that boat, if I were to gaze down from the billboards in Piccadilly Circus in six months' time, I'd be . . . disappointed in myself. Because, Nancy – how could I ever let you go? Not for silver screen stardom. Not for anything. I'm home, Nancy. *You're* my home. I don't know

432

what I've been doing all year. I don't know why I didn't see it from the start.'

'Your dreams, Raymond, they matter too.'

'Then I'll find a way to fulfil them here, right here, where I don't lose the only other thing I dream about.' He stopped, kissed her on the brow. 'How did it go tonight, Nancy?'

'Oh, Raymond,' she said, and turned her face to kiss him full on the lips, 'it went better than I could have hoped. Mr Peel, he kept us waiting. I don't know why. Rich men think the world stops turning for them, don't they? That the hours don't matter . . . But, when he came, he came with the best news. He's going to underwrite the Daughters, and he's sending his son to work for us – something to make him see the value of everything he's been given. And . . .' She realised her words were running into one another in her eagerness to get them out. 'The rest can wait. It can always wait. This – *this* – is what can't.' She reached for the ball gown hanging on the back of the door. 'Frank and Rosa, they went on ahead?'

'They did.'

'And we—?'

'We'll jive with them another time. Tonight is for you and me.' He smiled. 'Shall we?'

The clock tower in Westminster was tolling out eleven by the time Raymond de Guise led Nancy Nettleton by the arm through the Buckingham Hotel's famous revolving doors. In his black dinner jacket and top hat, Nancy in her gown of golden silk, they came down the steps and walked, together, to the waiting taxicab.

The snow had stopped falling on Berkeley Square. Above the rooftops, the clouds were coming apart, revealing the moon, full and round.

As the car pulled away, Nancy nestling close to Raymond in the back, the silver light of that moon spilled down, illuminating the taxicab in which they rode, the banks of snow they passed, and the solitary saxophonist who – pausing before he reached the Buckingham steps – looked up at the façade of the hotel he had once called home, and which he would soon call home again. There was so little in this life that truly seemed perfect, thought Nancy, but right now, here in this moment, there was not a thing she would change. Let the war come down; let it tear London apart; let the Buckingham Hotel itself fall, if that's what the Fates had in store. All that Nancy needed was to ride through the night with the moonlight cascading down over Mayfair and Raymond by her side.

Right now, and forever after, it was enough.

Acknowledgements

Writing and publishing a book is such a huge team effort and I couldn't have asked for a better team to help me bring my imagined world of the Buckingham Hotel to life. Firstly, my wonderful editorial team – Sarah Bauer, Katie Lumsden and Kate Parkin, who have been on board from the very beginning and have helped me to shape my many ideas into a novel. Thanks for making the whole process so much fun and for letting me dance and even sing my way through the edits!

Great partnerships only get stronger the longer you work together – that's something I've found to be true in the world of dance and is equally as true in writing. I learned so much working on my debut novel with a writing collaborator and I am so pleased with how relationship has developed. Thank you for all your guidance, patience and, more importantly, the fun we're had weaved this enchanting tale.

I'm immensely grateful to the eagle-eyed Steve O'Gorman and Jane Howard for their detailed copyediting and proofreading, respectively.

Francesca Russell, my amazing publicist, has travelled all over the country with me. I've never known someone fall asleep so quickly – I must be captivating company! I'm lucky enough to work with two publicists, so thanks also go to the brilliant Clare Kelly.

A highlight in this joyous journey has been seeing the beautiful covers evolve, Alexandra Allden designed both this cover and the ones for *One Enchanted Evening* and I couldn't be happier with them. I can't wait to see what she comes up with for the next one!

It takes a whole army to market and sell a book so a huge thank you to Stephen Dumughn, Sahina Bibi, Nico Poilblanc, Stuart Finglass, Andrea Tome, Victoria Hart, Arjumand Siddiqui, Angie Willocks, Carrie-Anne Pitt, Amanda Percival, Vincent Kelleher and Sophie Hamilton.

I love audiobooks – I'm always listening to them in my car between shows – so it was a real pleasure to be able to record my own introduction for the audiobook of *Moonlight Over Mayfair*. Thanks to Laura Makela for organising this and for all of her work with Jon Watt on the audiobook.

Alex May and Jamie Taylor produce the actual book and the many, many pages I autographed for the signed copies – thanks for keeping me so busy pre-*Strictly*!

And lastly, but certainly not least, from the wonderful bunch at Bonnier Books: thanks to Ruth Logan, Ilaria Tarasconi, Saidah Graham and Shane Hegarty.

I am honoured to be able to call my agent, Melissa Chappell, a true friend. Thanks as always for your guidance, support and advice. Thanks also, to Hollie Paton Pratt for making sure I always know where I'm meant to be and what I'm doing. Thanks to Scott Mycock for all your support and hard work on this novel. I wouldn't be able to do so many exciting projects if it weren't for all of you.

Kerr MacRae, my literary agent, thank you for guiding me so seamlessly into my new life of being a novelist and for your intelligent input and suggestions on this series of books.

My dear Ruthie and Eamonn and the fabulous Chris Evans, thanks for all of your support for my novels – I appreciate it more than you know.

The biggest thanks go to you, the reader. Thank you for joining me on this new venture. It was so lovely to meet so many of you on both my book tour and my and Erin's dance tour, and to hear all of your wonderful thoughts on *One Enchanted Evening*. None of this would be possible without you. Thank you so much for welcoming Raymond and everyone at the Buckingham into your lives.

Hello my loves!

Thank you for choosing *Moonlight Over Mayfair*. If you're reading this, you've probably just finished the novel. I hope you enjoyed reading it as much as I enjoyed writing it!

When I finished writing *One Enchanted Evening* (which was a *Sunday Times* bestseller, don't you know?), I knew I wanted to write more about the Buckingham Hotel. I had fallen in love with the world and the characters I'd created. I'm glad so many of you have kindly told me you felt the same. I felt there were just so many more stories to tell about life in the hotel.

But even knowing I wanted to go back to the Buckingham, I still had a lot of decisions to make: should I continue it straight where we left off or jump further in time? In continuing the series, I found I wanted to focus on different characters to vary it a bit, but I also knew you, the readers, would want to know what happened next to those who featured heavily in *One Enchanted Evening*. The great thing about setting the novels in a hotel is that people come and go frequently, giving me lots of scope to introduce new characters – but who did I want to create and add to this world? Another *huge* decision for me was how to make room for these new characters. I had to choose who wouldn't feature in this story and why – have they checked out of the hotel, got a new job . . . or did I need to kill anyone off?

Once I chose to leap straight back into 1937, I knew certain historical events that took place that year would affect the Buckingham Hotel. This gave me some structure and a lot of ideas for plotlines both upstairs and downstairs in the hotel. It is such a fascinating period in history – in *Moonlight Over Mayfair*, so much is changing so quickly: London is still getting over the Great Depression, a new king is being crowned and the threat of war is looming . . .

Of course, a lot of the drama unfolds on the ballroom dance floor, but Raymond has even bigger dreams in this novel. Where will they lead him?

Oooh, it's all so exciting! Thank you for entering this world with me and embracing it. I was overwhelmed by your reactions to my debut novel and none of this would be possible without you.

I am very pleased to say that we will be returning to the Buckingham again soon! I'm already working away on the next book – between rehearsals. To be the first to hear the new title (and all my other news, too), do sign up to my mailing list. You can find all the details on my website: www.antondubeke.tv

Love,
Anton

P.S. Don't forget to follow me:
🐦 @TheAntonDuBeke
📷 @Mrantondubeke
f www.facebook.com/antondubeke

Turn over for an exclusive Q&A
with the author . . .

In Conversation with Anton Du Beke

1. Have you always wanted to write a book?

Writing a book is one of those things I've always wanted to do, but never thought I would or even could do. I suspect a lot of people feel the same way. Because I've become known for doing one thing, I never thought I would end up doing anything else. But that was the real joy and wonder of meeting my publishers for the first time. I went into their offices to meet with them and, to quote Max Bygraves (ask your mum or nan!), said 'I wanna tell you a story'. And the lovely thing was, they listened! I knew then that they saw me not only as a dancer, but as a storyteller too, and that we could do wonderful things together. And we have!

2. What inspired this story and setting?

The 1930s is fascinating to me. I think more happened and changed at the beginning of the last century than in any other equivalent time period before or since. The two world wars affected everybody in the UK and were a huge catalyst for change – good or bad.

Of course, dance was changing massively, too. Dance is always influenced by what is happening in society, and so these huge changes and the arrival of people from around the world, particularly the American G.I.s, were helping to shape and influence dancing.

I really enjoy fiction set around factual events or situations, so I've loved weaving in real historical events and having them affect my characters in the novels; I love that I was able to have some familiar faces from history arriving at the Buckingham Hotel, too.

I always say that the first book, *One Enchanted Evening*, is the story of my life without it being autobiographical, because it's full of things I'm familiar with. The Grand Ballroom is a combination of all the ballrooms I've danced in throughout my life and the characters are all inspired by people I've met and spent time with.

I think one of the greatest joys in life is listening to a terrific raconteur telling stories and I've been fortunate enough to have dance lessons from one or two wonderful raconteurs in my time. They would conjure up images in my mind of the people they knew and my imagination would run wild. It was magical. So, my books are about all these wonderful characters that I have heard about but never met.

3. How did you find the writing process?

Because the hotel and the characters are an amalgamation of places and people I know, I felt quite comfortable committing them to the page. I want to say it was easy, but it wasn't! However, it was a lot easier than writing something completely new to me would have been. If you were to ask me to write science fiction, I wouldn't even know where to start!

The hardest bit for me has always been how to start. I have the same problem with choreography – how do I begin in an interesting fashion? You want to grab people's attention from the very first step – or, the very first page. I know already how the next book is going to start and I've very excited about it. We've got a fantastic ending too, which helps me plot exactly what's going to happen in the middle, because I know what we're heading towards.

And of course, having a wonderful editor keeps me on the straight and narrow!

It definitely all takes longer than I first thought. Not just the writing itself, but the whole process from that initial meeting where I told the story to my publishers to seeing the books on the shelves.

4. Do you enjoy being edited? Is it similar to facing judges?

I've spent a lifetime being criticised. As a dancer, especially a ballroom dancer, it's very rare to get a compliment. Everyone's first port of call is to criticise, saying things like 'I didn't love the foxtrot, didn't like the shaping.' It would be nice for somebody to just say 'That was amazing!', but if they did, I'd be suspicious! So, I like receiving criticism – as long as it's constructive.

I love being edited. I have a million ideas and can go off on a tangent, so it's important that I get nudged in the right direction and reminded that there's only a limited number of pages to fill.

That's the beauty of a creative mind – it's the same with books and dance. I've done choreography for other people in the past and then the next day you come back and look at it from another angle and have new ideas. Fresh eyes always see things differently, whether it's dance or writing.

5. The books centre around two characters: the dancer, Raymond and the chambermaid, Nancy. Why did you choose them to be your key voices?

As a demonstration dancer, Raymond is in a unique position within the hotel. He's upstairs charming and waltzing with the high society guests, but he's also an employee and mixes with the staff. He gets to see it all, and that brings him power. What I like about Raymond is that he's not the man you first think he is – he's hiding a secret.

And then Nancy, being new to the city, is a brilliant character to introduce readers to 1930s London and to the Buckingham. She's very modern in her ideas and ambitions and that really helps to highlight how different this time period was.

Both of them are also working at the Buckingham to improve their lifestyles, which is quite a personal thing for me, because both of my parents moved to the UK to improve their lives.

6. How did you come up with the titles? Do you find it difficult?

I'm always happy to brainstorm this with my publishers. I'm very lucky to work with some of the best people in the publishing industry, and I always listen to their suggestions and advice.

For both novels, I wanted to make sure we reflected the importance of music and dance in the title, but also got a sense of the period. I confess I didn't have a set title for either novel in mind, but when we came up with *One Enchanted Evening* and *Moonlight Over Mayfair* I knew immediately that they were the right ones. For me, they really encompass the mood of the books.

7. How do you like to 'read' books? Audiobooks, ebooks or physical books?

I love the feel of books, especially a hardback – I love how tactile they are. I don't like reading on a screen, though; I've done it on occasions, using my phone on a plane, but if I'm on a beach or reading at home I like to have a physical book. If I'm reading at home, it's normally to the babies. So if I'm reading a 'real' book it's often a children's book.

My favourite way to read is with audiobooks. When I'm in the car, I always have an audiobook on, rather than the radio. Of course, I'm in the car all the time – touring the country! – so I get through a lot.

8. Has fatherhood changed your perception of books?

Definitely! I've always loved books, but seeing my children fall in love with stories has been magical. They both like reading and being read to. It's become part of our bedtime routine: bath, book, bed.

9. What are your favourite books to read to the twins?

Anything by Julia Donaldson! Her rhymes are just so clever and Axel Scheffler's illustrations are brilliant. She's just tremendous. Her books are the perfect length, too – not too long that the little ones get fidgety, but enough to get into a proper story. We started with *The Gruffalo* but I think *The Snail and the Whale* might be the new favourite. The twins love *Zog* as well, of course!

10. There's a line in *One Enchanted Evening*: 'That was the thing about dance: it did not care whether you were good or bad, just so long as you loved it.' Is this how you feel? Do you think everybody has the ability to learn to dance?

Absolutely! I think people sometimes forget that dancing is not about being judged. Beyond ballroom dancing and ice dancing, dance is purely a performance art – you're doing it for yourself, not someone else.

Dancing is natural. It's just moving your body to music. I've noticed it with my children – they dance for no reason, bouncing along to a TV theme tune or the radio. It's only as adults that our inhibitions get in the way and I think that's such a shame.

11. If any of your readers are thinking about taking up dancing – or writing – what would your advice to them be?

Do it, absolutely, have a go! Any form of expression for me is to be applauded and encouraged. As long as you're doing it for yourself – don't go in expecting to win the Booker Prize or perform with the Royal Ballet!

If you're taking up ballroom dancing, my advice is to be patient. Whatever mental image you have of dancing, starting ballroom will feel like the opposite. You might as well be doing maths equations, because your brain will hurt more than your feet!